Journey of Honor

By

John F. Schork

Journey of Honor is a work of fiction. Any resemblance to actual persons, living or dead, business establishments, events or locales are entirely coincidental.

Copyright 2019 by John Schork

First edition: December 2010

For Captain Roger Hanson, USN (Ret.)

A physician, a mentor and a friend.
If all healers had his level of caring, the world would be a much
better place.

Chapter One

Cheltenham Manor
Kent, England
June 12, 1944

Commander Erich Von Wollner stood at a large window overlooking the expansive lawn of the manor. He was a tall, slender man with dark hair and pleasant features, not at all the stereotypical German officer. Until a month ago he had been a personal assistant to Adolph Hitler. Now he spent his days at a stately English manor in the Kent countryside. But Von Wollner wasn't a prisoner and the security troops who guarded the manor were for his protection.

In a lightning raid by the British Special Operations Executive, he'd been pulled out of Hitler's headquarters near Rastenburg, East Prussia. The rescue had concluded Von Wollner's role as Britain's most strategically placed spy in the Nazi command structure. For over three years he had been the director of the Fuhrer's Secretariat responsible for coordinating all communications to and from the supreme leader of the Third Reich. In that role Von Wollner was privileged to view every critical decision by Hitler. Now he was at the disposal of MI-6, the department of the British government responsible for all intelligence efforts in occupied Europe. Wounded during the escape this time at the manor also allowed him time to recuperate from his injury.

The door to the study opened and a young woman in the uniform of a WRNS Leading Petty Officer entered quietly. "Good morning, commander. Beautiful day isn't it? May I bring you some coffee?"

Erich smiled at her. "Good morning, Miss Andrews. It is a beautiful day. I can't think of a better way to start it than with a cup of your marvelous coffee."

Gillian Andrews smiled and said, "I'll be right back." Originally a driver for the Naval district in Portsmouth, she had been reassigned to MI-6 as an interpreter. Von Wollner knew some English but most of his communication was still in German.

After several minutes the young woman returned with a tray. Walking over to the table she put the tray down and poured a cup of steaming coffee.

"There you go, sir. I know you normally don't eat breakfast but can I bring you anything?"

"Thank you, no. This is fine. Do you know what's on the schedule for this morning?" Erich sipped the coffee, easily forgetting the terrible ersatz coffee used in Germany after the war began.

"I believe Commander Stewart is due here within the hour."

"Good. I'll read until then. It will help me with my English."

Erich looked forward to his meetings with Jack Stewart, leader of the team, which flew him out of Germany. The two officers had hit if off and were working together on Erich's extensive debrief of his years at Hitler's side. Stewart was focusing on the Nazi's efforts to develop new weapons, which might still turn the tide of the war. The Royal Naval officer was head of a specialized group within MI-6 called Section F. Over the last two years the team had conducted several operations against some of Germany's newest weapons systems. The senior leadership of MI-6 wanted to exploit Erich's knowledge of the efforts within Germany to field new and more deadly weapons.

Sitting at the desk in the study Erich glanced over the front page of the Times trying to recognize words and patterns. He was determined to learn English as quickly as possible. Erich felt he might never be able to return to his homeland. Many Germans would view his actions as those of a traitor and the German people did not tolerate disloyalty. In his mind, he was trying to help wrest Germany away from a madman. Initially a patriotic and loyal officer, over time he had watched the Jewish persecution and was sickened. Every day the Gestapo would arrest people and they would never be seen again. He could see the hopelessness of the war and ultimate destruction of Germany. The very future of his country was being destroyed by the loss of an entire generation of young men in the snows of Russia, the deserts of North Africa and the immense North Atlantic. They could call him a traitor but his conscience was clear.

Reading the paper he sat very upright. The wound to his back was still tender. He'd been hit by a round, which glanced off his shoulder blade during the escape. After the wound was bandaged, he rode the right seat of a Mosquito fighter bomber in a four hour flight to England. Jack Stewart, a former U.S. Naval Aviator, flew a second Mosquito in the flight. The pilot had been wounded and Stewart filled in to get the pilot back home. On arrival at RAF Biggin Hill, Erich had been met by Prime Minister Winston Churchill. During the period of Von Wollner's work for the British, as code name "Bishop", the Prime Minister was only one of three people to know his actual identity. Churchill not only appreciated the efforts by Erich but saw the potential for further exploitation of his knowledge.

Von Wolner heard the sound of a car and glanced out the window to see a black sedan pull into the enclosed area. The car stopped on the circular driveway and he saw Jack Stewart get out. With Jack was Major Phil Hatcher, Jack's second in command. A former Scotland Yard inspector, Phil was a veteran of several clandestine missions into Europe.

Erich watched the two men walk toward the kitchen entrance. The two men had the easy gait of well-trained, physically fit men in their prime. Both were wearing the brown battle dress of the British Army.

From the outside, the manor appeared as it did before the war. The brick main house was surrounded by well manicured lawns and gardens. There were a host of large and stately oak trees, which provided shade and privacy to the estate. The only visible changes were the sentry stations at the entrance to the grounds. Not readily visible was a large cadre of personnel within the manor who provided security. The house was used regularly for MI-6 guests who needed the most secure surroundings.

Erich heard footsteps on the hardwood floor outside the study. There were two quick knocks and the door edged open.

"Hello, Erich." Stewart smiled as he pushed the door open and entered the study. A tall man, he had sandy hair and blue eyes. Hatcher followed, a stocky officer with a ruddy complexion and a perpetual grin.

"Good morning, Jack. Please come in. Hello, Phillip, good to see you again."

Phil answered in German. He and the rest of Section F had been actively learning and using French and German for the last eighteen months. Jack had studied both during his undergraduate days at the U.S. Naval Academy. At their headquarters in Baker Street, the section would often conduct business in German or French to keep them sharp.

Jack walked over to Erich and they shook hands. "I hope Petty Officer Andrews is taking good care of you?"

"Of course, no complaints. She is a delightful young lady."

"How's the back?"

"Better each day. I'm lucky the Gestapo weren't better marksmen."

"You and me both," Jack laughed. He could see a new man emerging from Erich Von Wollner. The stress of years as an agent for the British had taken a terrible toll. He was finally beginning to relax.

Over the next two hours the three of them conducted a give and take exchange. Previous sessions helped to identify the research effort and proposed production schedule for a new class of submarines with a revolutionary propulsion system. If those boats were produced in any large numbers, the war in the Atlantic could tip toward the Germans. A bombing program was already underway specifically targeting U-boat production plants and ship yards.

This morning the conversation concentrated on the German's chemical and biological warfare programs. Jack and Phil wondered why the Germans hadn't used poison gas. The conduct of the war by the Germans could only be described as ruthless. It made sense to Jack that the use of poison gas, particularly in Russia, was a natural step to be expected from Hitler. In his position in the Secretariat, Erich had been able to monitor correspondence which went back and forth on the subject. It came to light there were many requests by the Wehrmacht to use poison gas on the Eastern Front. Erich said he was frankly surprised it wasn't used particularly when the German Sixth Army was trapped in Stalingrad. He felt Hitler's personal experience in the First World War was a major reason why the Fuhrer wouldn't authorize its use even in the direst of situations.

"What happens as the Allies close the ring around Germany? Is there a point he'll be pushed to use those types of weapons?" "There was one program which addressed that situation specifically. But after a very intense period of discussion among the senior leaders it dropped out of sight."

Hatcher frowned. "Tell us more about the plan and how it would be terminated."

Erich looked grim. "The code name was the "Valkyrie Contingency." It was a plan to use the new V-2 rocket to deliver large amounts of the nerve agent Sarin against London. The thought was the huge loss of life would give Germany some option other than unconditional surrender. Sarin or "GB" was one of the nerve agents our scientists developed from their work on insecticides. Sarin is extremely lethal, an amount as small as the head of a pin is enough to kill a human. These rockets would carry thousands of kilos of the agent which would be dispersed over the city prior to the missile hitting the earth. Estimates of casualties were put at over 20,000 if an attack of ten V-2s were launched to impact during the work day. But after several months of messages and discussions at the strategy meetings no further mention was made of Valkyrie."

Jack asked, "And you have no idea why it would just drop out of sight?"

"That wasn't unusual. There were many programs that never got past the concept stage. Although, as I think about it, there were always reasons given as programs were terminated. In this case I never heard anything else about Valkyrie."

Jack was thinking the same thing as Phil. "It could still be active?"

Erich thought for a moment. "There were some things which were so sensitive the communication was done by word of mouth from Hitler to his most trusted lieutenants. Many of the Jewish issues were handled in this manner." He paused, "My God, this could be the special project Himmler would occasionally refer to when he sent messages to Hitler."

SS Headquarters
Unter de Linden
Berlin, Germany
Early June, 1944

The second most powerful man in the Nazi hierarchy was Reichsfuhrer SS, Heinrich Himmler. He controlled the entire state security apparatus for the German Reich. Himmler had risen to a position of such immense power because of his total loyalty to Adolph Hitler and his complete lack of conscience. Himmler did whatever was required to achieve the goals, which Hitler set for the party and the country. His pursuit of those goals was ruthless and uncompromising. He did not accept failure or mistakes by his police or SS units.

The escape by Erich Von Wollner from under the noses of the Gestapo and SS at the Fuhrer's Headquarters was a failure of the highest order. Himmler's wrath resulted in three summary executions within the security organization of the headquarters. His personal embarrassment in front of Hitler prompted him to assure the Fuhrer that Von Wollner would pay for his treason. Hitler's concern was more pragmatic, realizing that many of his most sensitive communications would be laid bare as the Allies debriefed the traitor. Within one day of the escape, an order was issued by Hitler for the location and elimination of Erich Von Wollner.

The door to Himmler's office opened and his adjutant, Sturmbannfuhrer Helmut Scheer, strode across the room. Sitting at his large desk Himmler was reviewing the latest figures from several of the death camps. He was frustrated. The lack of both rail transport and crematory capacity was limiting the processing of Jews in the "final solution." He made a note to talk with Albert Speer, the Minister of Munitions, to try and free up more construction material for both Treblinka and Auschwitz. The Fuhrer expected him to carry out the final solution to the Jewish problem and he would not disappoint him.

"Herr Reichsfuhrer, Standartenfuhrer Dietrich is here."

"Very good, send him in. I'll finish these figures later."

Karl Dietrich entered the large office, his boots echoing off the black marble. He strode up to the desk and came to a stiff attention.

"Good morning, Herr Reichsfuhrer."

"Dietrich, it's good to see you, as always. Please sit down."

Even sitting, the man looked to be at attention. His black SS uniform was impeccable. At his throat he wore the Knight's Cross with Crossed Swords, personally awarded by Adolph Hitler for a mission behind enemy lines in Russia. Dietrich was one of the most experienced commando officers in the German military. His exploits throughout the European theatre were legendary, from assassination to rescues, to key sabotage missions.

"I have a mission which is of extreme importance and urgency to the Reich. This mission has been personally authorized by the Fuhrer and you act directly with his authority. On May 28, the Director of the Fuhrer's Secretariat deserted to the British. He left the

11

Wolf's Lair compound in East Prussia, and after a gun battle in which several SS personnel were killed, he was flown to England. Over the last three years this man was privy to almost all correspondence to and from the Fuhrer. You can well imagine the damage this could do to the war effort. We believe he's still in England, although we don't know where. Certainly British MI-6 is directly involved. Your mission is to hunt down Von Wollner and kill him. Do you have any questions?"

Dietrich's pale blue eyes narrowed just slightly. "No, Herr Reichsfuhrer. I assume you want me to begin immediately?"

Himmler rose and came around his desk. "Dietrich, this is very important to me. Let nothing stand in your way. I want this traitor eliminated."

Standing, Dietrich nodded. "Yes, Reichsfuhrer, it will be done." Turning, he walked to the door. He was the perfect picture of Hitler's master race. Young, only thirty, he was in superb physical shape and his chiseled jaw complimented his blond coloring. The equivalent of a colonel in the Wehrmacht, he would probably be promoted to General within the year. But unknown to Himmler, Karl Dietrich had started to have doubts about the war. He had seen the trains loaded with Jews headed for the concentration camps. Although he had no contact with Section IVB of the SS, he wasn't a fool. He'd heard of the mass deaths taking place behind the barbed wire.

Life had been simple when he had joined the SS, embracing the ideal of a re-born German nation with Germanic pride and a view to the future. Dietrich performed bravely in combat many times but always against the armed forces of the enemy. He knew that measures must be taken in any country for security, but the more he watched Germany today the less he liked what he saw. For the first time in his life he felt confused about his life and the world he found around him. However orders were orders.

The adjutant Scheer handed Dietrich a sturdy envelop with the official seal of the Headquarters SS embossed on the front. Dietrich read the enclosed letter. It was addressed to "Whoever may read this letter". It directed all resources and assistance be rendered to SS Standartenfuhrer Karl Dietrich in support of a mission of critical importance to the Reich. It listed several contact numbers and accounting information, if needed. It also noted that failure to comply with this letter would result in immediate arrest by the Gestapo. The letter was signed "A. Hitler." He put the letter back into the protective holder, placed his cap squarely on his closed cropped blond head and strode out of Himmler's office.

MI-6 Headquarters
64 Baker Street
London

Immediately on return to London, Jack Stewart asked for a meeting with Director of Special Operations Executive, Brigadier Noel Greene. One of the key members of MI-6, Greene had been instrumental in Stewart's assignment as head of Section F.

"Brigadier, thanks for seeing us on short notice," Jack said as he and Phil walked into Greene's office. A third man came in with them, Colonel Tommy Hudson, the Operations Officer for SOE and Jack Stewart's closest friend.

"I suspect this has something to do with your latest conversation with Commander Von Wollner?"

"Correct, sir. Something came up that triggered Erich's memory. We believe there may be a Nazi plan to deliver chemical agents against England."

"Poison gas? At this stage of the war? Germany hasn't used gas anywhere during the war that we know of. Why start now? It simply doesn't make sense." Greene leaned forward.

"That's one of the problems, brigadier," Phil added. "This plan doesn't use gas. It uses a nerve agent called Sarin."

"Refresh me on nerve agents," Tommy Hudson asked.

"Nerve agents are much more lethal than any of the gases used during the First War such as mustard or chlorine. They interrupt the nerve signals, which travel throughout the body. This disruption destroys the ability of the system to function normally. Also, protection by gas mask isn't very effective. The agent can act simply by coming in contact with the skin."

Greene spoke up, "You said they were planning to use it against England. How would they deliver this Sarin?"

"According to Von Wollner their V-2 rockets which we know are almost operational would deliver large amounts of Sarin on London. He said they estimated 20,000 casualties from ten rockets hitting during the work day. They call their plan the "Valkyrie Contingency.""

Greene sat thinking for a moment. "Something like this could change the whole complexion of the war. If they could hit London, they could hit Paris, Brussels, Vienna or Rome. I'd better get this to the PM straight away. Assuming this is a real plan we need to figure out what we can do about it. "

Tommy Hudson spoke up, "Brigadier, I propose we let Section F put all of their efforts on this project for the time being."

"Agreed. Jack, I also want you to continue working with Von Wollner on the debrief. Who knows how his knowledge might help unravel this issue. I know the PM will also have some direction for us after I brief him. Let's plan on meeting tomorrow at 0900. I'll try to meet with Churchill later today."

An hour later, the key members of Section F were seated in Jack's office. Besides Phil Hatcher, Terry Howe and Hiram Baker sat around the table. Terry and Hiram had been members of Section F since inception. Terry had been on all of the missions conducted by Section F and was considered the team's weapon's expert. Hiram Baker, an army captain who'd been wounded and invalided out of his regiment, was an expert in logistics. There was a quiet confidence among the members around the table. They'd taken on a number of extremely challenging missions and performed successfully on every one.

"That's what we know at this point. We might be chasing a phantom or this could be a threat to our people unlike anything we've ever seen." Jack used the phrase "our people" easily. Born in Seattle, until two years ago he was a serving officer in the United States Navy. Shot down at the Battle of Midway, he'd been selected by the OSS to be the officer who would join MI-6 in an agreement between Franklin Roosevelt and Winston Churchill.

Hatcher spoke first. "We need to get a lot smarter about these nerve agents. We need to have Ian connect with his experts so we know what we're dealing with."

One member of Section F missing from the meeting was Professor Ian Thompson, professor of physics at Trinity College, Oxford. Thompson also worked as part of Section IX of MI-6, the technical analysis experts.

"He'll be back in town tonight and I'll talk with him," Jack offered. "In the short term let's work on getting some location data. By that I mean where Jerry would be working on, storing or constructing either the rockets or the nerve gas. I want to do a complete scrub of the classified archives. Hiram, we need to work our contacts with the code boys at Bletchley Park to do a scan for any messages, which talk about Valkyrie, or Sarin or GB. Phil, you and I will run out to see Von Wollner after tomorrow's meeting. We need to work on his memory to pull out any important detail, which might be connected to Valkyrie. OK, let's get going."

Headquarters Building
Kriegsmarine Intelligence Director
Kiel, Germany
June 13, 1944

Historically there were not strong links between the SS and the Kriegsmarine. The Navy tended to be much more traditional and old school while the SS was the radical and more fanatic service. Karl Dietrich had developed a friendship with Rear Admiral Walter Kaltenbach during the Norway campaign of 1940. Intelligence information, which Dietrich gathered during two commando missions had been passed to Kaltenbach, who was then a senior captain responsible for the Navy's intelligence effort against the British Navy. Dietrich's information resulted in several crushing defeats and a humiliating withdrawal from Norway by the British. Two other collaborative efforts between Kaltenbach and Dietrich in the Crete campaign and again in Yugoslavia cemented their relationship.

After a warm reunion the two closed the door to Kaltenbach's office and sat at his conference table. Dietrich handed the letter to Kaltenbach who read it and placed it back on the table.

"I've heard of these letters but have never actually seen one. Very impressive."

"This is a matter of the utmost urgency and secrecy. I hope you can provide me with some help."

Kaltenbach smiled. "You know I'll help you anyway I can. With this letter we have all the power we need. Exactly what do you need?"

"I have to get to England with a companion. That's the easy part. My job is to track down a traitor and eliminate him. For that I need the use of any intelligence network or source you currently have in England."

The Admiral put his hands together on top of the desk. He sat there for a moment, and then replied, "We've had a bit more success than our army or SS counterparts in keeping agents in place on the island. It's been a very carefully guarded network which is one reason why it's survived all efforts by the Brits to break it."

"Walter, I wouldn't risk your network unless I feel there's some chance they can help us. Let me tell you what I need and I'll let you make the call."

"Fair enough."

"At the end of May, a navy commander, Erich Von Wollner defected from Wolf's Lair and was flown to England."

"I knew him when he was a junior officer at Flensburg."

"For the last three years he saw all of the incoming and outgoing message traffic of the Fuhrer. You can imagine the damage he can do when they debrief him. We suspect MI-6 was involved, but don't know for sure. It makes sense that he's still in Britain and being debriefed. I need to find out where he is so I can take care of him."

"You, personally?"

"I'll take Gerhard. It was clear to me that both Hitler and Himmler consider this a mission to be completed at all costs. I think I have the best chance of success, so I'll go. Do you think you can help?"

"We do have a network currently operating in England. Several agents are in the Norfolk area. They are the base for our operatives that work in and around London. Most of our recent activity has been directed at gaining information on the invasion. As part of that effort we did have some luck with several MI-6 personnel. We've discovered over the years how the Brits have dispersed from their Baker Street headquarters in London to many locations. We know some of the locations, but penetrating them has been a stumbling block. There are several sites that seem like logical places to hide him during debrief. I'd put him under lock and key in the Tower of London but they seem to like safe houses for their special guests. I'll bet you'll find Commander Von Wollner at one of those locations."

Dietrich thought for a moment. "Is there any way we can get your people to watch those locations until I get there? It might narrow the search and my plan is to make this a quick trip in and right back out."

"I don't think that would be a problem. Our counter-invasion efforts have obviously tailed off. We do have to be careful on our communication with the agents. The Brits have gotten very good at intercepting our messages. How about getting there? Are you thinking air or water?"

"With the massive air defence system over southern England my thought is to go by submarine. I want to talk with some of your experts to see what they think about getting in and out. It seems to me that coming in the back door via water makes more sense than trying a parachute drop."

Kaltenbach opened a folder on his desk which was labeled: 'Operational Schedule.' "You're in luck. Lothar Liche is back from patrol. He and the U-2321 are one of our most experienced boats. Let's see what he thinks."

23B Devon Street
Apartment 2
London, England

Pamela Thompson removed the hot water kettle from the stove and poured the steaming water into a blue porcelain tea pot. A slender woman with auburn hair and deep brown eyes, she looked very much like a young housewife in her dark green dress. Actually she was a Flight Officer in the WAAFs currently on convalescence leave. Sitting at the small table in the kitchen was her father, Professor Ian Thompson. He split his time between lecturing in physics at Trinity College and as a scientific advisor to MI-6, Section F. He'd just arrived back in town from Oxford where he owned a house near the college.

"How was the trip, Dad?"

"I didn't think the trains could get any more crowded but I was wrong. Even with the thousands now on the continent it seems there are more young men and women in uniform than ever before." He was glancing at a copy of the evening paper as he loosened his tie. In his early fifties, he had a closed cropped head of grey hair. His eyes were green and there were lines on his face from the stress of the last several years.

"Here, a hot cup of tea will soothe your problems away." She poured the steaming tea into a cup by his arm.

"Thank you, Pam. You do take good care of me."

She leaned down and kissed his head. "It's…it's…nice to have you here. Jack's been putting in long hours and until I get my medical clearance, I'm getting a bit bored." She sat down across the table from her father.

"Pam, there's no rush to get back on the job. You've had a severe injury and shouldn't be in any hurry to get back into that pressure." She was an operations floor controller at Fighter Command Headquarters.

"I guess I want to prove to myself that I'm back to normal." Pam had been run down in front of MI-6 headquarters in an attempted assassination of Jack Stewart.

"I'm just saying don't push yourself. All in good time."

She reached across the table and squeezed his hand. "All right."

There was a knock at the door. Pam got up and walked down the short hall. Unlocking the deadbolt, she opened the door.

"Hi, beautiful," Jack said. He kissed her lightly on the lips putting his hand under her chin. "Did your Dad get back from Oxford?"

"Only just. He's having some tea. Can I get you a cup?" She put her arm through his and they walked to the kitchen.

"Thanks, but after today, I think a little scotch is in order." They walked into the kitchen and Jack put his hat on the top shelf of the open cupboard.

"Ian, glad you're back. We've had a bit of a brew up while you were lecturing the young lords."

Ian closed the paper. "And what's that all about?"

Jack was pouring scotch into a glass. "If Pam would go get ready to go out for dinner, I'll let you know."

Pam smiled as she walked out of the kitchen. "All right, you've got ten minutes. Then I'm back and we're all going out for dinner."

Jack sat down at the table. "What do you know about Sarin gas?"

"Sarin? That's a name I haven't heard for a while. It must have been 1940. We thought there'd be an invasion and we tried to get as much information as possible on German chemical weapons. We really thought we'd have to deal with them. At the time, Sarin and Tabun were the two nerve agents we knew they had. However Jerry hadn't converted either one to full scale production. Damned glad of that too. We felt Sarin was the nastiest of them all. It kills quickly. By the time you know you've been exposed it's too late. It did appear the final product wasn't going to be hard to disperse in the atmosphere using bombs or artillery shells."

"Or V-2 rockets?"

"Especially rockets if you can get dispersal above ground using some type of fuse triggered by altitude. The liquid would come down just like a light rain, a death rain. You aren't telling me that we think the Germans are going to put the two together are you?"

"We don't know. But there was a Nazi plan to do just that and we don't know the status of the plan. Von Wollner seems to think it might still be operating under wraps with the SS."

"It's almost too hard to imagine. Over a city you'd have deaths by the tens of thousands. I'm not aware of any viable antidote either. If they've figured out how to convert the agent into a deliverable weapon we have real trouble, Jack."

Jack thought of his guidance from Greene, figure out what to do about this potential problem. *Where to start?* "How about digging up every shred of information we have on their nerve agents. Stop by in the morning and I'll fill you in on the rest." He heard Pam coming down the hall. "Now, let's be happily domestic for the rest of the evening." But he felt very unsettled. The more he learned about this threat the more he realized how difficult it would be to come up with any plan to protect England.

Chapter Two

Bletchley Park
Buckinghamshire, England
June 14, 1944

Captain Hiram Baker located a hut behind the main building labeled "6". He'd been directed to the temporary building, but only after the reception area checked his name against a master list. That was following the double identity check at the main security office to get into the compound. They obviously took security very seriously at Bletchley Park.

He was looking for a Mr. Simon Haskins who was aware of the tasking for Section F. Knocking twice, Baker opened the door and saw a Royal Marine security guard standing in front of a second inner door.

"Captain Baker here to see Mr. Haskins." Hut Six contained the crypto analysts who concentrated on German government and SS codes.

The Marine came to attention and said, "Identity pass, sir."

Following the security check Hiram went inside. The receptionist told him to go down to the third office where he would find Haskins.

"Mr. Haskins? Hiram Baker from MI-6. You're expecting me I believe?"

The large man in a bulky sweater jumped as if startled but smiled warmly. "Yes I'm Haskins. I've been assigned as your liaison. Do come in and have a seat."

A well kept secret, Bletchley Park was the most important part of the British code breaking organization. Utilizing some of the best and brightest minds from the world of mathematics, physics and statistics, the code breakers had been able to penetrate almost every enemy code in use at the time. The challenge was the collection of enemy signals to ensure that all critical transmissions were monitored. There was a tremendous volume of message traffic transmitted by the Germans.

Jack and Ian felt confident the codes currently in use for critical communication by the Germans had been compromised sufficiently to yield meaningful data. However the amount of traffic which must be screened might allow critical data on Sarin to be missed.

Baker went over the basic information points which the team wanted to start screening for immediately. Baker supplied Ira Haskins with forty seven key words, including several place names, which intelligence felt were the most promising.

Haskins went down the list. "Quite specific, this will be very helpful. My job will be to write the screening plans which will help us flag these words or combinations of these words in the decrypted messages."

"Do you think this is achievable?"

"I should think so. It's simply a matter of constructing a screening protocol and applying it rigorously."

"How long will that take you?"

"This has the highest priority. Not more that 48 hours."

"Marvelous."

Killian U-Boat Pen
Kiel Naval Base

Karl Dietrich was impressed with the sheer size of the concrete shelter constructed to protect Kiel's U-Boats from air attack. Built with walls over eight meters thick and a steel and concrete ceiling, "Killian" could withstand direct hits by the largest of Allied bombs. The structure was massive enough to provide shelter for a dozen of boats at the same time. As Kaltenbach walked Dietrich down the covered quay he could see eight boats currently in refit getting ready for their next war patrols into the Atlantic.

"Liche is one of the few 'old gang' remaining on active service at sea. Headquarters has tried many times to get him to come ashore but he refuses. His success had resulted in his command of the 2321, one of the first type XXIII boats to be put in service. These are the future of the submarine service. With new powerful engines, coupled with a special hydrodynamic hull, they can actually go faster submerged than on the surface. If anyone can get past the Allied screen, he's the one."

Dietrich was taking in the sights and sounds, the sharp salt air seemed so fresh, while the rancid smell of oil, flotsam and garbage that washed against the concrete pier made his stomach turn. "I told my assistant to meet us at the boat. I hope you don't mind."

"Not at all, Karl. I'm looking forward to meeting him. There's the boat now. She's finishing a month long maintenance period and is just about ready for sea." The pier sentry by the gangway came to attention as the two senior officers crossed over the dark water to the submarine.

A junior officer stood on the deck with a clipboard. He wore a pistol belt around his waist and had the relaxed look of a seasoned hand. He came to attention. "Good morning, Herr Admiral, and welcome aboard." They exchanged salutes. "The Kapitan would have met you but he's in the forward battery room with the yard superintendent."

"No matter, we'll go down to the wardroom. He can meet us there when he finishes." Kaltenbach knew his way around a submarine and moved toward the forward access hatch.

The young officer called after him, "Another officer is also waiting, sir."

Hauptman Gerhard Lutjens came to attention as the two senior officers entered the small wardroom. There was barely room for the three to stand as Dietrich made introductions. Lutjens, like Dietrich, wore the Knight's Cross at his collar. The two had inadvertently met when Dietrich passed through German lines on a mission to assassinate a Russian corps commander. A chance encounter with Gerhard, who was a young officer in charge of the scout/sniper platoon of the 46th Infantry Division, resulted in his being drafted to accompany Dietrich. The mission stretched to three days and culminated with a single shot by Lutjens which killed the Russian from over 300 meters. During the mission Dietrich had come to realize the natural talent of the younger man and also appreciate his total control in all situations. That mission began a unique partnership between a Waffen-SS senior officer and a Wehrmacht junior officer. They'd become close friends and Lutjens was on permanent loan to SS-Headquarters. Kaltenbach knew of the young officer who'd been with Dietrich in both Crete and Yugoslavia but this was their first meeting.

"It's a pleasure to finally meet you, Lutjens." The Admiral seemed sincere and the younger man was embarrassed. "I've benefited from your activities on several occasions. But every time I meet with Karl you're already off on the next assignment."

"Sir, the Standartenfuhrer likes to keep me moving. He says that's how he keeps me out of trouble." Gerhard grinned at Dietrich.

Dietrich laughed. "Gerhard has a way with the young ladies and it's my duty as his superior to keep him focused on his military tasks."

All three men turned as Commander Lothar Liche pushed through the curtains at the wardroom door.

"Admiral, my apologies for not being on deck to greet you. I'm sorting out some battery relay problems with the shipyard." The U-boat commander was wearing a white turtleneck sweater and his cap with the white cover, the mark of a captain.

"Kapitan Liche, may I present Standartenfuhrer Dietrich and Hauptman Lutjens. They are on detached duty from Reichfuhrer Himmler's headquarters." The men shook hands and then sat at the small table. Kaltenbach continued, "We're looking for a boat and crew to make a small boat insertion into England. This mission has the highest priority and my feeling is that you'd be the best choice of all the Kiel boats."

Liche said nothing for a moment. "Always an interesting mission. I've been on several of them. It's a navigational challenge putting someone at the right spot on a dark coastline. There are also seamanship issues. But the crucial matter is the party who has to leave the submarine and paddle into the unknown. Who's going to make this trip?"

Dietrich spoke up, "The two of us. We go ashore for as long as the mission takes and then you come back and pick us up."

Liche's eyes narrowed. "You make it sound routine. But I can assure you that any small boat insertion at night is difficult at best." He paused. "If you want to go I'll take you. Where specifically are we going?"

Kaltenbach pulled a folded chart from the inner pocket of his coat and spread it on the table. "Our agents tell us there's a good site for a landing on a remote beach about six kilometers west of the town of Sheringham." He pointed at the circled site on the chart.

Looking at the chart, Liche said, "We'll work up a navigation plan. When do you want to depart?"

"The day after tomorrow at dusk. Can you do it?" Dietrich asked.

"If the yard gets in here today to work on those relays I'll be ready."

Kaltenbach stood up. "Very well, I'll speak with the shipyard commander. We'll be here at noon Thursday with our two passengers and their gear. Anything else we need to discuss?"

"Yes, sir. How do I know when to go back in, to pick them up?"

Dietrich said in a low voice, "We'll have a radio. But don't worry; you won't have to wait long."

64 Baker Street
London

The conference room table was covered with maps and several manuals. Jack Stewart sat back and rubbed his eyes. "All right, let me try to pull this all together." Besides the key members of section F, Colonel Tommy Hudson sat at the table, taking notes. Jack continued, "We know the Germans have used a secure production facility on the Oder River to develop the industrial production capability for both Sarin and Tabun. We don't know what success they may have had but we'll assume they've figured out how to make large amounts. The next piece of the puzzle is the mating with the V-2 rocket. Is that hard or easy? Do they have to do it at a special facility? Can they transport the rocket with the nerve agent loaded or do they have to load it right before launch? We need to find out what our top scientists think."

Ian Thompson spoke up, "Let me take those questions out to Section IX and I'll get their thoughts." Section IX was the technology research working group for MI-6 located at a country estate called Frythe.

"OK, Ian. Let's also try to find out where we sit on any kind of antidote for Sarin."

"Bletchley Park thought they would be in business by tomorrow on the signals screening program," Hiram Walker said.

"Stay on top of that, Hiram. They might provide the best indication whether this is a wild goose chase or the real thing. Tommy, any feedback from the Brigadier's meeting with the Prime Minister?"

"I haven't heard anything but the Brigadier hasn't come in yet. I'll let you know as soon as I hear anything."

Jack nodded. "Phil and I are going to head out in about an hour to meet with Erich. If anybody has anything specific they want us to ask about let me know before we leave."

The group got up and headed to the door. Hudson remained seated at the table. Jack stood up and stretched his back as he asked, "Tommy, I've see that look before. What do you really think?"

"I'm thinking I wish I was on a tropical island with a scantily clad wench and not having to worry about this shit."

"Well said, my friend." They both laughed.

"Jack this one feels bad in my bones. From what we know the Krauts have the weapon and the delivery capability to get it to London. We're destroying every major city in Germany with our bombing campaign. If the situation were reversed, wouldn't we use the Sarin if it meant saving the country?"

"I think we would. What the hell's the difference if you die by high explosive or poison gas?"

"That's my point. We must assume they'll try it and then figure out how we stop them. I don't know what we can do but at least we'll be trying." Hudson sounded tired. He'd been running the MI-6 operational effort for almost four years and it was taking a toll.

"Tommy, let me worry about that. You go find Greene and see what he found out from the PM."

Hudson got up and walked toward the door. "Right."

Jack reached in his desk drawer and removed the shoulder holster. It carried the Walther PPK he had worn ever since the attempt on his life. Slipping his arm through the circular strap, he brought the connecting strap around and buckled it quickly. Pulling on his uniform blouse he walked into the outer office and told his yeoman he'd be back later that afternoon. The phone on the desk rang.

"Commander Stewart's office," Yeoman Buckley answered.

Jack paused for a moment.

"Yes, brigadier, just a moment." Buckley handed the receiver to Jack who listened briefly.

Jack looked at his watch. "Yes, sir, I can make it. I'll see Von Wollner later this afternoon."

Phil was waiting at the sedan. The driver sat in the idling car. Jack strode up. "Bit of a side trip, Larry. We need to head for Downing Street." Jack looked at Phil and said, "The PM wants to talk to us."

U2321
Kiel Naval Base
June 16, 1944

A working party of sailors moved the equipment bags from the back of a covered truck to the submarine. The bags contained an inflatable rubber raft, weapons, civilian clothes and a portable radio set. Liche's second in command, Lieutenant Hans Ulricht, met the two commandos and coordinated moving their gear down to the aft torpedo room. The Lieutenant told them the repairs were almost complete and they expected to get underway at 1930 hours.

Dietrich checked the gear was stowed and then found the captain in the forward battery compartment. Liche was down on his hands and knees looking behind an electrical panel near the deck.

"Kapitan Liche, our gear is stored and we're heading over to the headquarters building to see the Admiral."

Getting up from the deck, Liche wiped is hands with a rag and looked at the two. "Please be back by 1800. I'd like to do one run through of the deck launching. We won't inflate the boat but it's good to go over the sequence so everyone understands the procedures."

"We'll be back well before then," Dietrich said.

Twenty minutes later they were in Kaltenbach's office, the three men sitting around his desk.

"We've confirmed with our agent in Norfolk the location and time for your landing. 2030 tomorrow night on the Sheringham beach that was noted on the nautical chart. Our agent is a woman. The name she'll be using is Mrs. Hodgkins. She'll be on the beach with one other agent, Mr. Lowell. For navigation the group on the beach will use a flashlight. Every minute they will make two quick flashes. This will help you deal with the drift or tide as you make your way in to the beach. I talked with Liche and he's comfortable with water depth of two thousand meters off the beach. We've confirmed that only one of the MI-6 locations is currently manned. It's a small country estate in Kent called Farmingham. You have diagrams of the manor in your envelopes. This is a long shot but the Farmingham location had a great deal of increased activity at the time Von Wollner defected. You're still willing to go on such sketchy information?"

"Himmler made it very clear he wants this taken care of quickly I don't think I have much choice." Dietrich knew the information was not much. But from what he had learned of MI-6 procedures it was worth the chance.

"My people will be there to assist you in every way possible. I think you'll find they are very good. They report that there's not much military activity in the area and they'll have a truck to transport you to Farmingham."

10 Downing Street
London, England

An unusual agreement between Franklin Roosevelt and Winston Churchill had put the American born Annapolis graduate, Jack Stewart in the uniform of a King's officer. Because of this very unusual situation, Jack had come to know the Prime Minister. Following his first mission into France, Jack had spent time as Churchill's junior aide on one of his trans-Atlantic trips. The PM liked Jack and was pleased when his efforts to retain Jack in the Royal Navy permanently, paid off. Major General Bill Donovan, the head of the United States Office of Strategic Services had believed Jack would return from England and work for the OSS. Churchill had called in a personal favor from the President and now Stewart was committed to British Intelligence for the future.

Stewart knew his way to the office of Churchill's aide, RAF Squadron Leader Hugh Wylie. The two were both fighter pilots by training and had become friends over the last two years.

Jack opened the door to Wylie's office. "Good morning, Hugh. How about some tea for a couple of your favorite spies?"

"Jack, Phil, come please in. I'm afraid there won't be time for tea. After your Brigadier left here yesterday the old man has been cutting a pretty wide path through a number of ministries." He stood up and guided them both to the door. "He wanted to see you as soon as you arrived."

"Come in, gentlemen." Churchill was sitting at his desk reading from a folder. "Sit down. I'm just going over a report from our civil defence authority." In a moment he finished and laid the folder on his desk. "Jack, I'm very concerned about the potential problem you uncovered when debriefing Bishop. We know the Hun is close to having those rockets operational. We can't destroy the

33

rocket once they launch it. At least we can shoot down the damn V-1s. But we can't stop a missile that's coming down from outside of the atmosphere."

Jack had seen the many moods of Winston Churchill. It was clear he was worried over this latest development. "Sir, we don't have concrete evidence this plan is operational."

"I fear that a monster like Hitler wouldn't hesitate for one moment if this was technically feasible." He motioned to the folders on his desk. "I've just looked at our civil defence plan for gas attack and it simply doesn't address these nerve agents. The accepted antidote is Atropine and we not only don't have enough of it, we barely have enough of the substitute Lachesine. To add to the problem the antidote has to be injected in response to an attack. Imagine trying to get thousands of women and children to start injecting themselves, to say nothing of the potential side effects of the antidote."

"We're trying to see if there have been any references to the plan in intercepted radio messages. Bletchley Park has been working on it for several days. I'm hoping that any project of this importance would take a great deal of coordination between different commands and there would be message traffic." Jack knew this was a slim hope.

"What do we know for sure, at this point?" Churchill asked.

"Based on reliable information from the resistance, we know the V-2 is rapidly approaching an operational capability. The main production effort has been moved to the Harz Mountains and is being accomplished in underground caves. The use of foreign and conscripted labor has resulted in a great deal of information making its way out of Germany. I think it's interesting the two German rocket weapons have come under the control of different commands. The Luftwaffe is still running the V-1 program but Hitler gave the V-2 effort to Himmler and the SS. The Sarin facility near Breslau is under the command of the Wehrmacht as best we can determine. So there would certainly be big liaison problems for something like this."

"Quite so. I know how hard it is for us, can't be any different for them. By the way, how is our German doing?"

Jack smiled, remembering Churchill's concern when Von Wollner arrived in England with a bullet wound. "His wound is healing and I think he's getting more comfortable with us. I've had a little experience in switching allegiance and it's not as simple as people would think."

"The difference, commander, is both of your countries were fighting the same battle. I suspect he has many more doubts than you ever would."

"Yes, sir."

Kiel Naval Base
1800 Hours

Lieutenant Hans Ulricht stood on the deck of the submarine U2321 and watched the dock crew pull the metal gangway back and set it on the concrete wharf. The deck of the boat was empty except for ten sailors who were stationed at the mooring line attach points on the hull. There were also two officers standing forward of the conning tower both dressed in the jump suits worn by SS parachute troops.

On the bridge Commander Liche pushed the intercom switch and said, "Main control, bridge. Stand by to answer all bells." There was a rumble and diesel exhaust flushed out of the after engine manifolds. The deck passed on the vibration of the engines to all hands. "Single up all lines, number one."

"Aye aye, sir," Ulricht yelled back and he passed on the command to his line handlers.

It took a minute for the lines to be unwrapped from the bits and pulled back by the sailors remaining on the wharf. The submarine was only connected to the pier by two single lines, one forward, one aft.

Liche leaned over the metal conning tower shield. "Let go, aft," he yelled to Ulricht while selecting the intercom, "Left full rudder, engines back slow."

Dietrich watched as the rear of the submarine slowly moved away from the concrete wharf.

"Let go, forward"

Operating in the tight quarters of the submarine pen, the two thousand ton boat slowly turned to parallel the pier as the bow moved toward the darkened sky. There was a light wind blowing across the quiet harbour was quiet.

The two passengers walked forward. The U-boat cleared the concrete overhang and moved into the harbour basin. "Another adventure, eh Gerhard?"

"One to tell my grandchildren about, I'm sure."

Dietrich waited for a moment as his junior partner headed for the deck hatch. *Another adventure. How many more and how many before our luck runs out?* He shook off his thoughts and followed Lutjens down below.

As Dietrich grabbed the rungs to the ladder and made his way down into the submarine, a phone rang on in the office of Brigadier Noel Greene. It was from his counterpart in MI-5, the organization which controlled the counterespionage effort for England.

Chapter Three

Norfolk County
Southwest England
June 17, 1944
1815 Hours

A covered truck moved down the costal highway west of Sheringham. Painted on the sides were the words, "Thomas Furniture Moving LTD, Cambridge." The man driving the truck wore the brown coat and cap of a laborer. Sitting beside him and wearing a plain blue dress, was a woman in her late 20's. Mrs. Amanda Hodgkins blew the smoke from her cigarette out the truck's window. She was attractive and wore only a small amount of makeup. Her companion looked the part of a furniture mover with one day's growth of beard and pants grimy from work. They hadn't seen any vehicles in over two hours. It seemed there wasn't much activity by anyone on this stretch of the coast. The weather was cold for June and the wind blowing off the North Sea did not invite visitors to the seashore.

The woman looked at her watch. It was two hours until they were scheduled to meet the agents coming ashore at the Whiteside Beach. This type of activity was very unusual for the two of them. Their normal activities were to keep very much to themselves and simply be the eyes of German Naval Intelligence in the southwestern England. Through a set of rotating codes and frequencies, they'd been able keep a continual flow of information going to Germany for over three years. Her fellow operative had been recruited from the SS when they discovered his fluency in English and that he had spent time in England before the war.

Hans Richter had been a steady partner for Amanda, whose real name was Eva Papenhausen. Their cover as business owner and worker had met the scrutiny of local authorities in Cambridge. Richter carried identity papers with the name of Harry Thomas.

Moving furniture provided them with an excuse to travel the roads of southern England. Their trips had taken them from Portsmouth to Plymouth and Southampton, allowing them to observe naval buildups and troop movements. They were directly controlled by Admiral Kaltenbach and he kept their identities very tightly guarded. Over the last three years they had not contacted any other German agents.

"We're early, let's slow down. I don't want to be sitting in one spot for too long." She was nervous.

"As long as we can get to the spot before I have to use the headlamps. That's too much of a giveaway." He seemed less concerned but was also nervous.

"All right, let's stop in Blakeney and get something to drink and kill an hour. The turnoff is only three kilometers past Blakeney and we can be there before sunset."

"I only hope the Kriegsmarine can meet the timetable."

"They'll be there," she said. Eva turned to look out at the passing countryside.

U-2321
Six Miles North of Sheringham
Submerged, depth 40 meters

"Prepare to surface," Kapitan Liche said to the chief of the boat who relayed the command around the control room.

Dietrich and Lutjens stood by the navigation table. They were wearing SS jumpsuits with leather jackets and dark ski caps. "Kapitan, we'll head forward and be ready."

The U-boat commander grinned. "Good luck, gentlemen. Don't take too long, I've got a date in Kiel." He waited a moment and turned to the chief. "Surface."

The chief swung into action. "Blow main ballast tanks, forward planes, up full, aft planes, down five." The submarine angled up, the depth gauge indicating the decreasing distance to the surface. The sound of compressed air hissed through the boat.

Liche moved to the aft periscope used for general observation. "Up periscope. Bridge watch, standby." Several sailors in oilskins moved near the vertical ladder at the forward end of the control room. The control room was in red lights for adapting to night vision. The two men were also wearing dark goggles.

The commander rotated around a full circle. "Horizon is clear," he announced. "Check the air picture first. I don't feel like getting a Brit depth charge from one of their Sunderlands," he called to the lookouts.

"Equalize pressure."

The chief announced, "Open the hatch, lookouts to the bridge."

The two men scrambled up the ladder followed by Liche. Once on the bridge the commander quickly looked around noting a clear horizon. He called down to the control room, "Tell the forward crew that we'll open the hatch in ten minutes." Rechecking the course he ordered ahead slow on the diesel engines and looked ahead at the low-lying coastline – England.

Ten minutes later Liche called down to open the forward access hatch. He could see crewmen appear and lift a bundle from the hatch. Four thousand meters ahead the surf line showed white in the moonlight.

It took ten minutes to get the raft inflated and the remainder of the gear on deck. He estimated the distance to go at a little over 2000 meters. "All engines stop." Liche leaned over the railing. "Standby to launch in five minutes."

"Aye, Kapitan," came the reply from Lieutenant Ulricht who was on deck supervising the launch.

Surveying the beach line with his binoculars Liche paused as he saw a brief double flash from the shore. He checked to make sure all forward motion had ceased. "Launch the raft. Tell them to steer twenty degrees starboard of the bow."

Dietrich and Lutjens heard the relayed heading and pulled hard on their paddles to move away from the steel hull. There was a ground swell but not enough to push them back into the submarine. Working hard they were quickly clear of the boat. After several minutes they were able to see the beach line and a double flash of light on the beach. "Did you see that?" Lutjens asked.

"I did. Now let's get there in one piece."

They soon developed a rhythm and with a light breeze blowing onshore they covered the distance in twenty-five minutes. The surf accelerated them and they used their paddles as guides over the last twenty meters as the raft ground into the sandy beach. The two men jumped out of the inflatable boat into the foaming water. Grabbing the rope handles on each side of the raft they made their way up the beach.

Two figures moved out of the low vegetation, one clearly a woman.

Dietrich and Lutjens continued to drag the raft toward the line of brush as the two agents ran up to them. Without saying a word, the two strangers grabbed the rope handles to help move the raft. Dietrich heard the man say, "Hurry up," in German.

"Over here, we have a truck," the woman whispered harshly.

The four of them laid the raft at the rear of the truck. Lutjens bent down and removed the two deflation plugs and the air began to hiss out.

"Help us get the air out," Dietrich said. The four leaned on the rapidly deflating raft. In a minute the raft was flat with only their equipment rising above the reinforced raft bottom.

"Gerhard, fold up the raft." Dietrich turned to the other two. "Help me move our gear into the truck." The man grabbed the container holding the radio. The woman hesitated, staring in the darkness at Karl.

Gerhard completed folding the raft and called to his partner, "Karl, help me with the raft." The two men laid it in the back of the truck, the rear doors wide open to receive their gear. The raft was the last piece to go into the back of the truck. The black rubber raft would be re-inflated with the small bottle of compressed carbon dioxide when they were ready.

"Get in the back. We need to get off the beach," the woman called. Dietrich and Lutjens climbed into the back of the truck. Richter closed the door and hurried around to get in the driver's seat.

As he started the truck and put it in motion he quietly said to her, "That went well."

The woman was staring straight ahead and said, "I'm not so sure."

64 Baker Street
London, England
2100, 17 June 1944

Jack Stewart had been surprised to get a summons earlier in the evening to a meeting at MI-6 headquarters scheduled for 2100. It was very unusual for Greene to call meetings at night, although he frequently worked late at night by himself. When Jack arrived, Tommy Hudson and Phil Hatcher were already there. Entering the Brigadier's office he saw there was a stranger sitting in one of the chairs that faced Greene's large desk.

"Jack, come in and have a seat."

The five men were seated, no one saying anything. Greene spoke first. "Sorry to drag you out at night but there's been a development with Bishop."

Jack was alarmed. "Is he all right?"

"Oh yes, nothing like that. But it's along those lines, certainly. Let me introduce Phillip Kent. He's with MI-5 and has been working one of their most successful and closely guarded programs for the last three years. Tommy knows a bit of it but I'll let Phillip bring you up to speed."

Kent was in his late 30's, with dark hair combed straight back and a thin mustache. "Gentlemen, since early in 1940 we've had very good luck intercepting and turning German agents. Through radio intelligence and using already turned agents we've been able to catch new agents and turn them also. The system has allowed us to feed bad information to the Nazis and make sure they don't know it. We call it the Wireless Board. One of our best agents has alerted us about a mission to locate and kill Commander Von Wollner."

"Son of a bitch." Jack wasn't surprised to hear of the mission but it made him angry.

Kent continued, "Two agents came ashore near Sheringham about thirty minutes ago. We have set up a false target for them at a country estate called Farmingham. We chose not to take them on the beach because we don't know if they had a radio contact plan with Germany. We didn't want to alert the Krauts something was amiss. After talking with the Brigadier we see an opportunity to orchestrate Commander Von Wollner's demise in the eyes of the Germans. Our agent will try to figure out any reporting plan before we take them into custody."

"Real cloak and dagger." Phil Hatcher, the ex-police inspector was impressed with the plan, "Let Jerry think Erich has been popped and then they're happy."

"Precisely. But we wanted to get some help with the firepower issue. These agents are trained SS commandos not the normal agents we have to deal with. We would like to enlist your aid in taking them into custody."

Jack smiled. "I've got a couple who can hold their own with anyone. But what's the plan?"

Kent opened a folder, "Our agent will make sure the team goes to ground tonight with the attempt happening tomorrow night at Farmingham. Here's the layout of the estate with the bedroom and living area where she'll tell the commandos they'll find Von Wollner."

"OK, let me talk with the lads and we'll put together a plan. I'll be ready to brief you and the Brigadier by 0700 tomorrow."

The Fletcher Farm
Six miles south of Sudbury, Essex
June 18, 1944
0030

The truck pulled off the main highway and bounced along a small side road for fifteen minutes before stopping at a darkened farm. Killing the engine Richter walked back and opened the truck's rear doors. "We're here. We need to get you inside. Leave your gear. I'll pull the truck into the barn."

Dietrich and Lutjens got out of the back of the truck and stretched to loosen their stiff muscles after four hours in the truck. They saw the woman standing by the open front door silhouetted by the light coming from the kitchen. As they stepped up on the porch she said "There's food in the box on the kitchen table."

Stepping into the large kitchen Karl walked over to the table and opened the wooden box. Inside there were several tins of corned beef, loaves of bread and several blocks of cheese wrapped in oiled paper. Next to the box were several large bottles of beer. "Everything a man needs," Dietrich said.

"That's good. I'm ready for food in any form." Gerhard had removed the twist key from the corned beef can and began to open it. "See if you can find a knife."

Dietrich crossed to a cupboard. He found a small knife and several glasses, bringing them back to the table. "Beer?"

"When have I ever refused a beer?" Lutjens placed the corned beef on a plate and began slicing it into pieces.

Dietrich poured the frothy beer into large glasses, sliding one in front of his companion. The door opened and the woman stepped into the light. Karl glanced at her as he took a drink of beer. Slowly, he looked at the woman. "I'm going to get some air. Make me a sandwich," he said as he walked toward the door. He put his hand on the woman's shoulder and gently pushed her out the door. Engrossed in making a sandwich, Lutjens didn't notice.

The two walked to the end of the porch and turned to face each other. "Eva, can that really be you?"

"I thought the same thing at the beach," she said, crossing her arms in front of her.

"What are you doing here?" He was whispering but his tone demanded an answer.

"Karl, it's a long story. There are too many things happening." She sounded frustrated and confused.

"My sister said she'd lost track of you after you left Cologne."

"Is she well?"

"She's fine, still in Cologne. Eva, how long have you been here?"

"Three years." She seemed to be gripping herself tighter, wrestling with her emotions. Before the war Eva had been Karl's sister's best friend.

He reached up and put his hands on her shoulders. "It makes me happy to see you." His enthusiasm was genuine.

Eva reached out and put her arms around him pulling herself to him. She held him tightly but said nothing.

Dietrich moved his arms around her and they held each other on the dark porch.

On missions, Dietrich's internal alarm would awaken him early and he would get a head start on each day. This morning was no different. He quietly dressed. Looking at his watch dial, he saw it was 0445. Opening the door of the bedroom he shared with Lutjens, Dietrich made his way down the hall to the kitchen where he saw light under the door.

He pushed the door open to find Eva sitting at the table. She raised her head when she heard him.

He saw tears were streaming down her cheeks.

She said, "We have to talk."

Sitting down, he quietly said, "All right."

"Karl, if you attempt to carry out your mission tonight you'll either be killed or captured."

"Go on." His voice betrayed no emotion.

"I work for the British and have for the last three years. When I got here I went to them. They offered me immunity and citizenship." The tears continued to run down her cheeks.

"That's why you've survived as long as you have." Karl's voice was quiet and detached. "But why? What could make you become a traitor to your country?"

"When I was recruited by Naval Intelligence, I saw it as a chance to escape from a Germany that I'd come to hate. The Gestapo, the Nazis, the hate , I wanted no part of it." She buried her face in her hands. "But I can't let anything happen to you."

Dietrich got up and walked to the window. The first rays of the sun were breaking through the trees in the orchard.

"Eva, what have you done?"

"Karl, I did what I thought was right. And I still do. This is a good country with good people and they're fighting for the right cause. I know you don't want to hear that but it's true whether you want to hear it or not." She stood and walked over to him. "And if it would have been anyone else but you, I'd have completed my mission."

"Why am I any different?" His voice sounded cold.

She didn't say anything for a few moments then slowly said, "I realized last night I still love you."

"What!" He turned to look at her with a shocked expression on his face.

"I fell in love with you in Cologne. You were too busy to notice. I almost thought I'd gotten over you."

Leaning back on the counter he lowered his eyes to the floor and slowly shook his head. A flood of emotion ran through him and Eva's confession of love left him completely confused. "I was sent on this mission by Himmler personally. The letter I carry for is signed by Hitler."

"I'll take you back to the Norfolk coast and help you get away." She was talking fast, the words pouring out. "I know I can keep away from the patrols long enough to make the rendezvous. But the mission has no chance. I don't know where they have the man now, but it's not Farmingham."

"And what happens to you when they find out you helped me escape?"

"I don't know. I'll make something up. Tell them you were recalled or something. But I know I can't let you be captured or killed." She sounded desperate, her eyes again filled with tears.

48

His mind in confusion, he was drawn to Eva, putting his arms around her and pulling her close. She hesitated and then put her arms around him. "We've got a problem," he said.

64 Baker Street
0730 Hours

The key members of Section F worked through the night to come up with a workable plan. The challenge was to capture the German commandos alive, if possible. Trying to disarm or overwhelm highly trained operatives without needlessly endangering your own people is difficult. In addition to Hatcher, Jack had Terry Howe and his two experienced commandos, Curtis Livesy and Jimmy Hunt. All of them had been on dangerous missions behind German lines and could handle themselves well. They also had the advantage of surprise which was critical. Using the floor plan of the manor house they were able to run several different scenarios and by 0600 they had a rough draft for Greene.

Briefing Kent and the Brigadier went well. Going over every option, the final decision was to have the MI-6 team inside the Farmingham mansion with MI-5 agents on the perimeter. Greene was also going to have a large number of MI-6 uniformed security personnel throughout the area. The only real unknown in the plan was the willingness of the Germans to die – but they'd have to assume they wanted to live.

When the group broke up it was agreed that all players would meet at the mansion at noon. There would be time for several run throughs and they would lock down the final sequence of events.

Greene's final guidance stood out in Jack's mind. "Capture these men if at all possible. But kill them in a minute before you hazard one of ours."

Jack liked the rules.

The Fletcher Farm
1000 Hours

The doubts which had begun to surface in Karl Dietrich's mind over a year ago now came brutally into focus. After talking to Eva for over an hour he told her he needed some time by himself to think. She looked miserable, her world turned upside down and most likely about to dissolve.

They didn't say anything to the other two.

Dietrich slipped away to walk in the orchard and think about the morning's events. Eva and Cologne was a time in his life he'd put out of his mind. They were young and life was good. He remembered thinking about her as something more than his sister's friend but nothing ever came of it. So she was thinking about him at the same time. He wondered how his life might have changed? Would he have joined the SS at all? No sense wasting time wondering about what might have been. He was in an enemy country on a deadly mission and it was falling apart. The smart thing would be to get out of here as quickly as he could. He didn't relish Himmler's reaction to failure.

But his thoughts kept coming back to Eva and her reason for leaving Germany and joining the British. Hadn't he felt the same way every time the Jewish issue came up. Always on the edge of those events, he had seen the terrible things the SS units did in

Russia. The extermination of Gypsies and Jews, people which Himmler and Goebbels called 'untermensch' – subhuman. He had never taken part, but he knew what was happening. He was fighting the good war for the real Germany. But was he really?

Thinking back to his neighborhood in Cologne there were many good Jewish families. He was friends with many Jewish students at University. How did we ever go down this road? Weren't they Germans just like he was? What was he thinking to look the other way? And now we are guilty of doing the same thing as the SS herd people into boxcars and send them off to death camps. My God, what are we doing? What have I done?

Karl Dietrich, SS Standartenfuhrer, holder of the Knight's Cross sat down on the grass in a British orchard. With his arms folded tightly against his body he stared at the ground and began to evaluate his life. Everything which defined his world and values for the last ten years, was crumbling around him.

Farmingham Estate
Essex, England
1315 Hours

Jack Stewart had been pleased with the practice session conducted by the team. The main house was laid out very well for their ruse to get the German commandos into the main reception area on the first floor. From there his men would be positioned in a pattern which would eliminate every option by the Germans. They'd have no choice but surrender or be cut down. Jack was counting on the experience of the Germans to recognize the futility of their position. If they did, the plan would be a success. If they didn't, they would die very quickly. In either case Erich would be safe.

Walking down the main corridor Jack was trying to think of anything they might've overlooked. He heard footsteps on the hardwood floor behind him. He turned to see Tommy Hudson walking alone. Smiling at Hudson it hit him how much it meant to have the quiet man as a friend and colleague. "You look like the cat just ate your canary."

Hudson smiled and shook his head. "I just had a call from the Brigadier, quite extraordinary."

"All right, you've got my attention."

"Kent received a call from their agent who's with the Germans. It seems the German commander wants to talk."

"I think I'd call that extraordinary. I can't wait to hear this story."

"You won't have to wait long. The Brigadier and Kent want you to make the initial contact. It would seem the two of them are a bit skeptical and still think we need a big stick to deal with them."

Jack grinned. "Never thought of myself as a 'big stick.' But if that's what they want, fine with me. What's the plan to make contact?"

"They're currently at a farm not far from here. They've asked for a 1500 meeting at the farm."

"We've got all our players here. They're armed and equipped for anything. Let's go look at a map."

The Fletcher Farm
1400 Hours

It had been an eventful morning at the farm. Richter was surprised, but went about his duties quietly staying out of the way. Eva had been shocked and happy when Karl had come to her and told her of his desire to talk to the British. Gerhard Lutjen's reaction surprised everyone.

Dietrich asked his young protégé to walk with him. He explained the connection with Eva and Cologne.

"Gerhard, she works for British Intelligence. We've been set up. If we continue the mission we'll be killed or captured."

"So what do we do now?"

"We do the honorable thing."

"Honorable thing, what does that mean?" The younger man stopped and was facing Dietrich.

"We do what's right in front of our people and God. I've never talked with you about this, but the path which Germany is following with the Jews has always bothered me. It's only getting worse. This situation allows me to make a break from the Germany that's destroying a people and in the process our national honor. Gerhard, I've asked to meet with British Intelligence."

The young man looked Dietrich in the eye. "Karl, when you found me I was a member of the Wehrmacht. I joined the army because I thought it was the patriotic thing to do. What I saw in Russia made me sick. When you offered me a chance to fight with you on the kind of missions that I felt were honest, it was a godsend. My loyalty is to you and the Germany we both remember. I'm with you whatever the future brings." He extended his hand and the two men shook.

"For better or for worse."

Karl looked out the kitchen window at the olive drab sedan moving slowly down the driveway. A large covered military truck followed fifty meters behind the sedan. Both vehicles stopped, the sedan now twenty meters from the farm house. No one got out of the truck but both doors on the sedan opened. Two men wearing brown commando battle dress got out and walked toward the building. The first man was tall, in his mid thirties and led the pair. His companion was the same age but shorter and more compact. As they approached the house, Karl opened the door and stepped onto the porch, his hands clearly empty and visible. His instructions to the others had been to remain inside.

The taller man stopped and began to speak in German, "My name is Stewart, British Intelligence. This is Major Hatcher, a member of my team."

"I am Standartenfuhrer Karl Dietrich, Waffen SS. I was sent on a mission by Riechsfuhrer Heinrich Himmler to kill Commander Erich Von Wollner. I am placing myself and my companion, Hauptman Gerhard Lutjens, at your disposal."

Jack said, "In view of the unusual circumstances I think it would make sense for us to sit down and discuss what's happening here before we go any further."

"I agree. Where would you like to talk?"

Looking around, Jack pointed at a shady spot, under several trees. "Over there."

From the kitchen window Eva watched the men. The concern within her was evident on her face. She didn't noticed Richter watching her from the hallway. He quietly went into a bedroom and closed the door.

The three men sat on the grass and for a moment there was silence. Jack could sense the man sitting opposite him was uncomfortable, but at the same time confident.

"Colonel, I'm not entirely sure what we're dealing with here. Is this a surrender to British authorities or is it more than that?" Jack chose to use his rank equivalent in the British Army.

"You did not tell me your rank," the German said without emotion.

Jack replied, "Commander Jack Stewart, Royal Navy."

Dietrich didn't say anything for thirty seconds trying to form the words which would describe his situation. "Commander, while I am and always will be loyal to Germany, I've come to the realization that the Nazis and Adolph Hitler have chosen the wrong path for my country. When I said I'm at your disposal I meant exactly that. I'm ready to cooperate with you to hasten the fall of the Nazis."

Jack looked at the man. Dietrich's pale blue eyes were piercing and seemed to say that this is not a man who lies. "I was involved in the extraction and debrief of Erich Von Wollner. I find it interesting that senior officers of the German military are coming to the same conclusion about Hitler. Von Wollner was able to see Hitler every day and watch how Germany was being slowly destroyed. I'm sure many people would call him a traitor but I think someday he'll be recognized as a patriot. But you admit you came here to kill him. How can you change your mind so quickly?"

For the first time since they met, Dietrich smiled. "I didn't know my English contact would be an old friend. She made me face the truth which I'd been ignoring for a long time. There are terrible things which have been done on both sides during this war. The Russians are no different than the Nazis in that regard. They are beasts. But I'm afraid when the truth is told Germany will wear a badge of shame for many years. In my own small way I want to try and regain some of Germany's lost honor. There're many good Germans. They've let themselves be led down the wrong road. Now it's time to change."

Jack sat there looking at Karl Dietrich. How do you judge a man's confession of change? Stewart spent many hours talking with Von Wollner and the situation was very much the same. Both were good men who originally fought for their country as good Germans. But each had come to understand their cause was flawed. How difficult it must be to arrive at that realization. But honorable men are no different regardless of the flag they follow. They will fight to the death for their country but will not commit crimes. If Von Wollner could reach that conclusion, why not Dietrich?

"Colonel, I think we have many things to think about. There's a country estate not far from here, Farmingham. Let's move everyone there, get settled and figure out the next step."

Dietrich said, "I'm assuming that includes Hauptman Lutjens?"

Hatcher spoke up for the first time, "Yes, Colonel. We'll have your team and the two agents that met you at Farmingham. It's a secure location and we can take our time figuring out a course of action."

"Very well, let's go."

"One matter I'm sure you understand, we'll need to take custody of your weapons." Hatcher added.

"Of course." Karl heard himself say. *Where will this lead us?*

Chapter Four

Professor Ian Thompson sat at the conference table with Hiram Baker and Jack Stewart going over select transcripts which had begun to come out of Hut 6 at Bletchley Park. Jack left Phil to get the group settled into Farmingham while he came back to report to Greene and check on the team.

Initially there hadn't been many messages containing key words which might alert the team to activity on Valkyrie. Thompson and Baker were both discouraged, thinking the idea might be a dead end. But an excited phone call from Ira Haskins sent Hiram over to Bletchley Park. It was the first evidence that Valkyrie was more than an obscure plan sitting on a shelf.

Ira Haskins was a mathematician by training and an obsessive solver of puzzles. From the Times crossword to any riddle, he reveled in the mental gymnastics to find a key or pattern or hidden message. Understanding the basics of the Valkyrie challenge he began by screening messages using both geographic location and then subject matter. Looking for any cross connection he was rewarded in short order when he found a unique shipping code in a message on V-2 logistics requirements and a request for shipping support from Dyhernfurth, which was one of the original locations noted by Hiram Baker. Haskins next cross-referenced previous messages from Dyhernfurth, the suspected location of the Sarin production facility. It was simply a matter of working backwards to check all records of contact between the two facilities. It was from these he deduced the project code – "SR". It appeared the Valkyrie Contingency had moved from plan to action.

Ira had been selected to head the small team which was now working the Valkyrie project full time. The group was re-checking for all messages for the suspended project code. In addition they examined all messages to or from the Dyhernfurth facility and the V-2 logistics support group at Nordhausen.

There was clearly an increase in messages using the special code. Once the team knew what to look for, it became clear that the Sarin production facility was working on a project which would provide the Sarin for warhead assemblies which were being fabricated at Nordhausen. There were coordination and logistic messages, which indicated the Sarin capable warheads were in fabrication. The two commands were now trying to determine the method for combining the finished assemblies with the Sarin. This was where Ian's contacts at Section IX came in handy with their knowledge of chemical weapons.

Ian explained "The problem, as with every chemical weapon, is that it can be as deadly to the user as to the target. These nerve agents are terribly more unstable than earlier types of gases such as chlorine or mustard. There was always the problem of gas blowing in the wrong direction once it had been delivered. But accidents behind the lines were not common. Now we have compounds that are not only more lethal, but they're more difficult to store and transport. Our best minds on this one suspect the Germans will have to use some type of industrial glass probably in multiple layers to contain the fluid. This doesn't make transportation an easy task in wartime."

Jack thought for a moment. "So what we may have here is a simple problem of how to get the container to the material and then onto a rocket."

"Exactly so. This stuff is so lethal an accident would potentially be catastrophic to the Germans. Just think what would happen if the Sarin was on a train going through Berlin during an air raid. The snake would turn to bite its handler."

Hiram put down the message he was reading. "How does that help us stop them?"

Shaking his head, Jack said, "I'm not sure. But we need to look at the known facts and try to find their weak point."

"How are our newest guests doing at Farmingham?" Hiram asked.

"I left Phil to get them settled. I'm supposed to brief the old man. He's on his way back from the PM's."

The Brigadier arrived back an hour later. They were joined by Tommy Hudson, who had just arrived from Farmingham.

"So, gentlemen, what do we have?" Greene asked as they sat down.

Tommy offered, "The German team is bedded down at Farmingham with a full security detachment. We asked MI-5 if we could keep their two agents on site until we decide what to do with the Germans."

"And do we know anything about our Germans?"

Jack spoke up, "Two man team. The senior officer is an SS Colonel named Dietrich. I've got our people checking on him now. His companion is a Wermacht captain. According to Dietrich, they were sent personally by Himmler to kill Von Wollner. Apparently Hitler was involved in directing the mission. It would appear they weren't very happy about Erich changing sides."

"So they land by U-boat, are met by what they think is a German team, kill our German and then back to the U-boat." Greene said.

"That's about it."

"Why go to such effort for one man? Does he know something terribly important and they're afraid we'll discover it? Or were they just taking revenge for such a rampant act of treason?" Greene's question didn't have an answer and neither man offered one.

Tommy said, "The key is to decide how we can best use this situation to deal with Valkyrie."

Greene looked thoughtful. "Let's step back for a moment. Perhaps we're victims of a sophisticated counter stroke by the Germans. Is this Colonel really a convert or is he playing us for fools?"

"I talked to him when we first got there and again back at Farmingham. I think he's telling us the truth, particularly the connection with the female agent," Jack said.

"Perhaps that's a ruse?" Hudson asked.

"There're no guarantees in this business, Tommy. You taught me that. But I think we need to approach it like he's telling the truth and then see if we can maintain some leverage. I think I've got an idea," Jack said.

Farmingham Estate
Essex
June 19, 1944
0725 Hours

Karl Dietrich had slept very little during his second night in England. Reviewing his decision and the events of the last twenty four hours he felt like he was free of something dark and sinister. But breaking his oath of allegiance made so many years ago, was something he couldn't shake off. He kept telling himself the SS had lost their ability to demand his loyalty once they began to violate every rule of warfare. But why was he unsure?

There was a knock at the door and it opened slowly. "Good morning, Colonel. Can I offer you breakfast?" Phil Hatcher stood in the open door.

"Yes, thank you."

The two went downstairs where Dietrich found Gerhard Lutjens sitting at a table with a cup of steaming coffee in front of him.

"Have a seat, Colonel. I'll have them bring some food out."

"How are you?" he asked his friend.

"Considering we're prisoners of British Intelligence with a totally unknown future, I'm doing surprisingly well."

Dietrich looked at Lutjens and asked, "Second thoughts?"

The door at the other end of the room opened and Eva entered. "Gerhard, good morning," she said and looked at Dietrich, "Good morning."

He pulled out a chair for her and said, "It's good to see you."

She turned her head as she sat down and smiled.

The two commandos moved to the library after breakfast, talking and perusing the bookshelves.

The door opened and Gillian Andrews entered. "Excuse me, gentlemen. I'm Leading WREN Andrews."

Gerhard Lutjens remembered the young woman bringing in a pot of coffee during breakfast.

"Can I bring you anything? Coffee or tea perhaps?" she asked.

Gerhard found himself staring at her. She had dark brown hair and deep green eyes. Her smile was friendly and warm. She spoke fluent German.

Karl spoke up, "Coffee would be very nice, thank you."

Gillian said, "I'll be just a moment, sir." As she walked out, her eyes met Gerhard's. "I've arranged for some clothes for each of you. If you need any additional toiletries, please let me know."

The door closed behind her. "You're very quiet, Gerhard. It appears the young English girl made an impression on you."

Gerhard turned to find Karl smiling.

The two German officers were finishing their coffee when Jack Stewart, now in the blue service uniform of the Royal Navy entered. Tommy Hudson and Phil Hatcher were behind Jack and finally a tall man in a civilian suit. Karl immediately recognized Erich Von Wollner.

"Good morning, gentlemen," Jack said in German. "We'd like to ask you some questions if you don't mind?" When there was no objection from Karl or Gerhard he continued, "Good. Let's have a seat and get started."

Phil Hatcher was quietly translating for Tommy Hudson, the only non-German speaker in the room.

The group sat down at the long table in the center of the room.

Jack said, "Colonel, I believe you've met everyone here except Commander Von Wollner."

The room was very quiet as the two men looked at each other.

"You are correct. It is now my honor to meet him."

Erich replied, "Herr Standartenfuhrer, I am pleased to meet you under these circumstances."

There was an uncomfortable silence. "Gentlemen, why don't we let these two get to know each other. Captain Lutjens, would you join us in the dining room?"

The younger man looked surprised and said, "Of course."

Karl and Erich remained seated while the others got up and left the room, closing the door after them.

Erich reached in his coat pocket and pulled out a pack of cigarettes. He took one out and offered the pack to Karl. "These are American cigarettes, they call them Chesterfields."

Karl took one out and said, "Thank You."

Von Wollner lit his cigarette and offered the lit match to his companion.

The two sat for a moment, smoking and looking at each other.

Karl broke the silence. "Wouldn't Himmler like to see this?"

Erich laughed. "A German with a sense of humor. You restore my faith in our people."

"I'm afraid the rest of the world might disagree."

"The German people will pay for this for decades," Erich offered

"How did we allow our country to end up where it is?"

Erich paused for a moment. "I think we were looking for easy answers and the Nazis supplied them. They knew who to blame for our problems and they had solutions that made most German's lives better, especially the military. Throw in the Gestapo and there you have it - a dictatorship like the world has never seen."

"But it didn't seem that way while it was happening."

"It never does," Erich agreed.

They stubbed out their cigarettes and Karl asked, "What do they have you doing?"

"An extensive debriefing about everything I can remember. They want to bring this war to and end and with as little loss of life as possible."

"I'm just a soldier," Karl said. "I can't imagine what good I can be to them."

"I think you'd be surprised. Let's go find Jack Stewart. I think there are some questions he would like to ask you." The two got up to leave and Erich stopped, turning to face Karl. "I may never be able to return to Germany, but I can face myself now. I hope you will feel the same way."

The Mittelwerk Facility
Nordhausen, Germany

The original limestone mines dug into the Harz Mountains proved to be a superb site to build an underground rocket fabrication factory. Essentially impervious to aerial attack, the security measures made this one of the most secure facilities in Germany. Over thirty thousand people, from scientists to engineers to slave laborers, worked twenty-four hours a day, seven days a week building the assemblies for the V-2 rocket. From this facility the rockets would be shipped to several sites in Northern Europe where the explosive warheads would be joined to the rocket. The assemblies would then be transferred to tractor-trailers of the operation launch units. The race was on to get the V-2 totally operational before the Allied armies overran the launch areas. At the same time a new project had absorbed many of the most talented design engineers.

Volker Fischer was the lead engineer in the "Special Design Section" of the Mittelwerk fabrication division. A mechanical engineer by training, he had become a specialist in ballistic charges and explosive design. He was very proud of the final design for the V-2 rocket warhead. However now he was heading up the design team for the special warhead required by Project SR. From an engineering standpoint it had been the greatest challenge of his career. The warhead was designed to carry almost five hundred kilograms of Sarin liquid which would disperse in the atmosphere on detonation. Fischer's challenge was to design a vessel which would safely contain the Sarin. In liquid form the agent was highly corrosive. Fischer had to design a warhead which could withstand the forces of launch and normal handling and still break apart effectively. His design team had worked a minor miracle. Using a dual walled container made from the strongest industrial glass, they invented a silk and rubber layered insulation blanket to separate the two glass vessels. Initial tests had gone very well and they were now working the final challenge of the design, a method to rupture both glass vessels at the right time.

"Herr Fischer, we're ready to test the explosive pattern when you're ready."

Volker looked up at his test assistant. "Let's head out to the boom room."

Located outside the Mittelwerk tunnels, the "boom room" was the explosive test facility for the factory. In today's test a mock up glass warhead vessel had been fitted with a pattern of small shaped charges connected to a common firing point. Upon detonation the sequenced small charges would rupture, but not destroy, the glass vessel. This would allow the contents to atomize in the wind stream created as the V-2 plunged to earth. It was using nature to accomplish man's tasking.

It was a fifteen minute drive to the fenced off enclosure two miles from the entrance to Tunnel A. When they reached the test site the glass warhead assembly was already on the concrete and steel testing frame. The two men went into the small concrete bunker and made sure all of the equipment was ready for what they hoped would be the final design test.

The actual detonation was not much to see. Fischer knew the real test would be reading high-speed photography of the rupture and examining the warhead remnants. It was later that afternoon when his assistant brought the results to his office that Fischer smiled for the first time in a long time.

Farmingham Estate
Essex
July 19, 1944
1000

The morning had been a remarkable experience for Karl Dietrich. The discussions led him to several conclusions. First, Erich Von Wollner was a thoughtful and serious man. There was no doubt in Karl's mind that he was looking at a man with a strong sense of conscience and shame for the conduct of Germany. Second, this group of British Officers was totally professional and knew their business. The questions they asked covered many aspects of the war, including the role of the SS. The British made it clear to Karl that they understood he was a member of the combat arm of the SS and not connected with the political or police arm of the organization. The men were not judgmental but were searching for answers. Jack Stewart asked a lot of questions about Karl's combat missions from Norway to Russia and the Mediterranean. In the third hour the conversation went in an entirely different direction.

"Colonel, we've had several discussions with Commander Von Wollner about a project which surfaced for a time and then disappeared from mainstream message traffic which he would have seen in the Secretariat. The name of the project was the Valkyrie Contingency. Does that sound familiar to you?" Jack had a notebook open and was making notes.

Dietrich thought for a moment. "I don't remember ever hearing any name such as Valkyrie."

Phil looked up from the note page on which he was scribbling. "We've also reason to believe the project may have been renamed "SR"

His head turned and Karl asked, "Did you say "SR?"

"That's right. We've seen it surface in several places which make us think the two are one and the same."

"Christ, I'd hoped it was just a drunk talking."

The rest of the men looked at him with puzzled glances.

"I have a friend who's on Himmler's personal staff. We went through initial training together and became good friends. Whenever I'm called to headquarters we see each other and catch up. It must have been in May. I was back in Berlin and we got together for dinner at his house. There were many bottles of wine and Dieter got stone drunk. When I talked about how the war was going badly for us he said that would all change 'after we unleash Black Rain on them.' I asked him what he meant and all he would say was there was nothing that could stop it and the enemy would die like flies. There's the connection 'Schwarze Regen', Black Rain."

The British sat in silence realizing that their fears were justified. Tommy Hudson asked, "What do you know of the new V-2 rocket the SS is preparing to use against England?"

"There are several operational launch units which are already trained and deployed awaiting the first operational rockets. Is that what SR is all about?"

Jack ignored the question. "Have you ever heard of the chemical weapon Sarin?"

"Yes, I know about Sarin." Dietrich recalled his conversation with Dieter. "…nothing could stop it, that's what he said. Sarin with the V-2……My God."

Karl Dietrich was laying on one of the large couches with his eyes closed when the door to the library opened. His thoughts kept returning to the discussion that morning. His Germany was ready to launch nerve gas rockets against the English people. In the eyes of the world the German nation would be no different than the most depraved killers in history. He wondered for a moment if the launch crews would carry out those orders? Of course they would launch the rockets. In the SS you follow orders. Eva entered the room.

"Are you asleep?"

Sitting up, he said, "No, come in please. I've just been trying to make sense of what's happening. I'm afraid I don't have any answers, just more questions."

"Karl, you're not a philosopher, you're a soldier. Asking those questions will drive you crazy. Just worry about yourself for now. Let the rest of the world take care of Hitler." She came over and sat down next to him on the couch.

"I'm afraid a lot of Germans will be saying exactly that, 'what could I do, I'm just a person'. And I suspect the world won't want to hear it either."

"But you saw it and took action. How many never would have done that?"

"Right, cornered on this island with the war going against Germany everywhere, I chose to desert and dishonor my oath. I wonder how noble people will consider that?"

"It doesn't matter what people think. You made the right decision." She put her hand on his arm. He put his hand on top of hers. "You made the decision when the situation was reversed. You made it when you had everything to lose. What do I have to lose? I'll spend the rest of the war in a nice safe prison camp. I'm sorry, Eva. I don't feel like I've done anything very noble."

Gillian Anderson sat at the table in the small pantry and reviewed the shopping list from the cook. As she went down the list and compared it to the planned menu, her mind kept returning to the young German captain. What was it about him? She knew from Major Hatcher that the man was an experienced commando and highly decorated. But he seemed shy and more like a boy than a man. His face was kind and nothing like the Colonel's. When she talked with Colonel Dietrich, she felt he was the image of the SS. His eyes were piercing, without warmth. What a strange pair she thought.

That afternoon Jack sat in the Brigadier's office with Tommy. The three met to discuss the morning debrief with Dietrich. Greene led off by reading from a sheet of paper. "It seems our Colonel Dietrich is a bit of a legend in the SS. A veteran of multiple missions behind the lines, he may be the best commando in the German Army. He's a recipient of the Knight's Cross personally presented by Hitler. It makes his change of heart that much more remarkable or improbable."

Jack shook his head. "Sir, I've talked to him and listened very carefully. If he's acting then he should get the Knight's Cross for the best performance of the year. I would bet my life he's telling us the truth."

"Unfortunately, if we believe him we may be betting someone else's life."

"I don't follow you." Tommy said.

"It's quite simply really. We can lock our Colonel away for the duration or we can try to turn him and use him actively."

Jack frowned. "What do you mean use him actively?"

70

The Brigadier had been at this business for much longer than the two younger men and he smiled. "There are unique ways to take advantage of Herr Dietrich assuming he really is desirous of working for us. Not that I think we have any certainty on that issue, not by a wide margin."

"Let me talk with Mrs. Hodgkins or Eva as he calls her. It's my understanding from Hunt that she's a true Hitler hater and has been a superb asset for MI-5 for three years. She knew him from before the war, knew his family and I sense cares for him."

"Good idea, Jack, but let's get on with it. If we want to pull any tricks on Jerry we need to have some action soon or we'll lose our advantage. And I still have my doubts in any case."

Late in the afternoon Jack Stewart found Eva in her room at the main house at Farmingham. He asked her if she would mind accompanying him on a walk in the garden. It was a beautiful afternoon, a light wind was blowing and there was the smell of lilac in the air. Jack walked slowly down the gravel path, which ran between the flour beds. "I understand you knew Colonel Dietrich's sister before the war?"

"We were friends for many years in school." She had her arms crossed in front of her as if she was protecting herself.

"This is a rather remarkable situation we find ourselves in. I'll be honest with you. We want to use the Colonel, but the chain of command has great reservations."

She smiled. "Commander, I can only imagine the questions that are being asked. All I can tell you is what I feel with all my heart. Karl Dietrich has turned his back on Hitler and the Nazis. Don't ever think he's not a proud German. But he is also ashamed of what the SS has become."

"I'd like to believe that. It's some of our more senior types who are skeptical."

"Do you know how I came to work for MI-5?" she asked.

"I assume you were turned by them on arrival." He remembered Phillip Hunt's description.

"When I arrived in England, I went to them. I only agreed to work for German Naval Intelligence because I saw it as a chance to escape the nightmare, which Germany had become. I'm now British as far as I'm concerned. My loyalties are to my adopted country. I've talked with Karl a great deal in the last two days. I believe what he says."

Jack thought for a moment of the irony. An American and a German, now British by choice. "I guess all we have to go on sometimes is instinct. Would you be able to remain here for a few days? Events are unfolding quickly and it might be important for you to stay involved."

She nodded. "I can stay. I'll send Richter back with the truck. That will make sure anyone who might be watching us sees the normal routine. I'll have him standby for any radio messages we need to send."

"Thank you."

The shadows were starting to lengthen when Jack found Karl Dietrich in the kitchen drinking a cup of coffee with Lutjens. They turned when Jack opened the door.

"Commander." He nodded to Jack.

"Colonel, I'm glad I found you. We need to talk and there's a time constraint that's starting to come into play."

There was a knock on the door from the hall and Gillian Anderson came in carrying several ledger books. "Excuse me, gentlemen. I'll just be a moment."

"Gillian, why don't you take Captain Lutjens out for some fresh air? I need to talk with Colonel Dietrich," Jack said.

"Ofcourse, sir." She turned to Gerhard. "Captain, would you like to take a walk?"

Lutjens was on his feet, looking embarrassed. "Yes, please, that would be very good." He followed her toward the garden door.

Stewart waited until the door closed behind the two. "I think your captain has spent too much time at the front. He seems out of his element with the young lady."

"He needs some time to organize a battle plan," Karl said dryly. He put the cup on the table. "Now, what were you saying? I don't understand. What time constraint?"

"I just had a talk with a lovely young lady who is convinced your pledge to help us is true and genuine." Jack moved over to the credenza and poured a cup of coffee for himself.

"What I said, I meant. I broke my SS blood oath and that's not something I do lightly. We Germans value honor and integrity. But the Nazi's have destroyed that honor."

"We're getting reports out of the continent which are hard to believe. Detention camps with thousands of people dying." Jack had read some of the intelligence estimates and it was beyond belief.

Dietrich took a long slow breath and said, "There is a point where a man can no longer support his country. It occurs when that country violates the laws of humanity. Most Germans are decent people but there is a dark side to Germany. Hitler and the Nazis have used that hate and obedience. I've seen things in Russia that I knew were wrong. I chose to ignore them. But it adds up and now I'm

73

done with it. I will have to live with what has already been done as will the rest of Germany."

Jack listened to this man, a totally professional soldier and killer when necessary. But his words sounded sincere and his eyes didn't flinch as he looked at Jack.

Walking over, he sat at the table. "Colonel, as far as your people know you're still on your mission, correct?"

"That is so," Dietrich said slowly. "We made our initial radio contact and were not scheduled to make another until we had hit the target."

The 'target' Jack thought, *total lack of emotion*. "And what was the time table for the mission?" Jack's questions started to come quickly.

"Flexible." Karl shrugged. "We were to reconnoiter and then make the hit. At that point we would work our way back to the coast. We were to call 24 hours before the desired pick up by the U-boat."

"So you could still make your way back to the coast meet the U-boat and return to Germany. Correct?"

Karl Dietrich was quiet for a moment realizing what Jack was proposing. "Correct."

"You'd be able to return to Germany as our agent?" In Jack's mind this was the critical point in his questioning.

Dietrich looked at Jack, his stare intense. "I said I would and I will. But anything I do must be directed at the Nazis." There was hardness to his voice and tone which Jack did not misunderstand.

"We have a saying where I come from, 'you want your cake and eat it too'. You want to pick and choose your fight. That's a luxury which most of us don't have."

Dietrich remembered Russia. He couldn't have it both ways – he knew that now. "The idea of killing my countrymen is difficult to consider. But like a cancer, sometimes you have to take some of the good to get the bad. I'll do what you request of me. It's the only way I'll ever be able to live with myself."

"That's all I wanted to hear from you. We'll get more people down here to set the plan in motion. For tonight, have a good meal, talk with Eva and try not to think about the future."

"Commander, that's all I think about."

The first traces of sunset were showing in the western sky. Gillian walked down the main path of the garden toward the rose bushes. "Did you ever visit England before the war, captain?"

"Please call me Gerhard. No, the only trips I made outside Germany were to Austria with my family."

Gilliam felt unusually comfortable talking with Gerhard. "Where did you grow up?"

Lutjens was walking slowly, matching her pace. He would glance at her every several steps. "My father is a doctor in a small village outside of Munich. I grew up there and attended university in Munich. Then the war came. Have you ever been to Germany?"

"No, but I want to very much. I was studying language before the war and would like to see the places I read about."

He found he was enjoying talking with the young lady. There was something about her that he found comforting. "I hope you are able to do that. This war will end someday."

She thought he sounded very sad when he mentioned the war. He was not at all like what she expected from a German commando.

Later that night Jack arrived at Baker Street to find his entire section working on the Valkyrie mission. Hiram and Ian showed the latest message traffic.

"Something's starting to accelerate with Black Rain. There's been a big pickup in messages. Between the boys at Bletchley and our analysts I think we've got a few pieces of the puzzle." Hiram opened a map of Northern Europe. "Here's Nordhausen where we know they make the rockets and more importantly the warhead assemblies." He pointed to a location in the Harz Mountains, southwest of Berlin. "Here's the Sarin Facility near Breslau on the Oder River." The Dyhernfurth location was about 220 miles due east of Nordhausen in Silesia.

Ian Thompson spoke up, "The real issue is how and where the Germans are going to combine the warhead assemblies with the Sarin. It must happen before the rockets are sent to the operational launch groups. That was the unknown, which I thought would stop us dead. Apparently the Germans are concerned about the potential release of Sarin near their major cities. We have a decoded message, which discusses the proposal to move the Sarin in a special train north from Breslau to a facility on the main rail line near Posen. This facility is in sparsely populated country and normally Allied bombers never go near it."

Hiram continued, "Once the rockets are mated with the Sarin warheads, tracking them or destroying them gets much harder. They can be transported by rail or truck individually or in groups. There are a number of potential launch sites the Crossbow Committee has identified but it doesn't take much to prepare a site.

76

The Dutch underground is trying to identify all of those locations and we'll send several teams of SOE agents in with radios in a final attempt to hit the rockets before they're launched."

Jack looked at the map and thought about the options. "So we try to gum up the works at Posen. How about an air strike? If we can totally destroy the facility we stop them before they can mate the warheads to the rockets."

"In my opinion it's a matter of timing, Jack," Ian sat back. "If we hit it before the components are there they simply take them somewhere else and we may have no clue where that is. No, we have to be able to determine when the key components are on site and then conduct some type of strike."

"Do we have any good data on this facility?" Jack asked.

"No, it's pretty new. We've put in a request for a photo-recon flight with the highest priority. Depending on weather I think we'll have something in three to four days, maybe sooner. We really need to get some eyes on the target up close." Hiram said.

Jack sat back in his chair. *By God, it might work.*

Chapter Five

15 Miles South of Allenstein
East Prussia
July 20, 1944

Jerzy Lubowisz opened the front door to the small farm house and stepped out into the warm summer morning. Although he could never truly relax, this morning was a pleasant reminder of the tranquility before the war. It seemed like a fairy tale after the last five years of war. A captain in the Polish Army, Jerzy's cavalry unit had been destroyed by the German mechanized units outside Warsaw in 1939. Barely escaping capture he had made his way to France and then to England via Dunkirk. As part of the Free Polish Forces he had spent almost three years training for the invasion of the continent. Frustrated at the inactivity, he had volunteered for the Special Operations Executive and played a critical role in the rescue of Erich Von Wollner from Germany. Following that mission, he remained behind in his native country connected by radio with London and MI-6. The band of partisans he had joined ceded leadership to Jerzy and now there were a total of fourteen men and one woman conducting reconnaissance for the British.

He could see Stefan and Dobry coming down out of the trees, which covered the ridge north of the farm. They'd set up an observation post on the top of the ridge, which gave them good warning of any approach to the farm. The men ran four hour watch cycles to ensure they weren't surprised by the Germans. With the Russian Armies still over two hundred miles to the eas,t the majority of German troop activity was movement of supplies to the front. Jerzy's group had provided valuable intelligence on the German's attempt to stop the relentless movement by the Russians toward Germany proper. He was uneasy about what would happen as the front moved over them and how to best ensure the safety of his group. His concern was more than just a military issue.

Behind Jerzy a young woman came out on the porch with a mug of tea in her hand. "All quiet?" she asked, handing him the mug. She kissed him on the cheek.

He turned and smiled. "Good morning. It looks quiet. Today we rest, clean the weapons, check in with London and have a nice dinner for everyone. Those last few trips were hard on them, it's time for a break."

Mariska was Jerzy's age, with deep auburn hair and dark brown eyes. They'd been engaged before the war and were torn apart by events. Their reunion two months ago had been a miracle for both of them. Tentative at first, they both now realized their love had withstood the test of war. They enjoyed each day and gave thanks they were together. The future was something they still chose not to discuss.

"We've got two good pork roasts and plenty of potatoes. I think we can have a feast." Her voice was light and eyes sparkled.

"When did you become such a good cook? In Warsaw you never cooked."

She slipped her hand around his arm enjoying their domestic banter. "I had to learn, I assure you. There were several ladies we stayed with when I joined the group. They helped me figure out the mysteries of the cook pot."

"I owe those ladies a great debt because I'm now in love with a wonderful cook, who's beautiful to boot." He laughed and squeezed her arm. "Stefan," he called to the tall man walking across the yard. "Did you see any activity at all?"

"Nothing, quiet as a cathedral."

"Good. There's tea inside and some of Mariska's porridge."

Jerzy had developed a strong bond with this group of freedom fighters. Most had been at it since 1940 and they knew the penalty if caught by the Germans. Operating primarily north of Warsaw they were able to harass the Germans and then fade into the large forested areas where the Wehrmacht chose not to follow them. While on one of their transits in the forest they had encountered Jerzy and the team of three other MI-6 operatives from Jack's team. Following the operation to pull Erich Von Wollner from Hitler's headquarters in Rastenburg, London had authorized Jerzy remaining behind with the partisan team. Equipped with two radios, they had become London's eyes, in an area the British felt was going to be critical as the war drew to a close. Neither Jack nor Jerzy realized at the time how critical that capability would be for MI-6.

64 Baker Street
London

"Have you lost your bloody mind?" Tommy Hudson didn't think Jack's proposal had much merit.

"Tommy, if we can confirm Jerry's plans to mate the warheads with the Sarin at Posen then we need to have someone on the ground to determine exactly when the components arrive. Then we destroy them."

"Jack, I agree in principle. But what makes you think we need the ability to penetrate the facility to make this work?"

"We'll get one shot at this. If we destroy the facility before the warheads arrive they'll just send them somewhere else. If we're late it's a moot point. If we destroy these warheads and the Sarin, by the time the Germans can produce more the launching sites will be overrun. We have to have someone who can verify arrival of the material and get that word back to London."

"And you think it's Dietrich?"

"Who better than SS Colonel who knows his way around."

"Bloody hell, Jack, you're missing the point. He's an SS Colonel or was. What guarantee do we have that he's not going to conveniently switch sides back to Mr. Hitler?"

"I believe he's honest. Also, we still have Captain Lutjens and Eva to hold over his head. And, I'd go with him."

Hudson shook his head and smiled at Jack. "You're lucky the Brigadier likes you, otherwise he'd have you committed."

Farmingham Manor

Essex

Brigadier Noel Greene had a great deal of confidence in the judgment and knowledge of both Jack Stewart and Tommy Hudson. However their plan to utilize Karl Dietrich in their efforts to derail Germany's chemical rocket program was more than he could take at face value. He listened to the argument for having an agent on the ground and in the facility. Their logic made sense and that prompted his trip from London to Farmingham. Perhaps if he met this German, he too would develop the confidence of Jack Stewart in the trustworthiness of Dietrich's intentions. It was still a big 'if' in his mind. How could he risk the success of a mission, which conceivably might mean life or death for thousands of British civilians on a man who four days ago was an SS Colonel in good standing? He couldn't imagine briefing the Prime Minister on this one.

Karl Dietrich and Jack Stewart walked up the stairs to the study where Greene waited. "Colonel, you'll be meeting Brigadier Noel Greene. He is one of our most experienced intelligence officers and he's my immediate superior."

"What's the purpose of our meeting?"

"He wanted to meet you before making a decision on a plan we put together which involves you." Jack didn't want to play games at this point, the German needed to know he was on line for active service.

After introductions, Jack took a seat as interpreter for Greene. Greene was interested in the German's demeanor and attitude as well as his words.

"Colonel, I'll come to the point. Our people have put together a plan, which includes your return to Germany. I will not lie to you. I have a great deal of skepticism over this plan. It seems too much of a stretch that you could have experienced such a remarkable transformation in the span of several days." Greene stared at Dietrich as Jack translated.

Dietrich returned Greene's look, his expression neutral. "Sir, what would you have me say? I would feel exactly as you if the situation were reversed."

"So why should I place the success of a critical mission in the hands of someone who could still be loyal to the other side?"

There was a slight smile at the edge of Dietrich's mouth. "I would guess because you need my services to ensure the mission success."

Greene ignored Dietrich's remark. "Commander Stewart feels your intentions are honorable, but the decision is mine."

Karl was surprised that Jack Stewart who was a stranger only three days ago would stand up for him. "As I told the commander, I'm at your disposal. You said he felt my intentions were honorable. Brigadier, I will do what little I can to begin to restore honor to Germany."

An hour later Stewart and Greene were sitting in the upstairs drawing room. The atmosphere was markedly more relaxed as they sat with Erich Von Wollner. Stewart knew that Greene was still debating the question of Dietrich, but he hadn't made any comments either way.

"Commander, Jack tells me the back is doing well?" Greene had been at Biggin Hill when Erich arrived wounded from Germany. Jack provided the translation.

"Yes, sir. It's better each day." Erich was relaxed with these two men whom he had come to trust.

"We have a problem and thought you might be able to offer some advice," Greene continued.

"I'll certainly try."

Jack laid out the issue. "You talked with Colonel Dietrich yesterday and then sat in on the group's debrief. We're interested in your opinion of the truthfulness of his offer to help us."

"You wonder if the tiger could change his stripes that easily?"

Greene's voice was quiet, but Jack heard the concern. "Commander, the life or death of many Britons may depend on our evaluation of his veracity. Did you sense anything from him?"

Von Wollner nodded. "I did and it surprised me. His name was well known at headquarters. I read of his many exploits and his being awarded the Knight's Cross came across my desk. My assumption was he would be like so many of the SS officers' I'd encountered: arrogant, brutal, with no regard for anyone outside the SS. That's not what I found." He paused for a moment, then continued, "He saw many of the things which I only read about at headquarters. Like the many 'special actions' conducted on civilians, particularly Jews, when our troops captured towns in Russia. No, I think he's a man who will fight you to the death in an honorable war. But when he saw his SS begin exterminating civilians, something happened. I only wish there were more people who would see the truth for what it is."

Greene smiled at Erich. "Thank you for your words. I'm not sure they made my job easier, but I have more to think about."

The phone call from Ian Thompson caught Jack sitting in the garden going over his plan one more time. Although he couldn't talk over the phone, Ian was adamant they must meet tonight. With most of the players at Farmingham, Ian and Hiram were going to drive out from London and should be at the farm by early evening.

It was a somber group which listened to an excited Hiram Baker recap the recent message decode from Bletchley. "Gentlemen, we have a message which directs the warhead production facility at Nordhausen to ship fifty modified warhead assemblies to the Posen Intermediate Engineering Depot. There isn't a set timetable, but if the message has been sent we must assume they are ready to execute in short order."

Greene asked, "Anything at all about the Sarin shipment from Breslau?"

"No, sir. Nothing intercepted or decoded. Of course we know we don't get every message. Perhaps it slipped by our screens," Hiram offered.

"Bloody good that does us, I'd say." Hatcher said.

"Gentlemen, I'd like your thoughts on how we most effectively move to counter this development." Greene looked around the table.

Jack had been going over the problem and spoke first, "We need to get some eyes on the ground in Posen. I think we need to get Jerzy headed there as quickly as possible."

"I have to concur with Jack," added Tommy Hudson.

"What's our next move after that?"

"Sir, we need to get a team to Posen that can penetrate the facility and verify the arrival of both components." Jack knew there were no other options and hoped the Brigadier realized that also.

"Be more specific, commander."

"Sir, I jump in with Colonel Dietrich and link up with Jerzy. We then penetrate the facility and if appropriate send the strike order for Bomber Command."

Ignoring the issue of the German Colonel, Greene turned to Ian. "Is there any idea what would be the effect of a strike on a target where this Sarin gas is present?"

"Our research tells us intense heat, over 1000 degrees, will destroy the chemical agent. But normal disruptive explosives will only spread it around the detonation site."

Greene pressed on. "All right, we lay on an air raid by Bomber Command and request a large percentage of incendiary bombs. Ian, I want you to get together with the weapons experts at Bomber Command Headquarters and make sure they understand the problem."

"Of course."

"Next, we start our Polish chap toward Posen. Tommy, you contact your liaison at Bomber Command so they can begin planning a strike. Jack, you and I need to check in with General Gubbins. I'm not totally convinced, but if you're willing to bet your life on Dietrich I'll support you."

Jack didn't say anything for a minute. He realized how far out on a limb this recommendation would put him. But he continued to believe in and trust the German he'd known less than a week. "We still need to close the loop with the Germans on the mission against Von Wollner."

The Brigadier nodded. "Quite right. Suggestions, gentlemen?"

Tommy spoke up, "Let's make sure they don't send anymore visitors. I think we must report Erich killed and then have the two Germans captured in the attempt."

"We can have MI-5 transmit those mission results and that should bring the entire event to a close," Jack added.

"I agree. Tommy, get a deception plan together which includes a mock attack at Cheltenham. Make sure there are police and ambulances, the whole show. Never know who else might be watching. Now, let's get busy with an operational plan and time table. I suspect we're already behind."

Jack found the two German commandos and Eva finishing their evening meal in the small dining room off the kitchen. They seemed relaxed and there was an opened bottle of wine on the table.

"Hello. May I join you?"

Dietrich didn't smile, but his reaction was friendly. "Certainly."

Karl said, "May I offer you some wine?"

"Thanks, wine sounds very good right now." Jack sat down at the end of the table facing Dietrich. The four made conversation as they finished their meal. Jack enjoyed the wine and he took the time to organize his thoughts and how he was going to present proposal. When the plates were cleared by the orderly, he refreshed the glasses of the other three. "There's something about a glass of wine that just makes life a little better."

Eva laughed. "You sound like a man who would love our German wines." She sounded happy and relaxed.

Jack grinned, "I think I'd like to try your beer also." He could sense the chemistry between Karl and Eva.

Lutjens joined in, "The best pilsner in the world."

Setting his glass on the table, he changed his tone. "There have been some decisions made today that affect all of us. I wanted you to know what was going to happen." The other three looked serious but not anxious. "Eva, we will coordinate with your MI-5 group to put together a mock attack on the Von Wollner location. Following that attack you'll be sending a message we draft which describes the death of Von Wollner and the capture of the two commandos."

Dietrich and Lutjens sat forward but said nothing. Eva crossed her arms in front of her and sat back in her chair. "I understand your plan. I think it's a good idea."

"It does take care of a number of issues and allows us the greatest flexibility in the future. Now, I need to talk with the Colonel, privately. Please stay here and enjoy your wine. We'll take a walk outside."

The sunset was pink in the west as the two men walked on one of the paths which crossed the estate. The two didn't say anything until they were well away from the house. Their foot steps crunching in the gravel was the only sound.

"There are a number of people in my organization who feel I've lost my senses to believe you've changed allegiance. And to be honest I'm not sure I can clearly say why I feel the way I do. But I believe we both think this war needs to come to a quick conclusion. I remember Erich Von Wollner saying the future of Germany was dying in the fields of Europe. You know what has happened to the Jews on the continent and it will only get worse the longer the war lasts. This newest wrinkle could result in brutal retaliation if chemical weapons are used against England. I don't know what would be the result, but nothing good would come from it."

Karl listened and said, "I agree with what you've said. But how does that affect me?"

"I'm asking you to accompany me on a mission into Germany." Jack turned and the two men now faced each other. Dietrich's face looked hard in the fading sunlight.

"For what purpose?" The German's voice was steady but questioning.

"To ensure destruction of the facility where they'll load Sarin into the V-2 warheads." Jack looked at the German's eyes, trying to see a reaction, trying to see if he'd made the right call.

"What do you think are the chances of success?" Dietrich continued to display no visible emotion.

"If you go, I think it can be done. If you don't, the chances are much lower." Jack was leveling with him. Someone who knew the system and had the experience of Dietrich would make all the difference in the world.

Karl Dietrich stood there looking Jack straight in the eye. "I'll go, commander. I'll go for Germany because she needs my help. And I'll go for you because you trusted me."

Jack extended his hand to Karl for the first time. The German took his hand and gripped it for a long moment. "And I'll go because you'll get me lots of Chesterfield cigarettes." He smiled at Jack.

"Colonel, that's a deal." He liked this man. But deep in his heart, there was still doubt.

"Commander, I detect an unusual accent. It is very different from most of the others. Am I right?"

"You have a good ear, Colonel. Until two years ago I was an officer in the United States Navy. Born and bred an American."

"An American? How did you end up as an officer in the Royal Navy?"

"As they say it's a long story. I was offered a chance to trade a desk in Washington D.C. for an active part in the war. It seemed like the right thing to do."

"So they had you at a desk instead of in the war."

"Oh, I had my war. I managed to get shot down at the Battle of Midway and lost my flight status. I couldn't face spending the rest of the war sitting on my ass."

Dietrich laughed. "I understand only too well. At one point Himmler wanted to make me part of his personal staff. Travel around the Reich and play at being a soldier. I respectfully declined his offer."

"Sounds like you and I feel the same way about a lot of things."

"Particularly that this war needs to end now."

Chapter Six

Old Maryle Road
Northwest London
July 21, 1944

The air raid sirens had sounded twenty minutes prior in response to a number of air contacts picked up by the perimeter radar stations south of London. Anti-aircraft crews in the gun belt which lay around the capital had manned action stations. They were trying to knock down the low flying V-1 'buzz bombs' before they could impact London. Fighter Command had vectored several flights of Mosquito fighter bombers and Spitfire MK XIVs in an attempt to destroy the intruders prior to the gun belt. Over the last year thousands of the twenty foot pilot-less weapons had been fired from France. Unlike the heavy bombing raids of 1940 these flying bombs would hit sporadically around the greater London area. The population, most of which had survived those terrible raids, began to downplay the danger of the V-1s and their one thousand pound warhead. Many of the small flying bombs were destroyed over the sparsely populated countryside south of the city. Some of them made it to London.

This morning, a single V-1, it's engine having shut down as programmed, nosed over and impacted a row of shops which lined the southern side of Old Maryle Road. The only significant loss of life was in a small tea shop, which had several customers in for an early tea and biscuit. The blast destroyed the brick walls and glass windows. The tile roof collapsed on top of the debris and bodies. It took the fire brigade rescue squad over an hour to pull the dead and injured from the impact area. The street was littered with thousands of pieces of broken glass lying amidst the bricks that were spread around the impact site. In a neat row on the sidewalk the victims lay covered with grey blankets provided by the air raid wardens.

Several police officers were starting the identification process for the dead when they found an identity card which made them call their sergeant over to the body.

"Sarge, we found an identity card from MI-6. What do ya want to do?"

"'ere now, lemme see that." The wiry man read the card and then down at the body. "Ian Thompson. Looks like he's a civilian. Get down to the call box and have the station call headquarters. They'll probably send someone down here."

Jack sat in the front seat of the sedan on the way back to Baker Street. Phil Hatcher drove while Karl Dietrich sat alone in the back seat. Hiram and Ian had gone back to London the previous night to start operational planning for the upcoming mission, now officially called Operation Whirlwind. When Jack walked into his office, Terry Howe looked at him, his face ashen.

"Jack, I just got a call from Metropolitan Police Headquarters. Ian Thompson is dead. It was a V-1 in that first alarm this morning."

Behind him, Phil and Karl Dietrich walked into the office. Jack walked into his inner office as Phil asked, "What's up?"

"Ian Thompson was killed this morning. V-1 over on Marley Road."

Jack sat at his desk, looking out the window. Ian, his friend and mentor since 1936. The man who was his second father and soon to be his father in law. The steadiest, most solid person you'd ever want to know. *Son of a bitch.*

Phil and Karl walked into his office. "Jack, I'm sorry. What can I do to help?" Phil asked.

Karl stood quietly behind Phil.

Jack was frustrated and angry. But there was nothing he could do. "God damn it, Phil. Why Ian, why now?"

"There aren't any answers to those questions, never will be, my friend."

"I need to go to Pam." Jack's mind was a jumble of thoughts. How do I help Pam? Does she already know? What will this do to her? He knew he must get to her. "Phil, I gotta get over there. Get going on the plan, we're running on a tight schedule." He looked up to see Dietrich looking at him with a very somber look.

"Commander, I'm sorry for your loss."

"Colonel, thank you. That's why we've got to stop this insanity."

"Someone is trying to," Tommy Hudson said, as he walked into the office.

Jack looked up to see his friend.

"I'm so sorry about Ian, Jack. I was on my way down here to see you when they handed me this message." Tommy gave the single sheet of paper to Jack.

He read it and then turned to Karl Dietrich. "Someone planted a bomb in Hitler's headquarters in Rastenburg. It appears he was injured but survived. There was an attempted coup in Berlin but apparently it has failed."

Karl looked at Jack shaking his head. "There will be a blood bath in Germany before this is over."

Twenty Miles East of
Posen, Germany
July 23, 1944

The main line of communication for the Wehrmacht from Stettin east toward Russia ran directly through Allenstein. When the partisan group's mission was keeping track of German transportation movements, being near the main road was crucial. Now Jerzy had to travel well south of that main road using the network of country roads, which connected the small farming towns of the region. The journey would be almost 130 miles from the farm outside Allenstein to the Posen depot.

Jerzy had decided they would take eight people, the others would maintain their watch on the road. Traveling in two groups of four they would move at night as far as Gniezno. From there they would move into the forested area east of Posen. The depot was located about 6 miles east of the city on a railroad spur off the main line. The message told him that photo recon noted a recently constructed facility in a large forested area, which had multiple fences and security areas.

Traveling for two nights in borrowed cars, the group avoided any contact with German military forces and now their vehicles were safely hidden off a small side road. They still faced a trek of twenty miles, but felt safer back in the forest. The team was traveling light, the big challenge bringing the portable radio set to communicate with London.

It felt good to be moving through the forest again, Jerzy thought. The time at the farm was starting to become routine. He did enjoy the time he could spend with Mariska, but there was still a war going on and he felt out of the action.

"Stefan, go up and take the lead from Dobry. We'll keep moving for another hour and then take a break." It was starting to get warm and the humidity was building. There was almost no breeze in the trees, which added to their discomfort.

"I'll scout on ahead after you stop and double back. Save some food for me." The large man grinned and moved off. Jerzy had come to rely on Stefan. The man was totally fearless and dependable. A farmer before the war, his farm had been destroyed during the German invasion. His wife had died when German aircraft strafed a column of refugees moving north toward Warsaw. Stefan's hatred of the Germans was total, uncompromising and lethal.

The group continued to work their way through the lush forest. The only sounds were their footsteps on the forest floor and equipment jostling on their backs.

Posen Intermediate Engineering Depot
Posen, Silesia

Standartenfuhrer Franz Schroeder stood on the loading dock of Warehouse A. He watched the laborers move wheelbarrows of freshly mixed concrete from the portable mixer to a line of freshly dug holes that ran parallel to the rail spur servicing the warehouse.

Schroeder wore his black SS uniform. On his left arm there was a red armband with the distinctive black and white swastika. His collars sported the double lightning flash of the SS and his cap insignia bore the deaths head emblem feared throughout Europe.

Franz Schroeder was not happy. This recent assignment as the commander of a backwater depot had taken him away from his duties at Treblinka where he had spent the last two years as chief of security. The Posen depot still was not officially operational. Despite promises from the regional SS headquarters, his force of security personnel numbered only one hundred officers and men. Currently the guards were occupied directing the work efforts of prisoners in a final push to complete the depot. The laborers had come to him from road construction duties in the east and they were barely capable of doing a days work. How did his superiors expect him to finish this facility when all they sent him were these sickly wretches who could barely stand?

There were a number of engineers on site already and they seemed busy enough. The men, mostly German, spent their time in the long assembly buildings which were connected to the warehouse area by concrete walkways. Two days ago, Volker Fischer arrived from Nordhausen to take over as Engineering Director. Schroeder's orders were to accommodate Fischer and his engineers in any way possible. This group was charged with the final check of the mechanical systems which were installed in the three assembly buildings, "A", "B" and "C". Schroeder didn't like the engineer. His air of superiority was unmistakable. These technicians didn't seem to realize the only reason they were able to get their jobs done was because the SS provided the labor and security.

Schroeder saw the working party supervisor, a senior sergeant named Littke. He called the man over to the loading dock. "We're behind schedule on this final section. I want you to work these people until the project is finished. There are some portable lights over by Tower Number Two. Rig those and add on additional guards after dark."

The sergeant realized this was not a discussion of the project. "Yes sir, Herr Standartenfuhrer, it will be done."

Schroeder knew this group of laborers was scheduled to be sent to Auschwitz. They were dead anyway. Why not get the last bit of work out of them before they were shipped out? At least everything of any importance was now finished and ready for the incoming shipments. Both were scheduled to arrive in one week.

He should also be getting additional personnel including medical specialists and a small fire fighting detachment. The one item which was not on schedule was the anti-aircraft battery which the Luftwaffe said would arrive last week. So far there was no word and he had not seen any rail transport orders covering the transport of the 88 mm anti-aircraft guns. Six of these guns were supposed to be set up around the perimeter of the depot. He must call the Luftwaffe sector headquarters and determine where his guns were.

His communications section was set up with all their equipment now operational. He had long-range radio communications with the SS chain of command and also a signal intercept capability. Although a small installation, the depot was equipped with the latest equipment. Schroeder reflected on his situation. He would have to make the best of it.

64 Baker Street
London
July 24, 1944

Sitting in his office, Jack looked at the couch were Ian had sat through so many meetings, always the steady voice of reason, coupled with a wry sense of humor. He remembered the year at Oxford when Ian had been his faculty advisor, their long discussions on physics and life. Jack realized in many ways he was closer to Ian than to his own father. It still seemed like a horrible dream.

The funeral at Oxford had been at the Episcopal Church the Thompson family attended. It was a beautiful warm summer morning and there had been a large turnout from the academic community and MI-6. Ian's son Dicky came home from RAF Tangmere where he flew in the Special Operations Section. It was a fitting tribute to a man who spent his entire life giving to his students and his country.

Ian's wife Mary had died in 1934 and Pamela became the lady of the house. The special relationship between fathers and daughters became even more special between Ian and his daughter. With Dicky gone in the RAF, the two of them came to rely on each other more and more. After Pam's terrible injury last year Ian spent countless hours at his daughter's bedside willing her to get better. Initially she seemed to handle the news of his death with stoic acceptance. She had seen many of her RAF friends die during the war. But in the last few days she seemed to withdraw, even from Jack. He tried to reach out to her but it was if she had gone into a room and closed the door. Perhaps the head injury had some affect on how she was reacting to this crisis. He would call Dr. Hanson and ask him. For now that call would have to wait. Whirlwind was accelerating and it must be his top priority.

His section rapidly brought together the operational plan and details for Whirlwind. Jack had made the decision at the beginning to include Karl Dietrich in all phases of the planning to take advantage of his experience. The effort by the section to learn both French and German over the last year paid dividends. Dietrich spoke a small amount of French but no English. He was showing an interest in learning the language but that would have to wait until after this mission. Most of the section accepted his presence. The only real stumbling block had been Terry Howe. The weapons expert had made it very clear he would be professional but he wanted nothing to do with either Dietrich or Lutjens.

The Brigadier's efforts to convince General Gubbins, the Executive Director of SOE, that this use of Dietrich and Lutjens made sense had been successful. This was unusual enough that it was taken all the way to Churchill who deferred to his subordinates.

Jack was in the conference room with Karl, Phil and Gerhard Lutjens when his yeoman swung the door open with a look of panic on his face. "Commander, the Prime Minister just arrived downstairs and is being escorted up here by the Brigadier."

Jack laughed, the two Germans had quizzical looks and Phil summed it up in one word, "Christ."

Turning to Karl and Gerhard, Jack explained, "Gentlemen, this section has managed to develop a relationship with our Prime Minister. It appears he has arrived at the building and is on his way up here."

For the first time since Jack met Karl Dietrich he saw what might pass for a look of panic. "Why is he here?" he asked.

"I expect he wants to meet you. He's a very inquisitive person."

Dietrich and Lutjens were wearing RAF flying suits without rank insignia. They both began making sure all zippers were closed trying to appear as sharp as possible.

The door swung and the Prime Minister walked in with Noel Greene. Churchill was wearing a dark blue suit with a burgundy bow tie. He stopped as he saw Jack. The Prime Minister's face was deadly serious, his jaw clenched. "Commander, after hearing of your little plan I decided a personal visit was most appropriate. If this doesn't work there will be many questions asked both in Britain and around the world. I want to be able to address those questions."

"Sir, I understand." Jack saw the PM looking at Karl and Gerhard, who stood at attention on the far side of the table. "May I introduce Colonel Karl Dietrich and Captain Gerhard Lutjens." On hearing their names, both men nodded their heads toward Churchill. The PM looked at both of them narrowing his eyes ever so slightly.

"Sit down and we shall discuss it."

Jack turned to his men. "Gentlemen, please have a seat."

Once sitting, Churchill looked at Dietrich. "You will understand that most people would look at having you on this mission as foolhardy. I must admit that it struck me that way. But I trust Commander Stewart and he trusts you."

While the translation took place the two Germans sat attentively. When Jack finished translating, Churchill continued, "I think that history will look back at this war as a time when humanity took a step backward. There's been death and destruction on a scale that makes the first war pale in comparison."

During the translation, Jack could see that Karl relaxed slightly. Gerhard was still sitting at attention.

Dietrich was thinking about Churchill's remarks, but also trying to bring this encounter in perspective. Here was the leader of the English people sitting across the table from him discussing the fundamental issues of war and peace. Could this possibly be happening? What stroke of fate brought an SS commando to this room preparing to strike a blow which might hasten the destruction of the SS and Germany's military. Karl was not an overly religious person but this experience was having a profound effect on him.

"However, gentlemen, this newest potential use of chemical weapons would take this war to a new level of barbarism. I don't know what Herr Hitler is thinking, but he must know that if these weapons are used on England we will respond in kind and do the same to German cities. Not one of the allies, President Roosevelt in particular, wants to use chemical weapons. We must find a way to stop it. You, gentlemen, must find a way. Your efforts will save countless lives in both England and Germany."

Karl sat for a moment then spoke, "Sir, I'm sure the world has more and more people on both sides that have begun to ask the question, 'how did we get to this point'. The German people embraced Hitler and the Nazis as a way out of the past. Unfortunately we were willing to follow them down a road to our own destruction. Now that has to change." He spoke his heart and waited for Churchill's response.

The older man sat there listening to the translation, his pale blue eyes piercing into Dietrich. The power Karl sensed from this man was tangible and Karl now knew his own decision was correct. "Colonel, this war will end. I'm sure the allies will be victorious and this time we'll try to rebuild a world that is safe from people like Hitler. If there are more people like you in Germany I don't think we'll have a problem."

Churchill stood up and moved around the table to the two Germans who now stood beside their chairs. He stopped, looked both in the eye, offered his hand and said "Good luck."

As Churchill and Greene walked out of the room, Jack followed. The PM stopped and faced Jack. "Once more into the breach," he said. "Jack, I pray you're successful. A great deal depends on this."

"Thank you, sir. We'll get the job done."

When Jack returned, Karl stood looking out the window at the street below. He turned to Jack and said, "I've now met Adolph Hitler and Winston Churchill. It's the eyes, Jack. Both of them, as different as night and day, have an inner intensity that radiates from their eyes. Hitler's a mad man, but the intensity is always there. I'm glad I had a chance to meet the Prime Minister."

Jack nodded. "I feel very fortunate to know him. I think history will look back and recognize his greatness once the daily politics are forgotten."

"Just as they will recognize the madness of Hitler." Karl sat down on the couch. "Jack, I have a request. Would it be possible to see Eva before we leave?"

"While MI-6 wouldn't object, we would have to coordinate with her boss at MI-5. Let me ask the Brigadier if he would make a call.

10 Miles East of Posen
Thuringia, Germany
July 26, 1944
1600 Hours

Jerzy's group was now conducting active surveillance of the depot. Since their arrival there had been no rail traffic of any kind at the depot. What they couldn't know was what had arrived before their surveillance commenced.

The depot had a double fenced perimeter with guard towers which were manned at all times. Random patrols also had been seen both on the perimeter fence line and in the depot itself. This was a much higher level of security than the Germans would normally put on a supply or trans shipment facility. Jerzy wondered what was happening there.

It was a quiet afternoon in the partisan camp. In the forest around the camp there was the occasional cry of a bird. The warmth of the summer sun filtered down to the forest floor. Several of the men were sleeping, getting ready for their night watches. Mariska was down at the stream with Patryk filling their canteens. The camp had settled into a routine of watches, patrols, meals and sleep.

Jerzy saw Stefan before he heard him. It was changeover time for the watch. "You're back early. You must be hungry." Jerzy grinned and noticed the normally reserved Stefan now looked excited.

"Jerzy, a train just arrived at the loading platform. I left Tomas there, but I thought you'd want to take a look."

Grabbing his Sten submachine gun, Jerzy put on his cap. "Let's go."

Twenty minutes later the two of them lay prone in the observation blind. Jerzy saw the train was small by most standards, one engine, a coal tender, five boxcars and a passenger car. It appeared they were beginning to unload the first car. There was a mix of uniformed personnel and civilians on the loading dock. The first boxcar's access door was open and a ramp ran from the concrete platform to the car. He saw a wooden crate on a small dolly appear in the door. There were four men manhandling the crate across the ramp onto the dock.

They watched the crate and dolly disappear out of their field of vision. Ten minutes later the process was repeated. Over the next hour, six crates moved from the train to the loading dock warehouse. Jerzy left his men to keep track of the progress and went back to send a report to London. The messages from London had not been specific on what was being delivered to the depot. His job was to report what they saw and he would. But since the first message came in, he wondered what could be so important that a special team would be used to monitor? He knew Section F focused on new weapons or improved systems of the Nazis. Perhaps this was a new weapon. In any case something was happening and London would want to know.

Assembly Building "A"
1730 Hours

Volker Fischer watched as his technicians removed the top of a reinforced wooden shipping container. The first seven warhead assemblies were in superb condition. As senior engineer Fischer was starting to relax. If there had been any damage, he would have been blamed. To make sure there were no problems the shipping containers were twice the strength of standard crates. Each boxcar also had one of his junior technicians riding with the crates from Nordhausen to keep an eye on them.

General Walter Dornberger, head of the V-2 program was a reasonable man. However he was responsible to Himmler who was known for his fury when projects were not successful. There could be no mistakes. Before they finished tonight, all fifty of the warhead assemblies would be in the three assembly buildings. The next step would involve the transfer of the Sarin from the large transport vessels to each warhead assembly.

Major Rosensweig of the Dyhernfurth Facility had briefed the transfer procedure to the assembly crews and it seemed straightforward enough. Each assembly building would have a large metal and glass lined storage container, which would arrive by train. Once the large container was transferred to the assembly buildings his people would connect the transfer hose to the special fitting in the warhead assembly. The transfer pressure would come from a hand operated rotary pump, which would transfer the liquid in very precise amounts. All technicians would be wearing protective garments and have externally supplied air delivered under positive pressure. Decontamination stations were located at each end of the building. Several of the laborers would be strapped into seats in the assembly area as added indicators for any leakage during the transfer. Fischer thought it was a good technical plan which only needed flawless execution.

The rail transport time from departure at the Sarin Facility near Breslau to the loading dock in the depot should be no more that two hours. Priority routing would ensure there were no track conflicts. The short journey allowed the entire trip to be completed during darkness away from any prowling Allied fighter bombers.

The Sarin transport was scheduled for the following night. An arrival time of 0200, would allow for all material to be unloaded and staged to the assembly buildings by daybreak. Fischer and Rosensweig agreed to complete the warhead loading in Building A initially to determine if there were any problems. If all went well, the total loading time for the warheads in Building A would be twenty-four hours. Buildings B and C would then report the process. All loading operations would be completed within forty-eight hours of start.

The next phase of Black Rain involved the transport of the fifty Sarin warheads via rail from Posen to Luneburg. That part of the trip would take place during the first night. The train would be hidden during the day. The next night it would move on to Stavoren in Holland. There the warheads would be turned over to the 441st Rocket Assault Group for mating with the V-2 rockets. Fischer would accompany the warheads and supervise the mating process. It was possible the first Black Rain V-2 could impact London within seven days. That would make all of his work worthwhile. It could not bring back his wife, killed in an American air raid in Frankfurt last November, but it would make him feel better.

Farmingham Manor
Kent
28 July, 1944

"Gillian, I was an engineering student in university. I never had to deal with sentence structure." Gerhard Lutjens was frustrated. It was two days since Karl Dietrich had told him about the mission. He was concerned that Dietrich was going alone. They had not been separated on a mission in over two years. But Dietrich had explained the other purpose for Lutjens to remain behind, although no one had stated it. He was the Brit's insurance policy. He trusted Dietrich and would follow orders. Those orders were to learn English as fast as possible and lend whatever help MI-6 might request. The most attractive aspect of the situation was Gillian's assignment as his language instructor.

"But I know you would love to learn about sentence structure." She was teasing him, and he didn't mind.

"I will do my best. Now let's get busy."

Over the last two days the two of them had made a great deal of progress. With Stewart and Dietrich totally focused on the mission, Gillian and Gerhard were able to spend hours in conversational learning situations. She was adding to his vocabulary by walking him around the manor and pointing our items using the German noun and then switching to English. Gerhard was a quick study and found he enjoyed the mental stimulation. The frustration only surfaced as she began to build small sentences. There were several fundamental structure differences between German and English, which he had trouble grasping initially. But his frustration with the language was a small distraction. He found himself watching this lovely young woman as she taught him words and realized he was drawn to her. He had no attachments in Germany. His time in university and the army never allowed anything to develop with the girls he had known. It was if he had emerged from years of brutal war and now was seeing life again from a different viewpoint. Trying his best to learn what Gillian was teaching, he could tell she enjoyed spending time with him. Often times they would both laugh as he made a simple mistake and she would patiently go over the vocabulary or structure with him.

It was time to break for dinner and she was going over more vocabulary in the study. "This is a pencil. Repeat, pencil." She was handing it to him and it slipped from her hand. They both reached down and their hands met. As Gerhard slowly stood back up, he lightly held onto her hand. She did not pull her hand away.

"Pencil," he said.

Chapter Seven

RAF Biggin Hill
July 28, 1944
2000 hours

Much of the general planning had been completed by the supporting SOE committees, but the final integration depended on Jack and Karl. Their work had become very collaborative when Karl realized Jack regarded him as a partner not just a participant. In short order the equipment requirements were laid out including uniforms, weapons and radios. The two men would be outfitted as SS officers with Karl wearing his actual rank. Jack would be the equivalent of an SS major. Both men knew the consequences of these disguises. They would lose all protection of the Geneva Convention. For Karl it made no difference. As a deserter from the SS his fate would be sealed.

The plan was to parachute into the Posen area to link up with Jerzy's group. If it wasn't possible to determine if both critical weapon components were present, Jack and Karl would attempt to penetrate the depot to find out for sure. When it was determined the material was present, a signal would be sent which would trigger an air raid on the depot. It was a straight forward plan which gave the best chance of catching the warheads before they could be deployed for launch.

Jack looked out on the apron where a Lancaster bomber was parked. This particular aircraft was from the Royal Canadian Air Force, 428 Squadron. The Mark V Lanc was equipped with the updated H2S radar which would permit the most accurate parachute drop possible at night. In a line next to the bomber were four Mosquitoes from the Royal Air Force, 85 squadron. Specially requested for this mission, they were led by Wing Commander Jack Whitney. The senior aviator had been part of two previous missions by Section F and Jack wanted him flying cover on this one. The Mossies were the night fighter version and would protect the lone bomber flying across Europe.

"Commander Stewart, we can't seem to be rid of you," Whitney ribbed Jack when he and Karl entered the briefing room.

"You're my good luck piece. I wouldn't think of making this trip without you," Stewart said as the two men shook hands.

"So you're really jumping out of the Lanc tonight?" His tone was still light but Jack could sense an underlying hard question.

"I know, perfectly good airplane and all that. You just make sure the Luftwaffe doesn't try to prevent it." Jack tried to keep it light but he could tell his friend of almost two years was concerned.

Whitney smiled and clapped Jack on the back. "Don't you worry about the Luftwaffe, we'll get you there."

Jack was now the serious one. "I'm glad you were available and congratulations on the promotion, wing commander."

"Jack, that simply means I'm getting older and probably not any better." Jack Whitney was known throughout the RAF as one of the best Mosquito pilots in the service.

"I guess we better get this thing briefed." Whitney walked to the front of the briefing room and after meeting the Lancaster crew began the briefing.

In a quick, efficient manner he covered weather, radio frequencies, speeds, altitudes, and contingency plans. It was a tribute to the high quality of training and professionalism that three very different groups could come together and in a short time have a complex aerial mission ready for launch.

The drop point was 700 miles from takeoff. In order to draw less attention to the small group of aircraft they would be joining a large raid, which was launching tonight on the German city of Leipzig. The five planes would descend out of the larger bomber formation prior to Leipzig and proceed to Posen.

Jack stayed busy with the many last minute details. Tommy Hudson and his core team were present and making sure everything fell into place. Both commandos wore dark blue jumpsuits without any marking or insignia.

Karl seemed relaxed during the briefing with Phil quietly translating key points and answering questions.

Terry Howe roamed the flight line making sure all of their equipment was loaded on the Lancaster. None of the aircrews knew his identity and none knew why the two were being dropped near Posen.

Flight Lieutenants Roger Halliday, Jeff Alwyn and Ian Parke the pilot, co-pilot and navigator of the Lancaster were briefed on the depot and surrounding area. Because this was a Pathfinder aircraft it carried two pilots. Normal Lancaster Bombers had a flight engineer instead of a dedicated co-pilot.

Parke's interpretation of the H2S radar and his ability to find the depot on radar would be one of the most crucial parts of the mission. The radar navigation would be aided by a transmission from Jerzy's team to provide a final refinement on the heading and a precise drop signal.

When the briefing concluded, Jack took Karl aside. "Are you ready?"

The German nodded. "I'm ready".

Jack walked out to the ramp with Karl. His mind kept returning to this morning at Ian's flat when he told Pam he was leaving. He remembered the hurt look in her eyes. She hadn't said anything and in many ways that was worse.

He had tried to get through to her. "Pam, I wouldn't go if it wasn't something critically important. Your father was working on this until he died. I've got to do this. I don't want to leave you, but I have no choice."

Her voice had been wistful, "Jack, there's always a choice." Pam still wouldn't look at him.

"Pam, I love you with all my heart. I want you to be my wife. But I am who I am. That's not something I can change."

"Jack, you know how much I love you. It seems this war and your job will destroy us before we ever have a chance to live our lives."

Why couldn't he push it out of his mind? He remembered his first flight instructor had said, "You have to be able to put your feelings into a box before you climb into the aircraft". Jack knew he now had to focus on Whirlwind. So much depended on it, but her words kept coming back to him.

"Son of a bitch," he muttered in English.

"Something wrong?" Karl asked in German.

"No, I'm all right. A few things on my mind."

"I know." Karl's response was slow and measured. His meeting with Eva had taken place in a safe house in London last night. She had just finished the deception operation to simulate the death of Erich Von Wollner and capture of his two assailants. He was allowed to tell her he was returning to Germany on a mission but no specifics. They had talked for over two hours. Perhaps it was the emotional upheaval of his defection or the accumulated effect of years of combat, but he felt a need to be with her. It had been difficult for both of them. She had told him that she loved him and nothing could change that. In less than ten days he had lost a country and found love. Now he had to focus on the mission or he might lose them both, forever.

They continued on to the aircraft in silence, both men lost in thought.

Outside of Posen
2200 Hours

"Ludwik, you checked the radio over well?" Jerzy asked the young partisan.

The former electrician, took care of and operated the two radios supplied by the British. They had only brought one of the radios with them but it was the more reliable of the two. Capable of both voice and Morse code, the set was powered by a hand-operated generator. A long wire antenna provided the needed signal gathering capability to ensure their contact with London was secure. Last night

113

they had received a message detailing the parachute drop. Estimated time for the drop was 0100 local and the drop zone was an area which was less heavily wooded, three miles southeast of the camp. The message had said that two men and equipment would be dropped and requested Jerzy transmit four Morse code dashes every minute from 0040 until 0120.

"Jerzy, relax. This radio is working perfectly and checking it one more time won't make it work any better." The young man laughed and poked Jerzy's arm.

It was good to be back with his countrymen and in his country, Jerzy thought.

Ludwik and Mariska would remain in camp and operate the radio beacon, while Casimire would stand watch on the depot from the observation position. Jerzy and Stefan would take the remaining partisans to the drop area, spreading out to cover as much area as possible. He walked over to Mariska who was sitting by the small fire, with her arms around her knees.

"It's time for us to go," he said quietly. "Everything is set with the radio and we'll get back here as soon as possible after we pick up the men."

"We'll be fine. You watch out. We saw the German patrol in that area just day before yesterday. Be careful."

He knelt down and kissed her on her cheek. She turned and kissed him back on the lips. "I love you," she said.

Jerzy stood up and called to the others, "All right, let's get going. Stefan, take the lead. Everyone else follow at a good interval and keep you eyes and ears open."

Canadian Lancaster Call Sign "Ghost Zero Six"
12,000 feet over the North Sea
2230 Hours

The big Lancaster with the four night fighters had joined the long stream of aircraft enroute to central Germany. Lower than the bomber squadrons, the small formation was now located in the middle of the long string of aircraft.

Karl had spent most of his time going over their equipment, while Jack had been in the navigator's compartment with Ian Parker.

The H2S radar was working well and Jack could see the coast of Holland on the nose forty miles ahead. The young navigator had told him the ground based 'Gee' navigation system would not do them any good tonight, the range from the ground stations in England to Posen was too great.

"We were lucky to get some radar pictures from the Mosquito recon mission last week. You can see I've made some radar templates. That's how the target should look on radar as we approach from the west. The main industrial buildup of the town ends about five miles before the depot." Ian pointed at a black sheet with bright marks indicating the radar return. "On the run in heading of one zero zero the depot shows up as the only major radar return in that area. We'll fly south of the depot on our drop heading. I'll have the ADF tuned to the partisan's ground radio to confirm the drop distance. When we get needle swing we'll be close to overhead the partisan camp. We'll give you a green light 30 seconds later. That should put you directly in the middle of the drop zone."

Jack knew enough about the systems to feel confident in the technology. He also knew how things seldom went as briefed during the last critical moments of any aviation evolution. But it was a good plan and this crew was one of the best pathfinder crews in the RCAF. "Almost like being dropped in Piccadilly, right?"

"Commander, if you don't mind me asking, you sound more like a Canadian than a Brit. Did you come from Canada?"

Jack laughed. "Actually, Seattle."

"No kidding. I'm from Victoria, B.C." He saw Parker's eyes light up. He looked like he was fifteen years old.

"My family used to visit B. C. every summer. What a beautiful spot." Jack remembered those carefree days before the war.

"I can't wait to get back. My wife had a baby just before we flew over here. I never got a chance to see my new daughter."

Jack looked at the young man, having trouble picturing him as a father. "The war will be over in a year, I'm convinced of it. Then home you go. Well, I'd better go back and check on my partner. Let me know if you have any equipment problems."

"Yes, sir," Ian answered. He returned to adjusting the scope on his radar.

The steady hum of the engines and relatively smooth air made the mission seem like a training hop over Kent. But Jack had seen the coastline approaching and knew this was perhaps the most dangerous and critical mission of the war for him. He saw Karl sitting on the floor, his back against the aluminum side of the Lancaster.

"Karl, how are you doing?"

"I'm alright. I've never been really comfortable in aircraft, especially at night."

Jack sat down next to him. "Between night and day, I'll take day anytime."

116

"I've been through several air raids in Berlin. Guess I'll see what it's like on the other side."

"Let's hope the German night fighters have the night off. At least with flak, you know where it is. With night fighters, you never know."

Karl Dietrich had always been fatalistic about enemy threats. He knew he was prepared for his missions and that was all he could do. Tonight his concern was for a woman he had left behind in London

Posen Depot Administration Building
2300 hours

Franz Schroeder slouched back in his high backed chair and watched the cigarette smoke rise from the ashtray. He was satisfied it had been a very productive day for the depot. The warhead assemblies were all uncrated. According to Fischer they were undamaged. Tomorrow the train with the chemicals would be on its way and by 0200 unloading of the transport containers would be complete. Himmler would be pleased. The operation was going very well and it would be a pleasure to take the credit. There was a knock on the door.

"Come in," he yelled, irritated with the intrusion on his moment of self congratulation.

"Herr Standartenfuhrer, we have received a second transmission on 13.222 megacycles and my technician feels the transmitter is near our station." Hauptman Scheer was officer in charge of the communication section.

"What's your recommendation?" Schroeder did not understand communications and Scheer knew it.

"I'd like to take the portable direction finder out tonight and see if we can determine if the transmitter is near us."

Easy enough. "Permission granted. Keep me informed."

"Yes, sir," Scheer said, and turned to leave.

"Scheer, go find Sergeant Littke and have him report to me at once."

Schroeder sat smoking his cigarette. Perhaps there was something to this strange transmission. In any case it would cost nothing to conduct a search in the area for anything out of the ordinary. He would send Littke and his platoon out with Scheer.

Ghost Zero Six
Approaching Leipzig
2345

Jack stood between the pilot and co-pilot looking ahead at the chaos overhead Leipzig. On the ground he could see fires burning. Occasionally there were searchlight beams searching the dark sky. Anti-aircraft bursts would flash bright orange for an instant in the darkness and wink out. Each of those flashes indicated more shrapnel being blasted into the night air in search of the big four engine bombers.

They were now inside the flak belt surrounding the city. For fifteen minutes the threat of night fighters would diminish although more and more reports were indicating Luftwaffe night fighters pressing their attacks into their own flak guns. The main bomber squadrons were staggered at altitudes from 20,000 to 24,000 feet. The

Whirlwind flight was at 17,000 feet. Roger Halliday was preparing for the course change that would send them toward Posen.

"Nav, Pilot, how soon before we turn?" Jack could hear the intercom communication over his headset, which was plugged into a receptacle behind the co-pilot's head.

He heard Ian Parker's voice come right back, "Turn in eight minutes. New course, zero six eight magnetic."

Halliday reached up and set the new course in the compass indicator on the instrument panel. "What's your estimate from that point to the drop zone?"

"Winds seem to be holding to the preflight estimates. I should think about fifty five minutes."

"Thanks, Nav." Turning to his co-pilot, Jeff Alwyn, he said, "Let's do a good fuel check. Make sure the numbers agree with the flight plan. It looks like the outboard wing tanks have all transferred."

Jack found the routine comforting, the flow of information and the steady progress toward Posen. He was glad to be up here watching the action, despite having to drag around the supplemental oxygen bottle. In the rear of the aircraft, Karl was alone with his thoughts. Their conversation had been very sporadic and only about the mission. Jack could only imagine what must be going through Karl's mind. How would he feel in a similar situation?

Fifteen minutes later they were twenty-five miles away from the large bomber formations, the small group of five aircraft moving steadily through the moonlit sky.

Hauptman Hans Albrecht watched the altimeter climb as he kept the throttle at full power and the nose attitude ten degrees above the horizon. *What in the hell am I doing up here?* Albrecht was in an 'on deck' alert status at the aerodrome at Finsterwalde. His day fighter group was made up of four squadrons of Focke Wulf 190A-Rs and protected the German capital to the south. Normally standing down at night, the group kept a small alert force that was occasionally used if the night fighters were overwhelmed or out of position. As a day fighter the FW-190 was one of the best. But at night, it was luck alone that might allow an intercept of the Allied bombers using Luftwaffe ground control.

Scrambled by the fighter defence sector headquarters, Albrecht scanned his altimeter as he passed through 11,500 feet still climbing at 4000 feet per minute. At least he was alone tonight and didn't have to fly formation. He keyed his radio, "Control, this is Bluebird 41, airborne for your control, ten miles north of station, heading zero one zero."

"Bluebird 41, steer heading one two zero. On completion of turn your target will be on your nose at 40 miles, multiple radar contacts."

He was already pulling the stick hard to the right, feeding in right rudder and rolling to sixty degrees angle of bank. "Acknowledge, heading one, two, zero. Do you have an altitude on the target?"

There was a momentary burst of static. Albrecht heard the controller say the target was estimated to be at fifteen to seventeen thousand feet. He checked to make sure his engine temperature and hydraulic pressure was within limits. Both looked good. He selected all of his six twenty millimeter cannons to fire when he pressed the firing button.

The moon was high in the night sky and behind him which would be ideal for an attack. If the controller could give him good vectors when he got in close, he might add to his score of seventeen Allied aircraft destroyed.

120

Jack Whitney watched the big Lancaster droning on steadily in front of his aircraft. The four Mosquitoes were flying a loose trail position. Two aircraft were on each side of the bomber about one quarter mile astern and stepped up five hundred feet. So far the mission was going as briefed.

It had been quiet when they left the large formation and headed east toward Posen. Mossies did a lot of their flying alone and at night, but not with a Lancaster in company. The huge speed advantage of the plywood fighter bomber was lost when flying with the lumbering Lanc. Their electronic warnings systems were quiet. Those instruments would be the first indication that German night fighters were in the area using airborne radar.

The Posen Valley

Two trucks moved down the main access road from the depot. Leading the trucks a small Kampfwagen bounced on the dirt road. Hauptman Scheer and Sergeant Littke rode in the smaller vehicle. The first truck contained the portable direction finder the signals section used to triangulate on radio signals. Corporal Unterriter was Scheer's best direction finder technician and was operating the equipment.

The second truck contained a twelve man squad from the SS security detachment. Scheer decided to head north and pick up the highway which ran east from Posen to Kostrycn. By covering the largest distance possible in the time allotted there was a better chance of attaining an angular displacement in the signal and that would supply the general location of the transmitter.

121

Scheer keyed the microphone on his portable comm set. "Corporal, is the equipment working?"

Unterriter replied, "Yes, sir. No problems."

Looking at his watch he noted the time as 0035. He liked to keep track for his signals reporting log. "Commence the search across the target bandwidth and let me know if you get anything."

Stefan led the small group of partisans to the east. Their progress was slow due to the darkness. It was only a mile to the designated drop zone when Jerzy decided to leave Patryk as the western lookout. By placing his men around the perimeter of the area it would allow them to locate the parachutists as quickly as possible. This area was far enough from the main road that he didn't worry about German troops. He was more concerned about the lone civilian who might see the drop and then report to the Gestapo. This area had both a German and Polish population, a result of the changing political boundaries from the last several wars. You didn't know who to trust and Jerzy chose to trust no one. It was the best way to stay alive.

Jerzy looked at the luminous dial on his watch. "Patryk, the drop is scheduled for 0100. It's 0041. They could be early or late. Listen for the aircraft. It should be coming in from the west. The parachutes may be visible in the moonlight." He could see the tense look on the young man's face. "Keep your eyes and ears open. Be alert for anyone on the ground before the drop. After the drop, if you see where they land, move toward the spot. Remember the challenge and reply is 'Warsaw – London', everyone got that?

The group nodded, but said nothing. Dobry spoke up, "What happens if no aircraft shows up?"

"If there's no aircraft by 0130, make your way back here. Use the tallest tree over there as the rendezvous. In any case, I want everyone back here by 0200 so watch your time. Be careful with weapons, we don't want to announce our presence here. The rest of you, let's go."

The remainder of the partisans disappeared into the night leaving Patryk standing by the trail looking into the night sky. He laid his rifle on the ground and sat down to wait.

Sergeant Littke watched the lights playing over the two lane road as they headed east. He couldn't understand what Schroeder was thinking by ordering them out at this time of night searching for phantoms. But he would follow orders. You could never go wrong in the SS if you followed your orders. He'd come from Treblinka with Schroeder. At the death camp Littke had been in charge of the twenty barracks buildings, which housed the inmates who were spared initial execution to be used as workers. As the section head he had life and death power over all in his barracks. He would decide who was no longer able to work and they would be taken away to the gas chamber. He found great satisfaction, as he would make his daily rounds of the barracks with the Jewish 'Kapos' or trustees, the men the SS used to man the crematoria. He loved to see the look of terror on the faces of those who knew they were too sick to work. It was entertaining to play with them as they pleaded for a chance. He would give them just a ray of hope and then direct their removal. His trips to the barracks were always the highlight of his day. Far different than driving a useless Wermacht captain down a deserted highway in the middle of the night. Littke wished he were back in his barracks at Treblinka.

The radio came alive. "We have a strong signal with a very good bearing cut."

Scheer grabbed the handset. "Note the bearing and our location and continue to scan." He had the original bearing line from the depot. If there were no other signals, they would still have two lines of bearing. That would give the approximate location of the mystery transmitter.

"Another transmission, same code, one minute interval."

This was too good to be true. Most direction finding efforts would get only a sporadic signal, making it very difficult to pinpoint the exact site. If this signal was repetitive they could very quickly locate the transmitter. This would be a good night for the Wermacht Signals Intelligence Service Scheer told himself.

"Estimate targets on your nose at seven miles, Bluebird," the ground intercept controller passed to Hans Albrecht.

Albrecht noted his compass heading one more time in his night instrument scan. "Copy, control," he said as he turned the 'Master Guns' switch from standby to 'Fire'. Adjusting the illuminated reticule in his gun sight as low as possible, he began to scan the sky ahead of him. Based on the estimated target altitude of fifteen to seventeen thousand feet he was level at fourteen. Given a choice he wanted to come in underneath the bombers, avoiding most of their defensive guns and giving him a better chance at hitting bombs or fuel tanks.

Scanning the night sky the fighter pilot felt his pulse quicken. It was always like this as action approached. Somewhere out there was the potential for sudden victory or death.

He began to see the illumination from exhaust ports on the engines of a enemy bomber. Albrecht instinctively made a quick adjustment with his stick and rudder. The target was less than 300 meters away. He pressed the gun trigger and felt heavy vibration as his six cannons fired their explosive shells. There was only time for a three second burst as he screamed past the target. Albrecht had seen some of his tracers impact mid fuselage on what looked like a British Lancaster. *Shit.* He'd seen the bomber too late to aim for the known weak points. His hits were in the fuselage, which normally would not knock down a four engine bomber. He'd only seen one bomber. It must be a single ship, perhaps a pathfinder. Unloading the aircraft by pushing the stick forward, he felt the powerful fighter accelerate. Continuing on course for one minute, he mentally laid out the aerial geometry trying to estimate the bombers location. I should reverse now, he thought to himself, as he turned hard left trying to maintain altitude in the turn. Pulling the aircraft around to a heading of 150 degrees Albrecht calculated the bomber would be somewhere in his eleven to one o'clock position at about six miles. His finger was poised on the gun trigger waiting to catch a glimpse of the bomber. Although he was down light from the moon, he doubted any of the gunners in the bomber would be able to pick him up with this head on aspect angle.

In an infinitely short moment while his mind could still register, Hans Albrecht understood his aircraft was exploding around him as cannon shells impacted his cockpit.

The FW-190 had registered on the radar of Jack Whitney's Mosquito long enough for Flight Lieutenant Glenn Farley to arrive at a quick firing solution. Whitney knew it was a slim chance he would kill the intruder, but he wanted to try and drive him off. It was both luck and skill resulting in a killing burst, which literally tore the German pilot apart.

Reversing back toward the Lancaster, Whitney was afraid of what he might find. He could see the big bomber flying on as before. Thank God there were no flames and he couldn't see any trailing smoke in the moonlight.

"Ghost, Bandsaw leader. Say your status?" Whitney waited for the reply.

"Bandsaw, we have some damage. We're sorting it out now," came the terse reply.

Jack Stewart knelt on the floorboards next to Flight Sergeant Kibby Landers. The wounded man had been manning the top gun turret when the cannon burst tore through the Lancaster's fuselage. The plexi-glass bubble was shattered, frigid air pouring into the center cabin. Stewart could see Lander's severe chest wound. His flying jacket was torn open and the man was gasping for breath.

"Get me a light and an aid kit," he yelled at Anderson, the crew chief. He turned and saw Karl Dietrich kneeling next to him.

"What can I do?"

"Take this oxygen bottle and try to give him as much as he can handle." Jack wasn't sure what else to do but stop the bleeding and keep him breathing. Reaching down he unzipped the man's leather jacket and pointed his light down at the wound. He immediately knew this was not a wound you survive laying on the bottom of an aircraft two hours from home. There was a large open wound covering most of the left side of his chest. There was steam coming from the wound. He could see the man's lung, grey in the harsh light. There was blood on the jacket and flying suit, but not much coming from the gash in the man's chest.

"Get me the largest bandage in the package," he called to the crew chief. The man shoved a pre-packaged bandage wrapped in heavy paper. He almost laughed. It was a four inch by four inch gauze bandage. The wound was bigger than the bandage. "Have any more of these?"

"One more, commander. Here it is." The man sounded apologetic.

Placing the two bandages to cover as much of the wound as possible, he called for tape and did the best he could to secure the makeshift dressing over the wound. Karl knelt next to Lander's head, alternately putting the mask over his face and then removing it to check on his breathing. Landers was continuing to gasp, but breathing easier. The man hadn't uttered a word since they pulled him out of the turret enclosure.

"Hang in there, sergeant. We've got the bleeding stopped. Keep working on your breathing," he yelled at Landers over the roar of the slipstream. "Hand me a morphine syrette." Jack stuck the needle into Landers shoulder pushing the plunger until the vial was empty. Throwing the empty syringe into the aid kit, he turned to the crew chief. "I'm going up to the cockpit, chief. You keep an eye on him." His eyes met Karl's and they both knew what the other was thinking.

Working his way forward, Jack could tell the aircraft had picked up a vibration, probably from the fuselage damage. Moving forward he saw the bombardier, Flying Officer Jamie Kelly, hunched over Ian Parke. The navigator was writhing on the floor of the forward compartment.

"How is he?" Jack asked the young bombardier whose eyes were wide in horror. Jack could see the twisted metal on the side of the fuselage where a cannon shell impacted. The shell had exploded against the transverse bulkhead and Parker had absorbed the brunt of the damage.

Looking back at Parker, Kelly quietly said, "Not good." The young man lay on his right side. Jack could see blood patterns all around the compartment, as if a can of red paint had exploded.

"What can I do to help?" Jacked asked.

As Kelly struggled with a bandage from the aid kit, he said, "I'm trying to stop the blood flow from his side. Check him over and see if I missed any other problems."

In five minutes they had stopped the blood loss from Ian's main wound, a puncture on the left side of his chest. Jack couldn't find any other significant bleeding. Parker rolled slightly and vomited on the floor of the compartment.

"See if you can find a blanket and keep him warm. I'm going to the cockpit." Jack climbed up between Halliday and Alwyn. The pilot was flying the aircraft. The co-pilot had his light on looking at a chart. "You've got two badly wounded men back there. I'm afraid Landers has no chance to make it back. His chest wound is massive. Don't know about Ian. He took a bunch of shrapnel. But other than a bad puncture wound, I didn't see anything else."

Halliday kept looking forward as he spoke. "The aircraft is in good shape, all engines normal and no apparent fuel loss. Other than a vibration we seem to be all right. What are your orders, commander? We're about fifteen minutes from the drop zone."

Jack knew that he might be condemning Ian Parker. The extra thirty minutes they could save if they turned back now might make the difference between life and death. But the lives of thousands of Britons might lie in the balance. Both Halliday and Alwyn knew the score and though Parke was a close friend they understood the importance of the mission.

"Press on"

"Right," he said. "Pilot to Bombardier. Jamie, you comfortable with running the radar for the drop?"

Jack heard his reply on the ICS. "I expect I can make a go of it. God knows I've watched Ian run it enough."

Halliday turned to Jack. "Commander, you better get ready. We're starting our descent to drop altitude. And, good luck." The pilot turned to look at Jack.

"Thanks for the ride."

Jack moved toward the rear of the aircraft stepping over the wounded Parker lying on the compartment floor. Kelly was busy adjusting the radar scope. He wondered if Parker would ever see his young daughter in Victoria.

Chapter Eight

12 Miles East of Posen
July 29, 1944
0055 Hours

Kneeling in the back of the direction finder truck, Hauptman Scheer couldn't believe his good fortune. As their little convoy moved east on the main highway the lines of bearing from the transmitter began to clearly cross at a point approximately four miles southeast of the depot. This was critical information which he must get back to Schroeder. Although the radio was manned in the communications building at the depot, this transmitter was line of sight and there was a ridge between their location and the depot. Looking at the local chart he noticed a secondary road which ran to within a mile of the where it appeared the transmitter was located.

He saw Sergeant Littke standing at the tailgate of the DF truck. "Sergeant, look at this map." The large man walked over to Scheer. "Did you see this road when we drove past it?"

Littke was not good at reading maps, but didn't want to admit it to Scheer. Luckily he remembered seeing a turnoff about three miles behind them. "There's a dirt road about three miles back, sir. Is that the one you are looking for?"

Scheer took another look at his map. "It must be. Stand by while I try to contact the depot for orders."

Littke was starting to get interested. There might be some action yet and that might help him with Schroeder. He'd do anything to get on the camp commander's good side. It would make Littke's life much easier.

Scheer's attempts to contact the depot were unsuccessful. He decided the advantage of an ongoing signal to help them locate the transmitter must not be squandered. "Sergeant, we're going to go back to that road and see how close we can get to that transmitter."

In the distance they could hear the sound of aircraft engines growing louder in the night.

Level at one thousand feet, the Lancaster had slowed to 155 knots. Karl Dietrich had convinced Jack that jumping at the lower altitude made sense for drop accuracy and a more effective rendezvous on the ground. Consequently they didn't need a reserve parachute, there wasn't time to use it. Karl had said, "You must have confidence in your parachute rigger." Jack was having second thoughts as he stood at the aft cabin access hatch getting ready for the jump signal.

Forward, Jamie Kelly watched the glowing scope. He had directed a small course correction based on radar return, and now adjusted his range ring to give him a reference point to order 'jumpers away'. The bright spot on his scope marched down toward the illuminated ring. Based on ground speed the range ring was the pre-calculated distance where he would start a countdown timer. At their ground speed, two minutes and thirty-five seconds after the timer started, the command would be given and the two jumpers would be on their way. The young bombardier held his breath as he always did during a bomb run. "Jumpers away, jumpers away," he called on the intercom.

Jack was standing at the edge of the lower escape hatch and saw Anderson drop his hand in the pre-briefed signal to jump. Taking a small step forward he dropped through the hatch and hit the air stream. Almost before he could realize he was falling, his parachute opened with a violent jerk. He looked around in the partial moonlight and saw he was approaching the ground rapidly. Jack put his knees together, ready for landing in what looked like a small tree. As the branches ripped by his face Jack closed his eyes and covered his face. Slamming into the ground he found himself with one leg on the ground and the other on top of a large branch.

He lay still for a moment, the only sound the faint hum of receding aircraft engines. Unbuckling his straps, Jack began to extricate himself from the combined tangle of parachute and foliage. Crawling out of the bush he grabbed his Sten gun and stood up. He moved and stretched slowly, everything apparently working normally. *That's a good start.*

Jack pulled out the compass and confirmed his bearings. He began to move toward the east. The moon was still providing good illumination and he could see the trees swaying slightly in a light breeze. Stopping for a moment he heard movement in the tall grass ahead. Freezing in position he waited. Someone was moving toward him. Quietly as possible he cocked the Sten and in a soft voice called, "Warsaw."

"London," was the reply in heavily accented English.

Cautiously moving forward he saw a man rise up from the grass. The stranger wore civilian work clothes and carried a rifle. The man was grinning in the moonlight. Keeping his Sten at the ready position Jack moved forward.

"Do you speak English?" Jack asked. The man did not react. "Speak any German?" he asked in German. The man nodded his head.

"Yes, little German. Name is Patryk." He smiled again.

"My name is Jack." He extended his hand which the man enthusiastically shook.

Patryk motioned for Jack to follow and in a minute they were standing by one of the mission cargo bags. *There's a bit of good luck.* How about other men?" he asked Patryk.

"No." The man shook his head.

The cargo bag looked to be in good shape. Jack detached the chute and pushed it under some scrub brush. "Here, help me." Jack picked up one of the carrying straps. Patryk saw what he meant and grabbed the other strap. Jack pointed east and said, "Let's go."

The two men moved steadily for ten minutes. Both stopped as they heard a noise in front of them. Crouching down, Jack motioned for Patryk to move behind a tree trunk. He also made a silent motion to the young partisan by putting his finger on his lip. Jack held the Sten ready and said, "Warsaw."

There was no answer and Jack moved to the left trying to work his way closer to the location of the noise. His heart was pounding. He heard the brush rustle off to his right. *One last time.* He said, "Warsaw," as he raised the Sten aiming at the noise.

"London." The reply in heavily accented English. The accent was definitely German.

"Karl?" he said quickly.

"Yes."

Jack couldn't see the surprise, then anger in Patryk's eyes when he heard the German speak. The partisan wondered what was really happening here. He decided to do nothing until they found the main group.

Mariska looked at her watch. "Ludwik, it's time to stop the signal." Twenty had minutes passed since the two of them heard the sound of a low flying aircraft pass south of the camp. Although she felt the signal was no longer needed, they kept transmitting, following Jerzey's orders.

A pleasant night breeze rustled the trees above them and they sat on the ground with their backs against a fallen log.

Ludwik pulled out a pack of cigarettes and lit one. "I hope we can get American cigarettes from our visitors," he laughed. The war time quality of cigarettes had declined each year due to the restriction on the flow of raw materials from outside Germany. The joke throughout the countryside was German cigarettes tasted like dried horseshit, but without as much flavor.

Grabbing a rock near her leg, Mariska threw it into the darkness. "I want to find out how the war's going. Sometimes I feel totally isolated." She got up and grabbed a small piece of wood, tossing it on the fire. "I'll get some water boiling. They will want coffee." She walked over to the hollowed out tree on the other side of the clearing where they kept their water containers. As she knelt down, men burst into the lighted circle.

"Stay where you are," one of the soldiers yelled in German. There were eight soldiers carrying weapons which were pointed at Ludwik and Mariska. Both of the partisans raised their hands. Several of the soldiers formed a perimeter, on guard against anyone coming out of the darkness. Two men dragged Mariska back near

Ludwik throwing her down next to his feet. Other men kicked Ludwik down on the ground next to her.

While two of the Germans kept their weapons leveled at Mariska and Ludwik, the others searched the surrounding camp. More soldiers appeared out of the darkness and she recognized one as an officer. He immediately went to the radio, examining it very carefully.

"Sergeant, here's the radio. I want two men to carry it back to the truck." Scheer was looking at the antenna set up with professional curiosity.

Littke walked over to the captain. "Sir, there must be more partisans near by. We need to be careful, they could be setting up an ambush. They know this area better than we do." It had been a good night for Littke. He didn't want to stumble into the rest of the group in the dark.

"You're right, sergeant. Tie their hands and let's get back to the truck."

Littke cut two long pieces of wire from the radio antenna and brutally bound Mariska and Ludwik's hands behind them.

In ten minutes only the small fire, which was almost out, gave any indication people had been there. The only sound was the soft rustling of the tree branches in the evening breeze.

It had taken almost forty five minutes for everyone in the drop area to make their way back to the rendezvous point. Jack's group was the last to arrive carring the heavy equipment bag. Patryk pointed to the very tall tree across a clearing and said, "Jerzy said meet there."

Leaving the cargo bag, the three of them slowly moved toward the group of trees.

As they approached the rendezvous, three figures moved out of the darkness toward Jack. He immediately recognized Jerzy's walk.

"Why is it that we always seem to meet in forests at night?" Jack said.

Jerzy smiled and they shook hands. "Good to see you my friend. I was worried. We didn't see any chutes when the aircraft flew over."

"We jumped very low, a recommendation of my partner. Jerzy Lubowisz meet Karl Dietrich." Jack said in German.

The two men shook hands, but said nothing. Patryk who had been standing to the side stepped forward. "What's going on here? Why do we have a German with us?"

Jack sensed the animosity toward Karl. This was something Jack didn't anticipate. He continued in German, "We have a German with us because he's on our side and critical to the success of this mission." He was tempted to say more but then thought more information might just complicate things. These men don't need to know Karl had ever been an SS officer, he told himself.

Jerzy quickly said, "Then let's get on with it. I want to get back to the camp and relieve Casimire at the observation spot. Jack, where's your gear?"

The group gathered together and started west in a single file.

Franz Schroeder did not like to be interrupted during the night. The call from his duty officer requesting his presence at the Admin Building had disturbed his already fitful sleep. Now he sat at his desk in full uniform with Scheer and Littke standing at attention in front of him. Their report quickly transformed him from sleepy and annoyed to focused and questioning.

"So you estimate there may be six to eight more partisans in the group?"

Littke answered, "Yes, sir. Judging by the size of the camp there were at least three or four, perhaps more."

He turned to Scheer. "What can you tell me about the radio?"

"It has a voice and beacon capability, normally run with a manual generator."

"And the prisoners?" He was leaning forward over the desk. He knew something important was happening.

Littke spoke up, "Both appear to be Polish. One man, one woman, in their late twenties, good health and neither's very talkative. We decided to bring them directly here for interrogation."

Schroeder thought for a moment. He should call 12th Group Headquarters in Breslau and request support. But that son of a bitch Kessler would get credit for whatever I turn up. I'll take care of this myself and let Kessler know after I've run this thing to ground. *Did this have anything to do with the warheads?* The Sarin was scheduled to arrive tonight. He must find out if these partisans have anything to do with it. "Sergeant, bring in the man. Let's see what we can find out. Who's our best Polish translator?"

"Sergeant Regein is fluent, sir."

"Get him in here first. Then bring in the prisoner." This would be very good for his career if he could crush a partisan operating group and make sure the warheads were completed.

After an hour of intense interrogation, the man continued to plead total lack of knowledge of why his group was watching the depot. It began to dawn on Schroeder that his failure to call headquarters could backfire on him if they didn't get the information. It was clearly time to take decisive action.

Ludwik lay on the floor, his hands still tied behind his back with the radio antenna wire. Blood oozed slowly from his nose and mouth. One eye was almost swollen shut, the purple and reddish skin pulled tight over his eye socket. Sergeant Regein continued to translate as Schroeder asked questions. Schroeder lit a cigarette and said in German to Littke, "Untie his hands and then hold one of his hands over the edge of that table."

Two of Littke's men carried Ludwik to the table. Schroeder picked up a wooden walking stick from the top of his desk. The shiny black shaft was topped with a heavy pewter fist. The soldiers now had his right hand pinioned on top of a large table.

"Tell him he has one last chance to tell me why they were watching this depot or he will never use that hand again."

Ludwik's head hung down, blood dripping on the wood floor. He shook his head 'No' but didn't say anything.

Schroeder slammed the metal fist into the Ludwik's outstretched hand, the impact shattering bones and tearing flesh from the fingers. Ludwik screamed in pain and fainted.

Not expecting any further information, the blow helped Schroeder deal with his own frustration. "Get him out of here and get someone in here to clean this mess. Take me to see this woman."

"Jerzy, no one's in camp." Patryk was breathing hard after running back to the main group.

"What do you mean there's no one, where did they go?" Jerzy's heart went cold.

"I don't know. The radio's gone, the fire's out and they're not there." Patryk's breathing was returning to normal. "I didn't go looking for Casimire. I thought I should warn you first."

"Jack, we need to hide your gear here and find out what happened in camp. If there are Germans around I don't want to take chances."

While the group hid the cargo bag there were multiple conversations in Polish, German and English.

Jack grabbed Karl by the arm and said quietly, "Any ideas?"

"The Wermacht has a good signal intercept capability. The signal they were sending to the aircraft could have been a perfect beacon for troops to find them. But a depot like this shouldn't have any signal corps teams."

"Shit."

They moved toward the camp very cautiously. Several times the main group stopped. Jerzy would send one man out to specific points to ensure there wasn't an ambush waiting for them. It took another thirty minutes to reach the camp which they approached from the south. It was quickly evident that Patryk's appraisal had been correct. Jerzy found where the radio antenna had been cut. There were no other clues to who had visited the campsite.

"Stefan, go out and see if you can find Casimire at the observation point. We'll get things ready to move here. Be careful."

Jack asked Jerzy, "Who was at the camp manning the radio?"

"Ludwik and Mariska." Jerzy sounded numb.

"Jerzy, we'll find out what happened."

139

"Jack, if they aren't here, there's a good chance the Germans have them. You know what the Germans do when they catch Polish partisans?"

"They might have moved out of here because they heard Germans in the area. Both of them could be hiding somewhere in the forest." Truthfully, Jack didn't believe that.

Stefan and Casimire emerged from the trees.

Jerzy grabbed Casimire by the jacket, "Do you know where they are?"

"No, Jerzy. I didn't hear anything from the camp. There was a lot of activity in the depot, but I heard nothing from here." The young man looked concerned and dejected.

Jerzy thought for a moment and then said, "Gather up your gear. We're going to move south. Jack, we'll swing back for your cargo bag on the way. Patryk, stay here until sunrise. If they don't come back, head south and find us."

Sergeant Littke unlocked the padlock on the door and swung it open. Schroeder saw the young woman lying on her side, her hands still tied behind her. She looked up at the men, fear in her eyes.

"Stand her up," Schroeder said to the men. When she was on her feet held on both sides by SS troopers he asked, "What is your name." She stared back at him, a look of confusion mixed with the fear. "Regein, ask her what her name is."

Sergeant Regein repeated the question in Polish, but the woman remained silent.

Schroeder thought for a moment, this may be my only chance. The woman either didn't know anything or is too stupid for her own good. I need to work on her to make sure she will tell me what she knows.

"Sergeant Littke, search her very carefully for weapons or anything else she may have hidden. Don't be too rough, but be thorough. When you're done let me know."

Littke looked at the woman and smiled. "Yes, sir."

As Jack and Jerzy began their discussion Jerzy was using English.

"Let's talk in German so Karl can join in," Jack said in German.

Continuing in English Jerzy asked, "He can only speak German?"

Jack replied again in German for Karl to hear, "Karl recently joined our group and hasn't had time to learn much English."

The three of them were standing in a group away from the others who were still gathering their gear.

Jerzy asked in German, "Where was Karl before he joined the group?"

Dietrich quietly said, "I was in the SS. Is that a problem?"

"The SS! Mother of God, Jack, what's going on here?" Jerzy was trying to be quiet but the words seemed to burst from him.

Jack spoke up forcefully, "That's right Jerzy, the SS. In fact Karl was a Colonel. He's in greater danger than any of us by being here on this mission. But without him, we may not be able to pull this off. And if we aren't successful, countless people in England are going to die. If you can't handle that let me know. You should be able to figure out that when German soldiers realize they must fight against Hitler, we're going to win this war. Now what's it going to be?" Jack was angry, but felt he knew Jerzy better than most.

"Jack, you don't understand. You don't know what the SS has done to my country. They are butchers."

"You're right, I'm not Polish. I'll never know what your people went through. But I've lost good friends to the Japs and the Germans. Just last week Ian Thompson was killed by a V-1. There's nothing I can do about any of that, but I can damn well try to stop the SS from killing even more people. And that's what Karl is trying to do. So make a decision, captain. You're either in this or you're not."

Jerzy stared hard at Jack, his features like stone. It was totally silent in the camp, as the others had stopped to listen. "Jack, you're right. When an SS Colonel begins to fight for England against the Nazi bastards the war must soon be over. We are with you."

Jack looked at Karl who stood quietly, showing no emotion. "All right, we need to clear this area but it's still very important to have the ability to conduct surveillance of the depot. Is that possible if we head south?"

Jerzy nodded. "The forest is much thicker. But because they built the depot in a valley that runs north/south we should still be able to see it from the hills to the south."

"Jerzy, we're watching for the arrival of a train." Jack hesitated then continued, "The train is carrying material which will be used to construct warheads loaded with a type of nerve agent. If those warheads are completed and then mated with the new V-2 rocket it could change the course of the war. This is a mission where we're all expendable if that's what it takes to destroy the warheads." Jack thought they needed to know what was on the line.

"How are you going to destroy these warheads?"

Jack heard the old Jerzy he knew. "Once we verify the material for the warheads is in place, we call in a massive air raid to level the depot."

"Can't they build them somewhere else?"

"Sure they can. But we'll set the program back and hopefully as our ground troops advance, the launch sites will be overrun. The V-2 is powerful, but the range isn't much over 200 miles."

The rest of the group was now standing around them. Jerzy turned to Stefan, "Ready to move?"

The large man looked grim in the dim light. "We're ready to move, but not with a fucking German."

Jack didn't understand what Stefan had said, it was more the way he said it. "Jerzy, is there a problem?"

The multiple languages added to the tension. Jerzy said harshly in Polish, "Right now we move. We can discuss this later. If that isn't good enough for you, Stefan, then leave."

The big man moved closer to Jerzy. "I was the leader before you arrived and I can take any of these men with me. I don't think they want to trust their lives to a damned German regardless of whose side he's on."

Turning to the other men, Jerzy said, "We don't have time for this. There could be German troops on the way here right now. I want to be four miles southwest of here by the time the sun comes up. Now get your gear and we'll talk about this later."

As the men slowly began to shoulder their packs, Jack pulled Jerzy aside. "What was that all about?" Karl stood next to them, saying nothing.

Jerzy said in German, "They know he's German and don't want anything to do with him. I'm sorry, Jack. There's hatred that goes very deep over what has happened in my country. These men are no different. They're good men, they would die for Poland. But they don't want to work with a German."

Jack flared up. "They're being foolish. Karl, let's go."

The two commandos picked up their weapons and moved in the direction of where their equipment was stashed. Jack turned and looked back at Jerzy.

The former cavalry officer looked at his band of men and said, "I'm going with those two. If I can do something to shorten this war and bring Germany to her knees then I will shake hands with the devil himself. Now who's with me?"

The entire group, including Stefan, slowly followed Jerzy into the dark forest.

Franz Schroeder had taken a nap. It was only for two hours but it made him feel much better. Following a hot shower and a hearty breakfast of sausage, eggs and black bread he was ready to continue. Walking across the compound Schroeder felt much better with his new strategy. He would take his time with the woman. Entering the bare passageway he saw an SS Private standing guard outside the heavy wooden door.

The man snapped to attention as he opened the door for Schroeder, "Good Morning, Herr Standartenfuhrer."

Inside, the harsh light revealed the woman tied in a simple wooden chair. Her arms were secured to the arms of the chair, her ankles and knees to the legs and finally several lines held her torso upright. Sergeants Littke and Regein stood to one side with two men from Littke's platoon and the company clerk. The woman's hair and clothes were disheveled as if she had slept in her clothes. There was a vacant look in her eyes, very different from the look of fear only two hours ago. It was as if someone had broken her spirit although there wasn't a mark to be seen on her body.

Schroeder sounded very upbeat, "Good morning, sergeant. I trust all went well with the prisoner?"

"Yes, sir, very well." Littke tried to maintain a totally professional tone.

"And did we impress upon her the need to answer all of our questions?"

"Without question, Herr Standartenfuhrer."

"Good, let's get started." He moved over in front of the woman and in a pleasant voice said, "I am the depot commander. It is my responsibility to determine what is going on with your little group in the forest. Do you understand?"

Regein was again doing translation duty. The woman nodded, her eyes still vacant.

"Very good, very good." Schroeder smiled as he paced back and forth in front of her. "Now, what is your name?"

She looked up at his face, but didn't answer immediately.

"Now you and I both know you have a name. We will find out in the end, so tell me your name."

Her lips started to move and she quietly said, "Mariska Komoroski."

"Thank you. Now, Mariska, where are you from?"

She only hesitated for a moment, "Warsaw."

"Warsaw, very good. How long have you been here in Posen?" He continued to pace. The company clerk was taking down the questions and answers on a tablet of paper.

She hesitated briefly then stammered, "Two…. no more than two weeks."

"And how many were in your group?"

Mariska lowered her head looking at her lap. She shook her head as tears started to fall on her trousers. She knew she couldn't resist these men. Their control was total. The nightmare of the last two hours with these animals kept returning to her thoughts. Never again, she just couldn't face it. "Eight."

"Thank you, Mariska. Would you like some water?" He smiled at her, this was working out well. He must do something for Littke, his preparation did exactly as expected and now she's ours.

Chapter Nine

Posen Intermediate Engineering Depot
0830 Hours
July 29, 1944

Standing in his office Franz Schroeder congratulated himself on a job well done. He knew enough about the group in the forest to send an alert to the SS commander in Allenstein. The partisans left behind by this group should be easy to round up with the information obtained from the woman. Two platoons of his troops were in the forest now searching for the remaining Poles and he was optimistic they would be found.

"Herr Standartenfuhrer, Major Rosensweig and Herr Fischer are here to see you." Turning, he left his thoughts and saw his adjutant standing at the door.

He moved over and sat down at his desk. "Have them come in."

The two men entered and stood in front of the desk. Rosensweig spoke first, "Sir, I've been on the phone with Dyhernfurth. Everything is in place for the departure of the train on schedule."

Schroeder did not offer them a seat. He asked, "Is everything ready for the arrival of the train?"

Rosensweig answered, "Everything is in order, Herr Standartenfuhrer."

He turned to Fischer. "And you, Herr Fischer, are you confident we are ready to make the transfer on schedule?"

"I am confident, sir. We've done several dry runs. Everyone knows exactly what is expected of them."

Schroeder thought for a moment. "We captured several partisans southeast of the depot last night. On intensive interrogation I've been able to determine they had no knowledge of this operation. It appears the new construction prompted interest by the British and this group was trying to gather information."

Fischer said, "Sir, doesn't it seem like too much of a coincidence their activity was taking place just as we are reaching a key part of the plan?"

Schroeder smiled. "Herr Fischer, you give these peasants too much credit. There's no reason for anyone to suspect the purpose of this depot. After we complete these warheads and they go on their way there's nothing to connect them back here. We'll continue producing warheads and no one will be the wiser."

"Sir, is there any chance this group would try to conduct sabotage within the depot or on the rail line approaching the depot? From a safety standpoint Sarin is vulnerable to even the most rudimentary attack."

Rosensweig seemed as concerned as Fischer and it was beginning to irritate Schroeder.

"I've thought all of this through. We're combing the forest right now to capture the remaining partisans. I have extra security troops coming in from SS Group Breslau, they'll be here by mid-day. An inspection will be conducted on the railway spur line, which connects to the main line beginning in about an hour. I have this well under control."

"Yes, sir, thank you," said Rosensweig.

"We will meet at 1600 to go over any last minute problems with the warhead assembly. Now get out of my office and let me deal with this partisan problem."

There was little talk among the men as they made their way slowly through the thick forest. Jerzy pushed them south west of their original camp toward a ridge, which he felt would be a good observation point. An hour after sunrise the group fell out to take a much needed rest. Once everyone was dispersed Jerzy set up two lookouts and ventured off with Stefan to find a vantage point to observe the depot.

The two men worked their way up the slope constantly checking the field of view looking north. Soon it became obvious to both of them it would require climbing to the crest of the ridge to give them a view of the installation.

In another ten minutes they were at the crest. The depot was in full view three miles to the north.

Looking through his binoculars Jerzy said, "This will do fine. You can see the railroad siding and main buildings in the compound. The lower ridge blocks the southern fenced boundary but it's the best we can do right now."

Stefan stood with his arms folded in front of his chest looking toward the depot. "Jerzy, are you going to trust the German?"

"Stefan, I trust Jack Stewart. That's all I need. Perhaps my military background makes it easy for me to put my personal feelings aside. No one hates the Germans more than I do. But I took an oath. That means sometimes you have to do things you might not want to. You're a volunteer. In the military we play by different rules."

"We're both Polish, Jerzy, and that means we hate everything and everyone German"

The Polish Officer shook his head, "Don't be so damned simple. There are good Germans just like there are bad Poles. If Jack Stewart tells me this Karl is a good German, I'll believe it until something happens to prove him wrong."

"If he does something to prove your friend wrong I'll kill him." Stefan's voice was hard.

Turning slowly, Jerzy looked at his friend, "Stefan, if that happens he will already be dead."

When the two men came back down the slope they saw most of the group sitting on the ground or lying down trying to rest. Jack and Karl Dietrich were standing together at the far side of the small clearing.

Jerzy left Stefan and walked over to the two men. "We found a spot where we can see the depot. Not as close as before but with glasses it's workable."

Jack nodded and said, "We've been talking and have a plan."

While Jerzy was the local commander, Jack still gave orders for this mission.

Continuing Jack asked, "How long would it take to get to the railway station in Posen?"

"Posen?"

"Karl has been through there before. If we can get to the railway station it should be easy to arrange for transportation to the depot."

Jerzy looked at Karl Dietrich whose face remained totally calm. "You're going to go to the depot?"

Jack smiled slightly and nodded. "No other way to find out for sure if the material has arrived yet. Also we may be able to find out about Mariska."

At the sound of her name Dietrich looked at Jerzy and said in German, "If she's there we'll get her out."

Although Jerzy hoped she was somewhere in the forest, he knew in his heart she'd been captured by the Germans. He wasn't letting himself think about what might happen. Now this man who had been his enemy was telling him he would rescue the most important person in his life. Jerzy looked Karl directly in the eye and said in German, "Thank you."

64 Baker Street
London
1130 Hours

Hiram Walker marched smartly down the waxed corridor floor and turned into Brigadier Greene's office. He carried a manila folder under his arm and said to the clerk, "Is he in?"

"Yes sir, shall I announce you?"

Knocking on the closed door he heard Greene acknowledge.

Hiram walked over to the desk and put the folder in front of Greene. "This was just decoded at Bletchley. It seems the second part of the puzzle is about to come together." He stood in front of the desk as Greene read through the message.

151

"Have Major Hatcher report to me as soon as you can find him. And tell my clerk to call Colonel Hudson. It seems we need to get the Air Force moving."

Over the last two years the ability to project airpower from the British Isles to the continent had grown remarkably. The Royal Air Force and U.S. Eighth Air Force counted over 8000 fighter and bomber aircraft at their many English bases. Launching a raid of 250 bombers on short notice would not have been attempted in 1942 or 1943. Now, one call from MI-6 to their Bomber Command liaison office had mission planners, maintenance technicians, aircrews and ordnance handlers gearing up for a raid, which would launch tentatively at 0200. Much of the advance planning had already been done once the target had been designated. Flight profile, navigation checkpoints, fuel figures and weaponeering were completed several days ago by a special planning group at Bomber Command Headquarters. The task this afternoon was getting the information out to individual bases for the squadrons and groups to put into action.

The message, which the cryptologists had decoded at Bletchley Park, clearly identified a "SR" shipment order departing from Breslau at midnight tonight. Hearing nothing so far from Jack, Noel Greene made the decision to launch. Tommy Hudson was concerned they might miss the Sarin in the event the train was delayed. The key was to confirm arrival of the Breslau train by Jack's group. The SOE communications section was attempting contact Jack, but so far they had been unsuccessful.

Posen Engineering Depot
1600 Hours

Franz Schroeder sat at his large desk and took notes as Rosensweig and Fischer briefed him on the sequence of events for tonight's arrival of the train from Dyhernfurth. They had put together a comprehensive plan and it appeared to Schroeder there was nothing else of significance to discuss.

"Very thorough, gentlemen. Congratulations on your efforts. I will meet you on the loading dock at 0130 to monitor arrival of the train."

As the men were leaving his clerk entered the room. "There are two officers here to see you, Herr Standartenfuhrer."

Schroeder was surprised. He wasn't used to getting visitors at the depot. It was new, out of the way and with the exception of the warhead project there was nothing happening to warrant visitors. "What?"

"Sir, Standartenfuhrer Kessler from the Reichfuhrer's Office."

Schroeder felt a wave of panic envelop him. *My God, what is going on here?* "Tell them I'll be with them in just a moment." He must think.

Jack Stewart sat in Schroeder's outer office trying to look bored. As the day unfolded he felt like an actor in a play. It was a blur, which would never make sense unless he took each event by itself. They hiked to the cars with Jerzy, Stefan and Patryk. At the cars they changed into their SS uniforms for the ride into Posen. Patryk drove the car with instructions to wait in a ravine off the main road until Karl and Jack returned.

153

Jack kept looking at Karl who was wearing his actual rank and decorations including the Knight's Cross. There was a way he carried himself when in the uniform which Jack didn't notice in England. Karl presented an air of authority and deadly efficiency.

Their first test came at the local SS detachment. Karl called and ordered a car and driver to pick them up at the railway station. It was disconcerting to watch Karl as the SS driver arrived. This was a senior German officer conducting himself exactly as if he was on a mission from Himmler. They stopped at the detachment where Karl notified their duty section he would need the car for at least a day. Jack stayed close to Karl while in the building. He noticed that as a Sturmbannfuhrer he was given a great deal of respect of his own.

Arriving at the Depot's main gate Jack's anxiety again peaked. His papers would have to pass the scrutiny of SS guards. The entire procedure was anticlimactic. The guards were completely intimidated by Karl. One young guard looked at his identity card, very quickly returning it to Jack as he came to attention and saluted. Karl was a picture of bored indifference telling the guards he wanted to see the depot commander.

Jack tried to take in as much detail as he could during their short drive to the admin building. The buildings were newly constructed, with many signs the construction was still in progress. While there weren't many personnel visible in the compound he did see a group of prisoners unloading cement bags from a truck. It was hard to believe the condition of the workers. Covered with dust and dirt they were emaciated. Wearing threadbare grey shirts and pants these creatures shuffled from the truck to the loading dock. These people were already dead he thought. This was what this war was all about.

The door to Schroeder's office opened and he walked out to meet them. Jack noticed the man didn't wear any personal

154

decorations. *He must be part of the security side of the SS, probably has never been in combat.*

Schroeder smiled and raised his hand in the traditional greeting of the Nazi Party. "Good afternoon, gentlemen. I am Franz Schroeder. Please come in my office."

Following Karl's lead, Jack returned the salute. Saying nothing he followed the two men into Schroeder's office.

"Please sit down," Schroeder said, gesturing to chairs in front of his desk. "Now, how may I be of assistance?"

When Karl spoke, his voice had a hardness that cut like steel through the room. "My name is Kessler. I am on a special mission for the Reichsfuhrer. This is my assistant, Steiner." Karl handed Schroeder a doctored copy of the letter he had received in Himmler's office before his mission to England.

Jack couldn't see any reaction from Schroeder while he read the letter, but noted his hand trembled slightly when he handed it back to Karl.

"I am at your disposal of course, Herr Standartenfuhrer."

"We have reason to believe there is a partisan group operating in this area. They might be attempting to disrupt the special project." Karl's voice retained the cruel tone. "Do you have any information which might help our investigation?"

Schroeder couldn't believe his good luck. "Actually, I've already arrested two of the group. My security forces are on the trail of the rest of them as we speak."

Karl's eyes narrowed as he looked Schroeder directly in the eye, "You have already captured two of them? Very good, Herr Schroeder. I shall make sure the Reichsfuhrer knows of your aggressive actions. What information have you obtained from your prisoners?"

"The man was very uncooperative and paid for it. The woman, after some time with my men, was more than ready to talk. She gave a complete rundown on the partisan group. Where they were before, the number in the group, names, and a great deal of information I will turn over to the Gestapo." Schroeder sounded like a young boy reporting to his teacher.

Continuing in a very detached manner Karl said, "Was there any indication they knew anything about the special project?"

"Nothing specific. But I found it interesting that when she was captured most of the men were out recovering parachutists from England." Schroeder was starting to relax.

"You're telling me you decided to keep the prisoners here and continue the interrogation at your level after discovering there were British parachutists involved?" Karl sounded like a prosecutor in a courtroom.

Schroeder realized his mistake. He was concerned and stammered, "Of course I was going to transfer them to Breslau very soon. I was making sure all of the details of tonight's arrival of the material were taken care of first. The senior Gestapo agent in Posen was called an hour ago. They told me he would be here no later than 1800."

Sitting there, Jack's mind was racing. Not only did they know many details of Jerzy's group, but they knew about the drop last night. *Son of a bitch! The Gestapo would be here in an hour.*

"Perhaps a trained interrogator will be able to get more information out of them. Now, tell me about preparations for tonight."

"The train from Dyhernfurth is scheduled to arrive at 0200. We'll have all of the technicians turned out to make sure the transfer of the material goes flawlessly. I've had a final briefing with my key people and there are no problems at this point. There will be

156

additional troops coming from Breslau this afternoon. We just received a message the anti-aircraft guns we were promised will arrive within the hour."

Karl sounded almost indifferent. "It sounds like you have this under control. The other material is in place with no problems?"

"Yes, the unloading went without a problem. There are fifty warheads waiting in the assembly buildings.

"Very well. Now I'd like to see the prisoners."

"Of course. I'll take you over to our holding cells," Schroeder said as he stood up.

Karl and Jack got to their feet. "That won't be necessary. Have someone escort us over. You have many things to attend to. We don't want to detract from your primary duties."

It was a short walk to the one story concrete building. The depot commander had called for two sergeants to accompany them. Sergeant Littke was a senior non-commissioned officer with the security detachment who had been involved in the interrogations. Sergeant Regein was with them as the interpreter. Karl and Jack followed the two men into a dark hallway stopping at a heavy wooden door.

Littke unlocked the padlock swinging the door open. "This is the man. We couldn't get much out of him."

Jack looked inside as Littke turned on the light. Lying on the bare floor the man was in a fetal position cradling his hand in his lap. He didn't look up when the light came on but moved his head slightly, moaning. There was dried blood on the new concrete floor.

Karl said, "Who was involved in the interrogation?"

Littke turned to look at him, "Sir, it was…"

"Spit it out, sergeant!"

"Sir, Standartenfuhrer Schroeder, myself, Sergeant Regein and two troopers from my platoon."

"And you got nothing from him?"

"No, sir."

The look from Karl to the sergeant would have frozen lava. "I'm not surprised. Now take me to the girl. And get this one some food, water and something to lie on. The professionals will need something to work with," he said with clear disdain in his voice.

Jack followed Karl into the corridor to the next door which Littke was unlocking. The sergeant's voice was hesitant, "Here's the girl. She was very cooperative."

Karl continued, his tone now sarcastic, "Yes, sergeant, I'm sure she was. And why do you think she was so cooperative?"

Littke paused for a moment, unsure of himself. He said, "Because we showed her what German soldiers do with captured women."

Karl walked into the room and Jack followed. Mariska sat on the floor, her back to the wall. She held her arms protectively around her bent knees. She didn't show any indication she knew they were in the room.

"Have you ever been in combat, Sergeant Littke?" Karl asked.

"No, sir, not actually." The man's voice trailed off.

"When you spend six months on the Russian Front you can call yourself a German Soldier."

Karl knelt down and looked into the girl's eyes. "Ask her to tell me her name."

Listening to the Polish words, she turned her head slightly and looked up at Karl. In a soft voice she said, "Mariska Komoroski."

Jack and Karl were walking back to the Admin Building as a train was pulling to a stop at the loading platform. The train was made up of flatcars upon which rested 88mm towed anti-aircraft guns. Jack knew the reputation of the 88 as the best all purpose high velocity artillery piece in the war. He counted six of the artillery pieces lined up on the platform waiting to be unloaded. On the last three flatcars were six large searchlights, obviously used in conjunction with the 88's. The train stopped and men began getting off the two passenger cars. They must be the Luftwaffe gun crews Jack thought and wondered how long it would take to get the guns operational.

Karl opened the door of Schroeder's outer office and said to the clerk, "Tell the commander I wish to speak with him." Turning to Jack he said quietly, "Stay out here. I want to act like I'm covering up for him."

Schroeder stood up as Karl entered the room. Dietrich walked over to him taking off his cap and placing it on the desk. In a conspiratorial tone Karl said, "The Reichsfuhrer would not be pleased. You must know his policy on interrogations by field units."

Schroeder's expression changed from interest to concern. "I was not aware of any policy. I assure you, Standartenfuhrer Kessler, I would never knowingly violate an SS directive."

Dietrich sat on the edge of the desk. "We're all in this together and you've done a fine job with a tough situation. I'll take the prisoners to Breslau and tell them any injuries took place during their capture. That way you can concentrate on the special project. It must come off without any problems. I can tell you Himmler is very interested in this project as it could affect the rest of the war."

Sitting down in his chair Schroeder said, "Thank you, thank you very much. I understand the priorities and was only trying to

159

solve the problem as quickly as possible." He looked like a man who just received a reprieve from a death sentence.

"One thing would help me. I need to send my car and driver back to Posen. If you could get me a vehicle I can take to Breslau. I need something bigger to take the prisoners."

"Certainly, take my car. I will put the prisoners in the small Krupp."

Karl stood and picked up his hat. "Very well. Steiner can drive the car. Would you send Sergeants Littke and Regein in the truck? They're familiar with the prisoners and one of them can return your car."

Two vehicles pulled out of the main entrance to the depot, a shiny Mercedes sedan and a medium size Krupp truck. As they accelerated on the road to Posen a smaller black sedan passed them going in the opposite direction.

Before departing, Karl had told Littke, who was driving the truck, to follow them. They would stop shortly to "solve one of the problems you created."

Four miles down the highway a side road led into the forest. The two vehicles turned onto the road and disappeared into the high trees. The dirt road was passable but certainly wasn't used often. Two miles into the woods the sedan pulled to a stop.

Getting out, Karl walked back to the truck. Quietly he said, "Bring the man. We need to take care of this." The two sergeants looked at each other and got out of the truck.

Supported under both arms, his hands tied together in front of him, Ludwik Kowalski was carried stumbling into a small clearing. The pain from his hand did not overcome his sickening awareness of what was about to happen. He knew there was nothing

160

he could do but hold his head up, maintaining dignity as he faced death.

"All right, that's far enough. Stand aside," Karl said.

The two sergeants moved five paces away from Ludwik who turned to face Karl and Jack. Bruised and bloody, the partisan looked defiant and said something in Polish to his two executioners. Standing very still he watched as Karl and Jack removed pistols from their holsters, each chambering a round. Slowly they raised their pistols up to eye level.

Littke and Regein were watching the Pole and didn't see the pistols as they swung together toward them. Two shots rang out. Ludwik flinched and his eyes opened wide as Jack rushed over to the two soldiers now lying on the ground. Regein had been hit in the head and was dead. He had been Karl's target. Jack looked down at Littke who was bleeding from a wound in his upper chest. His eyes were open and he was moaning. As Jack stood looking down at him Karl walked up pointed the pistol at Littke's forehead and pulled the trigger.

"He's no German soldier."

Jack knew he'd never get used to killing, but this time it had been easy.

Ludwik had fallen to his knees and was looking at them with both terror and bewilderment. Jack took a deep breath and walked over to him, holstering his pistol as he went. He pointed to himself and said "English...Englander..Jerzy."

Slowly the realization came over the partisan. He whispered, "Jerzy." There was a flash of life in Ludwik's eyes, a look of hope.

The two men helped Kowalski back to the sedan, lifting him into the back seat.

Jack walked to the truck where Mariska sat, her hands and ankles tied with heavy cord. There was fear in her eyes. Jack reached down and started to untie her hands. He smiled at her and said quietly in English, "Mariska, do you remember me? My name's Jack Stewart and I'm a friend of Jerzy." He finished her hands and started on her ankles. He continued, "I saw you when we brought the airplanes to Rastenburg."

Mariska reached up and put her hand under his chin, tilting his face toward her. She seemed to struggle for a moment and then said, "Jack?"

Stewart smiled and nodded, "Yes, I'm Jack. You're safe." Although he knew she didn't understand the English words, he thought she understood the message.

She reached up and put her arms around his neck as tears began to flow. Jack picked her up and carried her to the Mercedes.

Ludwik turned to see her and he smiled, saying something in Polish.

Mariska nodded as Jack laid her in the seat next to him.

"We need to get back and get word to London about the anti-aircraft guns and the scheduled arrival of the train tonight," Jack said as Karl started the sedan.

"That man is a fool. But if the Gestapo's brought in, it could get very nasty."

The sedan pulled on the highway and headed east.

RAF East Kirkby
Lincolnshire
1745 Hours
July 29, 1944

Flight Lieutenant Roger Halliday and Flying Officer Jamie Kelly sat at a planning table with the Group Operations Officer, Squadron Leader Michael Formsby and the strike leader, Group Captain John Worthington. The senior officer on the raid, Worthington was one of the most experienced combat aviators in Five Group. His assignment emphasized the importance of this mission.

Halliday and his crew had arrived an hour earlier in a Lancaster Mk. X, side number DX 02, call sign "Ghost Zero Two".

Worthington, known throughout the Royal Air Force as "Jocko," would fly as co-pilot in Halliday's right seat. His normal co-pilot, Jeff Alwyn, would ride in the navigation compartment.

Operating on only six hours of sleep, Halliday and his crew had volunteered to go back to Posen when asked. The flight back home early this morning had been difficult. Ian Parker, barely alive when they landed, was now in the hospital, his condition very serious. Flight Sergeant Kibby Landers died an hour after the parachute drop, never really having a chance. Normally a crew would stand down after a mission like this morning, but Jamie Kelly had seen the target area, both visually and on radar. They would be the best crew to lead the entire 250 aircraft mission back to Posen and attack the depot.

The mission would consist of aircraft entirely from Five Group. Primarily Lancasters, there would also be three squadrons of Wellingtons. Worthington went over the time line, order of battle, rendezvous plan and ordnance loads. The weapons would be an equal mix of 500 and 1000 pound high explosive bombs and 30 pound incendiary types. The pathfinder aircraft would carry both flares and high intensity target indicators. Ghost Zero Two would make the initial target identification and marking.

Halliday listened to Jocko Worthington with professional attention and a little bit of awe. The older man was a legend in Bomber Command. One of the youngest squadron commanders at the beginning of the war, he helped write the book on strategic bombing for the RAF. Spending more and more time behind a desk, he was still one of the best tactical aviators in England.

"All right, Michael, I think that about covers everything. Would you make sure the information gets out to the squadrons straight away." Worthington closed his notebook and sat back in the chair. "Mr. Halliday thanks again for mustering up for this one. I know last night's mission was tough."

"Yes, sir." Roger was surprised he even knew his name.

"How's your fellow in hospital?" The older man seemed genuinely concerned.

"Serious, I'm afraid. He lost a lot of blood on the trip home." Halliday remembered the look of concern on Jamie Kelly's face after he had bandaged Ian. The young bombardier didn't think Ian would last the hour. But youth and a little luck had made the difference. Not so for Flight Sergeant Kibby Landers. The 'old man' in the crew, Kibby was 26 years old and the most experienced gunner in the squadron. His death had hit the crew hard. It wasn't difficult making the decision to go back. It was their way of dealing with Kibby's loss.

"Sorry to hear that. Did the intelligence types ever figure out what hit you?"

164

"No, sir. Which was the queerest thing. No indications at all on our equipment. It seemed like the fighter just stumbled on us. Tough to do anything about that."

"It might have been bad luck or could have been one of their day fighters pressed into night service. We're seeing more of that lately. Why don't you get something to eat? We can get together for a crew brief in thirty minutes."

Posen Depot
1830 Hours

Standing with his back to the two men in his office, Franz Schroeder felt the first waves of panic. During the last fifteen minutes the senior Gestapo agent in Posen had informed Schroeder of his many mistakes in dealing with the captured partisans. At best it seemed Schroeder was guilty of incompetence. He didn't want to think about what might happen if they were not recaptured.

Kurt Pressler stood with his arms crossed and shook his head. "Herr Standartenfuhrer, didn't it seem unusual when two men arrived at your command right after you captured two partisans? And without authorization from anyone in your chain of command you let them drive out the front gate." His tone was both sarcastic and accusing.

His voice shaky, Schroeder said, "I assure you their identity papers were in perfect order. They were most certainly Schutzstaffel Officers."

"As you said, SS officers directly from the Reichfuhrer's Office. Did you think about verifying that with Berlin?"

Turning sharply to face his accusers, he said, "There was a letter signed by Himmler himself."

Snapping back, Pressler said, "And if you read the letter carefully, there are always numbers to call for verification."

Quietly Schroeder replied, "It didn't seem necessary."

"It didn't seem necessary." The words were slow and accusatory. Schroeder began to sweat.

Pressler turned to his assistant, Max Leingang and said, "Get on the phone to Berlin and see what you can find out about this Kessler and Steiner. Then call Breslau and alert them to call us instantly if the prisoners arrive."

Schroeder didn't miss Pressler's use of "if."

My God, what if they weren't who they said they were? He pulled out his chair and sat down heavily.

Overlooking the Posen Depot
2145 Hours

The forest had been quiet all day with no sign of any German activity. With the darkness he was confident they would have stopped searching, especially in the heavily wooded areas. But there was still tension within the group. Stefan had been very quiet, something unusual for him. Several other comments throughout the day made it clear to Jerzy his men had no confidence in the Englishman or his turncoat German.

Casimire had set up the radio from Jack's equipment bag and was trying to get it working. So far he had been unsuccessful which made Jerzy very uneasy. If something of note happened in the depot there was no way of getting the information to London.

166

"Any luck?" Jerzy asked as he knelt down by Casimire.

Without looking up from the small area illuminated by his torch he said, "No."

"Well, keep trying. Without the radio we're out of business and might as well leave." Jerzy wondered if that would encourage Casimire or have the opposite effect.

Dobry, who was on lookout duty, ran into the clearing and said, "Jerzy, I hear someone coming up the ravine."

Everyone picked up their weapons and formed a defensive line toward the ravine. Stefan kicked dirt on the small fire. Not a word was said as the partisans waited quietly. Two minutes later they could hear the sounds of movement down the slope, heading toward them. They could make out the faint light of a single torch moving their way.

As the light slowly approached Jerzy called out in German, "Halt!"

From the darkness he heard the familiar voice. "Jerzy, it's Jack."

The men stood up, but kept their weapons ready as they watched the small group approach. Jerzy made his way down the slope to meet the group and then stopped. In the flashing light he could see there were five people and one was a woman. "My God...."

The two lovers stood apart from the group holding each other. Jack held his torch as Stefan relit the fire. Patryk helped Ludwik sit down with his back against a large tree. Standing alone, Karl Dietrich said nothing but watched the activity.

In a moment Jerzy joined Jack at the now relit fire. "Jack, I don't know what to say. I thought I lost her again, this time forever."

167

"She had a rough time. Thank God Karl was here to get her out. Right now we've got to get a message to London. The Germans have brought in 88's and searchlights for air defense. The aircrews need to know."

Jack turned toward the radio but Jerzy grabbed his arm. "Jack, she said you killed the two men who tortured her. You ...... and Karl."

"Jerzy, we did what had to be done. But without Karl, none of this would have happened."

Jerzy saw the look in Jack's eyes and nodded. He turned toward the group. "Casimire, come here." He said to Jack, "He's been working on the radio. There's power and nothing seems to be wrong. But we can't receive or transmit."

Casimire came over and explained in Polish what he had done so far and Jerzy translated for Jack.

Karl walked over and asked Jack, "What's wrong?"

"The radio. Something's wrong and they can't figure out what."

Karl said, "I'll take a look. Probably not as good as German radios, but maybe I can fix it."

For the first time that day Jack laughed.

Thirty minutes later the signal was sent to London. One hour later, Jocko Worthington knew of the anti-aircraft guns at the depot and was able to make an adjustment to the plan of attack.

Chapter Ten

Posen Depot
2200 Hours

Franz Schroeder sat at his desk, staring at the blotter. The two Gestapo agents had left ten minutes earlier after relating their communication with Berlin. Kessler was an imposter. The Main Reich Security Office was extremely displeased with Schroeder's failure to report the capture of the partisans, the possible parachute drop and attempting to interrogate the prisoners without trained personnel. There would be an officer arriving in the morning from Breslau to conduct an investigation. The apparent disappearance of his two men along with the prisoners appeared to have some connection to the special mission. Because of the connection Himmler was being notified of the problem at Posen. *The problem at Posen* he repeated to himself. In a fit of anger the small man pulled out his pistol and chambered a round. He placed it on the desk looking at the cold metal. Deep inside he knew that he couldn't kill himself. He desperately hoped something would happen to deflect the wrath of Himmler. They must know he was doing his best. His loyalty was total. Hadn't his performance reports always noted his steadfast allegiance to the party and the SS? They should have left him at Treblinka. He wasn't trained for this type of work. He was a policeman, not a soldier. Schroeder reached into the lower right cabinet door of his desk and took out a bottle of brandy.

In Berlin the duty officer at the Reichfuhrer's headquarters received the report from SS Group Twelve, the report having been originated by the senior Gestapo agent in Posen. The duty officer was not aware of the special project or its timetable. He decided to wait until morning before bothering Himmler.

Near the Posen Depot
2215 Hours

Jerzy and Jack decided to split the group. Ludwik was injured too severely to stay with them. Patryk, Dobry and Stefan would remain with Karl, Jack and Jerzy. Mariska pleaded to remain with Jerzy, but ultimately she understood his group would be moving faster and covering much more territory. Aleksy would lead the second group to the vehicles and start working his way east toward a valley where they agreed to meet in one week. Jack's group would move south of the depot to observe the air raid and report back to London when able.

"Aleksy, you job is to get to the vehicles and then to the valley for the rendezvous. We'll be at the small lake on the north end of the valley on the 7th. Get the vehicles as close as you can. There are several roads in that area. Stay away from anyone you encounter.

I think the Germans will come after us once the air raid is complete. If, for some reason we're not at the valley, wait only one day and then go to the church at Zagdrow. We'll do the same and meet there on the 12th. If either group is not at the second meeting assume the worst and head east to our old area. Understand?"

"I understand. Are you sure this is a good idea?"

"We don't have any choice with Ludwik. Be very careful and don't be in a rush. That's when you make mistakes. Good luck."

The two men shook hands and Jerzy walked over to Mariska. She was leaning with her back on a tree looking into the night sky. "I'll see you in a week. I promise you."

She nodded her understanding to him.

He put his arms around her and they stood there for a minute.

"Mariska, we must go," Aleksy called.

As they separated, Jerzy said, "I almost lost you once, it won't happen again. I love you."

"Be careful, please be careful." Then she was gone.

Jack's group worked their way southwest toward a tall ridge, which overlooked the railroad spur running into the depot. It had been hard going in the dark, but they were now on top of the ridge.

"I like the view from here, Jerzy." Jack had his binoculars out and was looking north toward the depot. The lights of the city of Posen were clearly visible to the northwest. The only other lights were on the rail switching shed one mile south of their position. The rail line into the camp split from the main north-south line at that point.

Bringing his binoculars down to his chest, Jack looked around at the area. "Set the radio up over by the large rock. We can run an antenna across to that tree." Jack wanted to be able to send the strike report to London as quickly as possible. Three letter groups would enable Jack to make a summary report quickly. The three reports would indicate success, re-attack required or failure.

Jack thought about the aircraft preparing to take off from England. It was a long mission, directly into the heart of the Reich. The German fighter network was very effective when combined with their radar warning system.

Recently Bomber Command had been proving very effective against the Luftwaffe. The intelligence community felt that it was due to the attrition of experienced pilots, which the Germans could not replace. Certainly the technological battle was about equal with no side having a clear advantage. The dwindling oil reserves were also starting to impact the Luftwaffe's combat readiness.

Dietrich was sitting on a large rock, a cigarette in his mouth. He had been quiet during the march to the ridge. He still wore his SS uniform as did Jack. Until they were out of the area there might still be a need to use their disguises.

Jack walked over and sat down next to Karl. They hadn't talked since returning to camp earlier. The German looked straight ahead as he took a drag on his cigarette. "It's funny how the night gives us time to think."

"That sounds like something's bothering you," Jack said.

Karl exhaled and said, "I started thinking about the last ten days. The mission to England, finding Eva, returning to Germany."

Jack was silent for a moment. "They say 'life is a journey.' You're on the next part of your journey, but on a road you never would have imagined. Karl, this is the right thing to do, for England and for Germany."

Dietrich stubbed out his cigarette. "I know you're right. But that doesn't make it easy."

Stewart sat in silence. He liked Karl Dietrich and he trusted him. How could that be? He'd known him for less than two weeks. But there was something about the man. You could sense strength of purpose with Karl. Today's events had only reinforced Jack's opinion that Karl Dietrich was a man who would stick with you until the job was done.

Breslau Central Switching Station
2355 Hours

The light from the overhead lights reflected off the black enamel paint on Reichsbahn Engine Number 2323. The Type 52 engine was pulling Special Mission A386 from Dyhernfurth to Posen. Easily moved through the switching yard the eighty ton engine was pulling only five cars in addition to its own coal tender. In the cab of the engine, Kurt Addelsen peered ahead looking for the green switching flags to indicate his path was clear to the main rail line running north from Breslau. The large man was a career railroad engineer. Joining the Deutsche Railway System in 1928, he had worked his way up to engineer by 1937. When the army took over the rail system in 1939 he was exempt from military service due to his occupation. He had spent most of the war on the runs east toward the Russian front. It had been a hard war in the east. The miserable winters coupled with the increased attacks on the train system made Kurt long for peace. He looked at tonight's run as a break. This was a special run from Dyhernfurth, which he had picked up at 2200. Behind his tender was a troop car, a "Linz" flatcar with an anti-aircraft gun and three freight boxcars. The boxcars were already loaded and sealed when he had arrived at the small station

173

west of Breslau. There were ten SS soldiers on board under the command of a senior sergeant. Four of the soldiers manned the quad-barreled gun which sat behind several protective rows of sandbags.

Karl and his stoker Hans Leitzel were the only two train crewmembers. Such a small load did not require the extra crew of the large trains he would haul on the line toward Moscow. Leitzel was a large, powerful man. The two of them had been together and with Engine 2323 for almost nine months now. Both of them lived in Dresden but were seldom there. They had given the engine a nickname, "Gertie."

Tonight would be an easy haul to the Posen Depot. Located only six miles off the main line, it involved one transfer to the spur line, which ran directly into the facility. He did note that there were several men in civilian clothes in the troop car. They didn't look like Gestapo, but perhaps they were engineers. As the train cleared the final switching center he looked at his watch and estimated an hour and thirty minutes to Posen. He pushed the throttle up to 70% power. With this load he should be at 85 kilometers per hour in ten minutes. It would be good to get somewhere early for a change. It seemed like he was always late, either from bomb damage to the rails or late connections. He reached down and found his lunch pail. Time for a sandwich he thought, as his stomach growled. Leitzel was methodically moving coal to the combustion box.

Approaching the town of Lezsno, forty minutes from Posen, Addelsen saw the red "track closed" light ahead. He thought the priority code for tonight's run would have ensured they had the track cleared to Posen. But what did he know, probably some Field Marshall in a hurry to get to his mistress. He rechecked his route map and found the siding, which was on the south side of the town.

He began to work off steam pressure in preparation for slowing the big engine.

In ten minutes he was at the switching lane and had the train slowed to almost walking speed. Ahead he saw the indicator flag, which showed that the switch was set up to put the train on to the main siding. With such a small train this was a very easy maneuver for an experienced engineer. He brought the train to a halt, releasing the excess steam pressure. Setting the manual brake he opened the cab door and climbed down the ladder.

"What in the hell are we doing stopped here?" The senior sergeant was striding up the side of the train with his hands upturned in question.

"I followed the signals from the switching yard. There is no choice. You have to follow the signals. If you don't there could be an accident. There must be something happening we don't know about."

The soldier was frustrated. He had been told by his superior that they were on a priority train and must get the Posen by 0200. "So how do we find out what happened."

Addelsen was already walking toward the control shack for the switching yard. "We go ask the dispatcher. That's all we can do."

A very sleepy dispatcher named Voehoffer sat at a desk in the small wooden building. The man woke up very quickly when he realized he'd put the wrong train on the siding and off the main north south line. After Voehoffer rechecked his priority routing schedule he could not have become more solicitous. Addelsen didn't care, he only wanted to be on his way toward Posen. Twenty minutes later they had re-boarded the train and were getting steam pressure back for pulling out. The engineer sat back on his chair watching for the routing flag to switch from red to green. Leitzel stood with both hands resting on the large shovel he used for the coal.

These damn dispatchers, Kurt thought, sitting on their asses and getting paid well. We're out on the line with bombings and partisans but those shit heads get to make our life miserable. *What's taking so long?*

Kurt could see a lantern 200 meters down the track. It looked as though the man was inspecting the switching box. In a moment, he saw the lantern coming toward him.

"Herr Addelsen, the switching slide mechanism is jammed. I can't get the thing to move. This is an old yard and the rails are not in good shape."

"Shit, that's all we need tonight. How soon can you get it fixed?"

"I'll have to call in my two maintenance men. It will take them half an hour to get here. After that, who knows?"

God damned dispatchers. "I suggest you get on the phone to your district coordinator and explain the situation. And be sure to tell him this mission number is on the siding and unable to proceed north." Addelsen was angry and wanted to make sure everyone understood the situation. Who knows, he thought, it might get help here earlier.

Following a phone call to the district rail coordination office the Lezsno dispatcher realized the trouble he was in and pleaded with his two maintenance workers to get to the yard as fast as possible.

RAF East Kirkby
Lincolnshire
2355 Hours
July 29, 1944

A single green flare arched into the night sky briefly lighting up the many Lancaster Bombers sitting in their parking spots with engines turning. Roger Halliday signaled to his ground crew to remove his wheel chocks. With a slight addition of power the big bomber began to move. Ghost Zero Two was leading a procession of aircraft at East Kirkby, which was being repeated at Swinderby, Scrampton and Coningsby. Every squadron in RAF Five Group was putting forth a maximum effort for tonight's raid. In addition, there were eight Mosquito Mk. XII's, from 85 Squadron, which would be joining them from RAF Hundon. Sitting in the right seat, Group Captain Worthington was reading through the takeoff checklist, which Halliday would acknowledge. Takeoff was scheduled for 0015 hours. The airborne rendezvous would take an additional forty-five minutes. Worthington planned to push the strike group toward the target at 0100 for a target time of 0400. The weather report was good with scattered layers of clouds in the target area. There were several other large raids scheduled tonight during roughly the same time. The intent was to saturate the Luftwaffe fighter defences.

Halliday was doing everything strictly by the book. It was intimidating to have such a senior aviator in the cockpit. But Halliday and his crew were experienced Pathfinders. They had logged thirty seven Pathfinder missions as a crew and many had been on additional missions.

Worthington put the printed checklist in the map case next to his seat and leaned forward to see the procession of aircraft on the

177

taxiways. "Right then, checklist is complete. Nothing last minute from operations so we go as briefed. How're you doing?"

Halliday nodded his head unconsciously. "I'm doing fine, sir. Grabbed a quick nap. That's all I needed."

"Don't be a hero. Once I get this circus rounded up and on its way, I'll take my share of the stick time. We both want to be sharp in the target area."

"Yes, sir."

As they approached the duty runway, the tower cleared them into position. Behind them sixty two bombers were staging, some just starting engines, others completing takeoff checklists. Everyone saw the double green flare that shot skyward from the tower.

Halliday ran the four Merlin engines to full power as he released the brakes. Ghost Zero Two began to accelerate down the runway. With practiced procedure, the undercarriage was retracted followed by the flaps. Both pilots were monitoring engine instruments as they established a positive rate of climb. They were cleared to sixteen thousand feet, one of three altitudes allotted to the bombers from East Kirby. Each aerodrome was assigned three altitudes, one thousand feet apart. The aircraft would establish a stable left turn with the rendezvous aerodrome in the center of the circle. This was one of the most dangerous parts of the mission. Each crew must be right on their altitude and very conscious of where they were on the group before they moved into the rendezvous circle. Every man in the crew was at observation stations to ensure the risk of a mid air collision was minimized. There were some pilots who professed they would rather be over the target facing flak that trying to join up at night.

Tonight the weather and moon were on the side of the bombers and all squadrons were able to rendezvous and push on time. Phase two of Whirlwind was underway.

Posen Depot
0140 Hours

At one end of the flood lit loading dock three men stood alone. Major Rosensweig and Dr. Fischer both sensed something had changed with Schroeder. Although he had arrived as scheduled at 0130, he seemed distracted and unusually quiet. Other than a few perfunctory greetings the three stood in silence watching the activity on the loading dock.

At the far end of the dock they saw Corporal Unterriter running toward them. He was carrying a message pad. Stopping and coming to attention, Unterriter said, "Herr Standartenfuhrer, we just received this on the district communication circuit." He handed the paper to Schroeder who took a moment to read it.

"There was a switching problem in Lezsno. They estimate the train will be headed northbound within the hour," he said.

"But no problems otherwise?" Fischer asked.

"None indicated. Gentlemen, I suggest we meet back in one hour. If there are any updates, my clerk will contact you. Good night."

Schroeder turned to walk back to his headquarters.

Four miles south, Jack Stewart checked his watch. Where was the train? If the second train did not arrive the plan would be jeopardized. It was not too late to contact London and abort the raid. They were still hundreds of miles from Posen, fighting their way through the Luftwaffe defenses. Perhaps taking out the depot would be enough. And there was no guarantee the train would not arrive later tonight. No one knew how long it would take for the mating of the Sarin and the warheads.

"Are you thinking the same thing I am?" Karl Dietrich was standing behind him also looking west toward the empty rail line.

"I'd hoped to see the train from Dyhernfurth by now. Something must have happened."

"The radio's warmed up. Do you want to contact London?"

Jack thought for a moment. "How quickly will they be able to react if one part of the warhead is eliminated?"

"I don't know. It depends on what backup material is ready to be shipped. They built this special facility to do the job. Can they do it anywhere else? What happens if the bombing kills key people? Can they be replaced?"

"Good point. They must have the best people from the project here for the final phase."

"Probably," Dietrich said.

"OK, we go as planned. As soon as the attack is completed we send the message and get out of here."

Jack knew they would be faced with the sun coming up in five hours, making their escape more difficult. But he had to see the results of the bombing. London must know how much damage had been done to the depot.

Ghost Zero Two
21,000 Feet
0236 Hours

Although they had been receiving indications of German radar activity for forty minutes, the first confirmation of night fighter activity was the radio call from a Lancaster in 52 squadron. Flying in one of the lower Group 5 squadrons, XR 88 had been hit and was dropping out of the bomber stream. Now 60 miles north of Frankfurt, Worthington knew they would be under Luftwaffe attack for the remainder of the track toward Posen. There were several night fighter bases near their route and the ones near Berlin were particularly dangerous. Although advances had been made in electronic-countermeasures, a good night fighter with solid ground control could do real damage to the bombers.

"Radio, Co-Pilot, confirm Tinsel is working." Worthington was referring to the radio transmission system that transmitted engine noises over known German air control frequencies.

"Working fine, sir. Good power out and we are covering all the frequencies used in this sector."

"Radar from pilot, keep on the scope. Everyone stay alert, we know they're out here." Night fighters were like sharks attacking. Sometimes there would be a sign right before the strike, other times it came out of nowhere. With the communication jamming and use of radar scanning it was harder for the Germans to get in close to the bombers without detection. But it was still a brutal fight when you met the Luftwaffe.

If the enemy fighters could close the bombers, the crucial area for Lancaster's was the underside. This made the lower aircraft in the bomber stream particularly vulnerable. For that reason, this strike had two B-17G's along for the mission. They were dedicated to defeating the fighters with jamming, warning systems and radar. They were known as Fortress III's by Bomber Command.

Tonight's raid also had an additional wrinkle. Jack's message about the German flak guns going into position at the depot had resulted in a specific task for 85 Squadron led by Jack Whitney. Their job was to attack the searchlights and flak guns surrounding the depot. This tactic was effective on point targets such as Posen and greatly reduced the losses to anti-aircraft batteries. Eight Mosquitoes were flying in the front of the formation with Whitney in the lead Mossie.

"Nav, Pilot, how far are we from out next turn point?" Halliday asked.

"Twenty three minutes if the winds don't change."

Behind them there were sporadic bursts of tracer fire as Lancaster crews defended themselves from the marauding Messerschmitt 110's. There was an occasional radio call, but the strike was still largely intact. However it was still a long way to the target.

In Luftwaffe sector control, located in Finsterwalde, Hauptman Volker Mannheim watched the small wooden blocks being repositioned on the large map of Northern Europe. There were several medium sized raids proceeding across the map. The Finsterwalde center controlled all fighter and anti-aircraft units in a large box which covered Berlin south to Leipzig and east to Warsaw. His floor plotters also kept track of all activity on the continent. Mutual assistance was the key to the Reich's flexible air defense system. Tonight the raids appeared to be heading toward Munich, Hamburg and Leipzig. The central raid toward Leipzig was the only group his sector would actively engage. As the sequenced launches of night fighters began, he walked over to the ground defence control desk.

"Make sure we have sent notification to all command sectors within 150 kilometers of Leipzig."

"Yes, sir," the senior controller answered.

"And get Berlin on the phone. This may be a feint south and may head for Berlin after all."

Calls were going out to the entire command network of the very integrated German Reich. The national effort to defend against air attack combined both civil and military authorities. Each branch would pass the air raid warning, setting into motion a well practiced series of events. Warnings would be passed, crews would man anti-aircraft batteries, fire companies would go to alert and transportation networks would shut down.

Lezsno
0305 Hours

In what was becoming a frustrating night, the jammed switching slide broke while the two repairmen were trying to free it. The metal was corroded and constant wear over time had weakened the slide. Addelsen was surprised when the dispatcher told him they had a replacement slide in their supply shed. The two men worked as fast as they could while Kurt watched the time. He was sitting in the cab smoking a cigarette when the dispatcher climbed the ladder looking for him.

"We should have it working in ten minutes. I've checked the line from here to Posen and you are cleared 'priority one.' No one else will be on the line and the switching alignment for you onto the Posen spur will be set up as soon as you leave here."

Kurt was tired, but this was good news. "Go tell the sergeant we roll as soon as there's a green light. Make sure all of his people are aboard."

"Addelsen, I'm sorry this happened."

"Don't worry, I won't tell anyone. Just get me back on the main line." He turned and increased air flow to the combustion box to begin raising steam pressure. The dispatcher disappeared below the level of the cab floor. Leitzel sat on a stool at the rear of the cab. "All right, Hans, get stoking old Gertie. We've got some time to make up." The big man grumbled but got to his feet and grabbed his shovel.

Thirty minutes later the train was approaching the Posen Depot spur switching station. Kurt reduced power and the engine began to slow immediately. He sounded two short blasts on the whistle to make sure the switching station knew they were coming. He would expect to see the track switching signal indicating the spur open. The spur was recently constructed and according to the system map had a sharp curve as you left the main line for the Depot. Annotated on the new chart was a speed limit of 20 KPH for the turn. Ahead he could see the switching station. He looked and was surprised to see a closed signal on the track indicator.

"Shit," he said to Hans. "Voehoffer probably fell asleep and forgot to call. They will make me an old man, Hans." Kurt began bringing the train to a halt, bleeding off speed and steam pressure. He looked ahead and saw a lantern coming down the track, someone waving it vigorously. "Maybe now we'll find out."

Kurt set the brake and went to the ladder. A railroad employee was standing on the ground with the lantern in his hand. Addelsen open the small door and climbed down the ladder.

"We received a call from the sector dispatcher. There's an air raid coming this way. They want you off the main line onto the spur and make sure all your lights are off. I'll go move the switch now."

The man had already started walking toward the building. "Wait a minute," Kurt yelled. The man stopped and turned. "That's all you can tell me? What about my delivery? When do they want me to proceed to the Depot?"

"That's all I know. Pull on to the spur, turn off all lights and then come back here. I'll call sector and see what I can find out."

"All right, all right."

In five minutes the train had moved ahead 300 meters and was now off the main line. Addelsen walked by the troop cars and told them to turn off the lights or close the shutters on the windows. He headed back to the switching building in search of information.

Jack saw the train first. He'd been looking north when he heard two whistle blasts. All of them watched as the small train stopped on the main line.

"Could that be our train?" Jack asked.

Dietrich said, "Late, but why would it stop at the line running into the camp?"

They watched over the next five minutes as the train pulled onto the Posen Depot spur and came to a stop. They were less than a mile away and could hear the sharp hiss as steam bled off the boiler. The lights on the train blinked off leaving all cars darkened.

"That must be the train from Dyhernfurth. But why did it stop here? The Depot's only four miles away." Jack was thinking aloud.

There was a knock on Schroeder's door and his clerk entered.

"Sir, there's a call from Group in Breslau. They said it was urgent."

Still distracted he picked up the telephone. "Schroeder here."

"Sir, this is Sturmbannfuhrer Dietzel at Group. We have been notified by Luftwaffe Sector Control of an expected air raid coming toward Posen. You must go to condition red."

Posen? They've never bombed Posen before. "Of course, thank you." He hung up the phone. "Unterriter, call the guard shack. Tell them to sound the air raid alarm and also darken camp. Then get the Luftwaffe detachment commander on the phone."

One minute later the wail of a siren was heard across the depot.

Standing on the ridgeline the partisan group heard the shrill cry of the Depot's siren as it reverberated off the surrounding hills. The perimeter lights snapped off as did the depot's internal lights. Plunged into darkness the installation disappeared, blending into the dark forest. Jack saw lights begin to extinguish northwest of their position as the city of Posen went into black out.

"The raid, they're getting ready for the raid." Jack realized the Germans must have figured out the target was Posen.

Karl said, "The air defence network is very effective. They will have any city within the potential strike range blacked out and man the flak batteries."

"And there sits the train, the other part of the puzzle. Shit!"

186

"How long before the raid will be here?" Karl asked.

Jack looked at his watch. "I don't know. They could have adjusted the target time for lots of variables. If they've sounded the warning I'm guessing within thirty minutes. Once the first bombs start falling, the attack should last twenty minutes. If they're using pathfinders you would probably get target marking ordnance five to ten minutes before the main body hits."

Karl was talking quickly, "What is this target marking?"

"The pathfinders drop a special type of bomb that burns bright red. For the following bombers it provides a target for the bomb aimers."

"So we would have some warning of the raid beginning?"

"If it runs the normal pattern, yes."

"Then, my English American friend, I have an idea."

Jerzy walked over to them but said nothing.

Karl continued, "If you and I were to go down to the train, we should be able to figure out how to get it moving."

"OK, how do we do that?"

"You don't appreciate the effect an SS officer can have on the rank and file in Germany."

"We don't have much time. If the train has been ordered to stay where it is we need to force the issue."

Dietrich turned to Jerzy, "While we are keeping the security force distracted you can have your people ready to take over the train."

Jerzy said,. "If we can surprise them, we should be able to take care of any guards. Does anyone know how to run an engine?"

Karl shook his head. "We don't need to know how. We will make the engineer drive the train once we've taken control."

"All right," Jack said, "Get everyone together."

Dobry, Patryk and Stefan formed a semi-circle facing Jack.

"Karl, lay out your plan."

There was a different attitude from the three Polish men. They looked eager.

Karl began talking and Jerzy quietly translated for his men.

"Jack and I will go down and try to find the head of the security detachment or the engineer. We will say we are from the depot and want to find out what is causing the delay. While we're doing that I need you men to follow Jerzy and determine where guards are located. No shooting yet. If you can take out a guard quietly with no one noticing go ahead. At some point Jack and I will have to show our hand and then you must attack the remaining guards. I'll try to give you a signal, so be ready. We'll get the train moving toward the depot and then jump off."

The air raid siren at the depot stopped abruptly. There was total silence around the small circle. Jack said, "We came this far. I know this is tough, but we have to try. Remember that train is carrying some of the most lethal poison ever made. Be careful with any gunfire." The three nodded.

Karl finished his brief, "We need to get moving. Everyone meet back here when we're done. By 0500, we'll head east. Whoever is here start moving." His message was clear. This was one that not everyone would survive.

As the men were gathering up their weapons Dietrich found Jerzy. "In the cargo bag are two satchel charges. We may need them. Would you bring them along?"

Jerzy nodded. "Sure." He started to walk away but turned back. "Karl, good luck. If we don't see each other again, thank you for what you did for Mariska." He extended his hand.

Dietrich shook his hand. "We'll meet again. I think both of us are too mean to die." In that moment a unique connection was made.

Two men who were sworn enemies were about to risk both their lives for the common good.

Ghost Zero Two
0345

"Bandsaw Leader, this is Ghost. Target, twelve o'clock, twenty two miles." Worthington knew the Mosquitoes were flying a weave pattern on both sides of the point of the bomber stream. He wanted them to know they were only minutes from the target area. One of the Mossies had engaged a German night fighter fifteen minutes prior. Other than that brief exchange of gunfire, the fighter bombers were still waiting to attack the flak sites at Posen.

"This is Bandsaw, roger." Jack Whitney was watching his fuel consumption. His aircraft should have about 15 minutes of time in the target area before they hit their return fuel level. Whitney felt confident that if the Germans began any anti-aircraft fire he would be able to suppress that fire. If the pathfinders put their markers on target, he should find the flak batteries in some form of ring around that marker. If they tried to use searchlights the Mosquitoes would make the lights their primary target. He knew there was a rail line running in from the south but he didn't figure that would play into the attack. On his right, navigator Glenn Farley had his head down in the radar scope hood searching the sky in front of the bomber stream.

"See anything?"

"Nothing, but I shouldn't think they'd be coming in from the east in any case."

"Probably right."

Roger Halliday scanned his instruments: altitude, airspeed, heading, it was second nature. Without an engineer he was also watching the engine instruments and aircraft systems carefully. He had been thankful that Group Captain Worthington turned out to be a superb pilot and was proficient in the Lancaster. Too often the senior officers, while still on flight status, really had lost their edge. Worthington was on top of his game.

"I'm surprised we haven't had more night fighter activity," Halliday said over the sound of the engines.

"We're not there yet. They seem to hold back anytime you are near Berlin and when they decide you're not after the city they throw everything they have at you." Worthington had led several raids where the majority of losses took place after the target area. This could be one of those. It was a long way back to England from Posen.

"Pilot, Nav, I've got Posen on the scope. I'll have an updated heading to target in a minute."

"Roger." Halliday breathed a sigh of relief. Over two hundred aircraft were counting on them as the master Pathfinder. There were two airborne spares, but those aircraft were farther back in the stream. Because Kelly had found the town on radar, Halliday felt assured they would be able to get the target markers into the depot. After that it was up to the bomb aimers in each aircraft. They would stay in the target area to adjust aim points for the following aircraft as they picked up information from the target area. It was dangerous, but with a target coordinator, Bomber Command had found their accuracy had increased significantly.

Kelly and their new bomb aimer Flight Sergeant Blackwell were trading off duties on the H2S radar. Ghost Zero Two was fitted with the Fishpond antenna modification that allowed the radar to pick up airborne targets beneath the aircraft. Blackwell was watching the scope while Kelly made the final course correction to the target. "Top from radar, bandit moving in from seven o'clock." There was an urgent tone to his voice. "Estimate four miles and closing."

In the upper turret, Tommy Murphy brought the Browning . 303's around and began to search the left rear quadrant. Looking into the darkness, he was hoping the layered clouds to the north might highlight any fighter coming in from that direction.

The crew heard and felt the upper turret open up on the bandit. There was quiet on the intercom. It was an iron clad rule, no talking when night fighters were in the area unless it was a life or death transmission.

In the rear turret, Darby Quinn searched the sky for any indication of where the target may have moved. If there was no call from radar the German must be above them. Quinn's guns were cocked and ready but he saw nothing. The night fighter couldn't have been driven off by one burst from a Murphy, they never broke off attacks that easily. He hadn't seen any indication of the aircraft.

In the nose, Blackwell and Kelly were now both watching the ground return on the radar. Kelly knew exactly where the depot was in relation to the town. From this angle the long concrete loading dock should provide the biggest return. He began to see the tell tale bright line of the dock. He moved his range cursor out to the return.

Blackwell was watching and they compared notes. He keyed his intercom and said, "Opening bomb bay doors."

Karl Dietrich and Jack Stewart stepped up on the porch of the switching shed. Opening the door they stepped inside to find three men standing next to a table. One man had a phone receiver in his hand. The other two turned to look at Karl and Jack. One man was in the clothes of a trainman. The other was an SS sergeant.

Springing to attention, the sergeant said, "Good evening, Herr Standartenfuhrer."

"Good evening, sergeant. Who's in charge of this train?" Dietrich sounded totally professional.

"Sir, I'm in charge of the security detachment, Sergeant Fleisher."

"This is the train from Dyhernfurth?" Karl asked.

"Yes, sir."

"Why are you stopped here?"

The sergeant remained at a stiff attention. "Sir, we were directed to stop because of the air raid. This man is the engineer, Herr Addelsen. We're trying to contact sector control now to see what's going on."

"We need to get that train moving, there's a critical schedule to keep," Karl said.

Jack looked at the engineer. A working man in his mid forties, he wore a set of coveralls and grimy cap. He was smoking a cigarette and leaning back against the wall. Their eyes met for just a moment. A man trying to deliver his cargo, Jack thought. If only that man knew what was behind the doors of those boxcars.

There was a loud crack from the direction of the Depot. Karl knew the distinctive sound of an 88 mm artillery piece. The RAF was here.

The man on the phone looked through the window toward the depot and saw one of the searchlights come on, throwing an intense beam into the sky. "My God, it's an air raid. We must take cover."

"Look at that." Karl exclaimed and pointed out the window. As the three men looked out he removed his pistol from the holster. With two shots the dispatcher and sergeant lay dead on the floor.

"What!" Kurt Addelsen jumped to the side as Jack pulled his pistol and shoved it against the man's chest. "Be very quiet if you want to stay alive. Understand?"

"Yes." The man nodded, his eyes wide in horror.

Karl was looking out second window. He asked without looking toward the engineer, "How many security guards?"

There was no answer from the man and Dietrich came over and looked at him face to face. "Answer me or you'll die."

"There are ten. Four of them are in the gun crew. The others rode in the troop car with the civilians."

"What civilians?"

"They got on in Dyhernfurth. I don't know who they are."

Jack looked at Karl and said, "Let's get this train moving." He shoved his gun into the side of the engineer, indicating he should move. "Walk to the engine. Do what I tell you and you'll live."

As they exited the building, there was a large red explosion in the depot.

Halliday put the Lancaster in a gentle bank to the left, climbing to 23,000 feet. They would evaluate their target markers and then direct the subsequent attacks. Several searchlights had come on and were searching the sky. There were four distinct red markers on the ground. The search lights were ringed around the markers – the target marker was dead on target.

Worthington keyed the radio which was set to strike frequency. "All aircraft from Ghost, markers are on target. Bomb the markers. I say again, bomb the markers."

Halliday could see flashes from the flak bursting below them. To the west he knew the Lancasters would be opening their bomb doors ready to drop their high explosive and incendiary mix.

Franz Schroeder ran from his office as the first explosions erupted on the southern fence. The concussion was terrific and immediately there was a bright red fire rising in the sky no more that 100 meters from him. He was terrified. This was a air raid on his depot. They were attacking him. He ran toward the main maintenance building, stumbling once. There were no air raid shelters, he'd never thought they would be needed. My God, there was no place to go he realized. He ran into the open door of the maintenance building. He could hear sharp reports as the anti-aircraft guns opened fire. This was a nightmare. The smoke from the first bombs was now drifting over his area, an acrid and bitter smell. He turned back toward his headquarters and yelled, "Unterriter!" His voice was lost in the rising crescendo of bomb explosions and artillery fire.

Rolling the Mosquito wings level, Jack Whitney stabilized in a thirty degree dive noting his altitude passing 10,000 feet. He made one wing correction and put the cross hairs of his gun sight directly on one of the searchlights. He squeezed the trigger and all four 20 mm cannons began to fire. A three second burst and the searchlight went out. Pulling hard, he put 4 g's on the aircraft and began climbing back to altitude. He heard another of his aircraft on their squadron frequency. "Number three rolling in on the northern most light." Systematically his squadron was attacking the searchlights while looking for any muzzle flashes, which might betray the gun positions. Bomb impacts were continuous with the bright orange of high explosive detonations sprinkled between the white spots of magnesium incendiary bombs.

Jerzy and Dobry crouched in the grass looking at a group of people standing outside the troop car looking toward the explosions at the depot. They had split up from Stefan and Patryk who worked their way down the track and were opposite the flatcar. He could see what looked like three men walking up the left side of the train toward the engine. Looking closer he could see it was Jack and Karl with a third man. He was ready but not sure when to act.

"Is there anyone in the cab?" Jack asked Addelsen.

"Only my stoker, Hans."

"Your job is to get this train moving toward the depot. Do you understand? If you can do that, you live. Now get up there."

Karl had gone up the ladder and his pistol was leveled at the big stoker.

"Hans, it's all right. We need steam pressure right now. Get busy," Addelsen said.

"How soon before we can move?" Jack asked.

"Five minutes, but it won't be fast."

Flames from the depot were visible through the front windscreen of the locomotive. The two commandos stand at each side of the cab, their pistols leveled at the two trainmen. Hans kept moving the coal from the tender to the combustion box. Adjusting several valves, the engineer watched a large gauge on his control panel.

"All right, we can move," he finally said.

"Two short blasts on your whistle, no more."

Jerzy heard the blasts and knew it was Jack's signal. He raised his Sten gun along with Dobry and they cut down the group of men standing outside the troop car. Down the track two hand grenades exploded inside the sandbagged enclosure killing the four gun crew. Cautiously Jerzy approached the train. He kept his gun leveled at the troop car and motioned to Dobry. The young man ran up the steps to the passenger car tossing a grenade into the dark doorway. The train began to move. As Dobry jumped to the ground the explosion in the troop car blew the windows out glass raining on the grass. Jerzy broke into a jog toward the engine. Running up to the cab he saw Karl lean out.

"Toss me the charge then get back to the ridge."

It was a short distance to throw the satchel but this was an explosive. Gently Jerzy lofted the canvas bag up to Karl who leaned down and caught it. The two looked at each other as the train accelerated toward the inferno that the depot had become. Jerzy was shocked at the expression on Karl's face, a man resigned to die.

The explosions were growing larger as the engine gained speed. Jack estimated the distance to go at three miles. He could see the steam gauge was still building pressure and could feel the vibration increase with the speed. They were now moving at about twenty five miles per hour and accelerating. He pointed the gun at the stoker. "You, get on the ladder and jump." The big man took one look at the engineer who nodded, moved to the ladder and jumped. Jack turned to the engineer. "All right, your turn." The man looked at him and without a word, jumped into the night.

Two more miles to go. The explosions were now very close. There was a bright flash and a string of bombs went off several hundred yards to their right. Down the track looked like the fires of hell. "Karl, good enough. The train will make it to the depot. Let's

196

get off." Jack had to yell, the noise of the engine and the bomb explosions was deafening.

"After you." Karl looked grim.

"What's wrong?"

"Nothing's wrong. Now get out."

"Karl, don't do anything stupid."

"I won't. Don't forget, you owe me some cigarettes." Karl smiled in the flickering light of the fires.

Jack turned away from his friend, climbed down two steps and jumped into the darkness.

Sitting with his back against the concrete wall, Franz Schroeder stared straight ahead into what remained of the main corridor of the maintenance building. Pieces of broken concrete lay on the floor and smoke hung down from the ceiling. He'd lost track of time. The pounding of the explosions had driven him to the edge of madness. Sweat poured from his face as the temperature kept rising. The entire camp was on fire. No place to go, nothing to save, he was at the end. He was vaguely aware of the rumble as Reichsbahn Engine 2323 careened off the concrete loading dock and slowly rolled on its side. The train cars behind the engine derailed and crashed into each other like an accordion. Inside each boxcar, the double walled glass containers of Sarin liquid broke free from their insulating rubber grommets. The containers ruptured and liquid exploded up and out from the smoking wreckage. Bomb impacts continued after the train wreck for ten more minutes. The updrafts from the many fires combined with the Sarin vapors. A deadly mist swirled around what remained of the depot.

When rescue crews reached the depot at sunrise they found no one alive. All of the Luftwaffe gun crews on the perimeter of the depot were dead. The bodies of Volker Fischer and Major Rosensweig were never identified. Most of the bodies were burned beyond recognition from the intense fires. A number of the rescue crew also became very ill, one fireman dying later that day in Posen. The SS was called in to ensure security was maintained. The site was fenced off and entry forbidden.

Winston Churchill felt as though London had been granted a reprieve. But for how long, he wondered? At what point would the Nazis finally cease being a knife at the throat of Britain. He knew that time was fast approaching.

Chapter Eleven

Operations Building
RAF Tangmere
August 4, 1944

A tall pilot in an RAF flight suit stood in front of a large blackboard in the Operations Office. Squadron Leader Dicky Thompson held a clipboard and was comparing the flight roster from his schedule to the available crews. Thompson was the Operations Officer for 161 Squadron. Based at Tangmere, they provided flight support for many of the clandestine operations on the continent. Since the invasion they had been as busy as before with many operations deeper into Europe. The quick jumps across the Channel to a field in occupied France had given way to missions across the breadth of Europe.

Originally a Blenheim bomber pilot for the first two years of the war, Dicky had transferred to special operations support and learned to fly the Lysander. Recently he had transitioned to the Hudson bomber, a militarized version of the Lockheed Ventura. The Hudson had become a workhorse for Coastal Command and now 161 Squadron was using them for the longer range missions. Dicky had been flying the Hudson for almost six months. Most recent missions were airborne drops of people or supplies to the resistance forces which were beginning to be more active with the Allied forces now on the continent.

A phone rang and the Ops clerk answered it. "Just a moment, sir. Mr. Thompson, there's a Colonel Hudson on the line for you."

Dicky knew Tommy Hudson well. They had been involved in an operation with their common friend Jack Stewart a year ago. Due to Tommy Hudson's position in MI-6, he and Dicky had collaborated on a number of missions during the last year. He'd last seen Tommy at his father's funeral where they had shared a few pints at the wake afterward. "Hello, Tommy. Good to hear from you." Dicky stood listening for several minutes. "Right, I'll get back to you." He hung up the phone. "Damn."

Wing Commander Terrence Toms, DSO, DFC with Bar commanded 161 Squadron. Originally a Mosquito pilot, Toms had been running the special operations support squadron for over a year. Qualified in the Lysander and Hudson, he was fighting hard to get Mosquitoes assigned to Tangmere. He was in his office, sitting with flying boots crossed on the desk when Dicky Thompson knocked.

"Skipper, got a moment?"

Throwing the magazine on the desk Toms dropped his feet to the floor and smiled. "Right, what's up?" He had his pipe clamped in his teeth.

"Just got a call from Tommy Hudson. He's on his way down here. Couldn't give me details on the phone but he said they will need two missions flown in support of an op on the continent. One will be a para drop, the other an extraction."

"All right, why don't you scrub me from the schedule this afternoon. I'll see what he needs. Damn, it would have been a nice day to go flying."

Hudson had brought Major Phil Hatcher with him. The four officers sat in Toms' office drinking tea. When the orderly closed the door Toms was the first to speak. "Understand you have an op we need to support."

"We have a team on the ground in East Prussia. Radio contact was lost a week ago but we have no reason to believe they've been captured. We need to drop a team into the rendezvous area with a radio to set up the final extraction."

"How many are on the ground?" Dicky asked.

"At least two, perhaps more. Dicky, one of them is Jack."

Dicky had talked to his sister twice since the funeral but she hadn't mentioned Jack being gone. Maybe that was why she seemed so upset.

"Where do you think they are now?" Toms asked.

Tommy got up and pointed to the map. His finger circled an area 20 miles east of Posen. "This was the valley for the post raid rendezvous. The rally point was a small lake at the northern end of the valley."

201

"Nothing like having to fly through the entire German air defence system to get there." Toms had been on several recent missions southwest of Berlin and knew what they were facing.

"Looks like we need the Hudson for both of them. I'm assuming you made some provision for a landing area near the extraction point," Dicky said.

Hatcher spoke up, "The primary site is in this valley." He got up and put his finger directly on the map. "Our intelligence has several locations that should support rough field flight ops."

"But our first challenge is to get a team on the ground with a radio," Hudson said.

"So we pick up your two plus the two that are already on the ground."

"Right."

Toms stood up and walked to his window. There was the sound of an aircraft taking off at the field. Looking out briefly, he asked, "When do you want to fly the parachute drop?"

"Day after tomorrow. Sorry for the short notice."

When radio contact had been lost with the Whirlwind ground force, Noel Greene and Tommy Hudson had made a decision to insert a team to coordinate the extraction. They were concerned with the loss of communications knowing that Jerzy's group also had several radios. They chose Terry Howe to lead the team. His reaction was mixed.

"Right, I jump a radio into the rendezvous area, find Jack and the Air Force comes in for the pick up." Terry's extensive experience behind enemy lines in Africa and Europe made him a logical choice. Phil Hatcher's leg was still healing so the assignment of another team member would normally fall to one of the junior commandos, Jimmy Hunt or Curtis Livesy. Terry wasn't ready for Phil's selection.

"Terry, I'm pairing you up with Dietrich's partner Lutjens."

"What makes you think I'll jump with a Kraut."

"Because it's an order, captain," Phil said. "And you're still taking the King's schilling. You know how you feel about Jack?"

"Go on," Howe said.

"Gerhard Lutjens feels the same way about Dietrich. They've been partners for as long as you've been with Jack. When I brought it up to him he almost demanded we let him go. He knows the area from his time in the infantry and he's more experienced than Hunt or Livesy. We have to do whatever we can to get Jack back."

That afternoon the two met for the first time since Farmingham. Terry's study of German made the communication easy. The problem was the obvious friction between the two men. During the first two hours they went over maps of the area, equipment requirements and British jump procedures. They were going over the modified jump harness when Howe raised his voice to go over the attachment hardware again. Lutjens stood up and walked to the door. He stopped and turned around to face Howe.

"Captain, it is clear you would prefer not to have me along on this mission. To be perfectly honest, I think I understand. But we also have our orders. I want Karl Dietrich back as much as you want to see Commander Stewart alive. They have a better chance if I'm there. I know the area and how Karl thinks. It's not going to be easy finding them. So I propose we make the best of it for our friend's sake if nothing else." He turned and walked out the door, slamming it as he went.

"Bloody hell."

An hour later, Gerhard was sitting in a briefing room going over maps when Howe walked in. Terry was holding a Sten.

Howe saw the startled look on Gerhard's face and laughed. "Don't worry, captain. I'm not here to shoot you. Thought we should take a look at the Sten."

Lutjens paused, then smiled. "Captain Howe, I would enjoy learning about the Sten. Please sit down."

For the next two days the two men went over every detail of the mission. Howe had to admit that Lutjens did know the area. Many times when the map didn't show a detail he could remember a key point. Their plan was to drop into the northern end of the valley and begin an expanding search for any indication of the team. Expecting Jack and Karl to head for high ground they would concentrate on the ridge tops. At the same time they would determine if there was any troop activity in the area and try to select which of the several landing sites would be best for the RAF. Lutjens would be wearing the uniform of a Wermacht captain under his jump suit. If they were in a tight situation the two could use a captor-prisoner ruse. Everyone knew, just like Dietrich, Gerhard was a dead man if he was captured.

The final afternoon the two of them were going over the schedule for the next day when Phil Hatcher dropped by the briefing room.

"All set, are we?" he asked.

Terry nodded. "I think we've covered everything. What time do we leave for Tangmere?"

"We'll leave London at noon. I talked to Dicky and with the moon rise at 2230 they want to take off at sunset."

"Right."

Phil turned to Gerhard. "I understand there is a young lady who would like company for dinner tonight. Are you free Captain Lutjens?"

Gerhard smiled. "Yes, sir."

"She's downstairs at the security desk. You better get moving."

Lutjens stood up and nodded to Howe, then Hatcher. "Thank you." He walked out, the door closing behind him.

"How are you two doing?" Phil asked Howe.

"He is not a bad chap, actually." Terry hesitated. "You think they're still alive?"

Hatcher sat down and sighed. He pulled out a cigarette and lit it. "I don't know. What bothers me is no radio contact. They had at least two radio sets in the group. All we can do is hope they're out there and you two can find them."

Howe stood up. "Come on, the mess is open. Least thing you can do is buy me a drink."

Tommy Hudson had been instrumental in arranging for Gillian to use a suite MI-6 maintained at the far end of the Baker Street offices. Gerhard was happy to see her and surprised what she told him as they walked down the street.

"Where are you taking me, Gillian?"

She laughed. "I'm taking you somewhere I can cook a real supper for you."

"So you can cook too?" They were walking down the sidewalk toward the five story complex at the end of Baker Street.

"We English girls can do many things." Her voice was light and cheerful.

The suite was one of several maintained for out of town visitors who needed more security than could be achieved at a hotel. Phil Hatcher let Tommy know there was a friendship developing between Gillian and the German. It made sense to both of them to do what they could to provide one more reason for Gerhard to remain loyal to his pledge. They both understood the man's loyalty to Dietrich was absolute. With his talent and experience Lutjens might prove to be as valuable to MI-6 as Dietrich.

Gillian unlocked the door and switched on the light. The living room was well appointed and branched out into a kitchen and master bedroom. The dining room was an alcove off the living room. She turned on several additional table lamps and walked over to the small bar on one wall. Gerhard remained standing inside the door looking very awkward.

"Please sit down, Gerhard. Let me fix you a drink."

He walked over to the bar and stood next to her. "What are you having?"

"I thought a gin and bitters," she said.

"That sounds wonderful."

"Why don't you see if there's any music on the BBC?"

He saw a table radio on a shelf by the alcove wall. Walking over he turned on the power switch and heard the tubes begin to warm up.

She was standing next to him holding a tall glass. "Here, you work on the music and I'm going to start supper."

"Can I help?"

"If I need help, I'll call. You sit down and relax."

What was it about this woman? He felt like they had known each other for their entire lives. He should be uncomfortable in a situation like this but it seemed very natural. *Sit down and relax, Gerhard.*

He heard her working in the kitchen and couldn't resist seeing what she was doing. "Sure I can't help?"

Gillian turned and smiled. "All right, those carrots and potatoes need to be peeled." She was working on a whole chicken which was sitting in a roasting pan. "I'm fixing my mum's baked chicken. I hope you like chicken?"

He found a knife in the drawer and began carefully peeling the vegetables. "I love chicken. In the army we never get anything baked, everything is boiled."

She came over and stood next to him supervising his work. "Very good, Herr Lutjens. You may make a cook yet."

The two of them laughed and turned to each other. He leaned down and kissed her lightly on the lips. It was their first kiss.

Gillian looked up at him. This time she leaned forward and kissed him, lingering a moment longer.

After dinner they sat at the table lingering over their wine.

"That was wonderful. Please tell you mother her recipe was superb."

"Thanks." She hesitated. "I lost my mum in 1940. It was an air raid on London."

Gerhard looked at her. She looked a little sad but quickly smiled at him. "I'm sorry. I don't know what to say. You mother dies in a German air raid and here you are fixing dinner for a German officer."

"I fixed dinner for Gerhard Lutjens. I'm not sure what I expected when I heard about you for the first time. A fierce German commando, arrogant, brutal, I didn't know what to expect. But you're not like any other man I've ever met. I fixed you dinner because I have come to like you very much."

207

"And I, you." There, he said it. This girl had found a way into his heart, war or no war. "Gillian, there's something I have to do. But when I get back I want to see you."

"Gerhard, I'll be here. No matter what happens."

"Would you like some more wine?" He put his hand on the bottle.

She reached across the table and put her hand on his. "There will be time for that later."

Tommy Hudson had known Jack Stewart for over two years and Karl Dietrich for only two weeks. But he still felt a sense of responsibility for both of them professionally and personally. On the fifth day of no contact he took it upon himself to let Pam Thompson and Eva Papenhausen know that the two men were unreported. It would have been easy for him to hide behind security issues and do nothing. But the two women deserved to know that something might be wrong. Their reactions were very different.

He stopped by Ian Thompson's apartment in London knowing Pam had been staying there since the funeral. She had told him she didn't want to be in the Oxford house alone. As she opened the door her eyes flashed with dread at the possible reason for Tommy's visit.

Before she could say anything Tommy said, "It's not that Pam. I promise you. But I do need to talk to you."

She led him into the small living room. "Can I fix you some tea?"

"No, thank you. Pam, I probably shouldn't be here. But I felt you needed to know that we are concerned about Jack."

Pam was sitting on the edge of the couch, her hands gripped tightly together. She remained quiet but her eyes showed fear.

208

"You knew he was on a very important mission."

She nodded.

"We lost radio contact with him five day ago. That may mean simply nothing except their radio is broken. We don't know."

"What will happen, Tommy?"

Hudson shifted in his chair. "Pam, I can't be specific. But we're taking every possible action to regain contact and get them back."

Pam lowered her head and rested her forehead on her hands. Tommy saw tears rolling down her face.

"Pam, I'm sorry this came when it did. You've had to deal with more than anyone should in such a short time."

Driving back to Baker Street Hudson thought about how difficult this was for Pam. She had just lost her father, Jack might be dead and now her brother was preparing to fly two dangerous rescue missions. She's due for a break, he thought.

Eva Papenhausen met Tommy at a safe location in the West End. She was concerned and appreciative for Hudson's contact. "He's doing what he had to do," was all she said about Dietrich. Tommy could sense she was upset but maintaining a stoic attitude. He promised to keep her informed and they went their separate ways.

RAF Tangmere
August 6, 1944
1835 Hours

During Jack Stewart's first mission into Europe, the Lysander in which he was flying hit a drainage ditch on landing and crashed. The pilot was injured and Jack's efforts helped to get Brian Standish back to England. Standish recovered from his injuries and remained on active flying status in 161 Squadron. When Dicky mentioned his need for a co-pilot for the Hudson, Brian jumped at the chance. The mission was very straightforward, a long range flight to drop Howe and Lutjens into the Prosna Valley. However the mission covered over 1200 miles roundtrip, most of it over enemy territory. The plan was to fly single ship, low altitude, avoiding population areas and radar coverage. The 161 squadron navigators were the best in the RAF, many having spent time in Pathfinder squadrons. The Hudsons were equipped with the GEE navigation system and the H2S radar. Dicky felt confident they could put their two jumpers into the valley. There would be some moon illumination which would help their visual navigation. The parachutes would be dark to cut down on visibility from the ground.

During the brief Dicky noted that Terry Howe was translating into German for the other jumper. Thompson had learned not to ask questions on SOE missions. The other jumper certainly looked the part. He wore the standard jump suit but it was evident the man had been in these types of situations before. He would occasionally nod when Howe would make a point about the drop.

Thompson finished the brief and told the two agents they should be at the flight line at 1915. Lighting a cigarette Dicky walked out of the briefing room.

"Nothing else you can think of?" Terry asked Gerhard.

"It's a good plan. Our jump interval must be as short as possible. I want to join up and get away from the landing area as quickly as we can." Gerhard had mentioned before that he didn't want contact with anyone on the ground, it could only complicate the mission.

"If we jump at 140 knots, 800 feet like you wanted we should be able to hold hands on the way down." Howe grinned.

Taken back by the humor, it took a moment for Lutjens to understand it was a joke.

"Come on. Let's get this show on the road. We've got two friends out there counting on us."

Chapter Twelve

30 Miles East of Posen
August 7, 1944
0630 Hours

The last five days had taken their toll on Jack. He crouched down in a group of small trees and surveyed the forest in front of them. It was quiet this morning. The only sound was the chirps of birds out trying to find their morning meal. Feeling comfortable there were no Germans in the immediate area he began to work his way back to Jerzy and the group. The thick underbrush made the going slow and it was ten minutes before he moved back into the small clearing. He walked over to Jerzy. "It's clear ahead for about half a mile. The brush gets very thick at that point but I didn't see anything."

"Good." Jerzy nodded. He was sitting on the ground next to Karl Dietrich's litter. The Polish officer looked exhausted, as they all did. The rest of the group lay scattered around the area trying to get some rest.

"Do you think we should send someone ahead to find the others?" Jack asked.

How far do you think it is to the lake?" Jerzy lit a cigarette and exhaled.

"No more than five miles. Whoever we send could give us a warning if he runs into Germans. Think about it. I'll check Karl."

Jerzy grabbed Jack's arm as he headed for the litter. "Jack, it's not good."

"I know."

After he had jumped from the train, Jack found Karl face down in the long grass next to the rail spur. The German was groaning and Jack realized his left leg was severely broken. Dietrich knew he couldn't move and told Jack to leave him. The commando was beginning to go into shock from internal bleeding.

"I'll be back," was all Jack had said to Karl. It took Jack forty minutes to get back to the ridge where he found Jerzy. All of the partisans had returned safely from the valley.

"Where's the German?" Jerzy asked.

"I think he broke his leg or maybe his pelvis when he jumped from the train. He's going into shock. Jerzy, I need help to get him out of the valley."

"I'll go with you. I'll send Stefan on with the equipment and we can catch up with them later."

When Jerzy explained the plan to his men, they didn't react the way Jack would have expected. Every man told Jerzy they would stick with him and help with Dietrich. A litter was constructed from tree limbs and coats and they went back to get Karl.

Dietrich was in pain but still looked surprised when he saw the entire group. He said to Jack, "You took my gun."

"Of course I did. I wasn't going to let you do something Teutonic."

For the next several days the small group traveled slowly and carefully through the forest toward the Prosna valley. On several occasions they could see or hear troop activity but it was never a real threat.

The critical issue was Karl's leg. Each day his left thigh seemed to swell more. On the second day Jack had to slit Karl's trousers to allow for the swelling. The pain was severe but Jack didn't want to use the morphine. Karl was in shock and morphine might kill him. Although there were no bones protruding, Jack was sure there was internal damage in Karl's thigh. The discoloration had worsened each day. Karl had been running a fever for the last three days. They had to get him to a doctor.

Jack knelt next to Karl. The German's face was ashen, dark circles under his eyes accentuating the exhaustion. There was a sweaty sheen on his skin. "How are you doing?"

Karl turned his head slightly, grimacing in the process. "I've been better."

"We're near the valley. I'm thinking about sending an advance scout ahead to look for the other group. What do you think?"

"A very German thing to do. I like it."

"All right. You rest for now."

Fifteen minutes later, Patryk moved out toward the valley. His orders were to find the lake and then try to make contact with Aleksy.

The Prosna Valley

The jump had gone well. Terry and Gerhard linked up immediately and found their equipment bag. They were able to move northeast to await daybreak and pinpoint their position. When the sun did come up they saw they were on the northern side of the valley about five miles from the small lake. They saw several farms on the floor of the valley with fields under cultivation. Their immediate plan was to work their way down the ridge top to the south and see if they could locate with any of their people. The forest surrounding the small lake seemed to be the most promising location. Terry could only hope Jack was still able to get to the area. Otherwise they would be searching for a needle in a haystack.

They were making their way across the forested slope when Gerhard put his hand up to signal 'silence.'

Terry froze and tried to look down the slope to see what Gerhard had found.

The German turned slowly and motioned for Terry to work his way down the slope.

Terry moved carefully, being as quiet as possible. Finally kneeling down next to Gerhard he watched the German point to a small stand of trees. Looking carefully he saw the back of a man's coat.

Gerhard whispered, "That looks strange. No farmer would be sitting up here in this tree line. Could that be one of your group?"

"It might be one of the Polish partisans."

"Can you speak Polish?"

"Never had to," Terry said quietly.

"Nor I."

Terry nodded. "I'll lead. I knew the group. Hopefully they remember me."

Very slowly the men worked their way down the slope. A wave of relief swept over Terry. It was Aleksy.

"Aleksy," he said quietly.

The man turned quickly and his head dropped down behind cover.

"It's Terry Howe. Do you remember me?"

Slowly Aleksy's head moved up. The partisan was looking where Terry knelt. Howe stood up. He held one hand in the air, his Sten in the other. Gerhard remained under cover. Terry moved down to Aleksy and they shook hands. Another man whom Terry remembered as Alois was also there. He motioned to Gerhard.

They were lucky. Aleksy knew some German and they were able to find out about the group's separation. They had not heard or seen Jerzy's group for a week. Today was the scheduled rendezvous day. Aleksy told them about Ludwik's injury. Fortunately they had found a doctor at the southern part of the valley in the town of Kalisz. Mariska was there now. She had one of the vehicles. The other was hidden off the small road they had followed south.

This was a good start, Terry thought. Now they had to find Jack.

For almost twenty years Rolf Brandt had been the only doctor in the valley. Although German, the doctor had taken care of both Germans and Poles before the war. Once hostilities started the Polish farmers were relocated and several German families were brought in to takeover and farm the land. The war had almost bypassed the valley. The farms provided food for the Wermacht but there was not much in the way of Nazi infrastructure. There was a police station but no military or Gestapo in the town of Kalisz.

Mariska had been able to pass for a German and found out the doctor's address. Ludwik's hand was badly infected and he was running a high fever. The doctor had seemed to accept the story that he was injured while putting in fence posts as one of Mariska's conscript Polish farm workers. Not sure if he could save the hand, the doctor called the hospital in Breslau to talk with a colleague about possibly having to amputate. What the doctor did not know was the directive which required all hospitals to report major injuries to the Gestapo.

It was mid day when Jack could first see the lake east of them in the valley. There were several farms south of the lake, but nothing closer than a mile.

"We'll make camp here." They were three miles from the lake, about half way up the western slope of the valley.

Jerzy came up and was standing next to Jack. "We need to send someone down to the lake. If our people are there, they'll be watching the lake."

Jack nodded, "I agree. It's pretty open, but I don't think we have any choice. Still no Patryk?"

They both wondered what had happened to the young partisan. Not held back with a litter, he should have made it to the lake several hours ago. If anyone was there he would have had time to rendezvous and get back. Where was he?

He took out a canteen of water and went over to Karl's litter. They were out of codeine tablets and he still didn't want to use morphine for Karl's pain. There might come a time for morphine but not now.

"Thanks." Karl let his head drop back down on the litter. "You know I always thought it would come quick. This is a hard way to die."

"We're going to get you back to Eva. You have my word on it." Jack knew it sounded hollow. He didn't have any idea how they would arrange an extraction with no radio capability. Then he heard Stefan yell.

"It's them, Jerzy, Jack, they're here."

He turned to see Terry Howe walk out of the trees behind Patryk. He thought his eyes were playing tricks on him when he saw Gerhard Lutjens following Howe.

Karl's eyes were open, looking up at the sky when Jack reached down and grabbed his arm. "You're going to make it, Karl."

Terry walked up extending his hand. "Knew it would take the Army to get you out of trouble." The commando was grinning.

"Am I glad to see you," Jack said, shaking his hand.

Gerhard had seen Karl lying on the litter and was kneeling next to him. Dietrich looked confused.

"Gerhard?"

"Of course, someone had to come and get you."

Through the pain, Karl said, "This is good." He closed his eyes.

Gestapo Headquarters
Breslau

Felix Steinhauer enjoyed his job. As the senior Gestapo agent in Breslau, he spent most of his time investigating any activity which might be connected to underground or subversive activity. The regional director from Warsaw left him alone and there was enough to keep him busy, but not too busy. It was just after lunch when he started going through the daily messages. He paused when he saw the note on the call from a Doctor Keller at the hospital. It sounded like something a little different and a good excuse to put off the rest of his paperwork.

"Come on, Reitzler. We're going to the hospital," he said to his assistant as he walked through the outer office. Karl Reitzler hurried after the senior agent.

It took the two policemen thirty minutes to drive across the city to the main hospital on Giegerstrasse. They quickly located Keller in the hospital's administration office. The doctor was a small, nervous man with large bulbous eyes and a bald head.

Doctor Keller was very specific about his call to headquarters. As soon as he realized there was a major injury he had telephoned. He assured the agents that this hospital always obeyed the directives from the Reich Security Services. The doctor was clearly not comfortable talking with the police.

"So the doctor in Kalisz wanted to see if you would be able to perform an amputation?"

"That is correct. The patient was a Polish worker whose hand was crushed on the farm where he was working."

"Anything else unusual?" Steinhauer asked.

"When I called back to ask about the man's vital signs, I talked to the nurse. She seemed to think the lady who brought him in was not German but Polish."

"Interesting. So what is happening, doctor?"

"We will send an ambulance to bring the patient here. I will examine the man and if needed, operate."

Ten minutes later the two agents were sitting in their sedan. Steinhauer lit a cigarette and stared out the window. "Let's take a drive up to Kalisz. There may be nothing to this but you never know. Besides, it's a nice day for a drive in the country. The paperwork will have to wait."

His assistant smiled to himself. Kurt Steinhauer detested paperwork and would do anything to put it off. There was also a little café in Kalisz and Reitzler knew the senior agent liked to sit outside and drink wine in the summer sun. They should be there in less than two hours.

The drive was very pleasant and they encountered little traffic on the road. Rationing was making it more difficult for people to operate their autos. There were workers out in the fields, the summer crops were approaching time to harvest. They also passed a Wermacht column of a dozen trucks parked on the side of the road. It appeared they were eating their mid day meal. Poor bastards, thought Reitzler, on their way east to fight the Russians.

Mariska sat at the edge of Ludwik's bed. The young man was pale, his face covered with sweat.

"We have to wait and see what the doctor thinks is best." She felt like she was trapped in a nightmare. Jerzy was missing and she didn't know what to do with Ludwik. Did she let them take him to Breslau to have his hand amputated? What would happen then? Would he die if they didn't amputate? The doctor had been very thorough in his exam. He said the infection was spreading and it would be difficult to control. They didn't have any drugs to combat the infection.

She got up and went into the corridor running into Doctor Brandt.

"Fraulein Mueller, the hospital called and they're sending an ambulance to pick up your worker. It should be here within two hours. We'll get him down to Breslau and Doctor Keller will take good care of him."

"Doctor, is there any way to save his hand. All he knows is farm work. He'll be no good to me with only one hand."

"I'm afraid without the right drugs he'll die unless we amputate. The infection has simply spread too far."

RAF Tangmere
161 Squadron

"Skipper, we're on for the second flight on the Whirlwind recovery." Dicky Thompson was standing in the door to Wing Commander Tom's office.

Toms was standing by the window, his arms crossed on his chest. "What do we know?"

"They found the ground team. Tommy Hudson requested a pickup at sunset tonight if we can do it. They have a landing site one mile south of that small lake. Sounds like it's a pasture running almost north/ south."

Toms picked up his pipe from the desk and began to fill it. "All right, go get a quick look at the weather. Let the rest of the crew know we'll brief it as soon as we get the final data. I'll fly left seat, put yourself in as co-pilot. And call maintenance and make sure they have the aircraft ready. Let's get this thing rolling."

Thirty minutes later Dicky confirmed the weather was going to be good, as was the moon illumination. Because the inbound leg would be flown in daylight, they requested fighter escort for that portion of the mission. Fighter Command was able to get a flight of four USAAF P-51 Mustangs with long range tanks to take them in to the target. The Hudson would land, pick up the ground party and make the return flight under the cover of darkness.

A series of phone calls resulted in an agreement with the 357th Fighter Group, out of Leiston, to rendezvous with the Hudson over Tangmere at 1530 hours. The American fighters would be using "Angel" as a callsign. The flight plan had the bomber landing as sun was setting. The signal to land would be a red Very pistol flare from the ground party.

As Toms was going over the photo recon pictures of the valley Dicky came in with the final weather brief. "Still calling for scattered layers up to 12,000. Winds in the area should be light and out of the north. I had another call from Phil Hatcher. Sounds like they have injured people."

"That's all we know?"

"I'm afraid so. Sounds a bit ominous. Wonder if we should take a doctor or corpsman?"

"I'll call Andrews and see what he thinks. They're not keen to have our docs go on ops like this." Group Captain Harry Andrews was the senior aviator at Tangmere and would have to approve sending any medical personnel of the flight.

The Posna Valley
1530 Hours

"We've got to go get Ludwik and Mariska." Jerzy told Jack. "I want them back."

"All right. The aircraft will be here in about three hours. We can take the vehicle and go get them.

"You'll go?"

222

"No, Sturmbannfuhrer Steiner will go. As a German friend once told me, don't under estimate the effect an SS officer can have on the rank and file in Germany."

Aleksy left to retrieve the second vehicle, a 1938 Fiat 508 truck. While Jack was gone the others would work their way south to the primary landing site. It was about a two mile trip. They could remain well concealed by staying in the edge of the forest during the entire trip. They agreed to meet at the northern edge of the designated landing field.

1650 Hours

Gerhard, Jerzy and Jack drove south down the valley road. It would take twenty minutes to reach Kalisz. Jack had cleaned up his SS uniform and now looked presentable. He remembered how Karl Dietrich had acted in uniform and there would be no doubt from anyone he met that they were talking to an SS officer. Lutjens had switched from his jumpsuit to the Wermacht uniform. Jack sat in the front seat with Jerzy.

"Gerhard, I'm glad you're here. But I'll admit I was surprised to see you."

"When Colonel Hudson and Major Hatcher explained the situation it only made sense to come. I spent time in this area at the beginning of the war."

Jack didn't notice any change in Jerzy but he knew that comment would strike a chord with his Polish friend. Some of the bloodiest defeats of the Polish forces took place just east of here. "Have you ever been to Kalisz?"

"Once, a long time ago. I remember it was a small town, not much else."

The car was quiet as they approached Kalisz. Mariska had told Aleksy where the doctor's office was located. Jack hoped her directions were good. The town was small, perhaps five hundred people. According to her directions the medical office was on the second cross street off the main road. They saw a red medical cross on a sign as they turned up the street.

"Jerzy, you stay in the car. Gerhard, get out and keep an eye on the street," Jack said as the car pulled up to the building. He got out and pulled himself up to his full height. He hoped the several nicks from his hasty shaving were not too noticeable. There were only two other people on the street. He looked back and saw Lutjens standing in front of the truck looking very bored. Swinging the door open Jack stepped inside. It was cool and smelled of disinfectant. There was a reception desk but no one was there. Then he saw Mariska sitting in a chair down the short corridor.

He walked up to her. She seemed lost in thought. "Fraulein, good afternoon."

Mariska looked up, confused. The uniform was the first thing she saw. There was a brief flash of fear until she saw Jack's face. Involuntarily she reached up and grasped his left hand. She whispered, "Jerzy?"

Jack nodded, "In the car outside. We came to get you and Ludwik. Where is he?"

She nodded toward the closed door. "In there with the doctor. It's not good. They want to amputate his hand." She stood up, still holding on to Jack's hand.

"Have you seen any troops or security people around here?"
She shook her head.
"Good. How about in here? How big is the staff?"

"There is the doctor and a nurse. That's all I've seen today. But the doctor said they were sending an ambulance from Breslau to pick up Ludwik."

"We need to get out of here before then."

The door to Ludwik's room opened and Doctor Keller emerged. Mariska quickly let go of Jack's hand. The elderly doctor saw the uniform and looked very surprised. He walked over to Jack. "I am Doctor Keller, may I help you?"

"My name is Steiner. Do you have a Polish worker here?" Jack's voice was hard.

"Yes. Yes, we do. He's very ill. Why?"

Jack put his hands behind his back and said with disdain, "It is a matter of internal security. You will prepare the man to travel. I am taking him for interrogation."

"But, sir, he's not able to travel safely. He might die if he is moved."

Jack knew he had no option. Leaving Ludwik here was a sure death sentence. Better he die among friends. "If he dies, he dies. Now get him out here."

Mariska played along with the deception. "Please, don't take him."

"Fraulein, stay out of this. You're not aware of this man's true identity. He doesn't deserve your sympathy."

Jack turned to the doctor. "Now get him out here or I'll start my interrogation right here."

The doctor turned and went into the room. Jack maintained his hard gaze at the door but said quietly to Mariska. "Quickly, go outside. There's a Wermacht captain standing by the truck. He's one of us. Tell him to get in here. Stay outside with Jerzy and we'll bring Ludwik out."

She nodded and rushed down the hall.

225

It was another minute before Gerhard entered the office. As he walked up to Jack the door opened and the doctor came out supporting Ludwik. The young Pole's arm was supported in a sling, his other arm around the shoulder of the doctor. His face was pale but he held his head high. When he saw Jack his eyes flared in recognition for a moment.

"Ludwik Kowalski?" Jack asked.

"Yes."

"You will come with me. Hauptman, help him out to the truck."

Gerhard moved to Ludwik and put his arm under the young man's shoulder, taking some of the weight.

Jack turned crisply on his heel. "Herr Doctor, good day." The men walked out the door.

Rolf Brandt was incensed. *The SS taking a sick man out of my clinic. There is no excuse for the actions of those thugs*, he thought. He walked over to the window and watched the group getting the young man in an older truck. Strange, the doctor observed, how gently the Hauptman was while lowering the man into the back seat. And there was a third man, a civilian, perhaps the driver. But wait, the driver and Fraulein Mueller were holding each others hands? The doctor didn't know what to think. The woman and the third man got into the sedan while the officers were now in the truck. Both vehicles backed into the street and drove off toward the main road. "Very curious."

I'm too old to worry about those things. Brandt walked back to his office. He was reading the newspaper when he heard a car pull up outside. *What now?*

Two men in civilian clothes entered the door to the clinic. The older man approached the doctor and pulled out an identity card, which he saw was from the Gestapo. "Good afternoon, Herr

Doctor. My name is Steinhauer. We're from Breslau and are investigating the injured Polish worker you have been treating."

Brandt shook his head. "They already picked him up for interrogation. You just missed them."

The senior agent frowned.

"What are you talking about?"

"The SS officer, Steiner, he took the man into custody." Brandt was getting irritated.

"This was the Polish worker whose hand was crushed?"

"Correct."

The second agent was now standing next to Steinhauer, a notebook in his hand.

"And the hospital in Breslau was sending an ambulance later today."

"That's correct. Doctor Keller was going to do the evaluation."

"But you say an officer of the SS came in and took the man into custody. Did you see the officer's identification?"

Brandt's pulse increased. "No, I never thought about it. He was very direct and I just did what he ordered."

Steinhauer looked at Reitzler. "Are you aware of any activity by the SS in this area?"

"No sir," Karl answered.

Steinhauer turned and looked out the window. He stood silent for a moment then wheeled and looked at Brandt. "Is there anything that seemed unusual about these men?"

"They were driving civilian vehicles, a truck and a car. And in the street it seemed like they all knew each other."

Wait a minute, the senior agent thought. He knew of the incident in Posen and knew about the search, which was under way to the north. Could these people be connected to that? "Doctor,

227

where is your phone? Reitzler, get Posen on the line. I want to talk to Pressler."

It took fifteen minutes to connect with the Gestapo Office in Posen. Kurt Pressler was there. Steinhauer knew Pressler casually and liked the man. He briefed him on everything that he knew about this incident. When he mentioned the name Steiner the agent from Posen stopped him.

"Steiner?"

"Yes."

Pressler said, "That was the name of the second officer that pulled the partisan prisoners out of the depot right under the nose of that dumb shit commandant. Felix, this is one of the Reichsfuhrer's personal priorities. You must contact the Central Security Office immediately. They will descend on you but you have no choice. Himmler wants those people captured."

Steinhauer hung up. He didn't like this turn of events. Himmler personally involved. *My God.* But the word was out. He must do everything right, he must.

He connected with the local telephone exchange and requested a line to Berlin.

Whirlwind Recovery Flight
Over Europe
1710 Hours

Captain John Scrapper banked his P-51, "Razor's Edge," gently to the left as he flew in a slow weave back and forth over the RAF Hudson. He knew the bomber was cruising at its maximum speed. The Mustang was throttled back and using a weave to maintain contact on the other aircraft. Once they crossed the channel he had broken his division into two sections. One group was flying low cover three to four thousand feet above the Hudson, a mile in trail. He was in the high cover section at 12,000 feet, two miles behind the first fighter section. Three of the four pilots on this mission were very experienced. Scrapper was the only 'ace' with six confirmed kills, but the other two 'old guys' both had air to air kills.

Second Lieutenant Bennie Matthews was the rookie in the flight. Newly reported, he had been on four missions but hadn't seen any heavy combat. The Operations Officer thought this would be a great opportunity for the young pilot to get some more hours and not have to deal with the big formations of B-17's and B-24's. "Scraps" as he was called put Bennie on his wing to keep an eye on him.

The setting sun was making it difficult to keep a good look out doctrine. That bothered Scraps. That old axiom of 'beware of the Hun in the sun,' was not bullshit. The Luftwaffe day fighters made a point of using the sun during their attacks. If you could see the Germans the Mustang could easily hold its own with the 109s and 190s. It was the SOB you didn't see that was going to get you. Scrapper kept his scan moving across the clear sky.

The flight plan avoided built up areas and Luftwaffe aerodromes. Toms knew that at 2000 feet he would also avoid a large part of the German early warning radar net. There were also two flight segments that were specifically designed to confuse the radar warning net. In addition there was a fair amount of tactical air traffic over the continent. A large number of Eighth Air Force fighters were tasked to detach from the bomber formations during the return to England and go freelancing across the German countryside looking for targets of opportunity. There were three major raids on their way back to England, which put a large number of P-51s and P-47s working over Germany right now.

"Our little friends still with us?" Toms asked Sergeant 'Tiny' Scully in the dorsal turret.

"Like little angels they are." Scully's slow cockney drawl disguised the intense focus he brought to bear when it was time to fire the twin .303 machine guns in the turret.

Toms turned to Dicky Thompson. "This is going too smoothly. Good weather, hitting all the navigation points, fuel is good, it makes me nervous."

"Skipper, we get paid the same for the easy ones as the hard ones. I'll be pleased to log this as an easy one."

Kalisz
1740 Hours

The doctor left the two Gestapo agents alone with the phone. Steinhauer had been able to get a line to Berlin and was now talking with the Central Operations Office. It was very much a one way conversation. When he hung up Steinhauer said, "Let's go....now!"

Reitzler followed him as the older man stormed out of the office. They got into the car and Steinhauer told him to drive to the main road.

"We're going to have more company than we ever wanted. Central Security is sending people from every surrounding office. They will coordinate diverting an SS Battalion that is currently in Weilun on the way east. We can expect people to start arriving tonight. Stop!"

Reitzler slammed on the brakes and they slid to a stop. "What?"

"That man up on the roof. Let's go." Steinhauer was out of the car and striding up to a brick building on the main street before Reitzler could turn off the engine. Standing on the edge of the roof was an older man in work clothes. He was holding a hammer and a roof tile. "You, on the roof," Steinhauer yelled.

The man looked down. "Yes."

"Have you seen two cars or a car and truck go by here in the last 45 minutes?"

Nodding he said, "I did. They went north on the main road. Not much traffic today. Would have been hard not to notice them."

Back in the car, Kurt Steinhauer stared straight ahead. After a minute he said, "I'm not going to sit here and wait for more people to arrive. If these people went north, the sooner we follow the better. Let's go to the police station."

Ten minutes later Steinhauer was in the one police car of the town of Kalisz heading north on the main highway. Karl Reitzler had left to enlist the help of the Wermacht unit they had seen on their way into town. Steinhauer wasn't going to let anyone else take the credit for this.

Three hundred yards from the main road, the two vehicles were parked under a small group of trees. Heavy underbrush added to the concealment. Jack was worried about both Karl and Ludwik. The two lay side by side, Karl still in his litter. Mariska had an overcoat covering Ludwik and another rolled up coat under his head. It was now a waiting game. Jack checked his watch and looked at the fading daylight. They must be here soon.

231

Jerzy organized the remaining men into a rough perimeter. No one was in sight at the farm just south of their position. Terry Howe had the Very pistol ready to signal the aircraft.

Jack walked over to Terry who was looking south toward the landing field. "Ready to go home?" he asked.

Terry turned. "I just got here. Bet you're looking forward to a bed and a bath."

"You've got that right. This went well."

"We've come a long way from that first mission." Howe pulled a pack of cigarettes out of his jump suit, offering one to Jack.

"Thanks."

Terry produced a lighter and lit both of their cigarettes. They stood quietly, smoking.

It's been a long way from Midway to a field in Germany, Jack reflected. Then he thought of Ian Thompson. I have to find a way to reach Pam when I get back. She's shutting herself off as though she refuses to accept her dad is gone. I know how to fight, Jack thought, but I'm in over my head when it comes to dealing with this.

"It looks like you and Gerhard teamed up all right?"

Terry exhaled. "Can't say I started out liking him. But I figure he's committed to Dietrich and has no love for the Nazis. And he's damned good in the field."

"I'll tell you. Dietrich is as good as they come. He's the reason we pulled this off. I want him back alive and I want him on the team permanently. Gerhard too."

Terry laughed. "Quite a crew you're putting together."

They both turned as Patryk jogged over to them. "There's a car coming down the main road. It has police markings."

Chapter Thirteen

Whirlwind Flight
40 Miles North
Of the Posna Valley
August 7, 1944
1825 hours

"There's our final nav checkpoint," Dicky said, spotting the highway bridge that ran over the Wolna River.

Toms banked the Hudson to the final heading for the Valley. "All right, gents. Fifteen minutes out. Let's get everything ready," he said on the intercom.

Ten thousand feet above, John Scrapper was checking his fuel. All of the Mustangs had jettisoned their drop tanks twenty minutes ago and they were looking at almost full internal fuel. Checking his mirror he saw Bennie Mathews holding position one hundred feet away at his 5 o'clock position. Oil pressure, hydraulic pressure, engine temperature all within specs he noted automatically. Below, he could see the low section and the Hudson as it passed over the river. Not long now.

Jack knelt down. He saw a big sedan coming up the road. There was a large "P" painted in white on the side, "Poleizi." He hoped there was enough cover for their vehicles. The car was approaching where they had turned off into the woods. It continued past the turnoff but then rapidly slowed to a stop. Backing up, it stopped on the road exactly where the partisan vehicles had left the main road.

"Spread out and stay low," Jack said to the group. All the men were with Jack. Mariska stayed with Karl and Ludwik.

Two men got out of the sedan. One was in some kind of uniform and the other wore civilian clothes. They went to the side of the road and bent down to examine the ground. Looking up they stared at the small grove of trees where the vehicles were hidden.

"Shit," Jack muttered.

The man in civilian clothes turned around and went back to the car where he leaned down and talked to the driver. Getting out, the driver walked back and opened the trunk. The driver handed the man what looked like two rifles, one of which he gave to the other man in uniform. The two continued on toward Jack.

Jack knew he had to take the police out of the picture. The aircraft was due here at any time. He motioned to Jerzy. "Keep your men here. Protect the vehicles and Mariska. I'll have Terry work his way around to try and take the car. We'll stay under cover and take those two when Terry gets to the car."

"All right."

Jack stayed low and moved over to Terry, motioning Gerhard to join them. He explained the plan. Terry had his Sten and two high explosive grenades, which would be their signal to take the other two.

"Right." Terry began working his way toward the car, using the underbrush as cover.

"Gerhard, I understand you're a good shot."

The German nodded. "I won't be much good with this Sten at this range."

"Let's see what the Poles have."

Stefan was carrying the most promising candidate for use by the former Wermacht sniper. It was a German Mauser Model 98 carbine with an adjustable sight.

"Have you ever sighted it?" Gerhard asked Stefan.

He shook his head, "Not really. But the aim has always seemed true. I'm probably not a good enough marksman to tell the difference."

Gerhard held the weapon, flipping up the adjustable sight. He put the rifle to his shoulder. "This should work."

The plan was set. When Terry's grenade went off, Gerhard would attempt to take out the other men. Jack looked at his watch. Where was the plane?

Felix Steinhauer held the rifle at his waist as he walked toward the woods. There were several sets of fresh tire tracks in the dirt. Ahead he could see a grove of trees and stands of heavy brush. He knew this was a long shot but he wasn't going to sit in Kalisz waiting for more senior agents to arrive, this was his show. He stopped and listened. The Kalisz policeman, Herman Flosher stopped ten paces behind him. The sound was an aircraft engine growing louder. He caught a glimpse of the aircraft as it passed down the valley. It was olive drab and it didn't look like any Luftwaffe aircraft he knew. What was going on?

The sound of the grenade explosion was muffled. Terry had managed to toss the weapon into an open window.

Gerhard squeezed the trigger of the Mauser. His shot hit the farthest man directly in the chest, throwing him back on the ground.

Quickly reloading the bolt action he re-sighted on the man in civilian clothes crouching on the ground. Exhaling slightly, he rested the sights on the man's head and squeezed the trigger. In slow motion, his target collapsed.

Jack got up and ran to the edge of the clearing grabbing the Very pistol as he ran. He could see the Hudson turning over the small farm. Raising his arm he squeezed the trigger and felt the solid recoil as the flare left the barrel. "Get me another flare," he yelled at Gerhard.

The German commando, still carrying the Mauser, ran to their stacked gear. He grabbed the cartridge case for the Very.

Jack quickly opened the pistol, removed the spent casing and inserted another flare. The Hudson was turning back toward them. He raised his arm but did not fire. He saw the bomber's undercarriage swinging down for landing.

"Angel leader, this is Whirlwind. We see the flare now. Setting up for landing," Toms broadcast on the mission frequency.

"Roger, Whirlwind. We'll orbit the valley and keep an eye on things." Scraps could see the small lake and the long pasture was where the Hudson would set down. The sun was going down but there was still enough light for the bomber to land safely. He was now level at 4000 feet above the valley. Bennie had moved into tight formation. The other section was on the opposite side of a circle with the landing field in the middle. His stomach growled. He was going to be ready for chow when they landed.

The Hudson appeared to be on final, landing from south to north. There was a small farm just west of the field and a road running up the eastern side of the valley. Scraps looked again and saw three vehicles coming north on the road. *Better go down and take a look*. He keyed the radio, "Loosen up, two. We're going down to check out those trucks on the road." Obediently Bennie slid back into a combat spread.

Toms heard the transmission from the fighter leader but he was on short final and couldn't be distracted. Landing in these unprepared fields was the most dangerous thing he had done during the war including Mosquito bombing missions in the fiords of Norway. You never knew for sure what the surface would be like. Luckily it was summer and the ground should not be too soft. You could only hope there wouldn't be big rocks, holes in the ground, or ditches under what looked like a simple pasture of hay.

"Stand by," Dicky said in the intercom. The wheels touched down.

Toms pulled the power back to idle and stood on the brakes. The field had a slight up-slope, which helped slow the aircraft.

As his airspeed hit 350 knots, John Scrapper leveled out 200 feet above the valley floor, and adjusted his course to intersect what he now could tell was one car and two trucks. The vehicles were racing up the road, a trail of dust rising behind them. Flashing over the road, JC banked left and pulled hard. "Whirlwind, you've got two military trucks coming up the road. Looks like they're full of troops. Angel Three, do you have them in sight?"

Angel Three was Tony Fortino, a cocky Italian from New Jersey. He was a master with a Mustang and had three air-to-air kills to prove it. "Three's got 'em, lead."

"Take 'em, we'll follow you."

"Rog." Fortino turned on his master gun switch and rolled the Mustang to the left setting up for a firing run.

Jack and Gerhard both turned as the two Mustangs roared over the road and climbed back up over the valley. Looking back they saw the vehicles on the road, less than a mile from the turnoff.

The Hudson stopped 100 yards from the trees its engines at idle. The door opened and a ladder was extended down from the door.

"Get the wounded out to the plane. I'll get Terry."

"Yes, sir," Gerhard yelled and ran toward where Karl lay in his litter.

Jack sprinted toward the destroyed police car and saw Terry running toward him. Raising his hand, Jack waved at Terry to hurry. The commando stumbled as a shot rang out. Stewart ran toward Terry who crumpled to the ground. He realized the man in civilian clothes had not been dead and was able to get a shot off. Jack had his Walther out and put two rounds into the man, the second tearing off the side of the man's head.

He ran up to Terry who lay on his side, blood spreading on the right side of his jump suit. Jack rolled him on his back. Terry looked up, gasping for breath. Pulling a knife from his back pocket Jack slit the jump suit open at the entry point. Blood oozed from a single entry wound. He turned to see Gerhard run up.

"They're taking the wounded to the plane," Gerhard said. He knelt down at Terry's side. "Jack, we must move." They could hear the trucks on the road.

"Put Terry over your shoulder and I'll try to keep pressure on the wound." They could hear shouts from the trucks as they pulled to a stop.

Fortino made a quick check on his altimeter as he leveled his wings. The reticles of his gun sight were approaching the trucks, which had stopped on the road 500 yards from the Hudson. He squeezed the trigger and his eight .50 caliber machine guns fired a mix of armor piercing rounds interspersed with tracers. He held his finger on the trigger.

238

Jack and Gerhard both crouched down as the hail of tracers arched over their heads and impacted the parked vehicles. They rose up and continued to move Terry toward the idling bomber. A second Mustang began to fire at the trucks, the hail of bullets turning the trucks into smoking wrecks. Bodies were lying around the destroyed trucks, the destruction almost complete. Flames were visible coming from under the remains of the second truck.

"Whirlwind, this is Angel lead. We're making another run on those trucks. You should be all right. But I wouldn't stick around much longer."

Toms keyed his radio. "Roger, Angel. Thanks very much." He leaned over to see what was happening in the back. There were wounded lying on the floor of the center section under the dorsal turret.

Dicky was supervising the on load of the injured. Standing on the ground outside the door he saw Jack coming across the field. He started to run toward his friend who was helping another man carry someone. As he got closer he recognized Terry Howe and the commando who had jumped with him the day before yesterday.

Jack recognized Dicky and yelled, "He took a round in the side. We need to get him out of here." Thompson helped to support Terry as they approached the Hudson. Jack saw Jerzy in the door reaching out to help get Terry up the ladder. "Careful." As he climbed the ladder he heard another pass by the Mustangs. In the distance tracers lit up the grove of trees.

Inside the fuselage they laid Terry down next to Karl. Ludwik was sitting toward the rear of the aircraft propped against a rubber raft container. Mariska was leaning down talking to him.

"Jack, you need to get out of here and we do too." Jerzy was moving toward the door. The two men climbed down the ladder and saw Patryk jogging toward them.

"Jerzy, the Germans, they're all dead." Patryk stopped next to them catching his breath.

"Good. Go get Stefan and pull both vehicles out of the trees."

Patryk headed back toward the grove of trees.

"Jack, we'll head northeast. I'll try to establish radio contact with London once we're away from here."

"I wish there was room to take all of you out of here. We could take Mariska."

"As much as I'd like her to go, you and I both know she wouldn't."

Jack nodded. "She's a special lady. You need to invite me to your wedding someday."

"We'll drink a toast and dance all night."

Mariska appeared in the door and climbed down the ladder.

Jerzy said to her, "They need to go, we do too."

She reached out to Jack and hugged him for a moment. As she let him go she said, "Thank you."

"Now go," Jerzy said. The two men shook hands. Jerzy took Mariska's arm and guided her toward the trees.

Stewart climbed the ladder. As he entered the cabin he looked forward and saw Dicky was back in the co-pilot's seat. He heard the power come up on the engines and the Hudson began to move.

In less than a minute the bomber spun around 180 degrees and was pointed north for takeoff. Checking that the flaps were still down, Toms ran the pitch full up, put the throttles full forward and released the brakes. Accelerating slowly the bomber bounced on the uneven ground. Passing 100 knots indicated airspeed Toms pulled back slightly feeling the transition of the wings to lifting. With the wheels touching occasionally he kept the bomber in ground effect as he accelerated to 125 knots and began to climb away from the field. Off to his left was the small lake its surface almost smooth.

Overhead two sections of Mustangs maintained a watch on their charge. From 8000 feet John Scrapper watched the sun beginning to set in the west. Checking his fuel he adjusted his mixture a little leaner. No problem so far but better to be a little conservative early. It was a long way to England.

Jack sat with his back against the fuselage. He felt a wave of relief as the Hudson became airborne. During the confusion of loading he hadn't paid much attention to the crew of the Hudson. Now he noticed an RAF officer move back from the radio compartment.

"Commander Stewart? I'm Dwight Ashley, senior flight surgeon at Tangmere. Let's get busy on your man."

Jack guessed Ashley was forty. There was a self-assured air about the man. Kneeling down he began to examine Terry.

"Commander, I'll need light here. There are several torches in my kit up forward. Please grab them if you would."

Jack went forward and saw two large leather cases. He grabbed both and moved aft where he saw Gerhard kneeling next to Karl. The younger man was putting a blanket over Dietrich. "Gerhard, come here and give us a hand." Jack noticed Ashley turn and look at them. The spoken German must have surprised the doctor. Jack said in English, "Don't worry, he's on our side."

"Really. How interesting," Ashley said. He returned to his exam of Howe. Jack knelt on the opposite side from the doctor pointing a torch at the wound. There was still blood oozing from the bullet hole. The doctor pulled a large bandage from his case and placed it firmly over the wound. "Can you tell your friend to apply steady pressure?"

Gerhard knelt down and placed his hand over the bandage. The doctor pulled out a stethoscope and listened to different places on Terry's chest. "Damn difficult to hear with all this noise," he commented to no one in particular.

Jack said quietly, "Terry?"

Howe opened his eyes.

"It's Jack. How are you doing?"

"Hurts like hell," Terry said in a harsh whisper. He was fighting for each breath.

"We're in luck. They sent a doctor on the flight."

The doctor leaned over Terry's face with a small flashlight, shining it in Terry's eyes. "Doctor Ashley. And you are?"

"Howe..Terry Howe."

"Terry, I'm going to turn your head slightly." He examined the side of his neck. The veins were distended. "Bit of difficulty breathing, Terry?'

Howe nodded slightly and whispered, "Yes."

Ashley placed his hand on Terry's abdomen and began to slowly examine the lower quadrant. "Get some blankets and cover his legs," he ordered Jack.

Gerhard moved the bandage as the doctor continued to slowly press his two fingers to different spots on Terry's chest and stomach, occasionally tapping the two fingers with the fingers of his other hand. The doctor indicated to Gerhard to resume pressure on the wound. Standing up Ashley intercepted Jack who had two blankets in his hands. "Commander, your man is in a bad way. It appears to me the bullet has most likely missed the liver, which is good. But every indication is that the bullet has punctured the lung. As your man tries to breathe, the lung deflates as air is expelled into the chest cavity. The pressure often times affects cardiac blood flow. It can also make respiration difficult."

Jack did not like what he heard. "Can you do anything?"

"Actually, yes. It's a bit crude. I can insert a tube into chest which should solve the respiration issue. He's certainly going into shock. But if we operate quickly, minimize blood loss and keep him warm, he should weather the flight home."

"All right, what can we do?" Jack felt encouraged; at least they had a chance of getting Terry home alive.

"I brought most of what I need, but I didn't bring any type of rubber hose. I need 8 inches of sturdy rubber hose with an interior diameter the size of your small finger."

"Doc, you get everything else ready and I'll get your hose."

In ten minutes Doctor Ashley had laid out a small leather portfolio with an array of medical tools. Next to the instruments were packets of sulfa powder and petroleum jelly. Jack and Tiny Scully had cannibalized the rubber tubing from one of the fuel tank vents."

"Here you are, Doc. Will that do?" Jack asked.

"Splendid, just what we need. Now let's get all those lights down here."

Jack and Gerhard held lights pointed at Terry's side.

"Right, let's get started." He reached over and pulled a scalpel from the portfolio. Moving the bandage from the wound he carefully wiped the excess blood away with a gauze bandage. He fastened a smaller adhesive bandage over the bullet hole. Using his fingers to locate the gap between the ribs, he made a two inch incision horizontally about one inch above the wound. Laying the instrument down he inserted his index finger into the incision and probed slowly but deeply. "Good, now hand me the section of hose."

243

Jack handed him the hose which was smeared with petroleum jelly. The doctor left his right index finger in the incision and slowly worked the hose alongside his finger and into Terry' side. He continued until the tube was five inches into the incision. Grabbing a wad of petroleum jelly he applied it to the hose at the entry point making sure the outside of the wound was airtight.

"All right, Terry. I want you to slowly inhale. There may be some pain at first but I think you'll find it easier to breathe.

Jack watched in the pale light of the combined torches. Terry's chest was expanding as the wounded commando inhaled.

"That's...that's better." Terry's face was pale but there was a hint of a smile.

"Good, very good," Gerhard was smiling.

"Let's get him as warm as we can. I want you to try giving him sips of water every 15 minutes. Not too much. But if we can keep him from becoming too dehydrated it's that much better. I did bring plasma if we need it. Now let's have a look at the other two and see what we can do.

244

Chapter Fourteen

Baker Street
London
August 22, 1944

After two weeks of leave Jack felt better than he could remember. It would be good to get back to work and in the swing of things. Events on the continent were starting to move fast and everyone was looking at the war in a different light. It was clear the momentum of the war had changed dramatically. Surprisingly there was only one message on his desk when he returned. He was scheduled for an appointment with Noel Greene that morning. The location listed was not Greene's office. It was in the next building, 72 Baker Street. Although it seemed odd, Jack had learned that MI-6 could surprise you every day.

It was a beautiful summer morning and Jack enjoyed the fresh air on his short walk down the street. Security was thorough but did not delay him. He knocked on the door labeled 204. Pushing it open he saw a lovely young woman in civilian clothes sitting at the desk.

"Good morning, my name's Stewart. I was supposed to meet with Brigadier Greene."

She smiled and said, "Yes, sir. Just a moment please."

Jack remained standing, hat in hand, as she picked up the intercom phone.

"Commander Stewart to see you, sir. Yes, sir. Commander, you may go in."

Jack opened the door to the inner office and went inside. It was much larger than Greene's office and more lavishly appointed. Greene stood up to greet him. The Brigadier was wearing civilian clothes. Jack had never seen Noel Greene in anything but the uniform of a serving officer in the British Army.

"Hello, Jack. How was your leave?"

The two shook hands and Jack sat on the small couch.

"It was superb, sir."

"And how's Pam?"

Jack appreciated his interest. Her situation was the most difficult thing in his life right now. "Doing much better. I think it will take some time, but she'll move past this."

"I hope so. What a tough go." He leaned forward toward Jack. "There have been several developments while you were on leave. I know they will come as a bit of a shock. However I think you will grasp the logic when you hear the whole program."

Jack was not aware of anything big in the works, but then he had been totally focused on Whirlwind.

"Jack, two immediate changes. I have retired from the Army. On leaving active service, I was able to accept a new post which is part of a new division within MI-6. Section D has been placed under the military intelligence division of the Current Intelligence Branch. As Section F was an offshoot of Section D, we have terminated Section F."

"Just like that, sir?"

"Hear me out, Jack. We've have been grappling for some time with how we will make the transition to a post-war intelligence organization that can deal with what will be a very different world. A decision was made at the very highest levels that we would create an elite and streamlined group within MI-6 that would be able to deal with problems. What that means are operatives that are solely in the business of dealing with situations in the real world. No bureaucracy, no entanglement, just action. Handling problems that we don't want in the press. Taking care of situations that no one else can or will. "

The world was turning upside down and what Jack heard next sounded interesting.

"We want you to form the initial group. Although not by design, your work over the last two years has produced some very experienced and talented people. Our intent is to develop your group into one that will handle these new problems the world will face. I will give you as much latitude as you need to accomplish this."

"Our group remains intact, but under new management?"

"Exactly so. I will be your immediate superior. Although I can't identify the next person in the chain of command, I will tell you it connects to the top. We also want you to take a very low profile. For that reason we are shifting your operations to a secluded country manor in Kent. Corry Woods has everything we need to support operational missions. We've had people preparing it for some time. I think you will like what you find."

This was coming fast. Jack had already thought through many of the issues, which Noel alluded to over the last few minutes. The world was changing rapidly. Threats to the world's stability would only increase after the defeat of the Axis. Old empires would have trouble rebuilding what had been torn apart by the Germans and Japanese. The Russians were an unknown. Without the Germans to keep them in check, who knew what Josef Stalin would do. The countries of South America, who had only played on the periphery of the war, would now look to assert themselves. China was going to be the dominant power in Asia after the defeat of the Japanese. The United States was going to be a driving force in every aspect of world affairs of the future. Jack was convinced the world would need all the help it could get.

Jack stood up. "With your permission, sir, I'd like to go take a look at the new site."

"I figured you might. Phil Hatcher is waiting downstairs to drive you out to Corry Woods."

Jack paused for a moment. "One last question, Brigadier. Where does Tommy Hudson fit into this new scheme?"

"Good point, and by the way my new codename is "T." Tommy has taken command of Section D. I suspect he will stay there for the duration. After the war we expect he will follow me into this organization."

Every answer by Greene spawned more questions from Jack. "Do we have a name for this group, sir?"

"For now we are simply calling it the Double 00 Group. Very low key of course."

"Right, Double 00. And do I have a codename?"

"We thought we would use numbers, which would make you 001. How does that suit you?"

"Quite well I think, very straight forward."

As Jack walked down the steps, he laughed to himself. He'd been given a number at the Naval Academy in Annapolis, which was a six digit number, unique for each Midshipman. It had taken him several minutes to commit 387686 to memory. 001 was easy to remember.

Corry Woods
Kent

The drive to Kent had taken less than two hours. Jack enjoyed catching up with Phil Hatcher. Due to his leave, the two hadn't seen each other since the return from Germany. The time together gave Phil a chance to brief Jack on the rapid changes, which the team had been making over the last week.

"Hiram has been an absolute gem. I don't know how he arranged for the transport, equipment, paperwork, the whole works, but he did. We have our own communications section, which makes everything easier. The manor is very large and also secluded. There's the main house where we have the offices, and a number of outbuildings. We've got everything to be self sufficient."

"How about security?"

"We have a dedicated group of Royal Marines. Most of them are combat veterans, good group by my take."

The two covered every aspect of this new installation until Jack felt comfortable.

"Where are our people? It was deserted at Baker Street. I thought everyone was on holiday."

Phil laughed, "Holiday, not likely. They've been busting it getting everything running out here. Curtis and Jimmy have been on a dead run for Hiram. They have things pretty much under control now."

The car turned off the country road onto a narrow tree lined country lane. On one side was a stone fence which bordered a large open pasture.

"The entire area to the right is part of the estate, almost eighty acres according to the caretaker." Phil turned the car slightly to avoid a pothole.

"A caretaker?" Jack asked.

"Right, Mr. Jeffries. Must be 70 if he's a day. But make no mistake about it, Corry Woods is his purpose in life. He's been here since he was invalided out of his regiment after the Boer War. Quite a character I think you'll find. There's the manor house."

Jack could see a three story brick estate with a sloping copper roof. The rooms on the two upper levels had small balconies. There were trees on both sides of a long driveway leading up to the manor house. Jack saw the sentry box at the beginning of the drive. A Royal Marine snapped to attention and saluted. Phil brought the car to a stop. The Marine checked both their identity cards and then with a short, "Thank you, sir," waved them ahead.

As their car approached the manor Jack could see the drive split off and went behind the house on the left. Phil stopped at the main entrance.

"Here we are, our new home," Phil said.

"I'm impressed."

As they got out of the car another Marine opened the large front door and stood at attention. The man saluted with a snappy, "Sir."

The tour took almost two hours. Jack was impressed. The offices were set up and functioning. Billeting and messing for the entire command, which now numbered sixty two, was in place. Finishing up in Jack's new office the two men sat down at the conference table.

"Phil, I'm more than pleased. You and Hiram have done a superb job with the move."

"Everyone pitched in and it went much smoother than I would ever have expected. The big question around here is now what?"

"We've got to fill in the personnel holes, train where needed and be ready for whatever they throw at us."

Phil lit a cigarette. "And what exactly do we think that will be?"

Jack laughed. "I have no idea. But I think we have a chance here to put this group together and manage it without too much interference. I'm comfortable Noel Greene will give us a lot of room to maneuver. So intend to do just that." Getting up, he walked over to the window. "I want to use the people we've gotten to know over the last two years. Why not build this group with those you trust?"

Exhaling, Phil put the butt out in an ashtray. "So what are we really trying to put together? Greene must have given you some direction."

Jack sat down at his new desk. "We need to develop the most effective undercover operators in the world. They need to be equipped with the best equipment, armed with the best intelligence and capable of dealing with the most challenging situation."

"That's all?"

"Hell, Phil, we have some very experienced people right now. We continue to train our experienced people hard. And we recruit from the best we can find in the business. Our job is to put together an organization that can do that and do it quickly.

"Right."

"Now I think I'll snoop around the places you didn't show me." Jack stood up.

"Want me to go with you?" Phil asked.

"No, I'll just go where the mood takes me."

Jack walked the corridors of the manor house for twenty minutes. He stuck his head into several offices and greeted people he hadn't seen in almost a month. Walking through the kitchen he ran into Sgt Major McGinty, who was delivering rations.

"Sergeant Major, making sure our larder is well stocked?"

"Right you are, sir. Have some premium beef I think the lads will enjoy."

"I suppose the origin of the beef will remain a state secret?"

"Aye, sir. Fewer questions, the better all around if you know what I mean."

Jack laughed and walked outside into the rear courtyard. Looking across to the garage he saw an older man sitting on a chair adjusting the brakes on a bicycle. "You must be Mr. Jeffries," Jack said as he walked up to the man.

Looking up from his work, the man said, "It used to be Sergeant Jeffries of the 1st Royal Sussex. But that was a long time ago. And you might be?"

"Stewart, Jack Stewart. A pleasure to meet you, Mr. Jeffries." He offered his hand.

Jeffries stood up, wiped his hand on a rag and shook hands with Jack. "Stewart. You're the new Commanding Officer, right?"

"Actually we aren't that formal, but I do get to sign most of the papers they type up. Tell me, how long have you been here at Corry Woods?"

"Over forty years. I started working for Mr. Lawrence's father right after I left the regiment. Now the Lawrence's are in Canada for the duration."

Jack liked the old man. "Who was here before us?"

"A bunch of damned American officers from an infantry division. Noisy buggers. Coming and going all hours of the day and night. Parties on the weekend that would shame a Plymouth whore. Glad to see them gone. By the way, you sound like a Canadian yourself."

"If the truth be known, I was born in Seattle. A damned American as some would say."

Jeffries frowned. He looked at Jack's uniform for the country tabs that were worn by Commonwealth members of the Royal Navy.

"Don't worry," Jack said. I'm Royal Navy through and through. But you will hear some different languages from some of our people. We need to keep that piece of information to ourselves. Can I count on you?"

"I should say you can. Just make sure your gents take good care of the place. That's my job and I intend that the Lawrence's will find Corry Woods just as good as when they left."

Ramsgate Military Hospital
London
August 29, 1944

Karl Dietrich looked up as Jack walked into his room. He was reading a German/English dictionary. The two had seen each other several times since returning from Whirlwind but this was the first time since the move to Corry Woods.

"I brought you a present. But keep it out of sight." Jack handed Karl a small bag.

"What's this," he said, opening the top of the bag.

"Medicine comes in all forms."

Karl laughed and pulled out a bottle of Scotch. "You and I are of the same mind. Thank you."

Jack sat in a chair by the bed. "I talked to your doctor. He said you were ready to be released."

"I'm getting around fine on these crutches. But I have to ask the question. Released to where?"

"Karl, that's what I came to talk to you about." Jack could see a hard look in Dietrich's eyes like he was preparing himself for bad news. "I told you Gerhard had returned to Cheltenham."

"Yes."

"Well, I have a proposal for you to think about. You can return to the manor with Gerhard and we will run some debriefs with the intelligence people. After that probably a move overseas or to Scotland as you transition to being a private citizen."

"Not to a prison camp?" Karl asked quietly.

"No. By every measure your efforts may have saved the lives of tens of thousands of civilians. Great Britain will not forget what you did."

Dietrich nodded slightly.

"But I have another path to offer you and Gerhard. It is entirely up to you, but hear me out. I think we are at the end of the war but at the beginning of another period of conflict. The senior leaders of this government want to get ahead of events. They know there will be a need for skilled operatives to handle problems in the future. I've been tasked with building a group of agents that can handle these problems."

"Go on." Dietrich pushed himself up and was now sitting with his back against the headboard.

Jack outlined the new organization in as much detail as he felt he could. "You and Gerhard would be granted dual citizenship, British and German. A civilian grade commensurate with your former military ranks would provide a livelihood and everything that goes with being a government employee. The only drawback is having to put up with me."

Karl laughed and swung his legs over the edge of the bed. "Let's drive over to Cheltenham my English American friend and you can tell me more."

Standing up, Jack walked to the door. "Get ready. I'll let the doctor know to start the release paperwork. It will probably take half an hour. I'm going to go see Terry in B wing."

Captain Terry Howe lay propped up on two pillows reading a magazine. Although there were two beds in the room, the other was made up with no evidence of another patient in the room.

"What a life, reading magazines, great food and pretty nurses. We'll never get you back to work." Jack smiled as Terry looked up from his reading.

"You should taste the bloody food. I'm ready to get out of here now." Howe laid the magazine down on the bed and extended a hand to Jack.

"Good to see you, Terry. You're looking a lot better."

"Getting on pretty well. Doc says another week and I should be released."

"That's the same thing he told me. We're counting on it. I told Hiram to put you on two weeks convalescent leave and then back to work. We've got some new people who need your particular brand of training."

"New people? What's the story?" Terry looked interested.

Jack sat down. "Not only new people. We've moved to a new location and will be expanding the section."

"Tell me about it."

Jack put his hand up. "Plenty of time for that. You need to concentrate on getting out of here. But I'll tell you we have moved out of the city. It's a manor in Kent called Corry Woods. We'll run you out there when you're released then you can take off on your leave."

Howe put his head fully back on the pillows, "I suppose I should go see my parents. It's been a long time. But not for two weeks."

"Fine, you can come back to Kent whenever you're ready. But I want you to ease into it slowly."

There was a knock at the door and Karl Dietrich stuck his head around the door. "May I?"

Terry said, "Please, come in."

Dietrich was on crutches and wearing a civilian suit. The tie was loosened at his throat. He made his way over to the bed. "You look well."

"Thanks, getting better every day."

There was a moment of awkward silence and Jack spoke up, "I'm running Karl out to Cheltenham. We're going to see Gerhard."

At the mention of Lutjen's name, Terry smiled. "I look forward to seeing him soon." He paused. "I wouldn't be here if he hadn't come after me. I won't soon forget that."

When Jack and Karl arrived at Cheltenham it was almost 1800 hours. They were met by Gillian Andrews, who informed them Gerhard and Erich Von Wollner were outside getting some exercise. She asked them about dinner and they accepted her invitation to stay. Jack and Karl went up to the library to have a drink before dinner.

Jack poured a measure of Scotch into two glasses handing one to Karl. "It appears the commander and the captain are getting along with each other."

"I only saw Gerhard once since we got back and he didn't mention Von Wollner."

"Phil Hatcher did brief Erich on Whirlwind. His clues started the entire operation, it only seemed right he should hear the conclusion."

Karl put down his drink to light a cigarette. "Where does Erich figure into your new organization?"

"Our new organization, my friend. This will be a joint effort. What do you think?"

Karl looked at Jack but didn't say anything.

"I'm serious. What do we want to do?"

"You were serious when you laid out your plan at the hospital?"

"Of course I was. You didn't think so?" Jack asked.

"I guess you caught me by surprise."

"Well I was serious. You're going to be involved in this step by step. You will earn your pay many times over. Now what do we want to do with Von Wollner?"

Karl hesitated. "You've known him much longer. I sense he is focused and organized. Who do we have to coordinate all of the intelligence data and organizations?"

Jack could see Karl's interest and noted his use of the word we. "Right now Hiram Walker is running the admin effort. But as we build up the intelligence side will become too big for him. I think we should see if Erich wants the job."

"I agree."

Neither Erich Von Wollner nor Gerhard Lutjens would ever forget the conversation around the dinner table that evening at Cheltenham. The two men had gotten to know each other following Gerhard's return from Whirlwind. A friendship was formed and they had enjoyed the time and the opportunity to practice their English. Gerhard had been a particularly attentive student with Gillian Andrews as the instructor. Most of the dinner was in German but Jack was surprised how many times English vocabulary would come out in the conversations.

Gillian had the dinner served and then retired to the kitchen. Jack held his glass up in a toast. "Gentlemen, to friends."

Each of the men echoed "Friends."

Gerhard thought Karl was in a very good mood. Although he was surely glad to be out of hospital, Gerhard could tell it was something else. He'd known Dietrich for too long.

"So, Jack, tell me what you would have us do for the rest of the war?" Karl asked.

Stewart looked nervous. "Karl, let's just enjoy the meal. There will be plenty of time to talk about that in the future."

"Nonsense. What better time to share information between friends?"

Von Wollner and Lutjens sensed the mood change.

Karl had become louder and now downed half a glass of wine in one swallow.

"Karl, I'm sure Erich and Gerhard don't want to talk about that tonight."

"I'm sure they do," said Karl.

"Now is not the time," said Von Wollner.

"I say it is," Karl shouted.

"All right," interjected Jack. "I didn't want to bring it up but I've had word from London about the three of you."

"That's better," Karl said.

Jack looked down at the table as if gathering his thoughts. "It has been determined that the three of you will be sent to Glynne Meade in Scotland."

"Scotland?" Erich asked.

"And do what?" Karl poured more wine in his glass.

"You will be assigned to a sheep farm. There you will tend the sheep and learn a trade for after the war."

The simultaneous look of shock by Erich and Gerhard was all that Karl could take. He burst out laughing, followed shortly by Jack. Now the looks of shock changed to confusion.

Jack held his hand up. "Gentlemen, let me offer our combined apologies for playing a little trick on you. Trust me, you don't have sheep in your future. Karl and I do want to make a real proposal to you both. We think there's something important we can all do in the future and we'd like you to be part of it."

Over the next hour, Jack outlined the new organization. The four of them discussed everything from the most mundane administrative details to bigger issues of national sovereignty. As they talked through the issues Jack could see their decision being made.

Karl sat back and lit a cigarette. "Gerhard you know me better than most any other man. Erich we've just met. Just as Whirlwind was a step back toward a sane world, I think this organization is a vehicle for us to make sure the journey continues. It's an idea ahead of its time. Think about it. Experienced operatives from different countries and backgrounds working together to solve those shitty little problems that mankind seems to constantly produce."

Gerhard turned to Karl. "You're in, I take it?"

Dietrich nodded.

"I'm with you too," Gerhard said to Jack.

"Thanks."

Erich Von Wollner was silent. He picked up his wine glass and took a drink. "This is wonderful wine. And I think you have a great idea, Jack. You honor me by inviting me to be a part. How could I do anything other than accept?" He raised his glass. "Might I propose a toast? To the new world. Let us make it better."

The other three raised their glasses. A pact had been made.

Chapter Fifteen

23B Devon Street
Apartment 2
London, England
September 14, 1944

Jack felt like he hadn't stopped running since he arrived at Corry Woods. In the last two weeks the group had made significant progress on many critical fronts.

Erich organized an intelligence shop that was now connected to each major intelligence organization within the British Government and the Allies.

Karl assumed the advance training of all agents. The intent was for Terry and Gerhard to conduct most of the training with Dietrich teaching advanced techniques. Everyone was now billeted at Corry Woods and settling into a productive routine. But during the stand up Jack knew there was a problem waiting for him in London. Now he was going to have to face that problem.

Pam had been able to work her way through some of her grief over Ian. Jack was encouraged with her new, more optimistic attitude. But he knew the effort he must put into the Double 00 organization was going to take him away from London and her for a great deal of the immediate future. This included a trip back to the United States which Noel Greene had informed him of only that morning. The Prime Minister was meeting with President Roosevelt in Hyde Park and Commander Stewart had been ordered to be present. Jack knew Pam would not be happy with an increase in his time away from London.

They had made pleasant small talk since he arrived just before dinner. He told her as much as he could about the new location and then he broke the news. "Pam, this new job will require I spend most of my time at Corry Woods for awhile."

She was sitting at the kitchen table, a glass of wine in front of her. He wasn't sure what to expect but he knew this was not going to be a pleasant exchange.

"I understand entirely. It sounds very important and I know Dad would be proud of you."

Jack was stunned. Never would he have expected her ready acceptance.

"I'll try to get back to London as often as I can, I promise," he said.

She smiled. "Jack, don't worry. I've been cleared for full duty by the doctors and I have a new posting."

"That's wonderful, but you're sure it's not too early?" He wasn't sure himself.

"I had a complete check by Dr. Hanson. It's something I need to do. I can't just sit around. You must understand that?"

She sounded very earnest and he did understand how she felt. Perhaps this was for the best. "I do, Pam. I'm happy for you. When do you have to report?"

Pam got up and poured more wine into their glasses. "One week. I need to be in Scotland on the 21st."

"Scotland?" Jack expected she would be back at one of the aerodromes around London. If she was in Scotland she might as well be in Seattle.

"Jack, you go where you're ordered. I wouldn't think I have to explain that to you."

She was right, Jack thought. "All right, you've got me there. I just assumed you would be around London. I guess we both will be able to give our jobs full attention. But don't get swept off your feet by some dashing wing commander or something. I'm still going to marry you when this war is over."

"You've never asked me."

Jack knew he had never formally proposed, but they had discussed their future many times and he assumed marriage was part of their plan.

He walked over and sat down next to her. Taking her hand he said, "Then I'm asking you now. Pam, I love you with all my heart. I don't think I ever knew what love was until I returned to England and found you again. I will promise to love you always. Please marry me."

Pam sat looking him. There was a film of tears in her eyes and she slowly smiled at him. She put her arms around him and said, "Yes." She whispered again in his ear, "Yes."

The Presidential Compound
Hyde Park, New York
September 19, 1944

There had been a great deal of sitting and waiting for Jack over the last two days. The flight across the Atlantic was on a VIP transport, which had arrived at Dover, Delaware. His priority orders got him on a transient B-25 enroute to Floyd Bennett Field in Brooklyn. Finally he had enjoyed a three hour train ride north to Hyde Park. He was surprised and genuinely happy when he got off the train at Hyde Park and saw Brigadier General Bill Miller waiting on the platform.

The two men exchanged salutes and a strong handshake.

"Jack, it's good to see you."

"General, I wasn't sure if I was welcome back in the States." Jack laughed but did wonder how he might be received after making his decision to remain with MI-6 permanently.

"I think you'll be surprised. The welcome mat is out and we are delighted you could break away."

Jack wasn't sure if Miller was just making small talk or did he know something about Double 00? "Always busy of course. But when the PM calls, we all come running."

Miller knew of his friendship with Churchill, which began on Jack's arrival in England in 1942. "A lot in this war depends on friendships. I'd suggest the one between Churchill and FDR is going to go down as one of the most important ones in history."

They walked down the platform to a waiting Army staff car. Jack began to wonder what was going on?

A bitter Jack Stewart, then a U.S. Navy Lieutenant, met Colonel Bill Miller during his trip to Washington D.C. after being shot down at the Battle of Midway. It was Bill Miller who recommended Jack to Major General Bill Donovan, head of the OSS. The President and Donovan had arranged with Winston Churchill to take an American into the most secret section of MI-6, but that person would have to accept a commission as a King's officer. Miller saw something in the young officer, as did Donovan. What none of the principals foresaw was the desire by Jack to retain his Royal commission and accept permanent British citizenship. The original intent by all parties was that Jack would learn the intricacies of the European intelligence world and return to the OSS to help the wartime build out. Last summer Winston Churchill had made a personal request to FDR that Jack Stewart be allowed to remain with the Royal Navy. The President had reluctantly approved the Prime Minister's request.

Bill Miller drove Jack to a residence which was being used to billet Generals Donovan and Miller.

"You'll bunk in here with the two of us. Your meeting is scheduled for 1730. We'll have you back on the train tomorrow morning for New York."

"Any hint what this meeting is about?" Jack was presuming on their friendship.

"I have an idea, but wait to hear everything at the meeting. What I will tell you is that it is an extremely unique plan."

"All right. Like the lamb to the slaughter, I'll trust you."

Miller laughed.

Stewart wasn't sure what he expected, but he didn't expect to be in the President's sitting room with FDR, Churchill, and General Donovan. Bill Miller escorted him in and then left the room.

"Commander Stewart, it is good to see you again." FDR was smiling, but Jack could see he looked very tired.

"Mr. President, it's a pleasure to be here."

"Hello, Jack." Churchill nodded pleasantly.

"Sir," Jack said.

General Donovan was as impressive as always. "Good to see you again. Please sit over here."

Roosevelt started. "Jack, as much as our focus is on the successful conclusion of this war, we are spending almost as much time laying out the post war world. What we say in this room today must stay in this room."

Jack murmured, "Yes, sir."

"As the German Reich and Empire of Japan collapse, we feel there are forces waiting to surge into that vacuum. Specifically, the Soviet Union. If we sit idle and allow them to usurp the traditional balances of power, the world has the potential to become a very dangerous place. We feel we must do everything we can to provide a continuance of the ideals and freedoms of the western democracies. That is where you come in."

Churchill joined in. "Jack, when you returned from Whirlwind Brigadier Greene directed that you take the first steps to form the new Double 00 group. He was naturally vague as to the chain of command."

He knew something crucial was about to become clear.

"Jack, Double 00 is the operational end of a combined intelligence group which is designed to continue long after hostilities have ceased," Roosevelt added.

"And we will keep the group and its activities very close hold," Churchill added. "We don't know what will happen to any of us. But we owe it to all of the men and women who have died in this conflict to ensure it doesn't happen again. For that reason we are going to rewrite the rules. Everything that is being set up is being done by executive direction from here and in England."

"You are critical to making this work. As close as our relations are now, we don't know where the future will take us. For that reason we need someone who has their hat in both rings." Roosevelt was speaking with great intensity and Jack felt the enthusiasm of the President. "We never envisioned what would happen when we sent you over in 1942. But the way things have played out we have a unique opportunity. We want you to make this work."

Donovan had been silent, but now spoke. "Jack, your commission in the U.S. Navy is still active. You have the singular distinction of holding commissions in the navies of both the United States and Great Britain. You also hold dual citizenship and always will do so. There is a document to that effect signed by both the President and His Majesty. We need you to build this group to handle the most sensitive and critical operations for the United States and Great Britain. Brigadier Greene is the common conduit for requests from both governments. As you build up your operational capability you will have total control. We aren't going to tell you how to do your job, but we will be giving you the direction. You can assume any tasking you receive is coming directly from the White House, Downing Street or both."

"Yes, sir."

Churchill smiled, "Jack, we're concerned there is a huge amount of scientific and weapons research that might fall into Russian hands as they enter Germany. Important as the information are the people who have the knowledge to use that information. Not everyone was a Nazi and the Germans have always maintained one of the most advanced research establishments in the world. Jack we need to get to the information and people before the Russians. This has got to be your primary mission for the foreseeable future."

"Sir, I understand."

Roosevelt said, "Well done. Gentlemen, I propose a drink to seal our bargain. Commander, might I interest you in a martini?"

Corry Woods
October 11, 1944

Hiram Walker stood in front of a large wall map of the continent and read the morning's dispatches. He stuck a blue push pin into the map and said, "The German high command in the area has rejected the U.S. Third Army ultimatum to surrender Aachen. Looks like a nasty fight for General Patton."

Erich Von Wollner looked up from his desk in the intelligence office. "Aachen, a very pretty and ancient town. I am sure it will be destroyed before they are done."

Hiram had come to respect the tall German. Although Erich was totally dedicated to an Allied victory, it was clear the destruction of Germany was hard for him to watch. During their time together Walker was impressed with the hours Von Wollner had worked putting the entire intelligence picture together for the group. The insight he gained as a senior staff member for Hitler made his analysis very accurate and timely. The entire senior staff of Double 00 was wrestling with how they should lay the groundwork for their operations during the rest of the war and after. Many discussions ended up with only sketchy ideas.

The most highly trained agents in the world were useless without operational intelligence. Although this was not totally the responsibility of Double 00, Jack wanted them to have their own intel networks. It was his number one priority.

The phone rang and Von Wollner answered. He said, "In a moment." He put down the phone. "Jack wants us in his office."

When Erich and Hiram arrived Karl Dietrich was in the office with Jack.

"Sit down," Jack directed. "Karl, go ahead."

Dietrich remained standing as he spoke. "We've been trying to figure out how we build our own intelligence network to supplement what we know we will get from the larger organizations. The question we couldn't answer was how we build out that network. Since Norway I have worked off and on with a senior officer in German Naval Intelligence. His name is Kaltenbach, Rear Admiral Walter Kaltenbach. Currently he's stationed in Kiel. He is very well connected throughout the military intelligence world."

"I know of him. He had a good reputation with the high command," Erich said.

"All right, we have the name of a senior intelligence officer in Kiel. Where do we go with it?" Jack asked.

Karl continued. "I've been thinking about this all morning. Over the years I've gotten to know Kaltenbach well. He is a German not a Nazi. There is a long naval tradition in his family. Certainly he knows the ultimate outcome of this war and would understand our efforts to head off problems."

"Go on," Jack said. This was the first plan that sounded like it might have promise.

"I go to Kiel and talk to him." Karl sounded very matter of fact.

A year ago Jack might have rejected such an idea. With the experience of Whirlwind he knew that covert missions must be part of their capability. Ignoring the technical details of an insertion into Kiel, Jack looked at the more practical side. "Can you get close enough to connect with him and do it safely? And will he talk to you?"

Dietrich nodded. "I can get to him. Will he talk to me? I won't know until I try. But I think it's worth the effort."

Erich looked at Karl. "If you guess wrong he calls the Gestapo and you're a dead man."

"My plan would be to make sure he can't call anyone if it goes badly." There was no doubt among those in the room what he meant.

Hiram asked a key question. "How do you get into Kiel?"

"It would be an easy insertion by submarine assuming we can get the Navy to cooperate."

"I don't think that would be a problem. Do we want to bring him out?" Jack knew the answer to his question but wanted their opinions.

Erich nodded. "Of course. If we could get him back here, he would be able to provide an ongoing source of intelligence and contacts."

"I agree," said Karl. We need to have an alternate plan if he wants to stay. But if I know Walter, he'll come with me."

"Let me run this by the front office. For now let's start making an op plan."

72 Baker Street
London
October 13, 1944

The plan Jack took to Noel Greene was a good one. The senior staff had worked on it for two days and every detail was covered. Karl's recent time in Kiel made the planning much easier and gave Jack extra confidence for success.

It would be a two man mission. The plan called for an insertion by rubber raft to the east of Kiel, near the town of Laboe. From the town it was a short trip into Kiel and to Kaltenbach's residence in the Ellerbak section of town. Walter's wife had died of cancer in 1939 and he never remarried. The Admiral lived alone, with only a housekeeper, in an old turn of the century house the Kriegsmarine had commandeered. The second agent on the mission would be Jack. Although it made sense to send Gerhard Lutjens, Karl felt it was important to have a British officer with him. Jack would also be able to answer questions or make agreements that Karl could not. The unknown was Walter Kaltenbach

The brief took over an hour. When he finished Jack knew the answer was yes. Because of the support requirement by the Navy the Brigadier couldn't give Jack final approval. Greene told him there would be an answer within a day.

Jack didn't get into London often anymore. With Pam in Scotland there wasn't much of a reason to make the trip. He had received several letters, more notes actually, sending her love and pleading she was too busy for long letters. That was just as well for Jack. Although he had several talents, letter writing was not one of them. He hoped they would be able to arrange for some time together at Christmas if she could get leave.

He arranged to meet Sergeant Major McGinty at the main headquarters building down the street. McGinty had been Jack's supply coordinator since the original standup of Section F. Jack pulled him into Double 00 and the expanded supply needs were being well covered by the sergeant major. Never known for following the conventional supply chain, McGinty always got his hands on exactly what Jack and the men needed. This morning he needed to have Jack talk with several of the accounting and finance people to settle the costs of the initial move to Corry Woods.

Jack was standing at the security checkpoint while the sentry checked him in when he saw Major Billy McClaren, the director of training at the SOE basic school at Arisaig House in Scotland. Stewart had gone through the course when he arrived in England.

McClaren was walking down the corridor on his way out of the building and he saw Jack at the same time.

"Billy McClaren, what happened? Did they run out of scotch in Arisaig? I didn't think you ever left Scotland." The two shook hands warmly.

"Aye, Jack. One day in this bloody city and I'm ready to go back to the green hills. How have you been, my boy? You're looking well."

"Busy, but busy is good. Did you hear Terry Howe was busted up a bit? He'll be fine in a couple of months."

McClaren smiled, "Not supposed to know about those things but you know how rumors fly about. There was a very unusual rumor he was rescued by a German commando."

"Don't believe everything you hear, Billy." Jack took him aside, out of earshot of the sentries. "Billy, we're doing a bit of expanding down here. Very focused. We're looking for some new talent."

The Scotsman became serious. "Always ready, Jack. What 're ya lookin' for?"

"Language skills, French or German especially. But more than that I need people who can think on their feet. We're looking for the kind of agents who can talk and figure out how to get information. They still need to be able to take care of themselves, but I think the days of blowing up bridges are over for us."

McClaren nodded. "Understood. There are two going through now that fit that mold. I think you might even know one of them, Pamela Thompson."

SS Headquarters
Unter de Linden
Berlin, Germany
October 14, 1944

Closing a leather folder, SS Brigadefuhrer Helmut Stahel stood up at his desk and took a deep breath. Stahel was Heinrich Himmler's intelligence chief. His job was to coordinate information flow from the intelligence departments of the military and the internal SS intelligence web. This morning he was going to present a briefing to the Reichsfuhrer SS on the events at the Posen Depot in July. He was concerned about what Himmler would do when he had all the facts. The deteriorating course of the war was starting to take a toll on Himmler. The continued losses by the SS combat forces could no longer be replaced. There was no time to train the men, there weren't enough suitable men available and the equipment was running out. Despite his dark side Himmler had always been the most enthusiastic supporter of any order from the Fuhrer. Nothing would ever stand in the way of Himmler trying to comply with Hitler's direction. But Stahel was starting to see frustration and desperation from the head of the SS.

"There is no question, based on photo identification by agents from Posen and the corroboration by our agent in England, Karl Dietrich was a member of the Allied team that was involved in the destruction of the depot at Posen. It appears that team did escape from Wermacht forces in the Posna Valley on the 7th of August. Two Gestapo agents were killed during the escape."

Himmler had been very quiet during the brief. Only two of his most senior aides were in attendance and the tension was high when Stahel closed the folder. "Dietrich?" Himmler said very softly.

Stahel expected fury, but Himmler seemed stunned.

"I don't know what is behind this," Himmler finally said. "We may never know." He turned to his senior aide. "You will remove Dietrich from all SS rolls of honor. His name will never again be spoken in my presence. A warrant for his arrest will be issued across the Reich. I want his immediate family picked up for questioning." He turned back to Stahel. "Order our agent in England to kill Dietrich, even if it means breaking his cover. This entire event is a blot on the reputation of the SS. Now leave me alone."

Nissenstrasse
Kiel, Germany
October 29, 1944
2145 Hours

Two men walked down a tree-lined street. Anyone who stopped the men would discover they were Gestapo agents from Bremen with arrest warrants for several suspected Allied agents.

It was cold. There was a bitter wind blowing in from the ocean. Jack Stewart thrust his hands into the deep pockets of his leather overcoat. The insertion by the crew of HMS Satyr had gone as planned. Arriving in the small town of Laboe, they stole a car from a back street and drove to the outskirts of Kiel. Hiding the car in an alley about a mile away, they walked the remaining distance to Nissenstrasse. Karl had been here several times for dinner and knew this part of Kiel well. Their intelligence effort prior to departure from Portsmouth indicated Kaltenbach was in Kiel. Karl and Jack knew senior officers are often called away at short notice. It was a chance they had to take. Karl turned up the walkway to Number 46. There were steps leading up to the large two story brick house. Tonight the light by the front door was still on. Karl told Jack that Walter was a late night reader, sometimes staying up all night.

Karl grabbed the metal doorknocker and rapped three times. In a minute the door swung open and a stout woman peered out.

"Yes, may I help you?"

Holding up an identity card, Karl said, "Weiss, Gestapo. We're here on a matter of utmost urgency for Reich security. We must talk with the Admiral."

She was holding a shawl around her neck with one hand. "Does he know you were coming?"

"Our office was going to call his headquarters, but it was late and they may not have gotten through. I assure you this is a critical matter."

Opening the door wider, she said, "Come in."

Karl led Jack inside to a long hallway with a stairway to the right of the door.

"Please wait here. I'll let the Admiral know you are here."

When she had gone Jack whispered to Karl. "She didn't recognize you." Karl's hair had been dyed black. He now had a mustache and wore glasses. It wasn't a major disguise, but it was enough.

The woman returned. "The Admiral will see you. It's the door on the right."

Walter Kaltenbach was sitting at a large desk in the study and rose when Karl and Jack entered.

"Gentl...." The Admiral stopped and looked at Dietrich. "My God, Karl." He walked around the desk and offered his hand. "I never thought I'd see you again. Come in, sit down." Kaltenbach closed the door and returned to his desk.

"It's good to see you, Walter," Karl said.

"I'm assuming, with the disguise, that you are on a mission?"

Jack sat quietly watching the two old friends talk.

"Correct, Walter. I'm working for British intelligence."

Without hesitation, Kaltenbach said, "I know."

"You know?" Karl asked.

"We knew Eva had been turned by the British. What we didn't expect was your change of heart."

"So you were sending me into a known trap?"

276

Shaking his head, Walter said emphatically, "No. We didn't know when or if Eva might notify the British. Our insurance was our real agent. He was to take her out if she was going to disrupt the mission. Unfortunately for us everything happened too quickly."

"What do you mean your real agent?" His tone was urgent.

"Eva's companion, Mr. Thomas. His real name is Hans Richter. Although MI-5 thinks he's turned, he's still working for us. In fact Helmut Stahel called me as a courtesy to tell me that Himmler has directed Richter to kill you. It seems the Reichsfuhrer did not take your defection well or the mission to Posen."

"You know about that?" Karl asked.

"The German intelligence community is much more cohesive than their combat command counterparts. We have to be. But there must be more to your visit than a desire to see an old friend."

"Walter, you and I both know Germany is going to lose the war."

"Karl, we've known that since 1941 when the Americans entered the war. The only question was how long it would take."

Dietrich knew he must appeal to Walter's common sense and practicality. "The Nazis have destroyed our country and our honor. If we want anything to rise up from the ashes we must work to rid Europe of every vestige of the old."

"Karl, I don't disagree. But we are all playing parts in a play and no one can get off the stage."

"I did, with the help of this man. And that's why I'm here to talk to you. Walter, this is Commander Jack Stewart, Royal Navy. He is the head of an organization that is focused on helping to create this new world. From everything I know about you it's something you would want to be a part of."

Kaltenbach looked at Jack. "A new world? That's quite an order so forgive me if I am a bit skeptical." The Admiral lit a cigarette and sat back in his chair. "All right, you came this far, I'll listen to what you have to say."

Jack outlined the purpose and organization of Double 00. It took him ten minutes. Kaltenbach said nothing. When Jack finished the Admiral got up and went to a small bar next to his bookcase. He poured schnapps into three glasses and carried two over to Karl and Jack.

Picking up his own glass he took a sip and put it down on the desk. "Commander, I am a German. I will always be a German. But I do understand that what will happen after this war will threaten the existence of my country. The Soviet Union has shown what their intentions are as they have moved like a swarm of locusts across the eastern front. But what would you have me do?"

"Come back to England with us and become part of the organization," Karl said.

For the first time tonight the Admiral seemed surprised. "Me? Become part of a British intelligence team? And what would you have me do?"

Jack spoke first, "You would coordinate the network we intend to build using intel personnel across the continent. Your knowledge and contacts make you the ideal person. And you would be working directly with the number two man in the entire organization."

"And who would that be?" the Admiral asked.

"Me," said Karl. "Two old friends, working for the future of Germany and Europe."

"Karl, it sounds too good to be true. I guess my pessimistic side tells me it can't happen."

"Walter, I don't know what will happen. But I trust Jack and I trust the British. If you stay here all you will do is oversee the demise and surrender of the Kriegsmarine. That will happen whether you are here or not. If you come with us you'll have a chance to do something that might help Germany survive as a country."

"What are the arrangements?" the Admiral asked.

"There is a British submarine waiting to pick us up," Karl said.

"And if I say no?"

"We leave."

Kaltenbach stood up, "You would trust me to let you leave Germany?"

Karl finished off his drink. "Walter, I wouldn't be here if I didn't trust you. There comes a time when we have to trust each other. You and I are at that point." He stood up, as did Jack.

Kaltenbach extended his hand to Karl, then to Jack. "Gentlemen, shall we go?"

At 0230, there was an urgent coded signal from HMS Satyr to the Admiralty for relay to MI-6. The message requested immediate arrest of Hans Richter a.k.a Harry Thomas. When Noel Greene read the words 'double agent', he called Phillip Kent at MI-5.

"Phillip, I don't know the specifics but I can assure you I have every reason to believe the validity. There is the possibility that Harry Thomas is a double agent. We are concerned he has been ordered to kill one of ours. The smart thing would be to bring him in and give us time to get to the bottom of this."

"I wish I could do that, Noel. We've been trying to contact the two of them and it seems they've gone missing. Our understanding was they were on a reconnaissance of the southeast but we can't locate them." There was a tone of frustration in Kent's voice.

Greene knew Jack had found out critical information while ashore in Germany. If there had been time to deal with any problems in a measured manner he would have never sent a message. It must be life or death. "If we combine our efforts and bring in Scotland Yard we will have the best chance of finding them."

"I agree. Let me handle the police. Can you meet later at my office to take a measure of where we are?"

"I'll be there in two hours." Greene placed the phone back on its receiver.

HMS Satyr
Harwich Harbour
November 2, 1944
0645

The voyage from the Baltic had been as expeditious as Commander Keith Collingswood felt was prudent. Clearing the northern tip of the Jutland Peninsula he kept the submarine on the surface for most of the remainder of the transit. When Jack explained the situation back in England Collingswood recommended they divert to Harwich to get Jack and Karl ashore as quickly as possible.

There had been some very interesting looks from the crewmembers when Walter Kaltenbach had come aboard that night. Still wearing his uniform, the gold braid caught the attention of the British sailors. But like all submariners the crew of Satyr took it in stride. Tonight they were looking at a night of liberty in Harwich before the return transit to Portsmouth.

Jack guessed it was the only time during the war that a Kriegsmarine Admiral had stood on the bridge of a British submarine. The Satyr was a quarter of a mile from the entrance to the inner harbour. Jack felt like he knew the area well from his time spent here with the MTB squadron here in the fall of 1943. He remembered the men they lost on their mission into Oostende, Belgium. Although they had done what they set out to do, an MTB and the entire crew were lost during the mission. More and more often, Jack found himself remembering the friends he had lost in this war. It seemed like it would never stop.

As they moved closer he listened to the confident orders from Collingswood as he maneuvered the submarine alongside the pier.

"Keith, we'll be off as soon as the gangway is in place. Your crew was magnificent and the drinks are on me next time we're in Portsmouth." Stewart shook hands with him.

"It was our pleasure, Jack. A little cloak and dagger does wonders to break the monotony of everyday ops." Keith Collingswood grinned at Jack. "Don't worry, the crew will get the brief. They saw nothing, right?"

"Right you are." Jack headed down to join Karl and Kaltenbach who were standing by the forward access hatch. The Admiral was wearing a Royal Navy pullover sweater and an oilskin coat. There was no reason to advertise his presence in England.

There was a light breeze blowing across the water and it made the morning very crisp. The three men stood together taking in the activity on the deck. Jack could see several figures in Army battle dress at the end of the pier. It was Hatcher, Livesey and Hunt obviously up from Corry Woods. The message sent last night asked

Phil to set up quick transport for three back to the manor. It was time to take care of this double agent. They must also maintain heightened security for all of their Germans. With Admiral Kaltenbach now among that group it was more urgent.

They were up the gangway ten minutes later. The two sedans were on the road to Corry Woods straight away. Phil Hatcher brought a second car with four heavily armed security guards as an added escort.

Jimmy Hunt drove the large sedan with Phil in the front seat. Jack, Karl and the Admiral sat in the back seat. As they accelerated out of the main gate and headed south, Jack asked, "What have we heard on this fellow Richter?"

Phil twisted in his seat. "They've been missing since MI-5 started looking for them. The authorities are all alerted."

Karl's face was hard. "I assume they checked Cambridge at the business and at Eva's house?"

"That was the first thing they did, Karl. No luck. The plan is to widen the search. They may have headed north for some reason," Phil said.

"Richter has a reputation as an effective agent. I don't know if he has ever been given an assassination mission however. There's a difference between spying and killing," Kaltenbach added

"I would enjoy introducing him to the world of killing." Karl's tone left no doubt that if he ever met Hans Richter he would kill him without hesitation.

"We'll try to give you the opportunity, Karl." Jack knew Karl was not concerned for his own life, but for Eva.

Hans Richter did not like his options. He had received the coded message in the post. Although it took longer to get messages back and forth, the intercept capability of the British made the post the most secure method for receiving instructions from Germany. Routed through the Portuguese diplomatic pouch and coordinated by a deep plant Abwehr agent, the contact system was reliable but slow. The advantage was the detail this method could provide, something not always available when constrained by transmission limitations. The message contained orders to kill the SS defector Dietrich. If required to complete the mission his cover could be compromised. Richter knew this day might come but it was still a shock. If he needed to compromise his cover it meant killing Papenhausen. His challenge would be to make his way to the network that he had been told was in place to get him out of England into Norway and then back to Germany.

"There's the shop. Park around on the side street if you can." Eva was looking at a bill of lading.

Richter was brought back to his immediate task, the delivery of four chests to the shop in Buningford. They had been on the road for four days. Their primary mission had been to determine if there were still any major ground troop concentrations in southeast England. It had been easy enough to crisscross the main roadways looking for any troop movements or any signs that might indicate bases which were still occupied. On return to Cambridge they would transmit their findings.

To more pressing matters he had to locate Dietrich. Hans Richter knew the commando and Papenhausen had seen each other on several occasions. All she would tell him was that she had been to a country manor in Kent. That narrowed it down to approximately eighty manor houses. He had to find some way to have her lead him to Dietrich. Perhaps he should break cover and get the information from her by force. But she was a stubborn woman. It would be easier if she would cooperate unknowingly.

"Go in and see if they have anyone who can help me with these chests," he told Eva.

In short order a shop clerk came out and helped Richter carry the four chests into the shop. They saw a pub across the street and decided to get something to eat before getting back on the road.

The cold meat sandwiches were good and the two ate in silence.

"Nothing pressing to get back to Cambridge. You should try and see your friend since we're down in the area."

Eva looked up from her sandwich. "I didn't realize you were interested in my love life."

Richter tried to keep it light, "I'm not. But there's a lady I'd like to see in London. Thought we could both use a little break, if you know what I mean. It can't be that far. I can drop you off, run into London for the night and be back to get you tomorrow morning. We can be back in Cambridge by mid day."

"That might work. Let me think for a moment."

Twenty minutes later the furniture truck pulled onto the road heading south for the Kent countryside.

For the first two hours Richter followed Eva's directions. They passed through Harwood and Epping staying on the main road. Approaching Dartford Crossing she told him to take the

Chatham road. "Corry Woods is near a small village called Headcorn. I don't want this truck seen at the manor. I'll have you drop me in Headcorn. There's a small inn and I can use the bicycle. They always carried a bicycle in the back of the truck."

Staring ahead at the road, Hans decided that would fit his plan well. He could get rid of her, check out the manor before the sun went down and move in for the kill during the night. He knew he was taking a chance. If he was discovered, he could say he was looking for her. What would happen after Dietrich was taken care of was more of a concern to him right now. Could he get to Aldeburgh on the coast without getting picked up? He had the name of a man in the small coastal town that would help him on his way to Norway. Everything seemed to be happening too quickly. He had to take his time and think. There could be no room for mistakes.

It was another hour before they saw the sign for Headcorn. There wasn't much traffic on the road and Richter began to memorize the landscape and roads. "How far is this manor from the village?" he asked.

"The edge of the property is about a mile. But it's closer to two miles by road to the manor house."

"It'll take me about two hours to get into London from here. What time do you want me back tomorrow?"

Eva thought for a moment. "How about noon? With this light traffic, we can be back in Cambridge by five.

"Noon it is."

The cars from Harwich arrived at Corry Woods just before lunch. Hiram Walker escorted the group into the library where there were message and telephone summaries laid out for Jack and Karl to review.

285

"Hiram, please show the Admiral his quarters. And let's get some food laid on in the dining room in twenty minutes."

Kaltenbach turned to leave the room, but stopped. "Commander, I notice everyone calls each other by their first names."

"Yes, sir. We are a little unorthodox. It came from our experiences on missions, first names worked best."

"This is not something prevalent throughout the British military."

Jack laughed, "Not at all, sir. I am sure there are many senior officers who would be rather upset with the way we do business."

Kaltenbach thought for a moment. "Perhaps I should also use only my first name? Would that be correct?"

Jack shook his head. "No, sir. Once an Admiral, always an Admiral. It's the curse of being a flag officer."

The tall German laughed. "Very well, commander. I will comply with your wishes."

"In that case, sir. My name is Jack."

Kaltenbach smiled and followed Hiram out the door.

"He's a good man, Jack." Karl had watched the exchange between the two and walked over to Jack holding a telex message from MI-5. "They still can't find Eva."

There were four officers sitting in the dining room when the Admiral walked in with Hiram Walker. They all got to their feet. Kaltenbach nodded to Phil, Karl and Jack. His eyes stopped on Erich Von Wollner who had joined them from the intelligence office.

"Admiral, may I present Erich Von Wollner?"

Erich stood next to his chair, his face expressionless.

Kaltenbach looked Erich in the eye. "We have met before. Is that not correct?"

Von Wollner nodded. "Yes, sir. It was in Bremen, before the war."

The older man studied Erich. "It is a pleasure to see you again, Erich."

The tension drained out of the room. Von Wollner smiled and said, "The pleasure is mine, Herr Admiral." The two men shook hands.

As Kaltenbach sat down next to Jack, he said, "When we finish, I would like to meet with you and Karl for a moment. I think it will make any further discussions more productive."

After a lunch of chicken and potatoes Jack and Karl escorted the Admiral to Jack's office. There was a note on the desk to call Noel Greene.

"Please have a seat, Admiral."

"Thank you, Jack. I wanted to talk with your and Karl about something which you will find hard to believe. It concerns an organization of which I am a part. Let me give you some background which will make what I tell you easier to understand."

Karl and Jack exchanged glances.

Kaltenbach continued. "The German officer corps has been a critical part of the German state since the time of Frederick the Great. The tradition of service and loyalty has been strong for hundreds of years and particularly so since the era of Von Bismarck. What has happened in my country since 1933 has been a horrible offshoot of that loyalty and dedication. We have an officer corps and an entire armed force that swore allegiance to one man, Hitler. The national spirit has been made subservient to the political party. It led Germany down the path to ultimate destruction." He stopped to light a cigarette. "There has been an 'underground' organization within the armed forces formed to resist the efforts of the Nazis and Hitler. In some cases it was localized, led by junior officers who had more heart than brains. Sometimes it has led to overt acts including the July attempt on Hitler's life. Despite the horrible purges over the last several months there still exists a secret organization that links the army, navy and air force. As you might suspect the SS with their integration to the party was never considered for inclusion. Why do I tell you this? Because I am a member. Furthermore I have key contacts within the other services, who also feel as I do. Our aim is to try and preserve Germany as a nation state. We are concerned that the aim of Stalin is to destroy Germany and her people forever. We are also concerned the Allied powers will stand by while this happens. It is the fundamental difference between the democracies and the totalitarian states. The United States and the British Empire, the only two powers who could balance the Soviet Union, will be tired of the war and will take the path of least resistance." The Admiral got up and began to pace while he talked. "We in our organization were grappling with how we organize a resistance to the Soviet post war effort while still engaged in a two front European war. And then you two knocked on my door. Gentlemen you and your organization and its connection with the British and American powers are the answer to our prayers."

The importance of what Kaltenbach just said stunned Jack. "So you are telling me you have a network throughout Germany that is dedicated to taking whatever actions are needed to preserve Germany and protect her against the Soviet Union."

The older man nodded. "And ensure the Nazis do as little damage as possible during their final death throes."

"What is this organization called?" Karl asked.

"We call it simply the network."

Over the next hour the Admiral described the structure and capability of the network. The seniority of the officers involved gave the network both power and access. When Kaltenbach ran down some of the names Karl and Jack were impressed.

"Sir, we will arrange for you to go to London tomorrow. I want you to meet with my immediate superior, Brigadier Greene. He is the key conduit into this new combined organization of which we are only the operators"

"I will look forward to it. Perhaps we can arrange for a civilian suit? I don't thing it would go over well to see a German officer in uniform walking the streets of the British capital."

"We will take every possible precaution to guard your identity and location. At least here in the country we have better security." Jack looked over as his door opened.

"Sorry to bother you, Skipper." It was Hiram Walker. "We've just had a call from the gate. There's a young woman asking to see Karl."

"Eva," Karl said, getting up and walking out past Hiram.

"Karl, wait," Jack said. "Something's not right. I hope it is Eva. But stay here while we get one of the boys to go down and bring her up to the house. There could be a sniper waiting for you." Hans Richter was still not located and Karl was at risk. "Hiram, get down to the gate and escort the lady up here. We'll watch through the window as you bring her up the walk."

Karl nodded. "All right, Jack. But if this is Eva, where is Richter?"

In five minutes they saw Hiram emerge from behind the hedge, which paralleled the drive. There was a woman walking at his side, it was Eva.

Karl met her in the main foyer. She ran into his arms. "Karl."

Still holding her, he said softly, "You're all right."

289

Eva pulled away and looked at him. "Karl, what's wrong."

His eyes turned steel gray. "Your partner works for Abwehr. We think he has been ordered to kill me and perhaps you."

"That makes no sense. I've known Hans for three years. We've been side by side the whole time. How could he work for Abwehr?"

They were walking back down the corridor to Jack's office.

"We have it on good authority," Karl said. The two turned into Jack's outer office. Hiram, Jack and the Admiral stood there. "Eva, I believe you have met Admiral Walter Kaltenbach?"

"My God."

Hans Richter pulled off the main road onto a small lane which ran into a grove of elm trees. He continued along the narrow path and pulled in next to a large tree, which blocked the truck from the main highway. He looked at his watch. The sun would be down shortly. Under cover of darkness he would make his way across the wide field to the northern edge of the main manor property. He didn't remember seeing a moon the last several nights and hoped he would have a dark night to accomplish his mission. Propping his head against the driver's window Richter closed his eyes and tried to get some rest.

It was almost 2300 hours when he decided to put his plan into action. If he could get in and out by 0100, he could be north of Colchester by daybreak. That would put him into Aldeburgh by 0800 and in search of his contact. The quicker he could get out of sight the better chance he would have of making it to Norway.

Richter checked his pistol. It was loaded and he had two extra clips of ammunition. Reaching down he checked the straps of the commando knife strapped to his calf. He also carried a length of strong line with wooden handles on each end to use as a garrote.

There was a sliver of a moon. With the broken cloud layer the night was dark. Making his way across the road he climbed the stone fence that marked the edge of the Corry Woods property. In the distance he could see there were several of the windows in the manor house still illuminated. Moving slowly and carefully he made his way to the inner stone fence, which surrounded the manor compound. Watching for any patrols, he saw or heard nothing. Perhaps they only man the security hut at the main gate, he thought. Hans moved east behind the low stone fence to give himself the best vantage point of the rear courtyard.

His plan was to hold in this position and observe the manor for thirty to forty five minutes. He turned up the collar on his coat and got as comfortable as he could.

Twenty minutes later he heard a door open at the back of the manor house. He saw a figure walk from the main house to an outbuilding which looked like an automobile garage. The man opened a door, turned on an interior light and went inside. Richter knew this was what he had been waiting for, a source to get specific locating data on Dietrich. Slowly he climbed over the stone fence making sure no one was in sight. He crept toward the outbuilding pulling his pistol out of his pocket. Carefully watching his steps to ensure he made no noise he stopped at the door. There were no sounds coming from inside but the light remained on. Richter tried the doorknob very gingerly. It moved in his hand and he could feel the mechanism begin to open the latch. With glacial speed he opened the door a fraction of an inch. He could see a man sitting in an easy chair reading a book.

Swinging the door open he pointed the pistol at the man and moved directly to his chair. "Don't say a word or you're a dead man."

The man looked up, confused. "What's this, who are you?"

Richter put the gun a foot from the man's face. "Shut up."

The man glared at him, but said nothing.

"All right, that's better. I don't want to hurt you. I just need information."

Still nothing.

"I'm looking for a German. His name is Karl Dietrich. I know he's here, but I need to know exactly where he is in the building."

"How the hell should I know, I'm the caretaker. I don't know their bloody names."

Richter lashed out with his pistol striking the man a glancing blow on the side of his head. The man reacted to the intended blow by pulling his head back, the pistol barely grazing the side of his head. Reaching up he grabbed Richter's gun with one hand and wrist with the other. A vicious snap resulted in Richter simultaneously dropping the gun and yelling out in pain. The man was quickly out of the chair and pointing a pistol at the German.

"Move and you're dead, Richter," the man said.

Hans Richter, holding his broken wris,t looked closely at the caretaker. He realized this man was in superb physical shape and knew exactly what he was doing with the gun. Slowly the man walked to the window drawing the curtains aside. The man kept the pistol aimed at Richter's chest watching the German constantly.

There were sounds of footsteps in the courtyard. Jack Stewart appeared at the open door, a pistol in his hand. "Well done, Jimmy," he said.

Jimmy Hunt nodded. "Thanks, Skipper." He kept the pistol aimed at Richter.

Phil Hatcher and the head of the security detachment entered the building, both carrying pistols. Jack turned to the Royal Marine captain. "Keith, turn out your lads. I want this man in handcuffs and leg restraints. And while you're at it, strip search him. And I mean thoroughly. Keep him under constant watch."

The tall young officer nodded. "Yes, sir. I'll be right back."

Stewart turned to Richter as Karl Dietrich came into the room. "Karl, it appears we have captured the man who was determined to kill you. I believe you have met."

Karl walked over to Richter who had moved with his back to the wall. He looked at Richter with fury in his eyes. "You are lucky I did not get to you first," he said in German. "You have one chance to escape the hangman's noose. We are going to ask you some questions. If you answer them truthfully you might escape with you life, I don't care. But what we are doing may help save German lives and Germany herself. So you will have to decide. Throw yourself away for a failed cause or make the decision to help us."

Several Marines moved into the room and took charge of the prisoner. After putting on handcuffs they escorted him back to the basement of the manor house.

Karl turned to Jimmy Hunt. "Thank you. You did very well. I hope your head is all right."

"Glad I ducked. He was determined to ring my bell, if you know what I mean."

Karl laughed. "Ring your bell. That is good. Jack, I think this calls for a drink."

"Karl, let me make one phone call and then we need to open a very old bottle of scotch."

293

Chapter Sixteen

Corry Woods
November 3, 1944
1515 Hours

Jack looked out the window of his office as two black sedans with Army escort trucks pulled into the long manor driveway. His phone call to Noel Greene did not result in a summons to London. Instead, he was told to stand by for a high level visit. Jack put on his cover and headed down to the main entrance.

"Commander, good to see you as always." Winston Churchill grinned at him and Jack saluted. The Prime Minister offered his hand. Noel Green exited the PM's car and greeted Jack.

"I briefed the PM on your little excitement last night," Green said.

Churchill entered the large doors with Jack at his side. "Have we found out anything of value from the Hun?" the PM asked.

"The real interrogation is going to take place in London. We were able to get the name of a contact in Aldeburgh."

"Splendid. One more fox driven to ground. The reason we are here is to talk with your newest guest. You can imagine my thoughts when I received the briefing."

Jack led them into the library. "We were just as surprised, sir. Our intent was to use the Admiral as an intelligence source. This is clearly a tremendous opportunity for all of us."

The men took seats at the table.

"Sir," Jack asked Churchill, "I'd like to bring my number two in to this meeting."

"By all means. We need to set a few ground rules before we talk with the Admiral," Churchill replied.

Noel Greene spoke up. "Prime Minister, to remind you Jack's number two is Karl Dietrich. You met him prior to the Whirlwind mission."

"A unique perspective, I would imagine."

Jack walked to the door and asked Hiram to get Karl to join them. "He has been immersed in English and has made remarkable progress. I'll help with any translation we need."

While they waited, the men discussed several points of the Whirlwind mission. The PM had read the report and was very interested in Jack's entry to the Depot with Karl.

The door opened and Dietrich entered. He was wearing commando battle dress with no rank insignia.

"Colonel, do come in. Sit down here." Churchill indicated the chair next to his own.

Karl said, "Thank you, sir."

"I read the mission report with great interest, Colonel. Your participation was key to the success of Whirlwind. I would like to personally thank you for a job very well done."

Dietrich looked very self-conscious. "Jack's team and the RAF were superb, sir."

"You made him your second in command," the Prime Minister asked with surprise.

"Yes, sir. He's as good as they come."

"I hope it is an indication of what we can expect from Double 00 in the future." Churchill sat back in his chair. "Tell us about Admiral Kaltenbach."

Karl described his long relationship with Walter. He also briefed as much as he knew of the Admiral's family and reputation within the armed forces. "I have talked with Von Wollner. He also feels the Admiral is loyal to Germany, not the Nazis and certainly not Hitler."

The Prime Minister looked around the table. "So, gentlemen, what is the best way to utilize our newest addition."

"We've thought about it, sir. It makes sense to let the Admiral determine how we will use him."

Noel Greene said, "Explain what you mean, Jack."

Jack looked and Karl and began. "Sir, the network's primary purpose is to preserve Germany and the German people from the Soviets. That is very much in line with what we want to try and accomplish, although we have a larger purpose which is to contain the Russians. Who better to tell us what is the best way to use the network?"

Churchill turned to Karl. "Colonel, do you agree?"

Karl had been working very hard to stay up with the conversation. "Yes, sir. Let Kaltenbach guide us for now."

Jack looked at Greene, then Churchill. "Do you want me to bring the Admiral in, sir?"

"Certainly."

Walter Kaltenbach entered with Phil Hatcher who assigned as his interpreter for the meeting. Jack introduced him to Noel Greene who nodded as they shook hands across the table.

Churchill rose and stood in front of Kaltenbach. "Prime Minister, this is Rear Admiral Walter Kaltenbach."

Extending his hand the Prime Minister said, "Admiral, it is a pleasure to meet you.

The Admiral bowed his head smartly and shook the Prime Minister's hand. "It is my honor to meet you, sir."

Everyone took their seats. Jack took the lead and said, "Prime Minister, if you would care to offer your thoughts."

"Gentlemen, I find it heartily encouraging that we have two distinguished German Officers sitting at the table today. Each in their own way determined that the Nazi Party and Herr Hitler were not the destiny of Germany. We are at the beginning of the end of a terrible time in the history of mankind. This battle between the world's democracies and the totalitarian dictatorships will be resolved in favor of the free peoples of this planet. The Soviet Union is the exception. The Stalinist era has been as brutal as any regime on earth. The only reason for our alliance with Mr. Stalin was the fear that Hitler was the greater evil. The problem now will be containing a different monster. With more men under arms and a greater number of land and air weapons, what must be going through Stalin's mind right now? As his red tide flows across the steppes of Russia into Eastern Europe, where will he stop? My personal opinion is that if he had any Navy to speak of, he might try to drive to the Atlantic. As it is I have every reason to believe the Soviets will occupy every country east of the agreed line of demarcation. The question we must answer here is how do we ensure they are contained?"

Walter Kaltenbach looked at Churchill. "Sir, there was a group within the German intelligence committee which felt the war was lost when the United States entered in 1941. The rest of the realistic thinkers knew when Hitler invaded Russia in June of 1942 that it was just a matter of time. All of us were surprised at the early successes, but we held no illusions. The country is too immense, the weather too extreme and the Communists realized it was a fight to the death. The network was born during that summer. Slowly the contacts and feelers went from friends within the different services to other friends. From that point a shadow organization began to form. The purpose was simply to do everything in our power to preserve Germany and her people. We knew the might of the major powers of the world would be unleashed on us. The factor we could never overcome was the United States. They possessed resources we could only dream of. Two thousand miles of ocean between us, the country was totally out of our reach. Our U-boats could nip around the edges, but they could never stop the flood of tanks and planes and eventually men. Certainly we made some attempts toward attacking the United States. Large bombers were designed, to no avail. The V-2 program was precursor to the V-4 program, a missile with the range to reach New York. The key to both of these was the production of a chain reaction weapon." The Admiral stopped for a moment and cleared his throat. "We were overwhelmed by the lack of new material, the bombing campaign and the drain on our manpower. So we struggled on with the fight. What else was there for us to do? The reason I am telling you this is to provide some basis for what I feel is the most critical item we can do to save Europe for the future."

Churchill sat quietly as Phil Hatcher finished the translation. "Admiral, go on, please."

Kaltenbach nodded and continued. "While we were not able to produce these advanced weapons, that does not mean we did not have the knowledge to do so. There are two areas in which we have extensive knowledge and capability. Our offensive rocket program is very advanced. What you saw with the V-2 is only the beginning.

The other area which might surprise your analysts is our progress in developing a chain reaction weapon from uranium."

"You're quite correct, Admiral," Noel Greene broke in. "Our agents in Norway felt your heavy water project never was successful. We also had it from Hitler's secretariat that the program had been abandoned."

Waiting for the translation, they could see Kaltenbach was getting impatient with the language delay. "Yes, you are right. The heavy water project was abandoned. But that was the more visible effort. What was well concealed was a second program run by the Luftwaffe. That group designed what they call a production reactor, which will create the special uranium material needed for the weapon. They have also designed the actual weapon, which was to be carried by our largest bomber, the Focke Wulf 200."

Jack broke in, "If the design falls into Soviet hands, they will be able to produce an atomic weapon. And if they get the rocket experts too, they could possibly gain the ability to fire a long range missile with a weapon which theoretically could destroy a large city." He remembered his discussions with Ian Thompson on the potential destructive power of an atomic weapon.

"Exactly so." Kaltenbach answered.

Churchill was surprising quiet, looking at the table, lost in thought.

Noel Greene asked Kaltenbach, "Not to put words in your mouth, Admiral, but what I think you are suggesting is a plan to deny the Soviets the knowledge of the rocket systems and the weapon."

Nodding vigorously after the translation, he said, "That is exactly what I am suggesting. Furthermore I will interface with the network to take whatever action is needed to safeguard the people and information. There are two key members of the network we must contact, Reinhard Gehlen, the intelligence director for the eastern front and Wolfgang Froehlich, head of Luftwaffe intelligence. If we can get them to agree, this would be very powerful."

Jack looked at Karl. The implication of what the Admiral had said was clear in his serious expression.

The Prime Minister looked up from the table. "We have an opportunity that we must utilize to the fullest. Jack, you can count on Double 00 having the highest priority for material, transport and support services. I will ensure that includes the American forces. Noel, I want you on your way to Washington straight away. Plan on briefing the President, Leahy and Donovan at a minimum. However, our knowledge of the network will stay in this room. We will only say we have special knowledge, not how we came by that information. Does everyone understand?"

There was a chorus of assent.

What took place over the next two months would never appear in any official history of the war. Kaltenbach was true to his word and agreement by the key members of the network was obtained. There were also understandings reached on an individual basis which resulted in the eventual emergence of West Germany as a pillar upon which post war Europe would depend. The most striking example of this arrangement was the rise of Reinhard Gehlen to the head of West Germany's Federal Intelligence Service. This was far in the future as the Double 00 organization prepared for their last wartime effort on the continent.

November 27, 1944

"Commander, the new agents are standing by in the classroom." Gillian Andrews was now Stewart's administrative assistant.

"Thank you, Gillian. Tell them I'll be down in five minutes." Jack was not sure how this was going to play out. One of the four new agents was Pam. He'd received the call from Tommy Hudson last week. She was getting ready to pass out of the Arisaig training course with extremely high marks. Tommy had echoed McClaren's praises and reminded Jack that the expanding organization needed manpower. It took a long time for Jack to come to the conclusion that their personal relationship could not be an obstacle in front of Pam if this is what she wanted to do. However, Jack was now having second thoughts. The four new agents arrived earlier this morning and Jack had still not seen her. He stood up, tugged his tunic in place and strode out the door.

"Atten-shun!" Petty Officer Andrews called as Jack walked in the classroom.

The four agents stood to attention beside their chairs. Pam and Cynthia Birdwell were both from the RAF. One of their male counterparts, Steven Riggs was from the Royal Marines and there was one American, Lieutenant Andy Hallowell from the U.S. Army Rangers.

"Please take your seats." Jack waited until they were all seated. "Welcome to Corry Woods. My name is Jack Stewart. You are here because you were better than your peers during the training course at Arisaig. You are also here because you volunteered for hazardous assignment. At any time during your advanced training, if you decide this is not your cup of tea, you may leave without prejudice. What we do here is train you to do jobs that most people want no part of. Do not let the glamour of the secret service fool you. This is dangerous and dirty work. We are involved in a vicious fight and there is nothing grand or glorious about it. But is it necessary? We think so. Our job is to make sure our side prevails in any encounter, with whatever enemy we might have to deal with. You will be trained by some of the best operators in the world. They know their stuff. Learn quickly and learn thoroughly. I can tell you your life and the lives of your teammates will depend on it. Now are there any questions?"

Riggs raised his hand. "Sir, when will we start our training?"

Jack looked at his watch. "Your first meeting with Captain Howe will take place in fifteen minutes. There will be time later today to unpack and get settled in your quarters. Any other questions?" The other woman raised her hand.

"Sir, are we to expect to remain at Corry Woods full time, or will we have the opportunity to go into London?"

Jack put his hands behind him and looked at the four of them. "For the foreseeable future, plan on being here at the manor. Your training will be intense and we don't have a lot of time to get ready. If that is all, please carry on. Let Petty Officer Andrews know if you need anything right now." Jack turned and walked out of the room. The four agents had stood as he left. Jack felt very uncomfortable with Pam in her role and the junior member of his command. But it was what it was and he would make it work.

During the evening meal, there were introductions around the mess. Pam's classmates quickly realized there was an unusual connection when Phil Hatcher greeted her warmly. Jack guessed she would have some interesting explaining to do with Cynthia tonight.

After dinner Jack returned to his office. He really didn't have any pressing work to do, but he suspected there might be a visitor.

There was a knock on his door and it swung open. Pam looked around the door and looked relieved to see Jack was alone. "Do you have a minute?" she asked.

Jack stood up, grinning. "As your fiancé, there can only be one answer to that question."

She closed the door and walked over to him. They kissed and she said, "This is going to be a bit strange, I'm afraid."

"That, my dear lady, would be an understatement. But we will make this work." They both sat down on his couch. "I saw your training jacket from Scotland."

Pam leaned back warily. "And what did you find out?"

"It seems that you're pretty good at those things that we find valuable in our little world."

"Jack, I enjoyed the training. I suppose part of it was because I finally was able to appreciate what you do." She sat back on the couch and took his hand.

"Are you sure you are ready to take the next step?" Jack looked very serious.

"What do you mean?"

"This is not the training world, Pam. We are all getting ready for what may prove to be more dangerous than anything we have done before. That puts me in a tough spot. How do I assign you to a mission that I know you might not come back from?"

"You have to treat me just like everyone else. It's as simple as that."

"No, Pam. It's not as simple as that. I happen to love you. I want us to spend the rest of our lives together. It will not be easy to make those decisions. Not by a long shot."

"Let's deal with that when the time comes. Until then, I intend to be the best trainee you have ever seen."

"I wasn't kidding today. Terry, Karl and Gerhard, are very good. Learn from them and if the time ever comes, you'll do fine."

December 5, 1944
Corry Woods

"Brigadier, we have established a good working communication system with the network. From our contact throughout the key parts of the system we have been able to close in on what we think is the key element. It's now time to move to the next phase of this operation." Jack was sitting at the head of the large conference table. In attendance at the meeting were Dietrich, Hatcher, Von Wollner and Admiral Kaltenbach. Noel Greene had come alone from London, having just returned from his trip to the United States.

"Very well, Jack, proceed."

Jack opened a briefing folder. "Running parallel with the initial heavy water experiments in Norway was another group of physicists working from a different theory. Interestingly, all of them were at one time at the Kaiser Wilhelm Institute. The leader of the light water group was a fairly well known academic, Walter Heisenberg. It appears the groups diverged in their philosophies just as the war broke out. The second team we call the Leipzig group was under the leadership of Max Kleiman. This second group apparently was able to get support from the Luftwaffe. There was a connection with Ernst Udet, a well-known aviator from the first war, who had risen to General and head of Luftwaffe project development. Goering was determined to produce a weapon, which would make his bombers the most deadly force on earth. A country estate in southern

Germany was converted to a research compound, which housed the scientists and their families. There were also a number of industrial facilities in the nearby factory section of Leipzig, which were commandeered for research and development by the group. The compound is located about twenty miles north of Leipzig near the town of Falkenberg. According to General Froehlich, head of Luftwaffe intelligence, the group is still at the compound. There are thirty-three primary scientists and about one hundred family members. The entire area is under Luftwaffe special security. It is Froehlich's opinion that all the knowledge and files are at that location."

Greene held up his hand. "Jack, refresh my memory. Where is Leipzig in the agreed upon areas of occupation?"

"It will be in the Soviet area of responsibility. The U.S. Ninth Army is currently moving toward the Leipzig area, as is the Soviet 2nd Guards Tank Army. Our intelligence and the network have confirmed the Germans are putting up their strongest resistance on the Eastern Front. The Third Panzer Army is facing the Russians, on a line extending south and west of Warsaw. There are equipment and manpower shortages on the German side but there is still plenty of fight left. Everyone feels the Soviets will begin their next big offensive after the first of the year."

"So if we do nothing and the German scientists stay in Falkenberg they will be caught in the Soviet web?"

"Yes, sir, that's the way we see it." Jack glanced around the table and there were looks of agreement.

Greene rubbed his eyes. "Where are our closest forces right now?

Phil Hatcher pointed to the large wall map. "Units of the Ninth U.S. Army have reached the Roer on a line from Julich to Linnich."

"That's a long way to Leipzig," Greene said.

"Yes, sir. But we would still like to put together a plan to try and get our people in there before the Russians." Jack knew this was the time to get Greene's support.

"Let's see what can be done. Although I think it will be a serious problem any way you approach it. There's one more piece of information. General Bill Miller has taken over OSS forward headquarters in London. They have recent information that there is some remnant of the heavy water program located near Haigerloch. They will be trying to get a team in there as soon as possible. I think we can concentrate on the Leipzig group for now."

December 7, 1944

Erich placed all of the agents into planning teams to look at various aspects of the potential mission. For many of the new people this was the first time they had been briefed into the mission. Each team was sequestered in different rooms working on their portion of the plan.

Karl's team was looking at the security set up for the compound near Falkenberg. Terry Howe was examining photographs taken by a P-38 photo recon mission flown two days prior. There were a series of shots, which covered the main compound, the surrounding road system and forest. The definition in the photo left much to be desired but it did appear there was very little in the way of hard security points or a formal perimeter. The only unusual feature was a landing strip about four miles from the compound. It appeared to have been abandoned some time ago.

A partial list of German scientists and their families had been received from the network. Pam was looking at the list with Phil to determine logistic support needs when the time came.

"Phil, wait a minute. I know this name," she said.

Hatcher looked up as did Karl. "What do you mean? What name?"

"Kleiman, Max Kleiman. And there is his wife, Greta. Pam was going down the list with her finger.

Karl walked over to them. "How do you know Kleiman?" he asked.

"It was 1934 or 35, no it was 34. Kleiman was an exchange professor at Oxford and my father was his sponsor. They were there for three months. I know the whole family." Pam looked up at the two men. "We spent a lot of time with them while they were at Oxford."

Eva, Gerhard and Jack examined the logistical problems of how to get into Leipzig and return the scientists back to Allied territory.

"Jack, you're talking about trying to travel through two armies which are conducting active combat operations. Then try to travel back with over one hundred civilians, including children and all their records." Gerhard was looking at a map of central Germany.

"But it's not a continuous front. There must be gaps we could get through." Jack was thinking out loud.

"I spent most of my infantry time on the Eastern front. Sure there were large gaps in the lines. But it was often very fluid. You never knew where you might find combat units repositioning."

Eva sat down at the table next to Jack. "Unless you can come up with some method to move quickly across open country we'll be limited to traveling by road. That would increase the chance of running into combat forces, to say nothing of security police."

Late that evening Jack and Karl were sitting in the library having a drink when Walter Kaltenbach entered.

"Good evening, gentlemen. May I join you?"

"Let me get you a drink, Admiral." Jack went over to the bar and poured a measure of brandy into a large glass. "We're wrestling with the Leipzig problem. Do you have any thoughts?"

The Admiral accepted his drink from Jack and sat down on the long couch. "I have talked with each of the team members and I think we might be overlooking a possible answer to our problem."

The comment drew a quick look from Karl. "It must be the wisdom of age." He smiled at his old friend.

"Not wisdom, my friend. But simply the devious mind of an intelligence officer. You have been trying to figure out how to negotiate a difficult trip through very dangerous country. Why make the trip at all? The logistic effort to move that many people across hostile territory might be too difficult and certainly is dangerous to everyone involved."

"I guess I'm not following you, Admiral." Jack couldn't see the connection.

"It is very simple. Don't try to bring the scientists all the way back to Allied controlled territory. But get them out of the compound and to another location. One which can be reasonably reached by an armored spearhead with sufficient troops and equipment to ensure a safe recovery."

"Sounds simple enough, but I see two slight flaws. How do we get the scientists to trust us and where do we go?" Jack asked.

"The answer to one of those questions came in on the latest network dispatch. General Froehlich gave us the name of a scientist who is connected to the network. We can use him for verification to the rest of the group."

This sounded promising to Jack. "Who is this scientist?"

The Admiral smiled, "He is the only one of the group who is military. The man is Major Manfred Holz. Apparently Froehlich used Holz for keeping track of the group's activities.

Chapter Seventeen

Kielce, Poland
Headquarters
2nd Guards Tank Army
December 10, 1944

A Ford two and a half ton truck with a red star painted on the door bounced along the rutted dirt road, which led to a large farm house. It was bitterly cold and the heater of the truck barely put out enough warmth for comfort. The passenger was wearing a heavy great coat with the insignia of a major in the NKVD, the Main Directorate of State Security. Two days ago Dmitri Ivanov had presented his orders to Marshall Konstantin Rossokovsky, commander of the 1st Byelorussian Front. The orders, signed by Stalin, directed all support be provided to Major Ivanov on a mission critical to state security. Rossokovsky had been very busy, but made time to see Ivanov. Ten minutes after the meeting concluded the Ford truck left for Kielce.

The driver, Pushkin, saw a military policeman standing on the side of the road. "Comrade, we're looking for the 2nd Guards Headquarters."

Walking across the road the man pointed to the farm house. "It's over there. Now keep the road clear." There was a constant stream of tracked and wheeled vehicles moving west. Pushkin pulled over to the house and stopped.

After getting out and stretching, Major Ivanov walked back to the rear of the covered truck. Pulling open the canvas flap he said, "How are you doing?"

A large man wearing an Army overcoat and wool cap spoke up. "Ready for food and a piss break."

"Get the men out and see if you can get them some food inside. And, Reuss, keep everyone close. I don't want a lot of questions."

"Understood."

Ivanov walked up to the farmhouse porch. There were two soldiers standing on each end of the wide platform with machine pistols slung over their shoulders. One of the men saluted as Ivanov opened the door and went inside. There was a sergeant sitting at a desk reading an open folder. "Sergeant, my name is Ivanov. I'm looking for the chief of staff."

The man looked up, his face expressionless. Getting up he said, "Just a minute, sir. I'll see if he's available."

Ivanov looked around seeing the normal hectic activity of an operational headquarters.

"Please come with me, major."

Brigadier Vassily Rossovich was writing on a pad of message blanks when Ivanov entered the small bedroom turned into an office. "Please sit down, major. Give me a moment while I finish this." The sergeant remained standing while the chief of staff put down his pen, read the message and held it out. "Get this transmitted right away."

The man didn't answer but took the paper and left the room closing the door behind him.

"Now, what can I do for you?" Rossovich looked tired. His tunic was wrinkled and there was a food stain on the front.

"Here are my orders, sir." Ivanov handed him the packet of papers.

Reading through the packet Rossovich rubbed his bloodshot eyes. Turning the page he saw the signature. "This is quite clear. We are ready to do whatever you need."

"Sir, I have a special team with me. There are six men who have been trained for this mission. We have been traveling for over a week. I would like to get them fed and then billeted somewhere."

"That is no problem."

"Here is the difficult part. What I am going to tell you is highly classified. But it is essential you understand the type of support we will need."

The Brigadier nodded. "Go ahead."

"My team is made up of former German commandos. They were captured over a year ago. They have joined us and have taken part in several actions against the Germans."

"Very interesting. I would never trust a German."

"These men are the type who put their own survival first. And we have made it financially worthwhile and agreed that their families will be protected after the defeat of Germany. We have the missions against the Wermacht to hold over their heads. If they betray us we will make sure the story of their treachery is well publicized."

Rossovich smiled. "I understand. I agree we need to do whatever is required to win this war."

312

"Sir, what we are doing is trying to make sure we win the next war." Ivanov saw the quizzical look on the Brigadier's face.

"The next war? I'm working to prepare the Army for our next offensive against the Germans. It will take everything we have. Now you're talking about the next war?"

"Brigadier, when this war is over the world will be a very different place. Germany may cease to exist. France and England will try to re-establish their empires. This is the opportunity of a century for the socialist movement. The peoples of the world will have a chance to take their destiny in their own hands. But they must have the Soviet Union as their beacon. There must be a powerful force to counterbalance the strength of the United States."

"Major, I'm a dumb soldier. I understand tanks and how to attack the enemy. But I can't figure out what you're doing in this freezing cesspool worrying about the next war."

"Sir, we have learned of a group of German scientists near Leipzig. My mission is to find those scientists and make sure they are brought back to Russia."

The older man had a slight frown on his face. "Leipzig! That's over 600 kilometers from here. And if you haven't noticed, there are about 200,000 German soldiers between here and there."

Ivanov nodded. "I am not underestimating the difficulty of achieving our objective. That is why I'm here."

"Which brings me to that very question. If you're trying to get to Leipzig, why wouldn't you be talking to Koniev? His 1st Ukrainian Front will be moving toward that part of Germany."

"Because Marshall Koniev does not have Milachenko."

The brigadier's eyes opened wider. "What do you know of Milachenko?"

"We know that his reconnaissance troops are legends in the Red Army. If I am going to get my team to Leipzig, past the Germans and before the Americans, I need Milachenko."

"Well, if I had to select anyone who might be able to make it to Leipzig and back, it would be Aleksei Milachenko."

"It is imperative I locate Captain Milachenko and talk with him about this mission."

The older man laughed. "Finding Milachenko depends on whether or not he wants to be found. If he's on operations you will find it difficult to track him down. Although at some point he will return to the Division Headquarters for new assignments. I'd recommend you watch the 66th Division's headquarters. He'll show up eventually."

"Yes, sir. Thank you."

**Two Kilometers East of
Starachowice, Poland
December 10, 1944
2320 Hours**

Three men slowly worked their way from a patch of dense underbrush toward an earth embankment where lines of barbed wire were visible in the patchy moonlight. Each of the men wore the uniform of the Soviet infantry including winter forage hats. They carried silenced Makarov 9mm pistols and each wore a large killing knife in a scabbard. Edging toward what was now easily discernable as a reinforced infantry position, they made no sound. The lead man held out his hand to the other two who froze in position. All three could see a single figure emerge from behind the earth wall and stop.

The man leaned his rifle against a small tree and reached into his overcoat. As he struck a match to light his cigarette the man did not see a hand reaching across his face until it was too late. A vicious slash across the man's neck resulted in a gurgling sound but no scream. Laying the now dead sentry on the ground the first man motioned to his comrades to move forward.

Captain Aleksei Milachenko knew this position was the battalion command post for a large sector of the German line. By watching during the day they had learned the small headquarters was not well defended. He estimated no more than five Germans would be inside the crude wooden hut. "Put it on," he whispered to the second man.

Quickly the man pulled on the dead sentry's overcoat and grabbed the helmet. Sergeant Sergei Voloshin, now playing the part of the battalion sentry, walked to the corner of the building and casually moved around the corner. In a moment he reappeared and motioned Aleksei forward.

There were no windows on the front of the hut, only a wooden door. Light was visible under the door. Aleksei motioned to the third man, Corporal Anatoly Taisen, who understood the command. Dropping down on his hands and knees, Anatoly looked under the gap at the bottom of the door. He paused for a moment and indicated the number "four" with his fingers to Aleksei, who nodded.

The intent of this raid was to capture a prisoner. Ideally the prisoner would be a senior officer, but any information they could get would help the division breach this portion of the German line. Lining up at the door Sergei would be the first man through the door. His job would be to locate the senior person and neutralize him. Aleksei would be next and then Anatoly. It was up to them to take out the remaining personnel. Standing ready Aleksei whispered, "Go."

Bursting through the door, Sergei still wore the German overcoat. At the far side of the room a Wermacht major looked up from his desk with a look of surprise and confusion. Lunging across the room Sergei threw the German rifle at the officer, pulling his knife and extending his arm to put the knife against the man's throat.

Aleksei looked to the right and saw a man who turned toward him at the sound. One round from the silenced Makarov hit the man in the right temple blowing off the front part of his skull. Spinning to his left Aleksei watched as Anatoly fired and hit a third man standing on the left side of hut. The impact threw the man against the log wall. A fourth man was reaching for his rifle in the far back corner of the hut. Aleksei fired once more hitting the man in the upper left chest, knocking him to the ground. The entire event was over in four seconds.

Sergei stripped the officer of his pistol and was tying his hands behind his back with a small length of rope.

"Gag him." Aleksei ordered.

"These two are wounded," Anatoly said.

The captain walked over to the first man who had slid down the wall and was sitting against the wood gasping for breath, a large bloodstain spreading across his chest. Aleksei put his silencer against the man's forehead and pulled the trigger. There was a splatter of tissue against the wall and the man fell to his left. Walking toward the soldier he'd shot in the chest, he looked down to see a young Wermacht private, his face contorted with pain. The man's breath came in sharp gasps. Aleksei looked the man in the eyes, raised the pistol and aimed at the soldier's head. In a split second the young private realized what was happening, his eyes opening wide in horror. Milachenko pulled the trigger.

"Is he ready to travel?" Aleksei wanted to get away from the German lines as quickly as possible.

Sergei yanked the major to his feet. "Ready," he said. The German officer had a wad of cloth in his mouth and a piece of cloth holding it in place. His hands were tied behind him.

"Anatoly, you take the point. Back the way we came."

The corporal nodded and moved to the door. Cautiously looking outside he said, "It's clear"

Headquarters, 66ᵗʰ Infantry Division
December 11, 1944
1645 Hours

Steam rose from the metal mess cups in the men's hands. It was cold outside and the hot metal felt good to the tired soldiers. Aleksei Milachenko sat on a log next to the cooking fire and sipped his soup. Sergeant Voloshin and Corporal Taisen squatted next to their commander, quietly eating. The three men had turned their prisoner over to one of Milachenko's platoon commanders who would take the German officer to the field interrogators. Aleksei had watched several sessions conducted by the military intelligence group. It was very effective and often resulted in the death of the subject. That fact didn't bother Milachenko in the least. German soldiers had killed his entire family during the fall of 1941, in the Ukraine. The desire to kill Germans burned inside Aleksei Milachenko.

The twenty-four year old Russian commanded the Reconnaissance Company of the 66th Division. In the Red Army the Recon troops were the commando counterparts of other armies. Often operating behind enemy lines, the Recon companies were the most feared troops in the Red Army. It was common practice by the Germans to execute on the spot any Recon troops they captured. In a war of brutal hatred between the Germans and Soviets, the level of vicious retribution was highest in the Recon companies.

"Where to next, captain?" Voloshin finished his soup and lit a cigarette.

Milachenko wiped his mouth with the back of his hand. "I need to talk to the Ops section. Why don't you two go see if you can get some sleep. Tell Lieutenant Kalinski I'll be back at the command post as soon as I find out what they want us to do." Kalinski was Aleksei's executive officer of the one hundred man company.

"Yes, sir." The two men moved off toward a cluster of tents.

It took Aleksei ten minutes to walk to the ramshackle building which was serving as division headquarters. There weren't many buildings left in one piece after the recent fighting in this sector. He was able to find Major Ledbedev in the operations tent in back of the building.

"Aleksei, you look like shit!" The major was a larger than life character but a superb soldier and reliable in a fight.

Milachenko smiled, "It's that crappy food you keep feeding us. When are you going to get us some good beef instead of these scrawny Polish chickens?"

"I have it on good authority that after we capture Berlin we will get everything we need."

Aleksei laughed and sat down on a folding chair. "Promises, that's all you ever give me."

Ledbedev turned serious. "Aleksei, I just had a visit from an NKVD major named Ivanov.

On hearing the abbreviation for the Ministry of State Security, Milachenko's demeanor changed also. "NKVD? What's going on?" The less anyone had to do with the secret police organization, the better.

"It seems they want the use of your services."

"What? Me, work for the NKVD?"

The major nodded. "This Ivanov talked with the General and it seems he has permission to take you for detached duty."

Milachenko shook his head. "Detached duty? The big offensive is getting ready to start. Who's going to take my company?"

"We'll promote Kalinski to captain and he can take over until you get back. Any problem with that?"

"No, he's ready. That's not what's bothering me. This could be the last big push by the army. I've been with the Division since we started. I don't want to miss the final show."

"Out of our hands. Hopefully you'll only be away a short time. But for now you need to find this Ivanov and get your orders. They wouldn't tell me shit so let me know what you can after to talk to him."

Aleksei stood up. "Yeah."

Milachenko found Major Ivanov on the far side of the division assembly area. There were several men in army uniforms standing around a warming fire. The major stood out from the group in his heavy great coat. His uniform was too clean for the front.

The men turned as Aleksei walked up. He saluted. "Major Ivanov?"

Returning the salute, the major said, "Yes, I'm Ivanov."

"I'm Milachenko."

Ivanov nodded. "Let's go in the tent."

The two men sat on a thick tarp. "Captain, I have a set of orders I would like you to read." He handed the packet to Aleksei.

Milachenko opened the papers and began to slowly read. He turned the page and stared at the paper for a moment.

Ivanov took the packet back. "Captain, you have a reputation as one of the best forward operators in the Red Army. We have a situation that requires a mission far into German occupied territory, in fact Germany itself. The successful completion of this mission could very well decide the future of the world for decades to come."

"You say into Germany. I assume you mean before the army?"

"That's right. We will start the mission preparations immediately. The sooner we are ready to proceed to the objective area, the better our chances of success."

Milachenko crossed his legs, leaning toward the major. "And what are we going to do?"

"Captain, we are on a mission to take control of a group of German scientists who have been working on an extremely powerful weapon. If we can bring them back to Russia they will be able to continue their work and the weapon will belong to the Soviet Union. If we can get the weapon before the Americans or the English, no one will challenge us as we spread the socialist revolution throughout the world."

Aleksei Milachenko was not a devoted socialist, but he was a professional soldier. He understood the need to produce weapons that were superior to the enemy. "Where exactly do we have to go?"

The major pulled out a map of Germany and traced a path to the Leipzig area. "Our intelligence places this group in a research compound north of Leipzig, near a town called Falkenberg." He pointed to an area approximately 40 kilometers north of Leipzig, just south of the Elbe River.

"There happens to be a German Panzer Army in our path. How are we supposed to get through their defensive lines?" Aleksei had seen the German positions and knew it was going to be a tough fight for his division to punch through.

"That is where I come into the picture. Certainly there is no realistic way a Soviet unit can force their way to Leipzig. But a German unit escorting prisoners to the rear has a chance of making it. My plan, is to mix in with the shock troops during the coming offensive. The last major defensive barrier is the River Oder. The plan is to gather our forces at the Oder for the last big push into Southern Germany. From the River to Falkenberg is about 100 kilometers. During the confusion of the breakout from the Oder, with our Germans acting as guards…"

"Our Germans? What do you mean, our Germans?"

The major could see he had touched on a problem area with the young captain. "Those men you see standing out there are former German commandos. They saw the wisdom of switching allegiance after their capture over a year ago. I have used them on several missions and they did their jobs well. I hate the Germans as much as you do. But these men have performed for us and we need them to get us to Falkenberg."

Milachenko cut him off. "You mean we let them control us as we pass through units from their own army? What keeps them from switching sides again?"

"These men have no illusions about what will happen to them if we don't get back to our lines alive. They know that the

NKVD will be ordered to hunt down their families as the Red Army sweeps across Germany. They know they have to get us back to our lines."

This is crazy thought Aleksei, trusting our lives and the success of the mission to Germans. And these are Germans who have sold out their own country. My God, what could this man be thinking. "I don't know, I have doubts."

"Captain, we all have doubts. I am open to any ideas you might have."

"And if we make it to these scientists, then what? We'll be hundreds of kilometers behind the lines."

Major Ivanov sat back in his chair. "I can only tell you there is a plan for execution when we arrive at the compound. Right now I can't tell you anymore. You'll have to trust me and select your ten best men for the mission."

Sergeant Fritz Heigel formerly of the 14th Panzer Grenadier's sat next to the fire smoking a cigarette. He tried not to think too much anymore. Sometimes a man has to do what is necessary to survive. When he was given the chance a year ago to work for the Russians or march east toward the Ural Mountains and a freezing death as a slave laborer, it was an easy decision. He didn't owe Adolph Hitler or Germany a thing. He had joined the Wermacht in 1938. It was either that or go to prison. The army had been a decent life. Do what the officers tell you and you won't have problems. Food was plentiful and there was an occasional furlough where you could drink yourself into a stupor as long as you were back on time. Now Fritz Heigel only owed loyalty to himself.

When it's all over I'll still be around, he told himself, one way or another.

"Fritz, go with this man here and get our rations for tonight." Werner Reuss was the senior man among the Germans and Major Ivanov had given him the job of squad leader.

Heigel didn't much care for Reuss but it served no purpose to argue. He got up and followed the Russian mess sergeant who had been sent over from headquarters. God he hated Russian food. It was almost as bad as Russian cigarettes. These people were the scum of the earth.

Werner Reuss found escape in doing his job as a non-commissioned officer. As one of the most senior sergeants in his regiment, he had been given more responsibility as the junior officers were killed in combat. At one time he even imagined a battlefield commission. Then he and his platoon were captured following a confused battle outside Uriyusk. He had heard that German POWs in Russian captivity would not survive. Combat had never intimidated him, but when he saw the looks from his Russian captives, he was terrified. He would never see his wife and children again. When his interrogators found out he was a member of the scout platoon of his regiment they offered him a way out. He had never looked back.

Chapter Eighteen

Corry Woods
December 17, 1944

"Jack we just got a call from London. The Germans have launched a major offensive in Belgium. Sounds like they are driving hard toward the sea." Hiram Baker laid several pieces of notepaper on Stewart's desk.

"Major offensive? What with? Didn't all of our intelligence tell us they were trying to conserve what little fuel and ammunition they had? How can they go on the offensive?"

"It looks like there are three German armies involved. Erich is gathering additional information. We should brief everyone as soon as possible."

Jack got up and walked to the door. "Gillian, get in touch with Dietrich, Hatcher and the Admiral. Tell them we need to get together in thirty minutes. Enough time for you, Hiram?"

"Should be fine."

Erich Von Wollner stood at the large map of Europe and pointed to the Ardennes region of Belgium. "Yesterday morning, three German armies launched an offensive in the Ardennes forest of Belgium. Estimated troop strength on the German side, 200,000 men and perhaps 2000 tanks. They struck a portion of the Allied line that was relatively thinly defended and in some cases with units that were not fully up to combat strength. So far the Panzer spearheads are making progress. The weather is bad and has almost totally shut down Allied air operations."

"They are going for Antwerp. That is the only thing they could be thinking." Admiral Kaltenbach was pointing at the wall chart with his pencil. "But they are fools. The only way they could put together enough troops, fuel and ammunition for something of this magnitude is to strip the Eastern Front. They are opening the gates to the Soviets."

Karl Dietrich sat back with his arms folded on his chest. "This will affect our plans for Leipzig. If the Allies are focused on this offensive the Russians can attack and roll across Germany. The Soviet line of advance will take the southern units, probably the 1st Ukrainian Front, directly over Breslau, Dresden and Leipzig. And I suspect with the U.S. Ninth Army occupied with this offensive, they will get to Leipzig before the Americans."

Hatcher added, "If the Russians start flowing across the southern plain of Germany, who knows what will happen to our group of scientists. The government may move them but more likely they would decide to strike out on their own. Once that happens we're out of luck."

"We need to get someone in there now to lay out plans for our extraction of the group." Jack knew they didn't have any other option.

Karl looked at Jack and said, "I think I should go. I know the area well and we're going to have to figure out how the security troops will play into this."

"What if the troops recognize you?" Phil asked.

"We need to come up with a good disguise and a solid background story that will satisfy any questions," Karl answered.

Jack stood up. "All right, let's start getting a background story together and we'll reconvene at 1300 to work out the details.

As the others filed out of the room Karl remained in his seat looking at Jack. "You know what we have to do, don't you?"

Sitting back down, Jack shook his head. "I never thought it would come to this. How can I send Pam into Germany? Christ, Karl, she has no experience."

"Jack, none of us did before our first mission. She did very well in training and Terry said she excels at everything. If we go in as a man and wife it will be a better cover. Her connection with Kleiman and his family are crucial. You have to separate your feelings. The mission has a better chance of success if she's there. You've got to see that."

"Shit." Jack knew the right answer but he didn't want Pam going in harm's way. "All right, if we're going to do this, let's do it right."

A message was sent to the network asking for the best way to insert a team of two into Falkenberg. Over a period of ten days a plan emerged that had been coordinated by several parts of the network. As Karl and Jack watched the pieces come together it demonstrated a remarkable capability to operate within the bureaucratic world of the Third Reich.

Initially Karl and Pam would come ashore in occupied Denmark. Met by a member of the network, they would be given authentic identity papers and travel permits. They would travel by car to Hamburg where they would take the train to Leipzig via Berlin. Major Holz would meet them in Leipzig and bring them to Falkenberg. The military situation at present made this route by far the safest compared to any other. A parachute insertion at this time of year and in the heart of Germany made no sense at all. This was their best chance for success.

The battle in the Ardennes was now the major focus on the Western Front. Allied armies were repositioning to try and contain the German advance. It was still quiet on the Eastern Front.

Falkenberg Research Facility
Germany
December 24, 1944

Despite being surrounded by some of the most devastated cities in Germany, the Luftwaffe's main theoretical research facility remained untouched. Near the town of Falkenberg, the property was originally a large country estate, owned by a Jewish banker from Leipzig. Confiscated in 1939, the Luftwaffe had expanded the property with more buildings, which included some of the best research labs in the Reich.

Led by Max Kleiman, the Falkenberg group was convinced they had perfected a process, which would yield a particular isotope of uranium, U238. When sufficient material was present it would be possible to create a self-sustaining chain reaction. While the 238 itself could be utilized to manufacture a weapon, that was not their prime purpose. Instead the process itself would yield a more potent material for weapons production, plutonium. This effort had been overshadowed initially by the Heisenberg group, which theorized that a process using "heavy water" could be perfected to yield material which was then weapon capable. By the beginning of 1944, although the Falkenberg work was more promising, the means to take the theory to production were beyond the capability of a Germany, which was struggling to provide enough material to conduct a two front war.

Counting on a reversal of fortunes the German High Command hoped they could stabilize the ground war long enough to devote more resources to the implementation of the Falkenberg project. Hermann Goering personally monitored the efforts of Kleiman and his team. In order to control the team's effort and keep its activities secret, the scientists and their families had been moved into quarters built on the estate grounds. A company of specially trained Luftwaffe troops maintained compound security. Oberstleutnant Jurgen Kolb commanded the detachment and was the senior military officer at the facility.

"Nothing like snow to get us in the holiday spirit, right Holz?" Jurgen Kolb noticed his fellow Luftwaffe officer staring out the office window.

Major Manfred Holz was the only member of the research group who wore the uniform of the Luftwaffe. Despite being in the military his credentials as a theoretical physicist were strong. He had spent time at the Kaiser Wilhelm Institute in Berlin where he met Max Kleiman. "Peace on earth. Isn't that what they say?"

"Major, you sound melancholy. We have launched our great offensive on the western front and we will surely drive them to the sea." Kolb was a member of the Nazi Party and his constant propaganda on the war was tedious to most of the scientists.

"Of course, Herr Oberst. You're right, it's only a matter of time." *What a load of shit.* Any rational observer could see the Third Reich was in its final death throes. Manfred Holz's sole purpose in life was to ensure the safety of his wife and try to survive the war. His connection with General Froehlich was his single best hope. This morning he had received a message proposing insertion of an Allied team to coordinate their escape from the Russian threat. His anxiety was as great as after the July attempt on Hitler's life. Everyday he expected to be arrested along with his fellow members of the network. But a large part of their organization had survived and now they were desperately trying to salvage something from the ashes of Germany's defeat.

Kolb turned and walked toward the door. "Have a happy Christmas, major."

"You as well, Herr Oberst." Holz didn't hate Kolb, but he was wary of him. The security chief was not stupid and this new development could be dangerous for everyone involved. He must get several key pieces of information to the network to be passed to their people. The orders bringing them to Falkenberg required endorsement by Goering's staff. They also must have priority travel permits to allow them to travel during this critical time. Those were details he was sure the allies could solve. The toughest challenge would be talking to Kleiman. There was no way they could try and bring anyone into this group without the agreement of the senior scientist. Manfred knew this would be a life or death move. If Kleiman were to turn him in to Kolb, his life would be forfeited. Even his wife might be punished. But if they didn't take action to ensure they were captured, by British or Americans troops, what future would they have under the Russians. Holz knew he must go to Kleiman, but didn't know what Max would do.

Twenty minutes later the major knocked on the door of Dr. Kleiman, head of the Falkenberg group.

"Come in, Manfred." The senior scientist was sitting at his desk with a large notebook open to a page of formulas. "Please sit down. I was just thinking about those calculations you sent up two days ago. You are very close I think. If we had gone down the Bismuth Phosphate road in 42, we might have a weapon by now. But for now we will continue to focus on this very promising process of yours. Now what can I do for you?" Kleiman was almost 60 but still vigorous and outgoing. He smiled at his young protégé whom he had known for over ten years.

"I have something critically important to talk to you about. In talking to you, I'm placing my life in your hands." Holz saw a flicker of concern in Kleiman's grey eyes.

"Manfred, what do you mean?" the older man asked with a start.

"Max, who do you think is going to win the war?"

Kleiman looked at Manfred, his eyes searching his young friend's face for some sign of what this was all about. "Why would you ask a question like that?"

"Because we, you and I, have to make some decisions that will affect everyone here."

Kleiman looked confused. "Manfred, you're making no sense. What is this all about?"

"Max, let me state the obvious. There is nothing that can prevent Germany from losing the war. Nothing. Our country will suffer the punishment of all countries, which lose wars. But in our case it will be different. The Russians will not be benevolent victors. They will rape and kill at will. The Germany we know will cease to exist. The wrath of the Russians will be horrific. As scientists we are as vulnerable as any group. We may be singled out for punishment or even taken prisoner to work for them. I want no part of it and more importantly I want my wife far from here when it happens."

The expression on Kleiman's face showed he too understood the bleak future that awaited all of them. He sighed. "I am only human, Manfred. Of course I understand the inevitable. I guess I've been trying to ignore the problem hoping something would happen."

Holz took a deep breath and let it out. "I have an option which most people would call treasonable. But only to a corrupt government that has destroyed our country."

The look of alarm had returned to Max's eyes. "What are you saying? Treason? How? This is hard to believe."

"Max, I am part of an organization that is focused on after the war. We want to try and save as much of Germany and as many Germans as we can from the Russians. It's called the network. And it will give us a chance to escape with our families to the allies." Now he had committed himself, but saw no other way. "If you turn me into Kolb I'll be shot. Any chance of escape will be lost. If you work with me we just might save our families and our work for the future."

Kleiman put his hands over his face and rubbed his eyes. "Manfred, you know I would never turn you in to Kolb. But this sounds too hard to believe. How can the allies get us away from here to safety?"

"I don't know. But they want to send a two man team in here to figure it out," Holz said.

"May God help us. Allied agents here in Falkenberg. I don't know if I can handle this." Kleiman's voice trembled.

Holz stood up and walked over to the desk, leaning down. "Max, we don't have any choice. All I need you to do is work with me. Can you do that?"

"I'll have to."

Piaski, Poland
December 26, 1944

The integration of Major Ivanov's German team with the reconnaissance troops of Captain Milachenko had not gone well. Only direct intervention and threats of dire punishment kept their mutual hatred under control. The Russian soldiers, most of whom had been fighting the Wermacht for three years, could not accept the idea that these Germans were any different from the many they had killed. To add to the animosity many of the Russians, including Milachenko, had lost family to the Germans. Ivanov tried to appeal to the men's patriotism but in the end he had to hold the threat of the secret police over their heads. Finally the threats were enough to force cooperation from both groups.

Final preparations were underway for the next offensive, which was scheduled to get underway at 0500 on January 12th. Units of the 1st Ukrainian Front would attack across the Vistula River. Ivanov planned to follow behind the shock troops with his platoon which now numbered nineteen including himself and Milachenko. The plan was to utilize the confusion to commandeer German transport and begin to move west toward Dresden. Their cover story was that this group of Russians possessed valuable information and was being taken to headquarters of the Panzer Army for interrogation. German uniforms and arms would be stored in their trucks ready for the switch of roles.

Corry Woods
December 27, 1944

Jack felt like he was going through the motions of mission prep. His job was to oversee the details and planning for Karl's mission into Germany. However Pam's participation was still difficult for him to accept. The plan as it unfolded was as solid as he could ever have wanted. Karl and Pam would be traveling as man and wife. Klaus and Maria Haller had been in Kolding, Denmark where they met with a Danish scientist who had worked with Niels Bohr. Their route would take them across the border into Hamburg and then on their way to Leipzig. They were being outfitted with appropriate clothes and accessories, which were consistent with living in Germany. Every detail was checked to ensure nothing would betray their real origin. Both Karl and Pam had been working with the Admiral and Erich to develop a "depth of knowledge" which would support their story. An entire life history was put together for both of them using many of Karl's real life connections and locations. In this way he was able to brief Pam on many details that would fill in her knowledge of Germany and her life with Karl.

For three hours Karl had been going over details of Cologne and "their early life."

"Karl, I think I could walk down Fredrichstrasse and feel at home." Pam was finishing an entry in her mission background notebook.

"I hope we never need this information but it could be the difference between discovery or not." Karl sat back and lit a cigarette. "Pam, are you absolutely sure you're ready for this?"

She put down her pen and looked at him. "I'd be lying if I said I wasn't scared. But I feel like I'm ready and I want to go."

"It took Jack every bit of will to issue the order. You know that?"

Pam got up and walked over to the coffee pot on the counter. "As long as I've known Jack he's always put doing his duty ahead of anything else. At times that was me. There was a time I hated him for it. Now I think I understand. There are some men, like you and Jack, who have the ability to put honor and duty ahead of things that other men hold sacred. Whether it's money or fame or even family, you don't care. Duty to country and honor to your own set of values always take precedence. I know Jack doesn't want me to go, but he doesn't have any choice because it's the right thing to do for the mission." She poured a cup of coffee and walked back to the table.

Karl sat looking at her. "I don't know how this will turn out. You never do with missions like this. But I am very confident that you will do your duty. Now, when were you born?"

"May 7th, 1921."

"Where?"

"Saint Maria's Hospital in Cologne."

"Parents?"

"Jurgen and Liisa Swarze"

Jack had been in contact with Captain Ian Parker who was the Officer in Command, Coastal Forces, Harwich. They had worked together on a mission in 1943 using motor torpedo boats to penetrate the Dutch harbour at Oostende. Jack needed transportation to the western coast of Denmark and he felt comfortable with using MTB's for the insertion. A message from the network arrived which proposed a landing by the team on a beach six miles southeast of the Danish town of Esbjerg. There had been a noted decrease in German naval activity since the invasion but there were still occasional encounters with E-boats and coastal trawlers. Ian told Jack that the area proposed for landing had been relatively quiet recently but he wouldn't take anything for granted. Jack wanted the firepower and speed of the MTBs in case things didn't go as planned. The most important factor would be the weather. Landing on a beach would require using a small launch or inflatable boat. There were still frequent storms during this time of the year and the winds and waves during those storms made small boat operations difficult. Parker had talked with some of his more experienced boat commanders and they felt the sheltered nature of the Esbjerg beach would make the landing feasible. Parker also told Jack he would put together a complete plan and get his crews ready to shove off when called upon.

Jack was reflecting on his time with the motor torpedo boats when Phil Hatcher knocked on his door.

"Got a minute?"

"Sure, what's up?"

"I wanted to show you the identity cards and travel permits for the mission." Phil laid a folder on Jack's desk.

Stewart looked at the pictures of the Karl and Pam, now attached to identity cards for the Third Reich. He saw the eagle and swastika seal next to Pam's picture and a chill ran through him. "We're confident these are current and have all the required stamps?"

"The information from the network has been very helpful. Plus whoever meets them will be able to check everything over again." Phil said.

Whoever meets them. Jack tried to imagine the dark beach, the smell of MTB engine exhaust, perhaps a recognition signal from shore. "Right."

335

"I asked Ian Parker if Lee Powers was still on active ops. Turns out he is now a two and half striper and the senior flotilla commanding officer." Phil and Jack learned about the world of Coastal Command from then Lieutenant Lee Powers and the crew of his MTB. "I'd feel better if he was taking them in for the drop."

"You'd feel better if you were on the boat yourself, right?"

Jack smiled at his friend. "Right you are. And I intend to use my prerogative to accompany them for the landing. Think the Brigadier will come down on me for that?"

"No, he understands. Besides it never hurts to have some more experience along."

Jack shook his head. "Let's take a look at the latest intel on the Leipzig area. The rest of us need to be ready to get in there when Karl calls."

Several messages were received over the next twenty-four hours. The most important communiqué set the rendezvous time on the Danish beach at 0100 on New Year's Day 1945. According to the message, they would be met by two men, Pieter and Johann. There would be a light signal consisting of three rapid flashes seaward to help them find the correct landing spot.

Jack contacted Ian Parker and the mission was scheduled. The four MTB's would depart Harwich at 2300 on the 30th. It would take the boats twenty-four hours at ten knots to reach the coast of Denmark. Jack was going ride the MTB with Karl and Pam. Phil Hatcher, who had also been on the Oostende mission, was going to go along on a separate boat. The weather forecasts looked favorable for both the transit and landing ashore.

At Corry Woods there was an atmosphere of urgency and quiet professionalism throughout the main house. A small motor convoy would depart from the compound to Harwich at 1600 on the 30th. That left twenty-four hours for final briefings and any last minute changes. Jack felt they were ready.

"Gillian, I'll be upstairs," he said as he walked out the door of the outer office.

Jack knocked on the door to Pam's room. The door opened and she smiled at him. "Come in. I was just going over some mission notes."

He followed her into the room. She sat on the bed and he pulled out the chair to her desk. "All set?"

"I think so, but thought I'd go over everything one more time. I don't want to let Karl down. Next to him I feel like an apprentice."

Jack was trying to keep the conversation light, but they both could feel the tension. "Just do what he tells you and you'll be fine."

"I guess I should be scared but I don't know what I feel. More curious about what it will be like I guess. Does that make sense?"

Jack looked at her, remembering the young nineteen year old he had met so many years ago. Now he was with a grown woman, one he loved with all his heart and watched what could be the beginning of the end of her life. "Sure it does. All of us have felt the same way and wondered what our reaction would be. The hardest part is waiting to get going. Once you start, the jitters go away."

"I hope so. How about the MTBs? What's it like out there?"

He remembered the fire and explosions from his last time in the small boats. "Lots of noise and constant motion. But you'll find no tougher bunch anywhere in the Navy. We'll be on Lee Power's

337

boat. He's the skipper I met last year. They don't come any better. He'll get us in there for the drop."

She stood up and came over next to him. Putting her arms around his neck she pulled his head to her. "I love you, Jack Stewart."

Jack closed his eyes and held her close. "Please be careful," he whispered.

It was windy and overcast when the cars departed Corry Wood for Harwich. Besides two Jeeps with Royal Marine security troops, there were two sedans. Jack and Pam rode in the first with Gillian Andrews driving. Karl and Eva were in the second car. Gerhard offered to drive the car and Phil Hatcher rode with him in the front seat. They would arrive at Harwich after dark to meet Ian Parker and Lee on the MTB pier. The weather report was marginal. However this time of year a lot could change in twenty four hours. It would be a hard crossing with waves expected in the three to five foot range and winds of 15-20 knots.

With the Marine escort they quickly passed through the main gate at Harwich and proceeded to the MTBs. Ian Parker was waiting in the pier security office when they drove up. Jack saluted and the men shook hands.

"Good night for an ocean voyage, Jack."

"No place I'd rather be, sir." Jack made the introductions and a working party of sailors carried their gear down the pier to the waiting MTBs. It was quiet, the only sound the wind coming off the harbour.

"Let's get you aboard," Parker said as the group began to walk down the pier. "Lee's boat is the 5509. Phil, you'll be with Mike Smythe in the 5228 boat. Everyone is closed up and ready to shove off. We have an M class destroyer, the Meteor, waiting off Felixstowe Light to provide an escort for the division. She will provide better radar coverage and plenty of firepower if you should stumble into Jerry."

The group came to the 28 boat first and Phil turned to Karl and Pam. "Good luck," he said as they shook hands. Phil stepped across the short gangway as the rest walked to the next boat on the pier.

Lieutenant Commander Lee Powers was standing at the foot of the gangway next to a tall Sub Lieutenant. He saluted as they group walked up. "Good evening, sir."

Jack extended his hand, "Lee, good to see you again. This is Karl Dietrich and Pam Thompson; they'll be going into the beach."

"Welcome aboard. I'd like to introduce you to my number one, Brian Stoddart." Turning to Parker he saluted. "With your permission, I'll get the division underway."

"Permission granted. Please signal when you rendezvous with Meteor. Good luck."

One by one each MTB started their powerful Rolls Royce engines. Ten minutes after the first engine started Lee Powers called to cast off lines and began to back slowly away from the pier. Jack, Karl and Pam stood behind Lee on the open bridge. Once clear, Lee ordered all engines ahead slow and headed up the channel. The other three boats followed in his wake. Although it was last day of December and there was breeze blowing, the temperature was moderate. Jack found himself enjoying the sensation of being underway again. Pam had been quiet since they came aboard. Jack knew the next twenty four hours was going to be hard on both of them, but for different reasons.

Piaski, Poland
31 December, 1944
1540 Hours

"You wanted to see me?" Captain Milachenko stuck his head into the tent opening.

"Come in. I have updated intelligence just in from Moscow."

Milachenko entered the tent and sat down on one of the folding chairs.

"I haven't told you this because until now I wasn't authorized to do so. We have an agent inside the German group in Falkenberg. This person has been supplying us with some of the technical information he is able to smuggle out to our local contact. Now we intend to use him to ensure our success on this mission."

"What is this updated information?"

"The group has been alerted to be ready to move at a moments notice. Apparently there is some plan to move the scientists toward an area the Germans think will be the last stronghold of the Reich."

Aleksei thought about their schedule, which was critically dependent on the new offensive. "Was there any indication when this move might take place?"

"No. You and I are thinking the same thing. Can we wait for the offensive? I think not. We need to find a way to cross the lines prior to then."

"I think we have no choice," said Aleksei. "We need to move to the front now so I can have time to find an area to cross."

Ivanov nodded. "All right, we'll plan on moving out tomorrow morning. I want you to study the chart and our latest

340

estimate of the German's positions and decide where we should move initially."

"This agent in the group, what happens to the information if they start moving?" Aleksei asked.

"My indications are we will lose contact with him."

"Then we better get there quickly, or not at all."

Falkenberg Research Compound
December 31, 1944

"Herr Doctor, we must talk about plans to move your scientists to Urfeld." Oberstleutnant Kolb was standing in front of Max Kleiman's desk, his hands clasped behind his back.

"Colonel, how can you ask me to make plans to leave our families behind to fend for themselves while we go to Bavaria?" Kleiman's face was red, his anger evident.

"This is a time for everyone to make sacrifices for the good of the Fatherland. There are no provisions for families in the movement order. I am sure they will be fine staying here. We may be able to leave some of my troops here to provide security."

"And if my scientists do not want to go without their families?"

Kolb's tone was very clear. "That is not their choice. Tell them to be ready to move on my command. We could receive orders at any time, they must be ready. My biggest concern is the transport of all working papers and research material. Work must continue once we arrive in Bavaria. I will let you get to work; you have many things to accomplish and very little time."

Ten minutes later, Manfred Holz was standing in Kleiman's office.

"Manfred, they are going to move us to Urfeld, Bavaria. Kolb wants all scientists ready to travel upon receipt of the order. They will not take the families. What are we going to do?"

Holz knew this would complicate any plan by the Allied agents. "For the time being we have to comply with Kolb's instructions. The team should be here soon. If we can delay maybe they will be able to figure something out."

Chapter Nineteen

Two Miles off the Danish Coast
January 1, 1945
0030 Hours

"All hands closed up at action stations, Skipper." Sub Lieutenant Stoddart stood at the top of the ladder leading to the bridge.

"Right, Number One. Make sure we have complete quiet and no lights of any kind showing." Lee Powers lowered his binoculars to address his executive officer.

"Aye aye, sir." The young man disappeared into the darkness.

Power's plan was simple. His boat would proceed close inshore looking for the beach signal. The 5028 boat with Phil Hatcher aboard would remain a mile and a half off the beach, ready to react as needed. The other two boats were holding five miles off the coast as pickets against any German coastal forces. HMS Meteor was ten miles at sea using radar to provide coverage for the MTBs.

5509 was closing the beach south of Esbjerg at dead slow. The beach was visible with small waves breaking on the flat sand. There were two lights visible on the shore but nothing else. Jack stood on the bridge behind Lee. Karl and Pam were with Brian Stoddart on the fantail waiting for word to launch the inflatable raft.

The transit across the North Sea had been uneventful. The weather moderated as the sun came up. The slow transit had given Jack and Pam a chance to spend time talking about something other than the mission.

"Some day this will be a great story to tell the children." Pam had said to Jack over the wardroom table.

"I will look forward to it." Jack sipped his hot tea. "Let's see three boys and three girls. How's that sound to you?"

"My heavens. Let's take it one at a time, if you please." Turning serious, she looked at Jack. "I have to say this, so let me finish. I don't know what's going to happen out there. I know it could go bad. If it does, you can't blame yourself. I want to do this and I know how hard it is for you. Maybe that's one of the many reasons I love you so much. Very non British of you, by the way. I guess there's still a bit of the Yank in there."

Jack looked down in his cup. He couldn't say anything. He might be saying goodbye to her forever.

Now standing on the bridge, he tried to concentrate on the job at hand. At least he could take care of her for a little longer. Using a set of glasses he scanned for the signal. There was nothing to see except the two lights that had been visible for the last twenty minutes.

Without taking his eyes from the glasses, Lee asked, "What do you want to do if we have no signal from the beach?"

344

"I'll go ashore with Karl and we'll see what we can find out. If we can get the boat back out here, have it ready to come back in with Pam if we make contact."

"Fair enough," Lee said. "The bottom here is flat and sandy. I can get in pretty close. That should make for a quick boat trip." There were two crewmembers who would paddle the four person raft to the beach.

The two men continued to scan the darkness for five more minutes. Jack estimated they were idling about 200 yards off the beach. "Still no signal. I'm off with Karl. I'll have a torch. Four flashes means send Pam. Two flashes, there's a problem. If you lose contact with us, plan on trying to pick us up tomorrow night, same time, three miles south of here."

Lee turned to Jack in the darkness. "I've got it. Now off you go, and watch yourself."

Moving back on the deck Jack saw Karl and Pam standing with Stoddart. "Karl, there's still no signal from the beach. I told Lee you and I would go in and have a look. If we can make contact, I'll send a signal and they can bring Pam in."

"Pam, I'll leave my bag here. Bring it with you when you come."

Pam didn't say a word just nodded.

"All right let's get the boat over the side," Brian Stoddart ordered the deck crew.

"Commander Stewart?" The signals yeoman was standing behind him. "Commander Stewart, we just saw a three flash signal from the beach. captain said to launch the boat."

"Boat's in the water, sir," the Leading Seaman reported.

"Looks like we're ready, sir," Brian said to Jack.

The reality hit Jack. This was it. He turned to Pam in the darkness. Quickly he took her hand and squeezed hard. "Take care,"

345

he said softly. Letting go of Pam's hand he put his hand on Karl's shoulder. "Good luck, my friend." Then they were over the side.

Piaski, Poland
January 1, 1945
1145 Hours

Fritz Heigel stared out the back of the two and a half ton truck as it bounced down the rutted road toward Baranôw. The small town was near the forward edge of the Russian lines and bordered the Vistula River. They had been on the road since very early this morning. The word of their early move toward the front and their mission had been greeted with mixed emotions. Everyone was getting on each other's nerves but there was warm food and no danger. Heigel knew what would happen if they were discovered by his countrymen and he tried not to think about it. He had seen several Wermacht soldiers hanged for deserting their units during the invasion of Russia. There was no doubt in his mind that active collaboration would be handled with special brutality.

The German soldiers and Russians ignored each other unless duty required interaction. Each group realized it was the only workable solution with the sword of the NKVD hanging over all of them. The Germans had showed a grudging respect for Milachenko. He was an intimidating person and they had all heard stories of his actions behind the lines.

Talking with his comrades, Heigel could not get anyone to discuss the possibility of deserting once they were across the lines. All of the other men had families and they were driven by the promise of safety if the mission succeeded. Heigel had no ties other than a half brother in Munich whom he hadn't seen in ten years. As the jolting journey continued, Fritz Heigel was looking at all his options.

The three truck caravan arrived at the Battalion Headquarters of the 3rd Battalion, 1st Regiment of the Soviet 66th Division just before mid day. Major Ivanov had gone in search of the battalion commander. Aleksei had been directed to find an area to set up camp.

Later in the afternoon, Aleksei and Ivanov made their way down to the forward observation post overlooking the river. They found a sergeant in charge of the position. According to the man, the area had been very quiet over the last week. Battalion intelligence estimated the opposite side of the river was thinly defended by a Wermacht company. Based on the lack of any observed armor it was probably an infantry or Panzer Grenadier unit. The sergeant had reconnoitered the front line both north and south of the observation post and noted that there was an area of dense woods three miles north that appeared to be clear of enemy troops. Aleksei had his direction.

Walking back to the camp he told Ivanov, "Tonight I can take a small patrol across the river and see what I can find in those woods."

Ivanov said, "I know the battalion has a supply of small boats for the offensive. They can move them up to the river for us. How many will you take?"

"Myself and two or three others. I'll take my most experienced crew. Two man teams can cover a lot of territory in a short time. We need to get the latest maps they have for that side of the river and the best estimate of location of enemy troops."

"Done."

Approaching the German/Danish Border
January 1, 1945
1200 Hours

Karl Dietrich sat in the back seat of the 1936 Volvo sedan with Pam. The last hour had been quiet following several hours of briefing and quizzes by their two companions Pieter and Johann. The rendezvous on the beach had gone as planned. A small house about a mile from the beach was their first stop. Once there, Johann inspected all of their papers including travel permits. He carried a rubber stamp, which gave them priority travel on the Reichsbahn. Pieter checked their clothes and belonging to make sure there was nothing that might give them away. A small breakfast was followed with a complete background story on their visit with Hans Thorvelsson, a Danish physicist who had worked with Niels Bohr on atomic research prior to Bohr's escape to Sweden. The Danish scientist lived in Kolding. Pieter gave them a complete description of the town and the scientist's house.

Their plan was to drive to Süderlägum, arriving at mid-day and cross the frontier. That particular crossing point was normally very lax in their searches and questioning. It would then be a two hour drive to Hamburg where they would catch the afternoon train to Berlin. Johann warned them about the ongoing air raids by the Allies disrupting the rail system, but the main lines were normally repaired quickly in the event of damage. Barring problems, they should arrive in Leipzig about 11pm. Major Manfred Holz, a member of the network, would be meeting them there and then drive them to Falkenberg. On arrival at the main station in Leipzig, they were to go to ticket window number five. Holz would be in the area looking for them. He would be in a Luftwaffe uniform and carrying a blue paper folder. If Holz was not there they were to make their way to Lundeenstrasse and check into the Metropole Hotel. The major would collect them as soon as it was possible.

"We'll be arriving in Berlin at the Lehrter Station?" Karl asked.

"That's right. You'll have to change trains, but your ticket will be good for the transfer." Johann turned to look at Karl. "When were you last in Berlin?"

"I think a year ago, maybe more. Why?"

"The raids have done a great deal of damage. It's not the Berlin you remember. But if you can stay in the station, you will be fine. Try not to venture outside. There are too many ways to get in trouble. Between the air raids and Gestapo, Berlin is not a healthy place to be right now."

Karl looked at Pam, who appeared relaxed and enjoying the ride to the border. "Do you have any questions before we get there?"

She turned to him. "Would it be bad form to ask for a stiff whiskey?"

Karl laughed. If she could keep a sense of humor, she would do fine.

The crossing was anticlimactic. The border police only asked Pieter, the driver, for his papers. A cursory look in the car and he waved them into Germany.

As they arrived in Hamburg the evidence of air attack was everywhere. Detours, burned out buildings and cordoned off areas seemed to be every few blocks. Hauptbahnhof, the main railway station, was in the center of the city. There was bomb damage to several parts of the station but rail service was continuing as scheduled. Their priority travel papers put them on the afternoon train in a first class car. They said goodbye to Pieter and Johann and sat down to await the arrival of the train, which was coming from Kiel.

Karl purchased a newspaper, *Die Welt*. He handed the second section to Pam and began to read. She had been very quiet since they left the car. During their pre-mission briefs, he had stressed to always act the part in public. It was important to be very careful of what you say, as you might be overheard. He hoped she was not freezing up on him now that they were in public.

Looking up from the paper he saw two German Military Policemen. They wore their distinctive silver breast insignia and appeared to be on a routine patrol. He kept an eye on them as they worked their way through the benches occasionally stopping to ask a question. One of the men stopped at the end of Karl's bench and looked at him. The policeman must wonder what a man of military age, clearly in good shape, was doing in civilian clothes. The Volksturm or home guard was conscripting males from 16 to 60 for emergency war service. The two men walked up to Karl.

"May I see your identity card please?" the taller policeman asked.

Karl didn't say anything. He took the identity packet out of his breast pocket.

The man looked hard at Karl's features and then at the card. He must be searching for military deserters, a growing group in Germany. "You've never been in the military?"

"I work for the Air Ministry. We all serve the Reich in different ways."

"This woman is with you?" The shorter man motioned toward Pam.

With a slightly hard tone in his voice, Karl said, "Yes, this is my wife."

"Papers, please." The shorter man stared at Pam, who opened her purse.

"Here you are," she said quietly.

The tall man looked at her, "Where are you going?"

Karl pre-empted Pam. "We are going to a Luftwaffe installation near Leipzig."

Handing her papers back, the short man said, "Very well. Have a good day." The two men walked away.

Karl returned to his paper, but stole a quick look at Pam. He could see the slightest trembling of her hands as she closed her purse. When she picked up her paper and began to read he noted the tremble was gone.

The train departed twenty-five minutes late but everything seemed to be normal. Their small passenger compartment in the car was empty when they arrived and no one joined them by departure time. To Karl this was a blessing. It would give him a chance to talk with Pam outside of their cover. Once underway he held up the paper to give them more privacy in addition to the wood and glass partitions, which separated their compartment.

"How are you doing?" He kept his voice low.

"I'm all right. This is harder than I thought. But I can do it." Her quiet voice was firm.

"You did well back in the station. They were military police looking for deserters, not very sophisticated. If we are stopped by the Gestapo play it the same way, polite and respectful."

As the train cleared Hamburg the results of Allied bombing was left behind. The fields and forests only reflected winter, not war.

An hour and a half later they were in the outskirts of Berlin. Darkness covered much of the damage but there was still evidence of massive air raids as the train made its way to the station. To Karl it seemed there were fewer lights than he remembered. Perhaps it was due to the bombing, maybe because of a partial blackout. He recognized the area they were now transiting. They would be in the station shortly.

As the train pulled to a stop, many of the platform lights went out. Helping Pam down the steps he saw people moving away from the train. The public address system came on, "The Berlin Air Defence Sector has issued an air attack warning. Everyone is to proceed to the shelters located on Ledenstrasse." The warning was repeated. Karl slipped his arm inside of Pam's and held her close in the press of the crowd. They found themselves outside and moving down the sidewalk. Karl saw signs for air raid shelters at several points along the street. Sirens began to wail and there was the sound of distant fire from anti aircraft batteries. The first shelter was full and they continued down the street. People flowed into the second shelter and Karl pulled Pam with him.

"Don't push, we'll all get there." A woman in a threadbare overcoat sounded more bored than scared.

The shelter was a large underground storage room. There were small light bulbs providing minimal illumination of the bare concrete walls. Karl estimated there were two hundred people in the room, mostly civilians and a few servicemen. He held Pam's arm and they moved over to one of the open areas near a wall. Most of the people were beginning to sit down trying to make themselves comfortable. Someone closed the large wooden doors. Throughout the room there were quiet conversations, people killing time and dealing with nerves.

Other than the sound of anti-aircraft guns there were no indications of what was happening outside the shelter. Slowly Karl felt a vibration building in the concrete floor from the impact of

352

bombs nearby. There were several sharp thuds and the concussion could be felt in the room. Karl could sense the people in the room were more anxious, many staring up as if trying to see what was happening outside. Three very loud explosions in quick succession seemed to be right on top of them. Pam held Karl's arm tightly but said nothing. As quickly as the noise and vibration began, it stopped. There was a siren sounding outside from one of the fire brigades.

Forty minutes later there was a second siren, which Karl knew meant "all clear." The doors were opened and people began filing out into the street. There was a smell of smoke and dust in the air. Karl looked west toward the city center where the many fires created a crimson glow. "Let's get back to the station. I hope we still have a train to take," he whispered to Pam.

It was over four hours later when their southbound train for Leipzig departed the station. If they didn't hit any delays they would arrive at Leipzig's Hauptbahnhof around 0100. Karl wondered whether this Major Holz would be there to meet them. But now was the time to try and rest. He looked down at Pam who had her eyes closed with her head against the seat rest. The only other passenger in their compartment was a small man in his 60's who had not said a word since they departed. *I hope she doesn't talk in her sleep.* Karl decided he would try to remain awake and rest later.

The Vistula River
Baranôw, Poland

Beneath a sky of low scudding clouds, Milachenko checked his watch and saw it was almost 2300. His men knelt around a small boat at the edge of the heavy brush 40 meters from the waters edge. The Vistula was almost 500 meters wide at this point. According to the local troops, the current wasn't strong. He had chosen several of his best and most experienced men to accompany him including Private Vladimir Gorshin. Sergeant Voloshin would lead the second team with Corporal Taisen. Once across the river Aleksei would go north, the sergeant south. They were trying to locate any troops, verify the location of a road that was marked on their maps and possibly capture a prisoner for interrogation.

It was cold as they moved out on the river. It felt good to work the paddles, the warmth from their exercise helping fight the cold. Aleksei controlled the navigation. The current pushed them south, but with aggressive paddling they were moving straight across the river. It took twenty-five minutes of hard pulling before the boat's prow grated on the sandy bank. Pulling the boat into the brush they threw several tree branches over it. Aleksei and Voloshin checked their watches. The plan was to meet back at the boat at 0200. If one group wasn't back by 0330, the other group would return across the river. They would try to re-rendezvous the next night using the same time schedule and location. Voloshin and Taisen quietly moved off in the underbrush.

Milachenko took the lead and began moving northwest. According to their maps there was a road that ran parallel to the river about a kilometer inland. They would continue until hitting the road and then work their way north. There was a breeze blowing through the trees. Aleksei would have preferred a calm night, making it easier to hear the enemy. Watching for any lights from fires or cigarettes he moved forward carefully. It appeared the area was clear of any defensive positions.

Forty minutes later Milachenko could see a road running left to right, fifty meters in front of him. There was no sign of any activity. *Where are the Germans?* He waved Gorshin up to where he was kneeling. "Vladimir, I want to cross the road and work our way north. I'll cross first. Once I get over, I'll wave you across. Understand?"

The young man nodded, "Yes, sir."

Aleksei slowly crept out of the tall grass and crossed the road, looking both ways as he went. Pausing a moment on the far side he listened. He raised his hand and Gorshin followed him across.

In twenty minutes he could see lights ahead on the western side of the road. Moving closer it appeared that there were three large tents set back from the road in a grove of trees. There were several lanterns providing light for the compound. He slowly and carefully scanned the area looking for any sentries. Taking out his glasses he checked the lighted area. This appeared to be some type of communication station. There were tall antennae extending on rods alongside the tents. He could also hear a generator running on the far side of the area. One man was visible sitting on a chair outside the largest tent. Beyond the man he could see two large trucks and a smaller Kampfwagen. Milachenko had seen everything he needed to see. He motioned to Gorshin. Together they began to move south toward the rendezvous point.

The Hauptbahnhof
Leipzig, Germany
January 2, 1945
0050 Hours

Karl stared out the window at the dimly lit platform. The train had made good time and he hoped Major Holz would be waiting. The older man left the train in Wittenberg allowing Karl a brief nap. Pam was alert now and seemed rested. The train pulled to a stop. Car doors began to open, the passengers moving toward the main terminal.

Pam and Karl walked alongside the train making their way to the ticketing area. Turning the corner they saw a Luftwaffe officer standing at the end of a wooden bench opposite ticket window five. The man carried a blue folder under his arm. Scanning the area for anything unusual Karl walked up to the man who was watching them approach. "Major Holz?" Karl asked.

"You must be Dr. and Mrs. Haller. Welcome to Leipzig. I have a car outside. Please come with me." Holz picked up Pam's suitcase and pointed the way to the exit.

As they cleared the building, Karl said quietly, "Sorry we're late, air raid in Berlin."

"That's to be expected these days. I suspect you're tired and hungry." They crossed the street and Holz stopped at a Porsche sedan. "It's an hour and a half drive to the compound."

Holz started the car and pulled into the street. It took fifteen minutes to reach the Falkenberg highway detouring around two destroyed city blocks. "You'll find bread and wine in the bag on the floor. If you aren't too tired, I'd like to brief you on the current situation."

"Current situation? What do you mean?"

"The head of our security detachment has received an alert order for a transfer of all scientists to Urfeld in Bavaria. We don't know when the orders will come down, but they're pressing us to be ready." Holz kept his eyes on the road and continued, "They will only take the scientists. That would mean leaving our families alone."

Karl asked, "What's the total number of scientists and family members?"

"Perhaps a hundred and thirty or thirty five," Holz answered.

Pam said, "Are there any restrictions to traveling? Is anyone sick or requiring special procedures?"

Holz thought for a moment. "One of the wives, Greta Freihold, is within a week or two of delivering her baby. But that's the only problem I know of. Why?"

"We have no intention of not including your families in any plans we make for the evacuation," Karl answered.

"That will make the job of convincing my colleagues much easier. I think if you can convince Dr. Kleiman, everyone will follow him. But he's a born skeptic who is hard to convince of anything,."

"We'll see about that," Pam said.

Chapter Twenty

The Falkenberg Compound
January 2, 1945
1330 Hours

Manfred Holz knocked on the Director's door. Karl and Pam stood behind him as he opened the door. Holz pushed the door open and turned back to them. "Please come in."

Max Kleiman was standing behind his desk. His face showed apprehension as they entered. He didn't say anything but stared at Pam.

"Herr Doctor, this is Dr. and Mrs. Haller," Holz said.

With a start, Kleiman said, "Please do sit down." He continued to look at Pam with a puzzled expression.

Karl spoke up. "Doctor Kleiman, my name is really Dietrich. And I believe you have already met Pamela Thompson."

"My God, it is you. Pamela, can it really be?" The older man leaned forward as if the closer distance would help him verify Pam's identity.

"It's been nine years, but yes, it's me."

Manfred Holz looked more confused than Max Kleiman. "I don't understand."

"Pamela's father was my sponsor when I did my sabbatical at Oxford in '35. Our families became good friends. Pam, how is your father?"

She knew this question was coming and still found it hard to talk about. "He was killed last July. It was a V-1 launched at London."

The older man's face sagged. "Pamela, I am so sorry. I don't know what to say. He was such a good man and a solid friend to me."

Pam nodded. "He valued your friendship, war or no war."

Karl cut in, "Herr Doctor, I am German but work for British Intelligence. We feel your group will be a prime target for the Red Army as they sweep into Germany. I'm here to help get you and your families to the Allied lines."

"Certainly we have talked about this, Herr Dietrich. This is a constant topic among our families. I believe that most of my people would want to go with you. But I would have to put it to them."

"There are several things to keep in mind, Herr Doctor. This is not without risk. We have to assume the security detachment will try to prevent any evacuation. If word of this were to get outside of this compound you could expect Gestapo and SS action at the least. We must ensure that this is kept very quiet until we execute whatever evacuation is put in place."

Kleiman looked anxious. "There isn't a plan yet?"

"Pamela and I are here to evaluate several possible plans. When we send our input to London they will put together the final plan. That is why secrecy is paramount. All of this will take time," Karl said.

Holz, who had been standing by the window, took a step forward. "Dietrich, by being here you're putting all of our lives in danger. We need more than your offer to present to our people."

Karl's anger was barely concealed. "Don't lecture me about whose lives are in danger. We will do our best to put together a plan that will get you and your families to safety. That is the best I can offer. If that's not good enough, we will leave."

"Doctor Kleiman, I wouldn't be here if I didn't think we could do this." Pam looked at Max and then to Holz. "This has the highest possible priority in London. As quickly as Karl can get the information he needs, London can and will put together a plan. I know the men who will be working on this operation. They are the best we have and they will get you out. But we need your help."

"Herr Doctor, may I make a suggestion." The tone had changed in Holz's voice. "You and I know there are four or five key senior scientists who are the backbone of our group. If you talk only with them, and get their thoughts, that would at least confirm that they want to try and escape. Keep the plan among only a small group until the last moment. At that point if anyone doesn't want to go, they stay here."

Kleiman looked at Dietrich. "What he says makes sense. If my senior group says yes, will that be enough for you?"

Karl thought for a moment. "That will be fine. We'll put together a plan which will accommodate everyone. If anyone drops out at the last moment it won't be a problem. The other issue is the security detachment. I need to find out everything I can about them."

"Manfred, why don't you take Dr. Haller to meet Kolb. That will give me a chance to catch up with Pamela. Also, no one but the four of us must know their real identities."

Holz escorted Karl to Kolb's office. On the way he told him the detachment was made up of one platoon of thirty soldiers. They were from the Luftwaffe branch that provided security to installations and facilities. Kolb was a non-flier who had received his commission through his Nazi Party affiliation. "Be careful when you're around him. He's a dangerous man," Holz warned.

Kolb was not in his office so they left a message. Manfred took Karl on a tour of the grounds. It was clear which of the buildings were part of the pre-war estate. Built of brick, they were laid out in a symmetrical pattern from the large house. There were over thirty wooden structures that filled in around the original buildings. Karl estimated the total built up area covered fifteen acres. There were large fields surrounding the buildings where the horses were kept when this was a breeding estate. Surrounded by forests, the compound was in an isolated area. The nearest town was Falkenberg about five miles north toward the Elbe River.

The two men were walking back toward the main house when they saw Oberstleutnant Kolb striding across the graveled courtyard. Karl noted a lack of combat decorations on the man's tunic.

Holz saluted as Kolb approached. "Colonel, may I present Dr. Haller. He arrived last night."

Kolb returned Holz's military salute with the traditional Nazi Party salute. He extended his hand to Karl. "Herr Doctor, welcome. I am Jurgen Kolb, head of security."

Karl smiled at the man. "It is an honor to meet you, Colonel."

"What brings you here?" The question had an edge to it.

"I've been working with a physicist in Denmark and may have some valuable information to share with Doctor Kleiman. I am sure you will want to see my orders. I will drop them by your office."

Kolb stared at Karl. "Just a formality, of course. But we must comply with procedures."

Karl found Kolb's stare uncomfortable. "I'll bring them by this afternoon. I have orders for myself and my wife."

"You have your wife with you? I assume Major Holz has you in married quarters?"

"Yes, we're in bungalow 21."

"It was good to meet you, Herr Doctor. I must be off on my inspection," Kolb said. "Perhaps we can talk later?" With a nod the Colonel walked away from them toward one of the research buildings.

As they walked toward the vehicle park Karl said to Holz, "Policemen are all the same. What can you tell me of an airfield we saw on the photographs about five miles south of here?

"You're talking about Falkenberg Auxiliary Number Five," Holz said. "It was built in 1941 as an outlying practice field for the flight school at Leipzig. When they closed the school last year the Falkenberg field was abandoned. Why?"

"I need to get back to look at that airfield in the daylight. It might be critical to our plan. Can we get out there today?"

"I still have the sedan from last night. Let's go."

Baranôw, Poland
January 2, 1945
1700 Hours

Ivanov had been busy all day with final preparations for the mission. Following the debrief of the recon mission, both officers realized now was their best time to get past the German front lines and start their journey into Germany.

"Major, all uniforms and weapons have been inventoried. Everything has been packed into the traveling cases including the radios." Milachenkov had inspected all of the men in their German uniforms and now those uniforms were packed for the move. Their German troops would wear German uniforms from the beginning of the mission. Once past the front lines all of the Russians would switch to German uniforms. The Russian's uniforms would be from the 14th SS Panzer Grenadier Division, which was a unique unit. All members of that division were from the Ukraine. There was no reason for them to be fluent in German.

All material and personnel were scheduled to be at the river's edge by 2100. They would be ferried across the river by Russian engineers, who would then bring the boats back to the eastern side of the river.

"Thank you, Aleksei." Ivanov was reading from a folder of messages. "Is there anything that still needs to be done?"

"I want to get the men one good hot meal before we head to the river. The weather tonight is going to be cold and windy. I want them to start out in good shape."

Ivanov looked up from the folder. "Sit down for a moment, please."

Milachenko sat down and lit a cigarette.

"I know you're not enthusiastic about our Germans. But have you seen anything that might jeopardize the mission?"

Aleksei exhaled. "Major, I think most of the Germans are just like most of our troops. They will fight and do their job most of the time. What concerns me is the first time we're in a tight spot. How are these men going to react? Will they give us away? Will they try to turn the tables and return to their own ranks? I'm not worried about my men. I've seen them in tough situations. I know how they'll react."

"I think these men are motivated by survival, both of themselves and their families. At best, if they turned on us, they'd be sent back into the lines and have to fight the Red Army. They've seen what is descending on Germany. At worst, the Gestapo would interrogate them and they would be shot as collaborators. Their best chance for survival is to successfully accomplish this mission."

Stepping on his cigarette butt he looked at the major. "You've never told me what we do when we find these scientists. If you're killed tomorrow someone else better know the whole plan."

"I was going to brief you as we got closer to the objective to protect our agent. But you're right. Things do go wrong. The plan is to transport the scientists to a location near Torgau, on the Elbe River. There is an abandoned castle six kilometers south of the city where we can remain until our forces are closer. We will either wait for an armored spearhead to close on the castle or have reinforcements come in by parachute to help us hold until relieved."

"Major, if you don't mind my opinion that puts us out on quite a limb. What happens if our forces can't get to us? Suppose the Germans collapse in the west and the Americans take that area?"

"Then we kill every one of the scientists and make our way back toward our lines. But I don't think that is probable. Field Marshal Koniev has specific instructions to drive the offensive

364

spearhead of his armies directly for the Leipzig area. He'll be there before anyone else."

Milachenko wasn't sure he agreed with Ivanov but he didn't have any choice. "I have one last question. Who is our contact point inside this group?"

"The head of the security forces, a Lieutenant Colonel named Kolb."

The Vistula River
2215 Hours

Despite a stiff current and biting wind, the engineer detachment was able to transfer all of Ivanov's men and equipment without incident. With Ivanov supervising, most of the men were working on moving their equipment to the road, which ran parallel to the river. Through the swaying forest trees, Aleksei led seven men north toward the encampment they had seen the night before. Knowing tactical situations change constantly he moved cautiously along the road. It appeared there were no new units or positions since last night. The area was still devoid of troops or any human presence. His one concern was allayed when he saw the lights of the encampment still shining in the darkness.

His plan was to split his men into three teams. The first would look for any sentries. The second team would go after the main tent in the center of the clearing. Finally the last group was to attack the two billeting tents on the far side of the clearing. He would go with Sergeant Voloshin who was assigned the large tent.

Fifteen minutes of watching the encampment identified two sentries stationed on the edge of the clearing, one north and one south. They did not appear to be patrolling, but would occasionally move around, probably trying to stay warm. Gorshin's team moved out with orders to take out the sentries using killing knives only. Aleksei gave them ten minutes to accomplish their tasks before the other two teams would movie into action. Once the sentries were dispatched, Gorshin and Ledbeyev were to hold on the perimeter to intercept anyone trying to flee.

Aleksei watched the time. He knew his men and had confidence they would have no problem killing two unalerted sentries. His concern was the unexpected event which you could never rule out. Anything from a weapon discharged during a struggle to a third person appearing during the assault. He listened to the sound of the wind hoping that was all he would hear.

The two German sentries died without making a sound. Gorshin and Ledbeyev moved to the perimeter and waited for the next step in Milachenko's plan.

Aleksei crept toward the large tent, the silenced Makarov in his hand. He counted on surprise to overwhelm the Germans. Approaching the tent opening, he listened for voices. The only sound was the generator running behind the tent. Making sure Corporal Taisen was ready he made a hand signal telling him 'stand by.' The corporal nodded, holding the pistol at the ready. Aleksei took a small breath, exhaled and pulled the tent flap open.

The interior was lit with a single kerosene lantern. Three German soldiers sat in front of radio sets, one man wearing a headset. Aleksei shot the operator in the forehead, the back of the man's head exploding against the canvas of the tent. Moving into the room he put two quick rounds into the chest of a soldier who was trying to stand up. Taisen took the man sitting in a chair to the left, firing three bullets into his chest. The man still had a surprised look on his face as he fell to the ground. Quickly checking to make sure

366

the men were dead, they joined Kolchin, at the tent entrance. "Over to the billeting tents." Aleksei removed his partially fired clip, replacing it with a full one.

Sergeant Voloshin did not need their assistance. Five dead German soldiers were still in their sleeping rolls. They had been killed in their sleep.

Aleksei turned to his men. "Check around for any other Germans and meet back here in five minutes." The men fanned out while Milachenko went over to check the vehicles.

There were two large transport trucks with canvas covers over the cargo areas. The trucks appeared to be in good condition including the tires. Parked next to the trucks was a small Kampfwagen. It showed signs of heavy use and it didn't fit into their plans in any case. "Sergeant Voloshin, check the fuel. Then see if we can get these trucks started." Milachenko walked back to the main tent to look for anything of intelligence value.

In five minutes both of the trucks were idling in the cold wind. Aleksei made one last sweep through the encampment and ordered his men aboard the trucks. Pulling onto the road they headed south to pick up Ivanov. Aleksei sat in the front seat next to the driver. Looking out into the dark night he tried to remember when it had become so easy to kill other human beings?

Two hours later a heavy bombardment by Russian artillery effectively destroyed the area where the communications encampment had been. Over six hundred 155 mm shells turned the area into a twisted maze of broken and burned trees. Interspersed in the target area were bits and pieces of equipment and human remains, however nothing was recognizable.

Corry Woods
January 3, 1945
0745 Hours

Hiram Walker rushed into Jack's office without knocking. "Skipper, we just got a message from the network. They made it to Falkenberg."

Jack looked up from the message board. A flood of relief swept over him. He had spent the last three days waiting for some indication that Pam and Karl were still all right. Judging by the look on Hiram's face his friends understood.

Handing the message brief to Jack, Hiram added, "There's a note directly from Karl."

Looking at the end of the transmission, Jack saw words that made the trip worth the risk. "AF looks good, proceed." He told Hiram to get the senior officers together in the conference room as soon as possible. For the first time in three days Jack took a deep breath.

"Karl has been able to check on the airfield and passed on that we should proceed with the operation. I know we've laid out the requirements but we need to start operational coordination straight away. Phil, I want you to work with the 1st Special Air Regiment to get their people queued up and ready to go on four hours notice. Terry, get into London and work with Noel Greene on the final arrangements for the Glider Parachute Regiment and the Fighter Command cover. I'd like to be able to forward deploy within twenty-four hours if at all possible. I know we're pushing this, but every minute we delay hurts our ability to pull those people out quickly if needed. Admiral, do you have any thoughts?"

"The most crucial issue is going to be the weather. We're counting on good flying weather to pull this off. The area south of Berlin is notoriously hard to predict because of the weather systems coming out of Bavaria." Kaltenbach moved to the map and pointed out the normal weather flow. "Anything we try to do in the air could be jeopardized by a winter storm."

"Terry, when you talk to the RAF see if they will spare a weather expert we can use for the rest of the operation." Jack made a note on his folder. "Erich, we need a decision on our being able to stage from the Y.42 Airfield southwest of Nancy. That would put us only 250 miles from Falkenberg. See if we can get Tommy Hudson to pull a little pressure on Supreme Headquarters for us. Hiram, I'd like to get a doctor to go along on the mission. That last go around it make all the difference in the world. All right, I want everyone ready to travel tomorrow morning at 0700. We'll make the final decisions on assignments at that time. Let's get moving." Jack stood up, as did the rest of the officers.

Erich walked over to the map and circled the small airfield symbol. The plan was bold and would take many units operating as one. He watched the group of men from different countries and services filing out of the room. *We can do this.*

Ten Miles West of Krakow
0830 Hours

Despite initial slow going as they made their way south on the river highway, they were able to clear the majority of the military activity by dawn. Once on the main highway to Krakow they made good time due to light traffic on the road. A military police traffic director gave them directions to the fueling facility on the outskirts of the city. After topping off with petrol, the two trucks continued west.

Major Ivanov, in the uniform of a Russian sergeant, sat in the back of the first truck with half of the Russians. Aleksei, also dressed as a sergeant, was in charge of the second vehicle. Werner Reuss sat in the front of the first truck where he was able to talk with Ivanov through the cab window. They were looking for a discreet location prior to their arrival in Breslau where the Russians could change into their SS uniforms. They carried orders directing the transfer of the platoon to the Buchenwald concentration camp north of Weimar as new guards. NKVD intelligence knew the Ukrainian troops had been used as concentration camp staff in the past. The cover should be sufficient for any reasonable challenge.

Traffic picked up twenty miles outside of Krakow. There were numerous military truck convoys heading east and a large number of civilian vehicles going west. The Germans were much quieter once the sun came up and they encountered Wermacht military units. Aleksei wondered what was going through their minds as they got closer to German territory. Most of them had been gone from home over two years. Many had no word from their families since well before they were captured. The need to know would get stronger as they began to see their homeland. This was not an aspect of the mission, which Aleksei saw as positive. Seven men must be wondering what happened to their families and friends since they left. All he could do was watch them carefully. He had no qualms about killing any of them that got out of line.

Two hours later they turned off onto a side road leading into a forested area. In twenty minutes they were in a secluded area and were able to stop for the uniform change.

It felt good to stretch his legs after so many hours. Aleksei walked over to find Ivanov who was relieving himself behind a tree.

"This stop was necessary for more than one reason." The major closed his trousers and came around the tree.

"Do you want to try and eat or just change uniforms?" Aleksei asked.

"Have them pass out loaves of bread. We can eat once we get back on the road. I want to get changed and take a look at everyone one last time."

"Yes, sir." He was pleasantly surprised. Ivanov had done well so far. Perhaps the NKVD weren't the worthless shits he had always thought.

It was a strange sensation as Captain Aleksei Milachenko of the 66th Russian Infantry Division surveyed the platoon dressed in uniforms of the Waffen SS, their blood enemy. Their Germans stood to one side talking among themselves. Milachenko still did not trust them.

Dmitri Ivanov, now dressed as an SS major, walked up and down the row of men with Sergeant Reuss. They found no problems with the uniforms and were now making short exchanges in German with the men. During their training time the Russians had been taught some basic military responses and conversation in German. Milachenko had changed into an SS captain's uniform and stood waiting for Ivanov to finish his inspection.

"Aleksei, the men are doing well. I want all Russian uniforms to be buried here before we depart. Make sure they are covered well."

In another thirty minutes the trucks were loaded and ready to move. Ivanov had moved to the front seat of the first truck, Milachenko did the same in the second truck. The next stop was

Breslau and then to Görlitz, where they would pass from East Prussia into Germany proper. Milachenko looked at his German wrist watch. They should reach Görlitz by early evening. Their arrival in the Falkenberg area was planned for sunset the following day to take advantage of the darkness. He was confident his men could take care of any security detachment, particularly if the head of security was working with them. This was certainly something he would be able to tell his grandchildren about.

Falkenberg Research Compound
1020 Hours

Karl and Pam spent the morning walking the area immediately surrounding the main building. They were able to get a good idea of the location of personnel, facilities and vehicles. Of particular interest was Building Four, the guard room and armory. There were heavy wire mesh screens over the windows but nothing else indicating increased security. Holz told them there were normally four security troops on duty at any one time. They did maintain a 24 hour patrol around the main compound. The perimeter security was primarily accomplished by a tall wire fence, which encircled the main compound. According to Holz only random patrols were conducted along the fence line. There were a large number of external lights, which illuminated the buildings at night. Holz had seen the troops carrying pistols and machine pistols during their patrols. He knew they also had several MG34 machine guns in the armory although he had not heard of them exercising with them within the last year. There were no heavy weapons or tracked vehicles closer than Leipzig.

The two agents stood at the edge of the parking lot for the main building and looked across the wire fence at the wide fields surrounding the compound. "Do we assume the message got through to Corry Woods?" Pam asked as she looked around to make sure they were alone.

"That's all we can do. Holz told me he expected to get some communication later tonight. Hopefully there will be a reply."

Pam wrapped her arms around herself, holding her coat close. "I've only seen one large truck and no buses. How will we get the people to the airfield?"

"Use every vehicle and make as many runs as necessary. That's all we can do." Karl pulled out a pack of cigarettes and lit one, the smoke drifting away in the light breeze. "I'm more concerned we keep this dry weather until we can get this thing started. With low ceilings we're out of business. Holz has a connection at the Leipzig airport so we should be able to get updated weather forecasts as we get closer."

Pam said, "Let's walk, I'm getting cold."

They headed back toward the main building. "Have you gotten any feedback from Dr. Kleimen yet?" Karl asked.

"He's meeting with his key people this morning. Once he's talked with them, he'll let me know. I do know he's doing individual meetings so it will take him some time."

Ahead, stepping out of one of the main building side doors, they saw Kolb and a soldier carrying a rifle. The two men approached and Kolb was smiling.

"Good morning. Out for a morning walk?" Kolb asked.

"Exactly. Getting some fresh air," Karl replied.

"I would have thought you would be busy briefing your work to the group."

373

"Doctor Kleiman is arranging that now, as I understand," Karl said.

Kolb had a slight, ingratiating smile on his face. "Herr Doctor, I understand you have worked with Doctor Kleiman in the past? Was that in Berlin?"

Karl sensed the man was searching for information, not being social." "I was at the University of Cologne. We collaborated on several projects over the last few years."

"I see. It seems you would have joined our little group sooner."

"Colonel, we are doing research that is more advanced than anything man has ever done. I hope you understand it is difficult to find the correct path. Many of us have been exploring different avenues. Only recently did Doctor Kleiman and I agree that we were arriving at the same conclusions. Because of that we decided it made sense for me to join the group." Karl tried to sound like a teacher talking to a slow student.

Kolb's face flushed slightly. "Very interesting. I hope you can make a positive contribution to the group. If you will excuse me, I have my duties." He nodded to Pam, turned and walked away, the soldier hurrying to catch up.

That man will be a problem Karl thought as he took Pam's arm and walked her back to the building.

After lunch Pam and Karl joined Kleiman in his office. Manfred Holz was also there when they arrived.

"I believe I have good news," the director said. "Meetings with my five key people went well. Every one of them was in agreement with your proposal. Several had concerns or questions, but I told them we could ask you for clarification."

Karl nodded. "Good. I would like to talk with them as quickly as possible to solve any problems. When we are ready to execute this evacuation, it will happen very quickly."

Kleiman leaned forward. "Can you tell me about the plan?"

"Let me give you the basic concept. Many of the details were being worked out when we left England. Right now there are a great many very specialized people putting together the final details." Karl took ten minutes to describe the basic plan.

"Karl, Pam, I appreciate your courage in traveling here to help us. But it seems very dangerous and I'm concerned for the lives of my scientists and their families. I don't think I could deal with their deaths."

"Doctor, this is the only way," Holz interjected.

"I understand your concerns, Herr Doctor," Karl said. "But we have looked at every possible way to get a group this size to allied lines. We must do it by air and there is always danger. But I think it is a reasonable risk compared to being captured by the Russians. I know you can't appreciate what happened on the Eastern Front. Millions of troops and civilians have been involved in a 'no quarter' fight to the death. Both sides have been cruel and brutal. Now, we're losing and there will be retribution against everything German. I'm telling you that your group does not want to be here when the Russians arrive."

Kleiman stared at Karl. "I'm sure you're right. It's difficult to move from our quiet research world to what you describe. I will arrange for my people to talk with you and we'll get everything ready to move."

"Herr Doctor, the transport is limited. You can only take the minimum in the way of personal effects. You must make sure that the files and records you bring are only the most essential. Everything else must be destroyed," Pam said.

375

"We also need to get everyone organized into groups, with a leader. That will allow us to have some control when things start happening. I'll leave that up to you but we need groups of about ten. Make sure they have a designated spot to rendezvous and a secondary leader in case something happens to the primary. We'll let you know as soon as we get word from our people when the operation will take place.

"So the time has not been set?" the Doctor asked.

"It could be tomorrow or next week. We are at the mercy of logistics and weather. I know it will be as soon as possible." It was all Karl could offer.

Corry Woods
1815 Hours

The light was shining under Phil Hatcher's office door. Jack knocked and opened the door. Hatcher sat at his desk with a phone to his ear. He motioned Jack in and continued to talk.

"Well done, Terry. Hope you didn't have to use Churchill's name too much today. I'll ring off but if you can get me the updated flight info tonight that would let me lock things in here." Phil sat listening to the phone and simultaneously gave Jack a thumbs' up signal. "Right, I'll expect your call within the hour." He hung up the receiver.

"Good news?"

Phil smiled. "It sounds like Tommy Hudson called in some markers and they used the P.M.'s name liberally, but it worked. Here's where we are. The air transport boys will have two Dakota's ready to leave from RAF Down Ampney tomorrow morning at 0700.

The SAS will have two platoons standing by to meet us at the airfield. The flight will be direct to the Nancy airfield. We have permission from the U.S. Ninth Air Force to stage out of the field. They've been operational since mid October so no problem with fuel, ordnance and support. This is going to be a combined air effort. The RAF is sending 198 Squadron down from their forward base in Belgium with sixteen Typhoons for ground support. The Ninth Air Force is going to let us have two P-51 squadrons from their 357th Fighter Group, the same chaps who covered you coming out of Poland. The most difficult task is to get two Horsa Gliders to Nancy. Terry said there are still several of them at Down Ampney that did not get the call for Normandy or Market Garden. They only need to get them checked out and ready to ferry to Nancy. The Glider Parachute Regiment has crews and tow ships ready as soon as the Horsa's are certified safe for flight."

"Remind me to buy Tommy a very large scotch the next time I see him." Jack was pleased so many different requirements could come together so quickly. It didn't hurt to have Churchill on your side. "So the only outstanding requirement is the extra DC-3's?"

"Exactly. We should have word later tonight. This little event in the Ardennes has pinched the available aircraft. Terry thought he would know within the hour."

"Any word on a weather guesser to go along with us?"

"We will be joined at the airfield by Squadron Leader Lee Philpott, RAF Meteorology. He's from 45 Group and will be with us as long as needed," Phil said. "All we need to do now is finalize our assignments and get a movement order on the street."

Jack paused for a moment. "I still think taking the new kids makes sense for the long run. Any second thoughts?"

"There will be enough SAS chaps around to keep them out of trouble. They have to learn sometime."

"Good then, let's get the word out. I suspect we need to be on the road by 0300?"

"Why do we always do this shit in the middle of the night?"

"Phil, you're starting to sound like an old man," Jack laughed.

Zgorzelec
East Prussia
2030 Hours

The proximity of German troops was disconcerting to Aleksei. There were Wermacht troops walking by their trucks. For the last hour they had been stopped on the side of the road a mile from the Viaduct Bridge over the Niesse River. The concrete and steel span had been damaged in a low level attack by several fighter-bombers of the Red Air Force. All road traffic was halted while engineers tried to determine if the spans would hold the weight of vehicles. Across the river was Germany proper, the town of Görlitz.

Milachenko lit a German cigarette and walked up to the cab of Ivanov's truck. Knocking on the window he saw the major turn to look at him. The door opened and Ivanov stepped down.

"Any new word?" Aleksei asked.

"I sent Sergeant Reuss up to see if he could get any info. They told him they were still waiting for the engineers to report back." The stench of burned buildings was strong, several still smoldering from the earlier attack.

"I checked the map. There's another bridge on the river about forty kilometers north. Do you want to try to get out of the line and make our way north?" Aleksei threw his cigarette butt into the mud.

"It would be a lot harder in the dark. We're making good time. We could get up to that bridge and find out it was down also. Let's give them some more time. How are your men doing?"

"Starting to get cold. These uniforms are not as warm as ours. If we're going to stay here we need try and find someplace to stay for the night." Milachenko did not like this situation. Caught in a military traffic jam, they were surrounded by German troops. Their chances of discovery went up the longer they remained here. But Ivanov was running this mission. Perhaps the engineers would get the bridge fixed and they would be on their way.

Ivanov agreed and sent Sergeant Reuss to see if he could find any shelter.

Chapter Twenty One

RAF Down Ampney
Gloucestershire
January 4, 1945
0600 Hours

It was a cold morning with a light drizzle blowing across the airfield. Home of 46 Group of Air Transport Command, there were numerous DC-3 Dakota Transports parked on the apron. Painted a drab olive green many still wore the black and white triple stripes painted on all allied aircraft for the Normandy invasion. Arriving on station Jack and Phil had met Wing Commander Trafford Jones, the commander of 48 Squadron. A big burly man, he filled out his flying coveralls and towered over the rest of his pilots. He was going along as the senior transport commander. There would be ten Dakotas making the trip to Nancy. Two would be carrying the SAS platoons and Jack's crew. The others would follow empty. Two of those aircraft would be towing the Horsa gliders.

Major Colin Herrick would lead the SAS contingent. He was on his way to Down Ampney from London. His troops were already in the holding area. Although they had been preparing to deploy back to Belgium after a refit and rest, this mission took priority. Terry had briefed Jack that the two platoons were all combat veterans and had been on the continent since D-Day. They had come back to England for three weeks to prepare for the last big push into Germany. "Jack, we were lucky they were back here. These men have the combat experience, but more importantly they were involved in the glider assaults during the invasion. They are the perfect match for our mission. By the way I found out Major Herrick was awarded the VC two days ago by the King."

Jack sensed a quiet professionalism among the Special Air Services troopers. They all sat quietly by their kits, a few smoking cigarettes. There was none of the obvious tension or excitement you often saw with inexperienced soldiers. An official sedan came around from behind the dispersal building and stopped next to the SAS troops. A slim officer in battle dress got out of the front seat. The troops began getting to their feet but he told them to stand easy. A sergeant approached the major, saluted, reported and motioned toward Jack and Phil. The man walked over to them.

"Good morning, sir. Colin Herrick, 1st SAS."

Jack returned his salute and offered his hand. "Jack Stewart and Phil Hatcher. Glad to meet you, Major Herrick. Can we buy you a cup of tea?"

"Sounds bloody wonderful, sir. Do you want my people to start loading?"

"I'll have my Captain Howe get them started while we grab a cup," Jack said.

Three cups of steaming tea sat on the table. They were alone in the corner of the Operations Office.

"Major, sorry to bollix up your redeployment plans, but we need your help," Jack said. He had immediately liked the young officer.

"Ready to help, sir. What can you tell me now? They were a bit vague in London."

Jack put down his tea. "We're trying to pull a group of German civilians out of a research facility north of Leipzig. These men could be very valuable after the war. There's an abandoned airfield several miles south of the facility. We plan on landing empty Dakotas to pick up the civilians. Luftwaffe security troops are guarding the facility. We intend to put a Horsa right in their front door with some of your men and some of mine. Not sure what we'll find, but we have to neutralize the security troops. Once we do that, the challenge is to get the civilians to the landing field for pick up. We will have already secured the field."

The man's brows arched briefly. "That's quite a trip. My lads have done some of this before. They'll do the job. Do you have any maps or photos?"

"I have a full packet for you," Phil answered. "It's on the first aircraft. We had planned to get your key people and ours together during the flight to start working out any issues."

"I'll bring my platoon leaders and their sergeants. If you'll excuse me, I'll get them moving. See you aboard."

Jack and Phil followed Herrick to the parking apron. Several of the Dakotas were starting engines and the smell of burned aviation gas drifted across the tarmac.

"That smell always gets my blood flowing, Phil." But he was thinking of Pam. This was the first part of his journey to bring her back to him. Climbing the boarding ladder of the transport he knew he was ready to get going.

As the Dakotas were rolling down the runway at Down Ampney, twenty four American P-51's were departing from Leiston on their way to Nancy. This mission would be a break from daytime bomber escort and the pilots were looking forward to a change.

Görlitz, Germany
0830 Hours

It felt strange to Aleksei Milachenko, knowing he was on German soil. The town itself was almost undamaged. Once the traffic jam on the other side started moving, they had crossed the river quickly. There were twenty different military vehicles making their way west. The procession was made up of different units and Ivanov's group welcomed the additional camouflage. None of the other groups appeared to pay any attention to the two covered trucks. The road was in fair condition and soon they were making good speed west. Fully fueled last night, they would be able to refuel in Dresden, which would take them the rest of the way to Falkenberg. They should reach the outskirts of Dresden within two hours. Their only challenge was to find enough fuel for the trucks.

All of the men had been quiet today. The reality of their situation was coming home to both the Germans and the Russians. If they did not succeed, their chances of survival were slim. Every minute took them farther away from any possible reinforcement and made their escape that much harder. Aleksei could see the look of resignation in their eyes. While never giving up hope, they understood the odds were very much stacked against them. He couldn't think about that now. They were within hours of their objective. Regardless of what happened, he would do his duty.

Falkenberg Compound
0900 Hours

Karl Dietrich sipped the ersatz coffee they had been issued. There was a small box of staples from the supply room for their bungalow. Pam poured herself a cup and sat down at the small table in the kitchen.

"There's some bread and sausage if you'd like me to slice some for you."

Smiling, he said, "It would have to taste better than this coffee. I'd forgotten how really bad it was."

Pam took a sip from the steaming cup. "Oh my, that is very unusual. What is that taste?" She put the cup down and pushed it away from her.

"I believe they roast the shells of several types of nuts and then grind those shells into what they call coffee. Sorry there's no tea. We stopped seeing tea several years ago."

"I'll be fine. But let me fix you something to eat." She got up and went to the counter. "Karl, no matter what happens, thank you for all of your help."

"I promised someone we both know that I'd make sure you got back all right." Karl got up and walked over to the counter. He picked up a piece of sliced sausage and took a bite. "Now that's something we can do better than anyone else, make sausage." He

384

looked up and saw she was staring at him. "What is that look all about?"

"I'm sorry, I guess I was staring. I was thinking how strange and wonderful it was that you two met each other in the middle of a war and how everything has turned out." She put her hand on his arm. "Your friendship means a lot to Jack."

"He's a good man. I'm pleased things worked out the way they did. For the first time in many years I truly believe in what I'm doing." He smiled momentarily. "And to think I would find Eva in the middle of all this change."

"Will you stay with Jack when the war is over?" Her voice was quiet, as if she was afraid to ask the question.

Karl shook his head. "So many unknowns. What will happen to Germany? What will happen in the world? I think Double 00 will be someplace a person could affect the course of events. If it works out I think I would very much like to stay with Jack."

"I know he wants to keep the entire team together. It sounds like there's support from the government at the highest levels to keep Corry Woods in operation." She walked to the counter but turned as she heard a knock on the door.

Karl opened the door. Colonel Kolb stood on the porch with four of his soldiers standing behind him. "Dr. Haller, you are under arrest." Glancing down, Karl saw the pistol in Kolb's hand. "Take them," he ordered and his men pushed into the small room.

"What are you doing?" Karl asked. The soldiers roughly grabbed he and Pam by the arms, one soldier on each side.

"It seems that Luftwaffe headquarters did have a copy of your orders. But when we traced your service file, you do not exist. Until we can determine the truth, you will be detained. A special investigator is traveling from Berlin to review the case. Take them to security."

385

The four soldiers manhandled Karl and Pam out the door and toward the Security Building. Karl saw Kolb still had his pistol drawn making any attempt to overpower his escorts futile. He would have to bide his time.

Following a thorough search, Karl found himself locked in a small room with a single window, which was covered with a heavy mesh wire. The door was wood, reinforced with steel straps. Sitting down in the single chair he tried to look for anything he might use for a weapon or to help him escape. Beside the single chair there was a small table and a metal frame bed. There was nothing else in the room. For the time being I'll stick with the cover story, Karl thought. If they are sending someone from Berlin they aren't totally convinced what the truth is. He could only hope Pam would do the same thing. It didn't seem likely that any hard interrogation would take place until the Berlin people arrived. Before that happened, he had to find a way for he and Pam to escape. As sharp as she was, no one would hold up for long under professional interrogators, not even him.

Pam sat in her room staring out the wire mesh at the grey sky. She shivered slightly, although it wasn't cold in the room. Although she had always known something like this could happen, only now did she realize how frightened she could be. Her thoughts drifted to Jack. A thought crossed her mind she might never see him again. Perhaps Holz is still undiscovered and can get word out to the network. Until then, she was on her own.

Airfield Y.42
Near Nancy, France
1330 Hours

The last aircraft landed at 1225, a Dakota from Down Ampney. Forty-six aircraft were now on deck and the airfield personnel were commencing fueling operations. All of the fighter aircraft had been loaded with ordnance prior to departure from base. The P-51's were carrying full .50 caliber loads, while the Typhoons were loaded with 20mm cannon ammunition. Jack scheduled a meeting for all mission participants in the one remaining hangar on the field. Left over from before the war, the wooden structure was laced with bullet holes, probably from Allied fighters on low level strafing missions. Most of the men were standing around talking or smoking when Jack walked in front of the group.

"Gather round, if you please." He waited as the group moved in closer. "Welcome to lovely Nancy. I'm Commander Jack Stewart, Royal Navy. I'm the officer in tactical command of this mission which has been codenamed "White Arrow." We have members of the Special Air Service with us, along with the Royal Air Force and two fighter squadrons from the U.S. Eighth Air Force. There are Typhoons from 198 Squadron for ground support and the Dakotas and Horsas from 48 Squadron to get us where we need to go. It's important you understand that this is a unique and very critical mission. You are participating because you are combat seasoned and will get the job done. Our plan is to fly two hundred miles behind the German lines, take over an airfield, rescue some scientists and fly everyone back here. We have the unusual opportunity to have both the ground and air elements together before the mission to go over all details. When we break up here, I want senior officers from each unit to gather at the operations tent on

387

the flight line. We must be ready to launch at dawn tomorrow. You know what you need to do to be ready. Stand by for word on the final briefing time for tomorrow. That is all, carry on." Jack jumped down and fell instep with Phil as they walked toward the Ops Tent.

"Quite a show you're putting on, commander. Should be one for the history books." Phil grinned at Jack.

"As I recall there are plenty of disasters in the history books I've read."

"Jack, this is a sound plan. If we get a break with the weather and can get the gliders on target, this will work."

I know, Phil. I guess having Pam right in the middle of it is tough to get used to. Let's just make sure we get it right."

The two waited in the tent as the senior officers filed in and sat on the wooden benches.

Jack asked the senior officers from each unit to introduce themselves. Besides Colin Herrick and Trafford Jones there was Wing Commander Guy Ashford from 198 Squadron and the American senior officer, Lieutenant Colonel Steve Ames. A quick rundown on aircraft and personnel status left Jack feeling positive about the start of White Arrow.

"Gentlemen, we have a very short time to sort out the details of this mission. We are working against two time constraints. The German authorities are trying to move the group to Bavaria. In addition we have two of my people on the ground and I would like to get them out of there. You've seen the overview in your mission packets. Let's cover some of the key points. Steve, we need air superiority over the formation to and from Falkenberg. We also need to have air support while we're on the ground, both at the compound and the airfield. Guy, those will be your lads. It's up to the Horsa pilots to get the ground contingent to their respective targets. I know this show will be very weather dependent. The question I need you to ask is what our minimums are before we abort?"

The American spoke first. "My guys have plenty of low altitude experience. We'll go as low as the transport pilots are comfortable."

"Our limiting factors are the glider requirements. We can go as low as 5000 foot ceilings and 5 miles of visibility," Trafford Jones said.

Guy Ashford, commanding the Typhoon squadron nodded agreement. "That's fine for us."

"All right then, it's up to our weather expert to do his magic. This is Squadron Leader Lee Philpott. What's it looking like for tomorrow morning?"

A tall gangly man stood up, remaining by his chair. "Borderline, commander. The route to the target will be under the influence of a system that is stalled over the Bavarian Alps. We'll know more later tonight, but if we have 5000 foot ceilings, it will be just barely." He sat down.

"There you have it. Let's take a second look at the navigation route. We originally set it up based on staying away from Luftwaffe aerodromes and built up areas. Take a look at the terrain and see if we need to modify the route. If the weather is that bad, we may not get much in the way of hostile fighter activity." Jack looked at the men, most in their mid twenties, but old for their age. They had that look of men who had seen too much death and stress for one lifetime. But he knew they had what it would take to succeed. "Phil Hatcher, my Ops Officer, has an updated timeline that replaces the one in your packet. Please take a close look at the sequence of events and make sure you have no problem with your assignment. Let's meet back here in an hour. That will give you time to get your men settled. We'll work out the final details at that time. Thanks, gents."

The men headed out the door. Looking past them, Jack could see low clouds moving across the field. It was going to be tight.

Twenty minutes later Phil had assembled all of the Double 00 personnel. Although they had been over their assignments multiple times, Jack wanted to run through it one more time.

"All right, I'll be in the Horsa designated Able Able. With me will be Phil, Jimmy, Curtis and Gerhard. The second glider is Baker Baker and we'll have Terry leading the airfield crowd with Steve Riggs and Andy Hallowell. The remainder of the Horsa seats will be full of the lads from SAS. The mission at the compound is to neutralize the enemy guards, organize the evacuees and arrange transportation. Terry, your job is to secure the perimeter for the Dakotas that will follow. We will have radios to coordinate between us and if needed we can use the Typhoons for radio relay. Terry, you'll have Major Herrick's number two with you. The major will be with me at the compound. Set up your command post to have a good view of the surrounding territory. The Typhoons are your primary line of defence against any intruders. Keep us informed if there is some reason not to start the evacuees toward the field. Once you have a transport filled, get it out of there as quickly as possible. Wing Commander Jones will be remaining on deck coordinating the transports from his aircraft. He will have extra radios to ensure we can talk to each other. Any questions so far?"

The group sat silently, a few taking notes.

"We've gone over the layout of the compound. At that time of day the scientists and their families should all be in their quarters. We will move to the bungalows as fast as we can, telling them to remain in their houses until we call for them to exit. We will repeat

390

we are British forces who have come to take them to allied lines. The SAS will be moving toward the security building to take out any armed and uniformed Germans. Don't let your guard down. We don't know where the security forces may be at that time of day. If you see a soldier in uniform and he's armed, be ready to shoot. Don't take chances. I'd rather see every Luftwaffe guard face down than lose any of you. Once the guards are neutralized we will use Erich and Pam plus their contact to start the evacuation process. If no has anything else let's get some rest and be ready to go for the final briefing."

Falkenberg Compound
1530 Hours

"Fraulein Haller, we can find no record of your service with the Luftwaffe Technical Branch. Can you explain that discrepancy?" Kolb stood in front of Pam's chair where she remained sitting as he paced the room asking questions.

Pam was surprised her fear had subsided. "Herr Oberst, I don't know what to tell you. My husband and I have been working in the Armaments Section since 1943. Perhaps in the air raids the records have been lost or damaged. Maybe it was because we worked directly for the University of Cologne and contracted with the Luftwaffe? I don't know, but there must be a good reason." It sounded improbable, but she had to try.

"And where were you again before coming to Falkenberg?" He had asked the question before but maybe she would let something slip if she was hiding something.

"I have already gone over where we were and what we were doing. Why can't you check with Dr. Thorvelsson in Denmark?"

"We will, you can be assured of that." He turned and opened the door. "Tomorrow there will be a new group of men asking the questions. I'm afraid they are not as civilized as I am. You might think about that tonight. If you decide to talk to me, perhaps we can forgo your appointment with the Gestapo." He smiled and closed the door.

Pam felt she had done well but the word "Gestapo" sent a chill through her body. She had never felt so alone.

Max Kleiman remained in his office since receiving word that Kolb had arrested the two agents. Manfred Holz brought him the news with no other explanation. He looked at his watch and saw it was now 1715. He had not seen the Colonel or heard from his security office. What would he tell the man? Surely their story would start to unravel if questions were asked outside of the compound. Wouldn't that immediately implicate Holz and himself? Maybe not, perhaps he could plead that he was only complying with Haller's written orders. Did I ever tell Kolb anything about Haller that would betray the truth? He felt sick and was too scared to think straight.

Karl heard the sounds of heavy trucks pulling into the main parking area. The sun was almost down but he could see there were two Wermacht troop carriers. He watched with curiosity as the truck doors opened. In the fading light it looked like the men were wearing SS uniforms. He thought it would be ironic if any of these SS men were from one of his former units. Not likely, there were almost eight hundred thousand SS men between the different branches.

Aleksei Milachenko sat in the office with Ivanov and Kolb. This was one time he knew that Ivanov was better suited to deal with the situation. The final part of their journey had been uneventful and included a delay to arrive at the compound as the sun was setting.

"We will tell your men that this is a special unit which was sent to move the scientists to a very secure location." Ivanov sat smoking a cigarette. "Tomorrow we will depart with the scientists and you will tell your men they are to maintain security at the compound. We will tell them our destination is Bavaria, while it is really the location at Torgau. What problems do you foresee?"

Kolb looked nervous. "The scientists will not want to leave their families. This was the problem they brought up when the move was first mentioned."

"Tell them there will be transport sent for the families at the end of the week. But make it very clear operations are now in the hands of the SS. I don't think you'll get many objections from a bunch of paper pushers," Ivanov said.

"What about your men? What do I tell them about the language?"

Ivanov stubbed out his cigarette. "These men are a special security detail chosen from the 14th SS Panzer Grenadier Division. Tell them they are here at the direction of Himmler himself. If there are any problems, let me know. We will take care of them quickly. It's time to go talk to the director and tell him the plan."

"Dr. Kleiman, the immediate issue is to get your people ready to go tomorrow morning. It is out of my hands. We have our duty to the Fatherland and I will do my duty. I hope I can count on you to do yours."

Kolb's voice had an edge on it that Kleiman had not heard before. This new development coupled with the detention of the two agents was almost more than he could handle. He slowly nodded. "I will get my people together tonight. You are sure there will be transport for the families within the week?"

Kolb smiled slightly. "Of course, I have confirmed it with Berlin already. Berlin wants the men on their way to Bavaria. The facility is ready and they want the work to continue. It will make it easier for the families if the men are already there and settled in. You can see that, can't you?"

Kleiman hesitated then said, "Yes, I suppose you're right."

"We will depart at 0800 sharp," the Colonel continued. "Tell your men to be in the parking lot at 0730. They will only need to bring one bag. The rest of their belongings will follow with the families.

The three men got up and moved to the door. Ivanov turned to look at Kleiman who sat forlornly at his desk. "Herr Doctor, this move will take place as directed by my superiors. I want no problems from your people. Any trouble will be dealt with in a most severe and permanent manner. Do you understand?"

"Yes...I understand perfectly."

Airfield Y.42
1900 Hours

All key officers had gathered in the operations tent for a final run through. For two hours every detail of the mission was covered until all participants knew the plan cold.

Jack listened to the discussions but his concern kept returning to the weather. As solid as the plan on the ground was, ceiling and visibility would determine if they could make it into Falkenberg. Once on the ground he was confident they could deal with the German security force. The German troops were rear echelon guards. He suspected they had little or no ground combat experience. Jack was sending heavily armed, well trained commandos to overwhelm them. There was no doubt in his mind that Colin Herrick's men would show no quarter in the assault.

According to the last report the auxiliary airfield was still deserted. It seemed reasonable to assume it would take time before any units from the Leipzig area might be mobilized against his force on the ground. In any case they would be under the constant protection of the Typhoons, their own airborne artillery. In the air over the objective, any attempt by the Luftwaffe to interfere would be met by very experienced pilots flying combat air patrol.

He looked at the assembled men and finished by asking if there were any further questions.

"I'm assuming you are buying at the bar when we get back?" Trafford Jones's question brought a chorus of laughs across the tent.

"That's right. Drinks on the Navy when we get everyone back here." Jack smiled and waited for any more questions. "All right then, final brief for all section leaders right here at 0315. The field kitchen will start serving breakfast at 0300. Try to get some rest. That's all, gentlemen." As they were filing out, Jack called out, "Colonel Ames, a word please?"

Steve Ames was a tall muscular man who looked completely comfortable in a flight suit. "What's up, Jack?"

395

"Your fighter group flew a four plane that provided cover for a Hudson that picked a few of us up near Posen in the first part of August. Any chance any of those pilots are on this trip?"

Ames thought for a moment. "I remember that. Yeah, the four plane single escort. Long range. They talked about the Hudson landing in a valley and having to strafe some army trucks. That was John Scrapper leading the section. He's here on this one. Good stick. He knocked down his ninth Jerry fighter last week."

"I'd like to thank him in person if he's still awake."

The two men walked into one of the large field tents being used to billet the transient crews. A lantern hung from a hook throwing a pale light over four men playing cards and smoking.

"There he is," Ames said. "Scraps, Commander Stewart would like to see you."

A tall man with curly hair and a small mustache stood up from the bunk. He walked over, grinning.

"Yes, sir."

"Captain, you flew cover for a Hudson mission to the Posna Valley back in August?"

"Yes, sir. That was a long one."

Jack continued, "It was my team the Hudson was picking up. If you hadn't spotted Jerry and taken them out, I don't think we would have made it out in one piece. I wanted to say thanks." He extended his hand.

Scrapper smiled and shook hands. "I'm glad we were there. Don't suppose you can tell me why you were there?"

"Wish I could, perhaps someday it will come out. Are any of the other pilots here?"

The young pilot paused. "One is back at Leiston, another was wounded and is back in the States and my wingman, Bennie Matthews, was shot down near Bremen two weeks ago."

"I'm sorry to hear that. There's nothing easy about losing a wingman. I lost mine at Midway, it's hard to get over it." Jack remembered a good friend from a long time ago.

"Midway? I thought your accent didn't sound too British," Ames looked at Jack curiously.

Jack grinned, "Annapolis, Class of '35."

"I'll be damned," the Colonel said. "West Point, '35."

"And here we sit on an airfield in France. Small world," Jack said. "Well it's an honor to be here with you guys. When we get back tomorrow I'd like to sit down and buy you both a large drink."

Walking back to his tent Jack felt good to know men like Ames and Scrapper were with him on tomorrow's mission. Never any guarantees, he thought, but I feel good about this one. He saw a figure coming out of the darkness.

"Jack." It was Phil, holding a message folder. "We just got a message from Kaltenbach." He handed Jack the folder.

Stepping into his tent, Jack opened the folder and held it under the light. "Network communication advises SS troops arrived at compound. Group scheduled to move tomorrow morning. KD/PT under arrest." The last words hit him like a blow. He read it again and took a deep breath. "Have you read this?"

"Yes. I'm sorry, Jack." Phil stood there unable to offer any help.

Sitting down on the bunk, Jack began to desperately think of what options were available. Could he get in there tonight? What would happen to Karl and Pam if the assault went according to plan? They might kill them before we take over the compound. "I need to get in there. How soon can we lay on a flight? I'll jump alone and make my way in and find them.."

"Jack," Phil interrupted him. "It can't be done. Between the weather, the darkness and lack of planning, it makes no sense."

"I'm not worried, I can make it." Jack stood up as if getting ready to move into action.

Phil put his hand on Jack's shoulder. "You might just do that. But if you make a mess of it you'll destroy any chance of our success tomorrow. You and I both know you can't jeopardize the mission."

Sitting back down on the bunk, Jack shook his head. "God damn it. I know it. That doesn't make it any easier." All of these men and their weapons of war and it doesn't make any difference he thought. Pam and Karl are in trouble and I can't do a damn thing to help them.

"Come on, let's go check the weather. At least we'll be doing something," Phil said.

"I need to find Gerhard. There's been a change in the assault plan."

The final brief was primarily focused on the weather. Unfortunately the sun was not up and there wasn't much new data for Squadron Leader Philpott to utilize for his summary. It was days like this when meteorologists earned their pay. Many years of studying the continental weather patterns had added a sixth sense to all of Lee Philpott's predictions. This morning he looked tired, spending all night going over all his current data and a large number of historical observations.

"What's you best guess?" Jack asked.

"I think you have an 80 percent chance of workable weather for the mission. It will be border-line as I said earlier, but the sketchy data I have for temperatures and dew points tells me we won't have fog. That was my biggest worry. You're still going to have to deal with ceilings at four to five thousand feet and there will be reduced visibility around rain and snow showers. But I think you'll be able to pick your way around them."

"That's good enough for me." He looked to each of the senior aviators who had been listening and they all nodded.

"I'll be the tug for the first glider," Trafford Jones said. "I've got one of my best men towing number two. I say we go."

"Lower ceilings are better for the Typhoons," Ashford added. "It cuts down on the bloody Messerschmitts jumping you from behind."

Steve Ames rubbed his eyes and said. "We can stay out of everyone's way. My guys will fly their CAP along the transport route and I'm going to put one barrier air patrol between our target and the Luftwaffe field north of Frankfort. It'll work."

"Fair enough," Jack said. "We'll stick with our original schedule, first aircraft off will be the two gliders at 0500. Good luck."

Chapter Twenty Two

Airfield Y.42
Nancy, France
January 5, 1945
0445 Hours

It was still totally dark as Jack climbed the steps into the glider. There were several dim battery powered lights illuminating the interior. He saw a full compliment of men in battle dress sitting quietly, some with their eyes closed. Major Herrick was sitting in the second seat back on the right. "Good morning, Colin. All well?"

"Right, sir. My lads are rested and ready."

Jack put his Sten gun down on the seat and went forward to the cockpit. The pilot in command was Staff Sergeant Harry Trent. Jack had spent some time with him yesterday going over the site maps. Sergeant "Digger" Collins was his co-pilot. "Morning, gents. All set to go?"

"Aye, sir. Just waiting for the skipper to start engines. I expect we'll be ready to roll in ten minutes or so." Trent looked like he was sixteen, but Jack knew he had flown in Normandy and in Operation Market Garden.

"We'll have you back here in time for tea today," Jack said.

"That's well and good by me. Last time I went on one of these, it took me twenty-eight days to make it back to my unit. This should be a piece of cake." Trent grinned in the pale light.

"Weather may be a bit doxey as we make our way east," Jack said.

As an engine coughed to life on the Dakota parked in front of them, Trent laughed. "Not a problem here, we just go where they tow us."

Jack knew bad weather in a tow situation could produce a variety of problems, all of which might be fatal. The second Dakota engine kicked over.

"Better get strapped in, commander. Should be ready to roll any time."

The takeoff roll was surprisingly smooth to Jack. He realized the tow rope and harness had absorbed the initial acceleration. It was remarkably quiet in the glider, the only sound being some structural squeaks and the airflow past the fuselage.

"Colin, I understand you've been in a glider assault before?"

"Yes, sir. I was in a group that attacked a bridge in Normandy during the invasion." Herrick appeared totally relaxed, like he did this every day.

"Landing a bit bumpy?"

"Actually every one is different. The hope is that you don't hit a fixed obstacle. These kites are made of wood and don't do well."

401

Jack looked around the cabin and saw what he meant. Colin Herrick had closed his eyes and appeared to be taking a nap. For the first time today he was left alone with his thoughts. He had been so busy with the final preparations that he'd been able to push Pam and Karl out of his mind. Now the reality of their situation came back to him. Would they still be there? Perhaps they had been taken to Leipzig. Once the guards realized they were under attack they might execute them. If they are still there I have to find them quickly. It was as though his entire life to this point had prepared him for what would happen during the next several hours. Nothing would stop him. If they were there, he would find them and bring them home.

One hour after the two Dakotas towing the gliders departed, the early morning came alive as Rolls Royce Merlin engines began to start across the parking area. The two gliders under tow would only be able to make 110 knots during their transit to Falkenberg. The Mustangs and Typhoons would begin their takeoffs in thirty minutes putting them up with the gliders approximately forty miles from the target. Guy Ashford would lead with a section of Typhoons. His initial mission would be to locate the compound and then provide navigation guidance to Trafford Jones as they approached the target area. One by one the fighter engines roared to life and soon there were sections of fighters taxiing out for departure.

Gerhard Lutjens sat with his back against the fuselage of the Horsa. He watched Jack Stewart knowing his friend was worried about Pam and Karl. Jack had briefed him last night on the situation in the compound. Jack decided he and Gerhard would join Colin Herrick's SAS troopers in the assault on the security building. While the SAS men would concentrate on taking down the security forces, Jack and Gerhard would try to find Pam and Karl. Gerhard knew

Karl could take care of himself but Pam's presence complicated things. All he could do was his best, that's all Karl would ask.

Trafford Jones checked the engine temps one more time. Always a problem on tow missions, today the temperatures were staying within limits. His greatest concern was the deteriorating visibility. Although the ceilings were staying near Philpott's prediction of four to five thousand feet, the visibility seemed to be getting worse. As the sun came up conditions might improve. His wingman was fighting a tough battle trying to maintain visual contact with Jones while making sure his glider did not stray too close to the other glider or tow line. The senior aviator's other worry was their dead reckoning navigation. If Philpott's wind predictions were not close they might miss the navigation check points which they were counting on to locate the target area. He checked his watch and estimated they were one hour from the target. The Typhoons should be within radio range in fifteen minutes. If all went well Ashford could give them a weather report on the target and help guide them in for the tow release.

Standing behind the pilots, Jack could see the navigation lights of the Dakota slightly above and three hundred feet ahead. The turbulence had increased and he noticed both of the pilots had their hands on the controls. The sky was starting to lighten. He guessed the heavy moisture had reduced visibility to less than a mile. There was no banter coming from Sergeants Trent or Collins. The two pilots were totally concentrated on keeping the big glider in position on the Dakota. His thoughts kept returning to Pam. Never before in the war, whether in aerial combat over the Pacific or behind the lines in Germany, had he felt the dread he felt now. He was afraid of what he might find. How would he ever deal with losing Pam, having made the decision to send her in harm's way? He wished they were there now, enough of waiting and not knowing. The Horsa lurched left as it hit some turbulence and Jack staggered, catching himself. Checking his watch he saw it was 0705. Twenty five minutes until their scheduled target time.

Falkenberg Compound
0715 Hours

Aleksei Milachenko released the clip of his pistol, checking to make sure it was full. He knew it was a habit of his, but going through the motion always reassured him. The night had been difficult. Billeted in amongst the Luftwaffe troops, his men had been subdued and anxious. He'd been with them too long not to sense their mood. Today would be better. Soon they would be away from this compound on their way to a location, which would be more defendable. Talking with Kolb, he and Ivanov decided to maintain their cover as SS troops. Better to let these men believe they were still part of the Reich organization than prisoners of the Red Army. Replacing the pistol in its holster he walked across the parking lot. Several trucks were lined up in addition to a passenger bus. There would be plenty of room for the scientists and their baggage. He saw Sergeant Voloshin standing by one of their original trucks smoking a cigarette. The wind was cold this morning and the sergeant was using the truck as a windbreak.

"Are we ready to move?" Aleksei asked.

"Nothing keeping us here, sir. I was talking to their Sergeant Reuss. It seems one of their men went missing last night." The man threw his cigarette on the ground not bothering to stamp it out. "That can't be good. Who knows what the man might do?"

"Make sure our men are ready to get the Germans on the trucks when they show up. I'm going to go find the major."

It had taken Karl several hours to work a metal support rod free from under the bed frame. He now had a weapon and a tool. Using the beveled edge of the rod Karl loosened the bolts, which attached the metal screen over the window. There were streaks of light in the eastern sky as he finished the final bolt. Could he get out the window and somehow get to Pam without being discovered? If he could get to her and they could get out of the compound he felt sure they could evade the authorities long enough to wait for the Double 00 operation. But could he get to her? As the sun came up he knew his window of opportunity was closing.

Major Ivanov looked up from the map he was studying when Aleksei walked into Kolb's office.

"I was going over the route to Torgau. It looks like we can avoid the main east west highway by taking back roads. See what you think." Ivanov pushed the map across the desk.

Milachenko began studying the map. "I heard one of your Germans has deserted?"

"It appears that Sergeant Heigel is no longer in the compound. I can only assume he has decided to strike off on his own." Ivanov got up and walked over to the window. "There's not much we can do. He could be anywhere."

Aleksei looked up from the map. "If he's picked up by German authorities he could reveal our plans."

"He could. But none of them know exactly where we're going. We can only continue with our plan. Are all the vehicles ready to roll?"

"I checked them all myself." He looked at his watch. "The Germans should start showing up soon, it's almost 0730."

Kolb walked into the office. "What do you want to do with that man and woman I told you about?" he asked Ivanov.

"Let's bring them along. If they are scientists, we want them. If they aren't, we kill them." He looked out the window. "We need to get on the road."

Kolb found his watch commander and told him to have the Hallers escorted to the trucks. They were not to stop for any belongings. Sergeant Wurtzler acknowledged the order and detailed Corporal Panke to get them from their rooms and take them to the assembly area.

Karl heard the key turning in the door and moved to the far wall. He held the makeshift weapon in his right hand down at his side. As the door opened he saw a young soldier with a machine pistol standing in the doorway. Behind him he saw Pam and she appeared to be alone.

"Come with me," Corporal Panke ordered. The machine pistol was slung over his left shoulder. The young man appeared to be bored.

"I need help," Karl pleaded to the man.

"What? What's wrong with you?" The corporal stepped over to Karl who was slightly bent over at the waist.

"Help me to the bed.....please"

The corporal bent over to grasp Karl's arms and in an instant the makeshift knife was at the boy's throat.

"What.." The man tried to move and realized Karl had him in a viselike grip.

"Silence or you're dead. Do you understand?" He pressed the point into the man's neck drawing a small trickle of blood. "Are you alone?"

Panke nodded.

Still holding the man, he moved with him until Pam could see them. Karl motioned with his head and she immediately moved into the room closing the door.

"Karl.."

"Is the corridor empty?" he asked quietly.

"Yes."

Holding the knife against Panke's throat he asked, "Where were you taking us? Quietly."

"To the trucks, that's all. The sergeant ordered me to." The panic was now evident in the man's eyes.

"Would he see you taking us out to the trucks?"

"No, there's a side door directly to the parking area," the man stammered.

"If you want to live to see tomorrow you will carefully unsling your weapon and hand it to her." The man did as he was ordered. "Now get on your knees facing the far wall." Karl took the weapon from Pam and checked the safety. In one sharp movement he hit the corporal at the of his neck. Panke crumpled to the floor. "Help me get his clothes off."

Wing Commander Trafford Jones did not like what he saw out the forward windscreen. In the dawn light the visibility was down to only a mile. Checking the altimeter he saw they were down to 3000 feet above the terrain. He was able to discern the landscape

407

below him but there was nothing that identified exactly where they were. He knew there was higher terrain to the south of their course. If they had strayed on this course, one of those clouds might hide a ridge.

"This is turning into a real clap up."

His co-pilot, Reggie Saunders, was leaning forward in his straps, a chart held in both hands. "Look up ahead."

"What? I don't see anything."

"Right ten degrees, see them?"

"I don't…..wait…..bloody wonderful eyes, Reg. The three lakes. We're back in business."

The three lakes just south of the town of Mülhbeck were fifteen miles due east of the Falkenberg compound. Jack Stewart had seen them as well.

"Colin, estimating six or seven minutes out. Let's get everyone ready."

Herrick stood up and began to walk back between the troops. "All right lads, time to earn the King's shilling. Five minutes to release. Recheck your straps are tight and any loose gear is stowed away. Lock and load weapons, safeties to remain in place."

Trafford Jones keyed the intercom line that ran intertwined in the towrope to the Horsa. "Trent, did you see the lakes?"

"Aye, Skipper."

"I'm descending to 2000 feet. You can see the east west ridgeline that runs into the compound. It doesn't look like there's too much wind on the ground. I'll plan on taking you about mile south and you can release when ready. Copy?"

"Looks good to me."

Digger was holding a map in his lap and looking forward. "There's the north south road, and there's the buildings. That's it mate, at 10 o'clock."

"Tallyho," Trent shouted. He checked his airspeed, leveled his wings and reached for the tow cable release lever.

The Horsa's nose pitched up slightly at release. Trent banked left, lowering the nose and lining up on the largest pasture on the east side of the compound. Knowing he had enough airspeed to reach his intended landing point he began to milk the big landing flaps down. The Horsa began to float slightly and then the rate of descent increased.

"Standby," Digger yelled back at the troops. "Brace, Brace, Brace."

Jack felt the landing gear touch down and the nose of the aircraft swerved left ten degrees. The noise from the aircraft grinding to a halt was louder than he had expected. In five seconds the glider was stopped. Men were up and moving toward the forward hatch as the explosive ring on the aft fuselage sheared off the tail assembly. Exiting from both ends of the aircraft, the men began to move toward the buildings.

Looking back he saw Gerhard trotting toward him carrying his Sten gun. He knelt down next to Jack. "There's the security building, let's go."

Colin Herrick motioned his men forward and they spread out in line abreast.

Kolb was standing in his office with Ivanov and Milachenko when they heard the gunfire. "What? Who's firing their weapons?" Ivanov asked. The three men ran to the window and saw two men in unfamiliar uniforms come around the corner of the supply building.

409

"Those are British uniforms," Kolb exclaimed.

Aleksei turned to Ivanov. "I'll try to find our men and rally them on the west side of the administration building." Grabbing Kolb by the arm he asked, "Do you have any weapons close?"

"Follow me. In the guard room." Kolb ran into the corridor.

Jack and Gerhard jogged forward on the left side of Herrick's line of men. Rechecking the safety off on his Sten he looked around trying to orient himself to the photos of the compound. He could see a number of vehicles parked in the area in front of them with soldiers milling around, German soldiers.

The SAS troopers knelt and fired at the Germans who immediately began to flee or take cover. There were several sporadic shots from the men under the trucks but they were not aimed or coordinated. As Jack suspected, these men were guards not combat soldiers. Running toward the building he saw several SAS troopers alongside him and Gerhard. Herrick was sending his men around to encircle the vehicles where the guards had massed.

Running up to the security building Jack pressed against the wall and peered around the corner. In the distance there were several civilian men in suits running toward the smaller buildings. Jack motioned to Gerhard that he would check the building entrance. Gerhard nodded an acknowledgement. Jack stepped up on the wooden porch in front of the door. The wooden wall next to the door was suddenly splintered from automatic fire from inside the building. Dropping to the ground, Jack rolled across the open door and reached for a grenade. Gerhard was now on the opposite side of the door, watching as Jack pulled the pin. Releasing the arming lever he threw the anti-personnel grenade into the room. He and Gerhard flattened themselves on the flat porch as the grenade detonated. Immediately they were up and moving through the door.

"Check him," Jack yelled at Gerhard, indicating a Luftwaffe corporal who lay motionless on the floor. Moving through the smoke Jack looked down a deserted corridor.

"He's dead." Gerhard was standing next to him looking around the building.

"Shit. There're two corridors. You take that one and I'll go down here. Check each room. If we can take a prisoner we might be able to find out something."

Gerhard nodded and turned for the far corridor.

Working his way carefully down the hall Jack checked the rooms, one by one. *Where are they?*

Karl was holding Pam's arm in one hand and the machine pistol in the other when he heard the first shots. "They're here. It must be them. Let's go." He pulled her toward the admin building. "We'll stay there until the shooting stops."

They ran onto the wooden walkway that separated the bungalows from the admin building. Sounds of firing increased in the parking area. They could see several Luftwaffe guards lying under the trucks firing their weapons. Running down the walkway they reached the main door and ran inside.

"Kleiman's office, there's a back door we can use," Pam said to Karl, her voice breathless.

The two of them ran into the Director's office and into Colonel Kolb who was holding a machine pistol aimed directly at Pam. "Doctor Haller, that uniform doesn't do you justice. Now place the weapon on the floor and step back."

Karl glanced around the room seeing two men in addition to Max Kleiman. Both were wearing SS uniform, but something wasn't right. He complied with Kolb's order and laid the machine pistol on the floor.

411

"Perhaps you can tell us who you are and who our visitors in British battle dress might be?"

Colin Herrick looked up as a Typhoon fighter flew directly over the compound. The aircraft was low enough that he could see the head of the pilot, as he turned west.

Guy Ashford, call sign "Lizard Six," banked the aircraft left and could see the Horsa sitting a hundred yards from the main building complex. The squadron commander was taking a close look at the compound. Three of his aircraft orbited a thousand feet above him. He had established radio contact with Trafford Jones, who had landed at the auxiliary field and was now acting as traffic director for the many aircraft operating in the area. The first Dakotas would be landing in twenty minutes. So far there had been no reaction by the Luftwaffe.

The German security guards began to throw down their weapons and were walking away from the trucks with their hands up. The tremendous volume of fire by the SAS troopers had convinced the Germans they were severely outnumbered.

Herrick saw Jack Stewart making his way across the grass from the security building. In the distance the rest of the MI-6 crews were working their way through the bungalows. Events seemed under control. He turned to his sergeant major.

"Major, the guards are being rounded up and weapons collected. They tell us there's another group of soldiers on the far side of that large building."

"Very well. I'll take one platoon with me. Have the second platoon secure this area and check the condition of these vehicles."

"Aye, sir." The sergeant major began yelling orders and men jumped to action.

"Colin, how are things going here?" Jack asked as he and Gerhard walked up to Herrick.

"This area is secured, commander. My men have been told there's another group of soldiers on the far side of that building. I was going to investigate."

"I'll go with you," Jack said. If you can get these vehicles ready to go, my men will start getting the people out of their quarters. Let's make sure we have the area secured first."

"Right, sir. My men are on it. Shall we press on?"

The SAS platoon was deploying in a combat formation and advancing toward the admin building. Three trucks were parked on the edge of the grass between the British and the building. Herrick's men split into two groups using the trucks as cover. Herrick crouched down and looked around the edge of one truck.

"Sergeant, fire team forward if you please."

"Aye, sir. McCullough, take your team and advance on the building."

Four men got up and moved forward, spreading out at the same time. Rifle fire came from several of the windows of the building. The four SAS troopers dropped to the ground and began to return fire as did the rest of the platoon from their covered positions.

"It would seem we have a group a bit more ready to fight. We can work our way around the right flank and go through the building or we could call in a Typhoon and destroy the target."

It didn't take Jack long to decide on the best choice. The Typhoon's 20mm cannon fire would easily destroy the wooden building and everyone inside. "Not worth risking your men. Let's get the close air support boys set up for firing runs."

Karl looked at the three men. The two in SS uniforms did not look like they were Germans. He recognized the unit insignia that indicated they were Ukrainian members of the 14th Grenadiers. Karl remembered hearing about them last year. But what were they doing here?

The door swung open before Karl had a chance to answer Kolb's question. An SS sergeant carrying a machine pistol entered the room and addressed the two SS officers in Russian.

"Sir, the British have moved forward and set up behind the vehicles. They will try to flank us. We're in a bad position for defence and the ammunition is running low." The man was breathing hard and now stood catching his breath.

"Sergeant, get back up there. Aleksei, go take a look."

Karl heard the major's response, also still in Russian. The younger officer left with the sergeant.

Kolb leveled his pistol at Pam. "Now, Dr. Haller, tell me who you are or this woman will die."

Karl knew he had no choice. "We work for the British government. Those men out there do also. You are outnumbered and even if you kill us, it won't help you." Karl stared at the two men, his eyes daring them to disagree.

The SS officer spoke. "Perhaps not." He walked over to the window for a moment. "You will go out to your people. Tell them if they allow my men and I to leave, the woman will live. Otherwise we all die. If you're after these scientists, you will get them. Either at no cost, or the life of this one woman. It's your choice." He turned back toward Karl and was now holding his pistol. "Move."

Four smoke grenades lay on the ground forty feet in front of the vehicles. The plume of smoke was one hundred feet in the air and climbing. Jack stood next to the portable radio with the handset to his ear.

"Lizard Six, this is White Rocket. Your target is a single story wood building one hundred feet north of the white smoke. Make your firing runs from south to north. Our people are east of the vehicles. Acknowledge, over."

"White Rocket, this is Lizard Six, roger. We will set up for south to north runs. Will be in position in one minute. Tallyho on the smoke, will call inbound."

"All right, lads, strafing attack in one minute. Everyone take cover and keep your bleedin' heads down until I call all clear," the sergeant major bellowed across the parking area. Everyone not already under cover headed to join their comrades.

Jack knew the Typhoons would be loaded with armor piercing and high explosive cannon shells. After the aircraft completed their attack runs the wooden building would be totally destroyed. Once the threat was eliminated they could get on with loading their evacuees. While they were loading the scientists and their families he would search for Karl and Pam. Perhaps some of the evacuees might know something. Either they escaped and are nearby or had been taken away by the authorities. He could hear the Typhoon coming in from the south. Jack looked around the corner of a truck for one last check of the target. In the distance a lone man emerged from the far entrance door. He was carrying a white flag over his head. *Christ!*

"Lizard Six, abort, abort, abort…acknowledge. I say again abort!"

Guy Ashford was watching his gun sight track across the ground toward the building. He had his hand on the firing switch when he heard Jack's frantic call. "Lizard Six, aborting run. Lizard flight, stand by. Everyone take orbit overhead."

The lone figure approaching them wore a white shirt and dark trousers. He walked directly toward Jack with both hands held high, the white flag in one.

Jack looked again and realized it was Karl coming across the grass. Turning to Herrick he said, "He's our man. Spread the word." Jack broke cover and jogged out to Karl. As he approached him Jack could tell it was not good.

"Karl?" The two men shook hands.

"Jack, they have Pam. I'm here with their demands."

The men walked behind the vehicle.

Karl began to speak. "There are between twelve and fifteen soldiers. I saw two officers and the Luftwaffe commandant. The two officers are Ukrainians according to their uniforms."

"Russians?" Jack asked.

"No, Ukrainians, recruited by the SS when we overran the Ukraine. They hate the Russians as much as we do. They are demanding two trucks and safe conduct away from here. If we don't comply they say they'll kill Pam."

Jack Stewart looked at Karl and said nothing. He turned to look at the building knowing she was in there. Now her life depended on his decision. "Will they do it?" he asked, already knowing the answer.

Karl nodded. "These men are not your normal infantrymen. They have a look that makes me think they are a reconnaissance unit. Perhaps commandos, something more than conscripts."

Jack realized he had to make a decision. "And they think we'll let them drive away?"

"They will hold her as a hostage until they are several miles away. Once away, they say they will release her."

The two men looked at each other. Each knew they would most likely kill any hostage once their usefulness was ended.

Gerhard walked up and the two old friends nodded to each other. The younger man had a foul weather coat for Karl and a weapon.

"I'm going in to talk to them," Jack said. "If I don't come out, I want you to order the Typhoons to attack the building." Jack checked his watch. "Tell them 0815 target time, it's now 0758. Karl, where are most of the troops?"

Karl pointed at the left side of the building. "At that end. They're using those far windows as observation posts."

Jack looked at the building again. "Where's Pam?"

"She is in the director's office with the three officers and Dr. Kleiman. His office is right by the entrance door on the right side."

"Have the Typhoons aim for the left half of the building and use south to north runs. Tell them we're in the right side. If I can't get them to release her, I'll use the attack to try and overpower them. We'll try to make our way out the back." Jack continued to look at building. "It's a long shot, but it's all we have."

"I'm going with you," Karl said.

Jack shook his head. "I need you here, my friend. We still need to move a lot of people to that airfield and I want you running it."

Karl looked hard at Jack, his jaw set. "Phil and Gerhard can take care of that. If you're going to try to overpower them I can help. She's my responsibility too."

Friends and comrades, Jack thought. "Thanks." He checked the clip in his Walther and grabbed his Sten. "Ready?"

Karl buckled on the pistol belt Gerhard handed him. "Let me have your knife," he said. Taking his friend's knife, he raised his pant leg and slipped the Fairburn killing knife into his right boot, pulling the pants back over the boot. "A little insurance," he said to Jack.

As they walked across the field the two men were silent. They both knew the odds were against them but they wouldn't have had it any other way.

"If we have to take them, the young captain looks like the one we have to kill. The other two are amateurs if my guess is any good." Karl kept looking straight ahead as he walked.

Jack held the same white flag above his head. "I'll try to get close to Pam and get her out of the way if I can."

They walked on in silence.

Jack and Karl stood ten feet from the building waiting for a reply after telling the faces behind the windows they wanted to talk to the commander. A door opened and a voice said, "Come ahead."

Inside the building they were relieved of their weapons and escorted down the hall to Kleiman's office. Pam was sitting next to Kleiman's desk and the Doctor was still in his desk chair. Karl and Jack stopped just inside the door.

"You've heard our demand. What is your answer?" The major asked.

Jack looked for an instant at Pam then directly at the man. "My name is Stewart, Royal Navy. I command this force and I will let you depart without the woman." Jack looked at the other two officers standing on either side of the Major.

The major smiled, "Royal Navy? And what is the British interest in this out of the way spot?"

"That is not important. I have a superior force surrounding this building. You have the opportunity to depart here with your men and survive. But the woman goes free." There was a no emotion in Jack's voice but his tone was clear to everyone in the room.

The major walked to the back window taking the time to think. "You offer safe passage for me and my men with no conditions?"

"Correct."

Ivanov pulled his pistol out of its holster, and pointed it at Jack. "Very well, I'll let the woman go. I still have two hostages."

Jack nodded. "Agreed. I watch the woman return to my men and I will tell them to give you two trucks. The two of us will remain with you."

The two other officers were watching for Ivanov's reaction.

"All right, let's go." The major pointed with his pistol toward the door. Pam and Kleiman stood up and began walking toward the door.

There were two soldiers standing outside in the hallway and they held their machine pistols at the ready.

Jack glanced at his watch as the group began walking toward the west end of the building. It was 0807, eight minutes to go. He turned to the major. "The woman can walk over to my men. I will have two of my men drive two trucks over here and you can load your men. Why don't you let the doctor go as well?"

"He stays here. I'll tell you which two trucks we'll take."

"Understood," Jack replied. He glanced at Karl who was walking on his right side. Pam and Kleiman were walking behind them with the two soldiers trailing the group. His friend nodded slightly, he understood Jack's plan.

They reached the last room. Jack could see the door leading outside was partially open. He turned to Pam seeing the look of despair in her eyes. "All right, which two trucks do you want?"

"My sergeant and another driver will go with the woman," he said.

"Let's get this going," Jack said.

419

"Sergeant Reuss, take Corporal Gorshin and bring back our two original trucks."

The sergeant nodded and put his hand on Pam's shoulder to guide her to the door.

"Jack?" She seemed frozen in place.

"Pam, go, go now. Everything will be fine." Jack reassured her knowing that what he said was a lie. He was ready to die to protect her. For a moment he felt sorrow. His friend would die with him and now Pam and Eva would be on their own. But he had to put that out of his mind. There was still a chance.

The sergeant pushed her outside. She was looking at Jack as she disappeared behind the door.

Karl stood next to Aleksei Milachenko. There were eight men in the room.

Jack could see the three walking across the grass toward the vehicles and his men. She was safe, he thought. Not wanting to look at his watch he estimated three or four minutes until the Typhoon attack. What would it be like he wondered? Twenty millimeter cannon fire was devastating. His only hope was that he and Karl could use the momentary confusion and destruction to make something happen.

Wing Commander Guy Ashford checked his watch and continued to set up for his first run on the target. He understood what was happening on the ground and would make his run exactly as directed. The big fighter was two miles abeam the target heading due south. Estimating a two minute turn he would extend on this course for forty five seconds and reverse course to the attack heading. He rechecked all guns selected and turned the master gun switch on. Watching the clock and constantly refiguring in his mind,

420

he reached the point he knew was right to commence his turn. In fifteen seconds it would be 0812.

Jack watched as Pam moved behind the first vehicle. He casually moved several steps back from the window and three feet closer to a large wooden desk in the center of the room. Four metal filing cabinets were next to the desk and should provide some cover during the attack. Looking at Karl he knew his friend understood what he wanted to do. Karl was standing next to the captain he had estimated to be the biggest threat. Jack was closest to one of the men who had his machine pistol slung over his shoulder. Glancing down at his watch he saw it was almost 0815.

Ashford stabilized in a ten degree dive, his gun sight set to a ten mil depression. Checking his airspeed at 310 knots, he began to watch the ground through his gun sight as it tracked toward the building. Glancing at the clock the second hand was approaching straight up. He depressed the firing button and applied the slightest forward pressure on the stick to maintain the impact pattern of his cannon shells in the smallest area. The Typhoon shuddered as shell after shell left the cannon muzzles.

Jack never heard the aircraft. No one in the room had any indication of the attack until the building began to disintegrate around them. Jack dove behind the desk as wood and metal splinters began to fly around the room, the noise was beyond painful. The barrage lasted for four or five seconds. Jack felt debris hit him as he put his arms up to cover his head knowing he had to be ready to act. As the violence ended he lunged toward the soldier who now lay face down on the floor. He grabbed at the machine pistol trying desperately to get the strap from under the man's arm. There were screams coming from several of the men and dust was everywhere. Jack pulled the gun free and looked around spotting two men kneeling down by the wall. He checked the safety off and fired a quick burst dropping both of them. Expecting the attack of the next aircraft he knew he had to get out of this room. *Where's Karl?*

Pam watched in terror as the west side of the admin building was brutally torn apart with cannon fire. "No!" She started to move around the end of the vehicle as Phil grabbed her.

"Pam, there's nothing you can do."

She struggled for a moment, tears streaming down her face. Phil held her, no longer to restrain her, but to comfort here.

The two drivers were now under guard, their faces showing resignation to their own deaths.

Aleksei Milachenko had reacted instinctively as the room began to come apart. Not knowing what was happening, he dropped to the ground and tried to find some protection from the attack. He felt a sharp pain in his back and knew he was hurt. More splinters flew around the room as every man tried to protect himself. He saw Kolb and Ivanov go down near the window. As quickly as it began, the violence was over. Getting to his hand and knees he heard a machine pistol burst to his right. *The British!* Dropping down he rolled violently to the left, pulling his pistol out of the holster. *Where was the shooter?* Lying on his back he saw the British commander's head above a wooden desk. Raising the pistol he fought the pain in his back and sighted at the man's head.

Karl had dropped to the floor as the first cannon shell impacted the room. The dust was immediate and made the hell of splinters and noise complete. He felt a burning pain in his left shoulder as he lay face down waiting for the attack to stop. Opening his eyes he could see the captain several feet to his left getting to his hands and knees. A machine pistol burst came from behind him as Karl reached down toward his right boot and withdrew the knife.

Aleksei tried to take a deep breath. The pain was excruciating, shooting deep into his chest. He put the pistol down on the floor for a moment to rest. With all his will he raised the pistol and sighted on the British commander's head.

Karl saw the captain raising his pistol and realized Jack was the target. With all his might he lunged forward, the knife extended as far as possible. The point of the knife entered under the man's jaw and Karl drove it into his skull as the pistol went off and the room began to come apart again.

In the space of four minutes the Typhoons completed their firing runs on the building. After the last attack the west end of the building was destroyed. Colin Herrick called on the radio to cease all attacks as his men moved forward to search the area. Phil held Pam back.

"Pam, I need you to do your job. We have to get these people on the vehicles and headed to the field. Do you understand me?"

There were tears in her eyes. "My God, Phil, Jack's dead, he's dead."

Hatcher pulled her toward the vehicles so she couldn't see the destroyed building. "Pam, I don't know. What I do know is he would want us to finish this mission. Now snap out of it. Go help Gerhard get those people out of their houses and into the trucks."

Pam looked at him without saying anything. She looked numb as she turned around and walked toward Gerhard.

Colin Herrick's men approached the building in combat formation. They had learned to always expect the worst from your enemy. Although to think anyone could survive the destruction of the building was hard to believe.

"Sergeant Major, one squad into the building. Have the others maintain a perimeter."

"Aye, sir."

With one hand holding their weapons the SAS troopers carefully went through the debris. Parts of the collapsed walls were horizontal, the high explosive shells having torn the support beams apart.

"Sergeant Major, there's one alive over here."

"Better go get the medic."

Epilogue

Corry Woods
January 9, 1945
1045 Hours

Flight Lieutenant Pamela Thompson sat in the outer office with Hiram Baker. Both had mugs of tea in their hands, a comfort from the cold and rainy weather outside the window. Pam had been back at Corry Woods for two days. The return from airfield Y.42 had been delayed when an emergency airlift near Cologne required the Dakotas of 48 Squadron. Stranded temporarily, it had actually been a blessing to have two days without the debriefers. Two days to reflect on the events of the past two weeks. She felt proud of what had been accomplished. Men had died and lives were changed, but they had completed the mission. The scientists and their families were now in England at a secure location and would be part of the allied technical effort going forward.

She was still coming to grips with the entire mission. Experienced hands had told her it wasn't unusual to feel confused and unsettled once you are out of danger. In a very short period of time she had felt more intense fear, joy and pride than at any time in her life. Now she knew there were decisions which must be made about her future. Was this where she wanted to spend the rest of her time in the RAF? What about after the war, was there a future for a woman in this world? For now she would take each day as it came and worry about the big picture later.

"What time do you have to be back with the debriefers?" Hiram asked.

She put her mug down on his desk. "They told me to take an hour and relax. I hope I'm giving them what they need."

Hiram laughed. "Trust me, dear lady, if you don't, they will be the first ones to remind you."

"Have you heard from Jack this morning?" Every time she said his name she knew how lucky she was to have him alive and unhurt.

Hiram nodded. "He called from the hospital. After the meeting at Baker street he wanted to check on Karl. It seems our commando is beginning to drive the nursing staff up the wall and so he'll be released within two days."

They all knew how lucky Dietrich had been in the Typhoon assault. A large wooden splinter had imbedded itself in the back of his left shoulder. Fortunately there was not serious damage to the arm, just a great deal of pain. Jack had been able to help him to the east side of the building during the subsequent Typhoon attack runs. When the two friends emerged from the far end of the building it was like a miracle to all present. Jack had Karl's arm over his shoulder as they made their way across the grass. We're comrades and friends and still alive to fight again. No one had attempted to restrain Pam when she realized it was Jack walking out of the smoke.

The transport to the auxiliary field had gone smoothly. There had been no attempt by German forces to move on the operation. Constant air cover resulted in all aircraft returning safely to Nancy. The total count for German scientists and their families was one hundred and seventeen. The only casualty was Max Kleiman who died in the strafing attack on the admin building. Operation White Arrow was considered a success on all counts.

Ramsgate Military Hospital
London
March 1, 1945

Jack turned down the corridor leading to D Ward. He was used to the journey now, having been a regular visitor for the last six weeks. D Ward was located in the rear part of the large hospital in the suburbs of London. There were Royal Marine security guards and the wing was hardened with steel bars and extra fencing around the perimeter. The patients included high ranking prisoners of war and occasionally defectors from the other side. The Marine sentry recognized Jack and came to attention.

"Good morning, commander." The young man handed Jack the sign in sheet as Jack flashed his military identity card.

"How are you this morning, Corporal Allen?" Jack noted his time of arrival and signed his name.

"Couldn't be better, sir." He walked to the door and held it open for Jack.

There were eight single rooms on the passageway. He knew his way to room D6, third on the right. Jack knocked lightly and swung the door open. The patient was lying with his head propped up on several pillows.

"Good morning, Major. How are you feeling today?" he asked.

"Very well, commander. Each day I seem to be a little stronger. They tell me my wounds continue to heal. That is all I can ask."

Dmitri Ivanov had been near death when the SAS troopers pulled him out of the wreckage of the collapsed admin building. Only the protection of Colonel Kolb's body, which they found on top of Ivanov, had prevented his death. Even with the protection of a body and the structure of the wall he was severely injured by multiple shrapnel wounds. Only quick attention by the RAF physician at the auxiliary field prevented his death.

Jack pulled up a chair to the side of the bed and sat down. "Dmitri, we have honored your request that your embassy or forces not be made aware of your status. I think it is time we talk about that. Are you up to it?"

"I thank you for doing what I asked. You won't understand my position but I owe it to you to explain. When I regained consciousness on the aircraft I realized I would end up behind British lines. You still thought I was a Ukrainian SS officer not a Major in the NKVD. I already knew my future was uncertain when I returned to the Red Army. Despite full support I failed at my mission. Marshall Stalin personally ordered the mission. He does not take failure well. Not only did I fail but the British did succeed in finding and taking the scientists. That is why I admitted my real identity to you and asked you to say nothing."

"Where do we go from here?"

Ivanov shifted slightly in the bed, the effort showing on his face. "I am a man without a country, Jack. I can't go home. I would be cashiered out of the service at best. Most likely I would be arrested and imprisoned. Now that I have been in your custody for a month and a half, my loyalty would certainly be questioned. I have nothing in my future. I hope I can ask for your help to change identity and move somewhere across the ocean. Perhaps to South America."

Jack got up and walked to the window. He trusted his instinct about men and this time was no different.

"Dmitri, I may have another choice for you."

Printed in Great Britain
by Amazon

21365464R10246